Kingmaker
Kingdom Come
TOBY CLEMENTS

arrow books

1 3 5 7 9 10 8 6 4 2

Arrow Books
20 Vauxhall Bridge Road
London SW1V 2SA

Arrow Books is part of the Penguin Random House group of companies
whose addresses can be found at global.penguinrandomhouse.com

Copyright © Toby Clements 2017
Map © Darren Bennett 2017

First published in Great Britain by Century in 2017
First published in paperback by Arrow Books in 2018

www.penguin.co.uk

A CIP catalogue record for this book is available from the British Library

ISBN 9781784752620

Typeset in 11.88/14.3 pt Fournier MT by Jouve UK, Milton Keynes
Printed and bound in Great Britain by Clays Ltd, St Ives Plc

'It is Clements' ability to excite both tender emotions and a capacity for bloodthirstiness that has allowed him to achieve what Shakespeare couldn't manage, and spin a consistently enthralling story out of the Wars of the Roses.' *Daily Telegraph*

'The narrative is quick-paced, direct, and written in the vivid present . . . the repression, anger and bloodshed of the Wars of the Roses was itself frequently beyond belief. Clements' pages are aflutter with that conflict's every emotion.' *Spectator*

'Fans of Tudor history in search of a post-Mantel fix will be intrigued . . . Clements' storytelling is evocative and direct.' *Independent*

'Toby Clements captures the grimness, grit and grime of 15th-century life, but with compassion and humanity, as seen through the eyes of common people . . . its period detail is wonderfully accurate as are the set-piece skirmishes and bloodbath at Towton.' *Daily Mail*

'If you like books that grip you from the very start, that are fast-paced with fascinating characters, then this is the book for you. Beautifully written, with an exciting plot, this book kept me engaged on every page.' *Historical Novel Review*

Also in the Kingmaker series

Winter Pilgrims
Broken Faith
Divided Souls

In memory of my much-missed friend and beloved brother-in-law,
Ian Hanbury Philips,
1972–2016

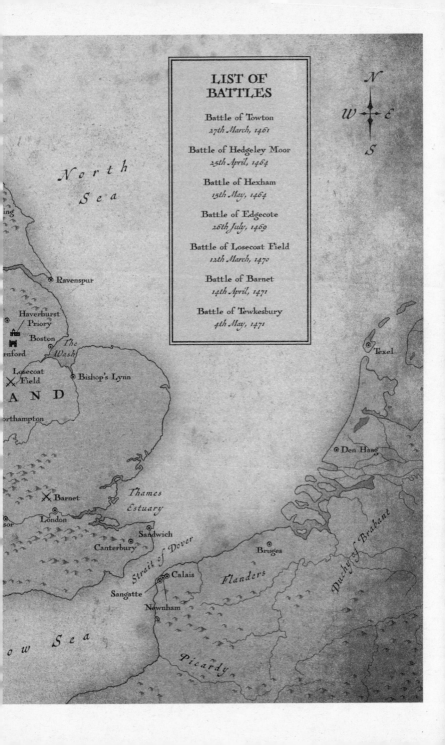

LIST OF BATTLES

Battle of Towton
27th March, 1461

Battle of Hedgeley Moor
25th April, 1464

Battle of Hexham
15th May, 1464

Battle of Edgecote
26th July, 1469

Battle of Losecoat Field
12th March, 1470

Battle of Barnet
14th April, 1471

Battle of Tewkesbury
4th May, 1471

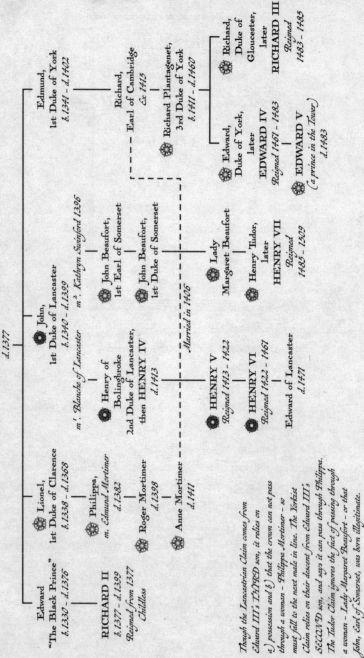

Key: York · Lancaster · Tudor

EDWARD III
d.1377

Edward
"The Black Prince"
b.1330 - d.1376

Lionel,
1st Duke of Clarence
b.1338 - d.1368

John,
1st Duke of Lancaster
b.1340 - d.1399

Edmund,
1st Duke of York
b.1341 - d.1402

RICHARD II
b.1377 - d.1399
Reigned from 1377
Childless

Philippa,
m. Edmund Mortimer
d.1382

m¹. Blanche of Lancaster   m². Kathryn Swinford 1396

Roger Mortimer
d.1398

Henry of
Bolingbroke
2nd Duke of Lancaster,
then HENRY IV
d.1413

John Beaufort,
1st Earl of Somerset

John Beaufort,
1st Duke of Somerset

Richard,
Earl of Cambridge
Ex 1415

Anne Mortimer
d.1411

Married in 1406

HENRY V
Reigned 1413 - 1422

Lady
Margaret Beaufort

Richard Plantagenet,
3rd Duke of York
b.1411 - d.1460

HENRY VI
Reigned 1422 - 1461

Henry Tudor,
later
HENRY VII
Reigned 1485 - 1509

Edward of Lancaster
d.1471

Edward,
Duke of York,
later
EDWARD IV
Reigned 1461 - 1483

Richard,
Duke of Gloucester,
later
RICHARD III
Reigned 1483 - 1485

EDWARD V
(a prince in the Tower)
d.1483

Though the Lancastrian Claim comes from Edward III's THIRD son, it relies on 1) possession and 2) that the crown can not pass through a woman – Philippa Mortimer – so must fall to the next male in line. The Yorkist Claim relies on their descent from Edward III's SECOND son, and says it can pass through Philippa. The Tudor Claim ignores the fact of passing through a woman – Lady Margaret Beaufort – or that John, Earl of Somerset, was born illegitimate.

Cast of Major Historical Figures

KING EDWARD IV:

Victor of the battle of Towton, crowned king in 1461, he has been on the throne nine years, but has yet to achieve real peace or fulfil his promises.

WILLIAM, LORD HASTINGS:

Ennobled after Towton and still King Edward's Chamberlain and procurer, now with a substantial power base of his own.

GEORGE, DUKE OF CLARENCE:

King Edward's younger brother, willingly used as a pawn by those seeking an alternative king.

RICHARD, DUKE OF GLOUCESTER:

King Edward's youngest brother. As staunch, loyal and honest as the day is long – for the moment.

RICHARD NEVILLE, EARL OF WARWICK:

Architect of the first Yorkist victory, later known as the Kingmaker, now dissatisfied with his lot and happy to make use of the Duke of Clarence to unseat his former protégé the King.

JOHN NEVILLE, EARL OF NORTHUMBERLAND:

Younger brother of the Earl of Warwick, used to be Lord Montagu, promoted for services to the House of York.

JOHN TIPTOFT, 1ST EARL OF WORCESTER:

Constable of England, later known as the Butcher of England.

LOUIS DE GRUUTHUSE:

Flemish nobleman who offered succour to the exiled Edward IV.

KING HENRY VI:

Last Lancastrian king, who spends most of *Kingdom Come* locked in the Tower of London.

QUEEN MARGARET:

Henry VI's almost indomitable wife, sometimes known as Margaret of Anjou, living in France, still trying to get her husband's throne back, either for him or their son.

EDWARD OF WESTMINSTER:

The son of Henry VI and Queen Margaret, sometimes known as the Prince of Wales. Rumoured to be extremely warlike, as befits Henry V's grandson.

Kingmaker
Divided Souls

Prologue

In the first few snow-girt weeks of the year 1470, the subjects of England held their breath. The Yorkist King Edward IV held the throne, while the old king, Henry of Lancaster, still languished in the Tower, his cause seemingly beyond hope. But in place of the old strife between the two royal houses, a new discord had arisen among King Edward's kinsmen. The truth is that during this summer last past, when King Edward was held at the command of his cousin and erstwhile ally the Earl of Warwick, the late-blooming seeds of war were planted deep in fertile soil.

And now, as the country wakes from winter's grip, it is widely supposed these barbed and iron-tipped seeds will soon break winter's hard-frosted skin and grow to bring misery to the land. And so it is that every wise lord keeps his men close by. And never were the country's smiths and bowyers so busy at their forges and benches as they are today . . .

PART ONE

Marton Hall, Marton,
County of Lincoln,
Before Candlemas, 1470

1

Thomas Everingham and Jack Bradford saddle their horses in the light of a rush lamp, and they are already on the road to Gainsborough when grey dawn makes itself known in the leafless crowns of the elms to the east. Snow lingers on the ground among the trunks of the trees, and even though Thomas is wrapped in twice as many layers of linen and wool as there are Evangelists, he still feels the ache of his old wounds.

'You're getting on,' Jack tells him.

And Thomas supposes this is so. He must be nearly thirty, he thinks, though he can't be sure. He pulls his rabbit-fur-lined cloak about his shoulders and settles deeper in his fine saddle, and he takes some consolation from the warmth of his smooth-pacing palfrey.

'My leg hurts a bit too, though, when it's like this,' Jack admits, straightening it to look at it in the stirrup. 'Where Katherine pulled that arrow out.'

Thomas laughs because Jack makes it sound as if it's Katherine's fault his leg aches, rather than one of Lord Montagu's archers who shot the arrow there in the first place, and he thinks of reminding him that Katherine did not so much pull the arrow out as hammer it through to the other side, and she did it with an old piss pot.

Instead he turns to the boy they've brought with them, a sort of servant, though you'd never say that to his face.

'What about you, John? You got any old scars to show us yet?'

John is about fifteen, Thomas supposes. His mother died in childbed and his father has brought him up in rough-and-ready fashion ever since, and he's a wild-looking boy, with a foul mouth, and it is broadly agreed that it is a miracle he has not been hanged twice over, let alone not lost both ears to the clippers. The boy extends his muddy wrist from his muddy sleeve and shows them a whorl of puckered pink flesh, only recently healed. Thomas and Jack suck their teeth sympathetically, though both have seen worse.

'Hog tusk,' the boy tells them proudly. 'Bled like a Jesus Christ himself – begging your pardon – till Mistress Katherine put some of that salve on it. Then it stopped.'

He tucks his wrist away proudly, as if it is something precious he did not want just anybody to see, and they ride on through a narrow defile in a dense wood of holly trees where birds cluster among the berries. Even their little bodies are steaming in the cold. Thomas wonders how much John Stumps must suffer in weather like this, with his arms cut so short just above the elbow? He hasn't complained of it yet, which is a surprise, for John Stumps takes much pleasure in complaint. He moans, Jack has told them, because he cannot sleep for any length of time before he is woken by pain in his arm where the imagined bracer on his left wrist is too tight, and it pinches him, and there's nothing more he'd like to do than run a finger under it, or loosen the strings, but he can't for he has long since lost the wrist on which it is strapped. So it is not his fault that he grumbles so, but it makes his company heavy, and is one of the reasons Thomas did not ask him to come this morning. That and the fact that it is hard for a man with no arms to ride a horse, even over these few short miles to Gainsborough, where they're riding this morning to see a lawyer named Mostyn.

They could have made this journey any time, Thomas knows. They could have made it in the spring, perhaps, when the road might be busier and so presumed safer, but Thomas is anxious to buy back the last of Sir John Fakenham's land that the old man's stepsons sold to ease their debts, and Thomas wants to do this as soon as he can, because he has become gripped by the unvoiceable conviction that his fortunes reflect those of the country at large, so that when he has been down, as he has been, so has the country, and when he has been up, as he is now, then so is England herself. So now he believes if he can restore Sir John's estate to wholeness, then England will knit herself up, and peace and prosperity will return.

It is a silly thing. A dream. A fancy. He knows that, and he has never mentioned it to a soul. And yet, and yet. Look around. Since he first took possession of Marton Hall, back in the autumn, have there been rumours of insurrections in the Northern Parts or in distant Wales as was once usual? Have armies been mustered? Have Commissions of Array been sent out? Has the country seen riot and affray? No. The peace may be imperfect, true, but that – in Thomas's mind – is because he has not yet reclaimed these last scraps of Sir John's estate. Once he has, and once he's ploughed his own furrows deep into its damp black earth, then everything – everything – will fall into place, and he, and England, will find this perfect, elusive peace at last.

This is why he has pressed so hard for the sale of these last furlongs, why he is paying so much for them, and why he is now riding out so early in the day, early in the year, when all decent men should be abed, or at prayer, and with only Jack and young John for company.

The sky above is a flat scrim of pale cloud, and the hard-frosted slips of snow and ice on the track remain brittle all morning. They ride north, with the river to their left, and all about them the sodden fenland in winter is cheerless, with rotting thistles struggling to keep their heads above the ice-veneered meres and the birch trees ringing with crows' dismal caws.

'Kind of weather you'd want to be hanged in,' Jack notes.

And yet Thomas is feeling buoyant and hopeful and his mood is contagious, and Jack and young John are cheerful too, and they greet those few cloak-muffled travellers they pass with blessings that are returned, and they raise the spires of Gainsborough by early mid-morning, to find a well-wrapped pack-horseman to point them in the direction of the house of Sir Thomas Burgh, Master of the King's Horse, Sheriff of Lincolnshire, and the present owner of the parcel of land that Thomas wishes to buy back.

Burgh bought it from Isabella's sons for a good price when they were hard-up this last summer, and it is not absolutely in the man's interest to sell it to Thomas, but Thomas offered him good money, and Burgh is one of the men who came to meet King Edward – and Thomas and Katherine, as it happened – in York the year before, when the King was released from the Earl of Warwick's custody. Thomas supposes that Burgh must believe him still high in King Edward's esteem, and this sort of exchange of favour, Katherine tells him, is how things are done among such men.

'Will he be there himself?' Jack asks.

Thomas supposes not. While Burgh is happy to do Thomas the favour, he is far too grand a man to receive him as an equal, and so they will only be seeing his man of business, this attorney, John Mostyn, who will give him the deeds and see to what is needed.

As they near the town, the woodland is better kept, and there are men and women in the fields with ox and plough, readying the soil for the pea and rye crop. They ride the familiar path towards All Saints, where the sun catches the vane on the spire, through the marketplace, deserted now, and past the road that leads down to the ferry dock on the river's bank, likewise still deserted. But in a small orchard that Burgh has planted to shield his house from the town, they find a man up one of the mist-dampened trees, pruning branches with a small saw. He is in russet, with no gloves, and a black cap pulled low. His breath is like a small cloud about his head.

'God's bones,' Jack greets him. 'Could you not find a better day for it?'

The man grumbles that pruning must be done when it must be done, and Thomas supposes this must be true, and wonders if it is the sort of thing they ought to be doing at Marton; he's about to ask a few more questions, but the horses are unsettled hearing anyone talking so high in the branches, so Thomas and Jack kick on down a gentle slope to find the house – a grand thing, far finer than Marton, but still no castle – hidden now behind ash-pole scaffolds. It is as if the place is still being built, though there are no labourers to be seen since, it transpires, it is too cold for the mortar to set right and the men Burgh hired to lay the bricks are from Flanders, and are back home for the winter.

'It's why you shouldn't build a house with those bloody bricks,' the man who meets them at the gate tells Thomas. 'Not that I blame them, mind, them Flems. And besides, imagine trying to daub wattle in this weather?'

Thomas and Jack, who have both tried daubing wattle when it is so cold the mud and straw are stiff enough to strip the skin from your fingers, agree. The man – huddled in Burgh's blue livery, with a long glaive resting on his shoulder – sends a boy off to find the attorney while Thomas and Jack wait in the yard, admiring the works; after a moment, Mostyn emerges to greet them. He's a thin-faced, quick-eyed little man in clacking pattens, long, very dark robes and a tall red hat made of folded felt that he removes to reveal a shiny pate.

'God give you good day, masters,' he says with a smirk and what might be an ironic bow. 'Come. Come. Warm yourselves by my fire.'

Thomas does so, but Jack is put off by the man's manner and stays with young John and together they go with the ostler to the stables to tend to the horses. Thomas is uncomfortable at the separation because he thinks of himself as no better than Jack; though, to be honest, he doesn't feel the same way about Foulmouth John, who is as likely to drink the ink as write with it.

Mostyn leads Thomas into one of the new-built chambers on the first floor warmed by a well-set fire of glowing coals. He has the papers they need weighted out on a desk alongside a jar of his pens, and a pewter jug and a couple of matching cups on a table nearby. He pours Thomas a drink of the dark wine while Thomas removes his fur-trimmed cloak to reveal his best clothes, worn in the vain hope of impressing Mostyn, and a boy is there to take it, and his hat, and Thomas rubs his hands over the flames, and then while they drink Mostyn tells him about the building works and about the Easterling builders. He speaks as if he is trying to soothe a dog, Thomas thinks. Soon the change in temperature makes Thomas's face and ears burn, and he wishes he had not gulped the wine so, and he starts to feel fuzzy-headed; and then Mostyn refills his cup and they drink some more, after which Mostyn sighs, takes out a set of horn eyepieces that he arranges on his nose and says: 'So, to business.'

This they then conduct. Money has already been deposited with a third party and these are only the final niceties, which Thomas must complete by attaching his sign to the bottom of the various papers that Mostyn has laid out. Thomas is thrilled. He can feel his heart thumping with the pleasure of it all, and as he first reads and then signs each, Mostyn, who had obviously understood Thomas to be unlettered, becomes more admiring.

'You have a right fine way with letters,' he says. 'Neater than mine and I make my living by it.' He speaks quickly, in fluting, breathy phrases.

'By that and other things, surely?' Thomas brushes aside the false modesty.

'Well, perhaps,' Mostyn agrees. 'But no, sir, really? I've scarce seen so fine a hand outside a cathedral cloister.'

Thomas enjoys proving his appearance has deceived Mostyn as much as Mostyn's flattery, but it is also a welcome thing to be discussing letters and ink and the quality of paper and so on when he is usually concerned with domestic matters such as whether the pigs need gelding or the privy is full. And Mostyn knows what he is talking about, because look: Thomas does have a nice hand. Beautiful regular letters.

'I was briefly in a priory,' Thomas admits. 'A little to the south of here.'

He has never spoken of his time at Haverhurst Priory to anyone save his wife Katherine, and he feels a guilty thrill in doing so now. But it was such a long time ago, and really, does his past matter so very much now that he has become who he is? But there is the briefest hiccough in the flow of Mostyn's words, and Mostyn blinks at him through the polished lenses that make his eyes very large.

'A priory?' he repeats. 'Oh.' And when Thomas can only nod, he goes on: 'It is a good life, I dare say, that of an ecclesiastic, though it is not for every man, is it? The privations of the body and so on. Though I cannot see you as a white friar, nor some brown Franciscan either?'

Mostyn is fishing for something and Thomas suddenly feels very vulnerable. He regrets saying anything of this, and shakes his head to change the subject, but Mostyn takes this to mean that Thomas was the other sort of friar.

'Ah,' he says. 'An Austin friar, then? And how did you leave them?'

Thomas knows he has already said too much, and so he ends the conversation more firmly, squaring the pages on the desk.

'In good order, master,' he says. 'Much as we leave these papers.'

Mostyn is brought up short and blinks, reprimanded.

'Quite so,' he says, and he leans forward to take them for filing, but there is a flicker of some satisfaction at the corners of his mouth, as if he's glimpsed the inkling of an opportunity, and so the event that Thomas hoped would bring him such satisfaction, which they would celebrate on his return to Marton, is spoiled, and becomes a niggle of worry. Mostyn hums through his smile as he files his copies of the papers in a pigeonhole before handing Thomas his, and then he offers to show him the rest of the house.

When it is done, and they have seen from cellar to attic, and they find themselves back in the courtyard, Thomas can only agree that it is very handsome.

'Though hard to defend,' he ventures.

'Defend, Master Everingham? Defend against what?'

'Attack?'

'Attack? Sir Thomas is Master of the King's Horse, Master Everingham. He is not some – some – some out-of-the-way man with no interests at court. Who would dare attack him? Besides, we have John here, and he is formidable enough to see off any mere bandit.' He jokingly indicates the man in livery, who has put aside his glaive and is wrapping his arms around his shoulders, letting his hands thump on his back to keep himself warm. He does not look very formidable.

'I dare say you are right,' Thomas says. 'I am sorry. It is a pre-occupation of mine.'

Mostyn raises his eyebrows as if to indicate he expected no less, and he walks on. Thomas watches him adjust the hang of a painted wool cloth on the wall, and he sees that Mostyn's problem is not that he believes himself so very much grander than Thomas – though he does and perhaps he is – but that he believes this hall is everything that the world is to become, while Thomas, with his clumsy heft, his sword and his mud-splattered riding boots, with his fears of attack by God knows whom, is everything the world once was, but is no longer.

Thomas trails along the corridor a step or two behind, and he finds himself hoping Mostyn is right, and that soon a man won't have to build a house with arrow slots and drawbridges, or keep a crossbow by the door. He finds himself hoping that soon the world will become dominated by corridor-stalking attorneys and black-coated moneymen such as this John Mostyn.

Mostyn suggests dinner, but Thomas is anxious to be away. He does not want to be on the road after dark, and he worries about what might be happening back at Marton Hall. He shakes Mostyn's hand, which is slim and cool, and he goes to find Jack and Foul-mouth John in the sort of stables one might expect the Master of the King's Horses to own.

'They treat horses better than they do any man I've yet to meet,' Foulmouth John says, but this comes as no surprise to Thomas or Jack; nor are they surprised to find the boy has stolen a handful of oats.

'Come on then,' Thomas says and they walk their horses out and back through the yard.

'Are you right well, Thomas?' Jack asks. 'I thought you'd be happy with having got that land at last?'

Any pleasure Thomas might have felt has been tainted by the bitter thought that he let Mostyn know he was once an ecclesiastic. He was a canon, true, rather than a friar, but that makes no material difference, for everyone knows that to become either a man must take a vow to follow the three evangelical counsels: of chastity, of obedience and, crucially, of poverty. You cannot go around buying land if you are – or once were – an ecclesiastic. You cannot go around owning land. Not if you are holding it for yourself, unless you have a dispensation from, of all people, the Pope in Rome, and who has that? Not Thomas.

Thomas mounts his horse in preoccupied silence and they begin making their way back though the orchards, following the winding track towards the tree-pruner, who has moved to a new tree and is working away. Thomas tries to think what use Mostyn might make of the information. Something? Nothing? Of course it is going to be something, but what? Thomas looks over his shoulder. He should not leave it at this, he knows. But what can he do?

The pruner sees them coming and waves his saw at them, but he does not seem to have done much work, Thomas thinks, and if it were not such a frigid spot in which to be working, he might believe he was malingering. But before they reach him, he stops his waving, and he glances back over his shoulder. Then he jerks his head around like an alarmed cock pheasant and stands upright in the branches and stares southwards.

'What's he up to, the idiot?'

Foulmouth John laughs.

'Hope the fucker falls.'

But there is something else odd happening. Jack turns and looks at Thomas. Thomas stares back, incredulous.

'What's that noise?' Foulmouth John asks.

Thomas and Jack both know what it is. They've heard it before, but why should they hear it here, now? A low rolling drum that comes from the ground. Horses. Many of them. Coming fast. Why? And the man in the tree can now see what they can only hear. He stands alarmed for a moment, staring. Thomas and Jack both pull their horses around.

'What is it?' Foulmouth John asks again. 'What's happening?'

'Come on!'

Thomas snatches the boy's bridle and hoofs his horse into a gallop, pulling the boy's pony with him, through the trees, away from the track, away from the house, out of the way of the horsemen. Jack follows. They ride as fast as they can, ducking low branches, through the orchard and out across some ridged furlongs where the horses need to step carefully. Beyond is the line of willows that must mark the river. They ride to them, and then, when they are under their tendrils and the river smell is strong in their nostrils, they slide from their saddles and lead their horses down to the frosted mud and the smooth black waters.

'Hold them,' Thomas tells Foulmouth John, 'and wait here.'

The boy nods. His eyes are as round as pennies. Jack nocks his bow and takes a handful of arrows, of the slim-shafted sort, better for hunting than for shooting at a man, but who keeps the other sort about his person? Thomas loosens his sword and they make their way back through the fields. Ahead is a great commotion of neighing and shouting. Thomas catches a first glimpse of the men coming through the orchard. There are perhaps fifty men, riding fast five abreast, all helmeted, all carrying some sort of weapon, and they are making for Burgh's new house with only one intent. It seems Mostyn spoke too soon. Thomas wonders what the soldier with the glaive will do. Run? It is what he would do.

'Who in the name of God are they?' Jack asks.

They are well organised for mere bandits, and this seems more than mere banditry. This is something planned. They've even brought those poles for pulling down walls and roofs. Thomas and Jack make their way through the trees to find a better view of the house. They crouch in some long withered grasses under an old pear tree and watch as the men climb down from their horses and flood through the gates and into the courtyard. They have sent the guard running, and now they are getting to work pulling at the scaffold. Someone has a fire burning. A woman screams and something smashes. There is much rough splintering. Another section of the scaffold teeters and then collapses in a ripple of cracks and snaps. Alarms are shouted. There is another scream. Dogs are barking as they are kicked and horses are skittering as they are dragged from the stables.

Thomas and Jack see windows knocked out and objects thrown or passed down. The place is being looted. A few men – of the usual sort – are still on horseback, directing the foot soldiers who are now investing the house. There's more smoke. More window frames are pushed out from the upper floor and lowered to hands raised below. Then someone is thrown out. A boy. There's a roar of soldierly approval and a woman starts screaming and it's obvious something bad has happened.

'Lucky we signed for the land when we did,' Thomas mutters. He swings the leather bag around his shoulder and clutches it tightly. What will happen to the men and women inside? A slim part of him hopes to see the lawyer Mostyn fly from an upper window. Grey and then black smoke begins to billow from another part of the estate, and a moment later the thatch below is cheerfully aflame.

'The stables,' Jack says. 'Said they should have used tile.'

As he says this the men start ripping tiles from the main house, one by one at first, and then there is a great sliding crash of them as they give way together.

'But who are they? Can you see a badge?'

Jack shakes his head. 'Could be anyone,' he says.

A couple of them wear black and red livery jackets, but what Thomas will have to see is a badge to know if this means anything. Another length of scaffold is levered from its wall and there's a further crash of masonry or something. A string of horses is brought neighing away from the stables where the flames have caught properly now, and the roofs of the barn and what looks like a dairy seethe with pale grey smoke. In a moment they will catch flame too, and then there'll be no stopping it.

They watch as men bring out coffers and furniture from the house and set them down a little distance off. Two or three men remain in their saddles. One of them gestures with his sword and, above the popping of the flames, Thomas can hear him barking instructions and the house Thomas had so recently admired is pulled apart, bit by bit, and everything – all the fine furniture and so on – is dragged out and carried away.

Two hatless men in hose and pourpoint appear behind the house and go running pell-mell towards the buildings beyond. More follow. Women too, hampered by dresses. One of them is clutching a bowl of something. Another, a babe in arms. More children come after them, scattering to the various folds where once they might have hidden in a game. Three soldiers in red and black come running out after them but after a very few yards they stop their pursuit, laughing, and they return to the house for better spoil.

At that moment Mostyn emerges, running awkwardly towards them, one hand on his hat, his coat undone, something under one arm.

'We could save him' Jack mutters. He nocks his bow.

'No!' Thomas says. He pushes Jack's bow down. 'No. There are too many of them.'

Watching Mostyn floundering towards the men, Thomas feels a sudden leap of hope, but then quashes it. He cannot bring himself to admit for a moment that he would see Mostyn dead, but at least that way – but then the useless soldiers let him go by. They hardly bother with him. It is as if they were meeting one another on the road, and after a moment he is past them and hobbling away into the gardens of the houses.

Thomas gasps with frustration.

'Look: just red and black. Anyone you recognise?'

Jack shakes his head again.

'They aren't all in red and black. Look. That one's in blue.'

Then it strikes Thomas. What about Marton Hall? If these men have come up the road from the south, they will have come through Marton. Past Katherine. Past Rufus. Christ! What if they have attacked them too?

'Jack,' he says. 'Let's go.'

They run, crouched, back to the willows where the horses and John wait shivering noisily and they fumble with the bridles and then lead the horses through the mud alongside the swirling black waters. They grab them and lead them on, keeping as low as they can.

'Ha!' Foulmouth John croaks. 'That fucker's still up his fucking tree. They've not touched him! They must think he's the biggest fucking crow what ever lived.'

There is no time to ponder this.

'Come on, damn you!' Thomas shouts. 'What about Marton? What about Nettie? And Katherine! Think of them!'

They mount up and ride until they find the track that takes them back on to the road south. Its mud has been much churned up by horses coming north. Seeing the tracks, Thomas knows it is as he feared: they will have come through Marton.

'Come on,' he urges. 'Come on!'

They should never have left the house, Thomas thinks. What good would John Stumps have been in protecting it? He sees dead bodies. Ripped clothing. Naked flesh. Blood. Soot. He can smell it. Hear it. He stands in the stirrups and kicks his horse into a gallop. Jack and John can hardly keep up.

'Wait!'

But he rides on across the mud stippled with the prints of their horses' hoofs. There are tears in his eyes. He looks up above the treetops. The sky is grey now, very pale, the colour of smoke and bone, of burning thatch, wood, rush. Jesus!

They reach the village and still there is nothing. No sign of any robbery. No dead bodies or burning buildings. The village is deserted, as it might well be in this weather, and the tracks run on south, past the track to Marton Hall, back down to Lincoln. All seems as it should. He allows his heart to slow, his fears to abate, his hopes to grow. He kicks on, up the track, past the church. There is a catch of smoke in the air, but once through the trees, he sees it is gusting from the hall's chimney.

Thomas reins in his sweating horse. Pats him on his neck. Both man and beast are steaming in the cold.

'It's all right,' he breathes. 'God be praised, it's all right.'

His heart slows. He is shaking, though. He had imagined such terrible things. Jack and John come cantering out of the trees behind him. Jack looks grim but relieved. Foulmouth John clings to his pony. They ride together into the deserted yard.

A face appears at the window, and a moment later the door opens and Rufus comes spilling out, laughing, clumsy, in his robe but no cap, his red hair springing everywhere. Thomas drops to the ground and bends to pick the boy up and hugs him. Rufus squeals and grabs his ears in both hands.

First Nettie comes to the door, and then Katherine, hand across her belly. They are shoulder to shoulder and they stare smiling at their men in mild surprise.

'That was quick,' one of them says.

'So who were they?' Katherine asks.

They are sitting in the hall at the table where Sir John used to sit and the fire is lit and there is bread and smoked cheese and some very salty ham and Thomas and Jack, still red-faced from their ride, are both drinking ale.

'I don't know,' Thomas admits.

'We didn't stay to find out,' Jack boasts. 'We were worried about you.'

Nettie is nursing their baby at the chair by the fire, and she is merely cross that Jack has been out and got himself involved in something that might endanger him, while Katherine looks more distantly worried. Thomas, whose recent desperate fears afforded him a glimpse of a different future, is so relieved to have returned to find the hall and his family just as he left it, and them, that he cannot take his gaze from his wife, unless it is to look at his son. She wears her dark green dress, which she will soon need to let out over her swelling belly, and she has on a bleached linen headdress that wraps under her chin. Time, or motherhood, or lack of want, has changed her face, and the austere, bird-like ferocity of her youth has softened into something more approachable, and she is to Thomas's eye ever more beautiful than ever she was. But there is something awry between them, some distance that he cannot cross, however much he tries, and however much he does.

And now he has said something to worry her, and there is a crease between her brows, and he feels that same old feeling, as if he has missed something.

'But they didn't look like robbers?' she asks. 'As you would imagine robbers to look like?'

Thomas thinks.

'No, I suppose not. They were like someone's household retainers, but they were in motley, weren't they, Jack? And they carried no flags, and wore no badges, or none that we were close enough to see.'

'And they were properly led,' Jack adds. 'Did you see their captain? Sat in his saddle all the while, pointing his sword and telling everyone what to do.'

'We can ask in the village,' Katherine supposes. 'Ask if anyone saw them passing through. We must find out who sent them.'

'Sent them?' Jack asks. 'They were just a band of robbers. A bit better organised than most, I grant, but the sheriff will have them hunted down—'

'But they attacked the sheriff. That is my point. They did not attack anyone else, did they? Not us, and no one in the village. No one as they passed. Only Burgh. Only the sheriff.'

'So? He is the wealthiest man in the county,' Jack says. 'And like to have the most things worth stealing.'

Katherine nods.

'He may do,' she says, 'but we have things worth stealing too, don't we? And yet they passed us by. Any normal band of thieves would have come here first.'

'But it is as I'm trying to tell you,' Jack says. 'They were no ordinary thieves.'

'Exactly,' Katherine says. 'So who were they? Why would they single out Thomas Burgh and his new house?'

'Because of who Burgh is?' Thomas suggests when he has finished chewing. He doesn't know where Katherine is leading them, but he knows her well enough to follow.

'And who is he?' she asks.

'He is the Sheriff of the Shire, and Master of the King's Horse.'

'So he is King Edward's man hereabouts, isn't he?'

'Yes,' Thomas supposes. 'Yes. He is.'

'And yet someone gathered, armed and then sent troops to attack his house.'

Now he sees what she means.

'They attacked him *because* he is King Edward's man? So it is an attack on King Edward?'

She nods shortly.

'Don't you think?' she asks.

'But – who would do that?' Jack asks. 'Only a man out of his wits.'

'That's true,' Thomas says. 'Do you remember King Edward saying how he had learned his lesson from last time when he was so slack? He'll not dither this time. He'll come with thousands of men to find whoever did it, and when he does, each and every one'll find himself hanging from a tree.'

Jack gallows-laughs.

'Saints,' he says. 'I would not wish to be in their shoes.'

Katherine nods, but Thomas can see she is concentrating on something beyond the thought of men hanging from trees, and that bird-like ferocity is back.

'But that's the point,' she tells them. 'Whoever did this, they did it knowing King Edward will react that way.'

Thomas is sceptical.

'How would they know that?'

She is becoming impatient.

'It is such an obvious affront,' she says. 'To pick out King Edward's man above all else. A provocation.'

There is a long moment's silence while they try to think what this might mean. The light is fading. A new log on the fire would be welcome.

'But why?' Thomas asks. 'Who would do such a thing?'

'Only someone who feels himself as powerful as the King,' Katherine tells them.

Thomas looks at her. He feels as if something is being spoiled. It's like finding the season's first lamb is stillborn.

'You can't mean the Earl of Warwick?' he asks.

'Oh Christ, not him again!' Jack moans, putting both hands to his face.

'But why would he do such a thing?' Thomas presses.

Katherine sighs.

'I don't know,' she admits. 'He might want King Edward to come up here. So he can cause trouble in London. Or wherever he is. Or there might be something else. I don't know.'

The thought that the strife is reawakened and might come again is too much to bear. He will not believe it.

'No, no,' he says. 'All that is over now. The two men are reconciled. Surely?'

'I hope you're right,' is all Katherine says, but she's looking at Rufus, their son, who sits dark-eyed by the fire, playing a complicated game of his own device with some blocks and a cloth doll. Thomas sees she has a discreet hand on her belly and her own eyes seem to have deepened in the shadows of her brow, and she looks, for the first time in a while, fearful.

So he repeats that the robbers were simply robbers, and that the wars will not come again, because did not the King prove to the Earl that only a king can rule the country? But Thomas finds himself less certain with each passing moment, and then John Stumps, who has been uncharacteristically quiet all this while, wades in with one of his predictions:

'It is well known,' he says, 'that if January the first is a Monday, as it was this year, remember, then sheep will die, and grain'll rot, and those of us that are not killed fighting in the field will die of sore throats.'

'Of sore throats?'

'Of sore throats.'

This might be a joke, but John Stumps doesn't joke. So Thomas tries to stop himself thinking about what will happen if Katherine is right, and the wars do come again, but he cannot. It is all he can think about, and so it is that he forgets the business of the day, and the attorney Mostyn.

2

In the night it snows again, a heavy dusting, and the next morning Katherine is out before daybreak, standing alone in the yard where the cold bites her to the bone. She stands for a long while, alone at the head of the track with the wind stirring her hems, her thick cloak clutched to her throat, keeping watch over the dark line of bare-limbed trees that mark the road. As dawn comes they begin to take on fantastical, cruel shapes, and they appear to stir of their own accord, and to convene and suddenly thicken, as if welling with a host of men, only to part again, and reveal themselves as they really are.

She waits until sunrise, then she turns suddenly and goes back into the hall to rouse her sleeping household, and by the time they've said their prayers, eaten their bread and drunk their ale, Thomas's new-purchased acres are forgotten, as he and Jack and the other men from the village set to work preparing the house in case the men who attacked Burgh's house should come calling on their own.

'So that is it?' she asks.

Thomas nods. He is evasive, refusing to catch her eye, and so she determines he has chosen to believe this one thing – the wrong thing, she is certain of it – over the other, right thing, and that for some reason he is sticking with his choice. She wonders what she can do about it. Nothing, of course, for the moment, and so while they all wait to see what will happen – if the men who attacked Burgh's house were robbers or not – she must lend her hand to the general effort.

Marton Hall is not any kind of castle. It is not made of stone and iron, with a moat, and a drawbridge, but Sir John Fakenham once single-handedly held off Giles Riven's attack for three days, killing most of his men with crossbow bolts shot from the windows, and even if there is no drawbridge, watchtower, moat or curtain wall, there are things that have been done to make the place less attractive to passing thieves: stout oak bars span the windows, and both doors, front and back, are four inches of solid oak, with two drawbars, also of oak, that can be dropped in place so that only a battering ram could open them.

Thomas summons everyone up from the village, in part, he says, for their own protection, but they are also useful with the work, and they gather in the yard with their families – thick-armed wives with children like grey mice, most of them – and bundles of their few possessions. Apart from John, who left his parish in Kent because his priest tried to kill him, and who towers head and shoulders over all save Thomas, the new men all look oddly similar, as if they might be the sons of the same fat-necked, deep-chested, short-legged father. If they are so, then he was a man with no great skill at anything in particular, save an ability to put his brawn to blunt use, and to travel widely too, for they've come to Marton from divers parts of England: Kent and Essex, mostly, but Robert is from a village in Devon where every man, woman and child died of plague while he was at sea, and there is a Bald John from Droitwich, who claims to be a reaper, whose wife it was who died, leaving him in sole charge of his son, the foulmouthed boy. More than that, the mythical common father must have been catholic in his tastes, for these men's eyes are blue and brown, and their hair is not only brown, but black, blond, non-existent and even (twice) red. They wear mostly patched russet and, observed from a distance, they seem to blend into the land, as if they are an elemental part of it, timeless as the soil they tramp.

Seeing them all together in the yard, they remind Katherine of the men of Sir John Fakenham's little company, most of them christened John, clucked over by Geoffrey, barked at by Walter, made to laugh by Dafydd and Owen — and all dead now. Thomas now has eight men, excluding John Stumps, who live on his land and who rely on him, just as those others used to rely on Sir John Fakenham, and over the last few months he has made them join him with their bows in the butts, where he and Jack have shouted at them and made them run to and fro, just as Thomas was made to do all those years ago by Walter in Calais. When Thomas comes in after one of these days, his voice is always hoarse from all the shouting, and he tells her they are improving, but they have a long way to go before — before what? Whenever he reaches this point in his account of his day's activities, he stops, and shrugs, and takes a drink of ale.

This morning Thomas has set two of the men to bring up water from the well to fill every barrel in the buttery that is not already filled with ale, not just to drink, he says, should they be forced to endure any kind of siege, but against the threat of fire started by arrows dipped in oil and then lit. A trench is dug through the yard, though why Katherine is not sure, and armless John Stumps is set to oversee the women and children bringing in the dried apples and the smoked meat and the salted fish from the barns, and to ensure the supplies are stacked or hung in the buttery or from the beams above the hall itself where she knows the fat will drip on those gathered below. When any complain of the weight they are carrying, John Stumps will tell them that he used to be able to carry a full-grown pig under each arm and still jump a fence.

Wood is brought in from the stack and arranged against the north wall. Logs are split end to end to provide extra planks to reinforce the window shutters. They bring in the cheese from the dairy and children are sent to harvest the medlars, even though they are not yet ripe. The few remaining pigs are penned close by, and the goats too, so that the geese have the run of the yard, and the sheep are put in the close fold, and the smell is rasping.

After dinner Katherine asks some of the women and children who have come up from the village if they saw the men ride through the day before, but none is able to identify them.

'They weren't overly friendly, like,' one says.

'Their horses were fine, though,' another tells her.

'They were all in green.'

'Red and blue.'

'Black.'

Thomas and Jack count their stocks of arrows and check the fat bellies of the various bows for cracking, and extra strings are wrapped around wrists. Knives and billhooks are sharpened on the wheel in the yard. A pile of hammers is made and then distributed around the doors and windows. Each man's protection is seen to, and the women are set the task of stuffing old jacks with tow and patching worn sleeves. Jack and one of the others ride with instructions for the blacksmith in the village a little further to the south, a man who can also do finer work including rough field harness, and while he is gone Thomas paces nervously, his bow nocked, ten or fifteen arrows in his belt.

'He will forget everything I've told him,' Thomas swears. 'Or they will be offered ale and that will be that: we'll not see them until after Easter.'

It is true that Jack is like to leave anything he has once held behind him in a trail to mark where he has been, but he says this helps him find his way back to collect what he has dropped, and it is true that since his wife Nettie gave birth to their daughter with her lungs like bellows Jack has taken wherever possible to ale and the company of strangers. But in the event the two men ride in, sober, just as it is getting dark, stiff with cold. They've brought back three dozen bolts and a new goat's-foot winding mechanism for the third crossbow, and they swear the helmets and breast-plates Thomas has ordered will be ready before Candlemas.

'How long does it take to make ten helmets?' Thomas asks. 'And we'll have no call for them if our heads are already stove in.'

Behind his back, John Stumps barks a sour little laugh, and says he thinks Thomas will soon be ordering them livery jackets.

'Building up a little affinity of his own, isn't he? Just as if he were a knight of the shire! Just like old Sir John!'

Thomas overhears him and flushes and Katherine realises this is probably not the first time Thomas has thought this, and she feels a curiously warm sense of satisfaction and even pride in her husband. If only he would listen to reason.

Now with these men up in the hall, and their families too, the smell of unwashed bodies mixed with dogs, wet wool and wood smoke becomes a powerful brew in so small a confine, as for the next few days they are compelled to remain shut up, never straying farther than the privy, where they go armed, and all are nervous, pacing, watchful, fingers plucking taut bowstrings, even Foulmouth John who is forever goddamning everything, worse than any of the older men, just as if he were an old soldier in France, and he seems to find the fact of animals covering one another almost endlessly entertaining.

But nothing happens that first day after the attack on Burgh's house, nor the second, nor the third. On the morning of the fourth day Thomas and Jack ride a circle of the estate and come back having seen nothing worth mentioning. Candlemas comes and they leave Jack at the hall while they go quickly to Mass as a household. The men keep their weapons close, even through the sacrament, and the priest is brisk. They take the candles with them back to the hall and then Jack rides over to collect the helmets and breastplates from the blacksmith.

'I feel immortal when I've got this sort of thing on,' Jack tells Katherine when he comes back wearing one. He raps the plate with his knuckles. 'Like no one can stop me.'

The following week passes slowly, and the men wait at the windows, if only to justify the wearing of their few pieces of plate, which they seem to love. Katherine sees Thomas actually wants these bandits to come, to be proven right, for he is still convinced the attack on Burgh's house was the work of outlaws.

It snows again, and thaws, and then there's a hard frost, and icicles hang from the hall's eaves like sword blades. Seeing this from the warmth of within, for a while each man and woman is pleased to have reason not to go out, but to remain gathered together about the fire in the hall, and at night the household sleeps around it as they used to when Sir John was alive.

By the end of the next week, it is felt they need no longer double up as night watchmen, and they need no longer put the dogs out when it falls dark, or constantly stand by the windows during the daylight hours, and still nothing happens. As the days eke past, the pleasure of idleness ebbs just as the earlier tension had, and the enforced stillness begins to rankle. Jack twitches and bounces and itches to be gone, out with the lurchers in the wood, or down at the butts, or anywhere away from his wife and noisy baby. Tempers begin to unravel at the close confinement and the lack of exercise, especially as the weather turns properly mild during that third week, and Thomas stands at the window, looking not at the road, as might be supposed, but at the fields they might usefully be ploughing and sowing with seed.

Katherine has not minded the time so much as the others, for she has been feeling the weight of the baby in her womb, but she has resented the isolation from the greater world beyond more keenly than them. It is the lack of news, the not knowing, that bothers her. And as every day passes without sight or sound of this band of robbers, she has itched to find some new proof that it was a deliberate affront to King Edward, a provocation, only for none to come – save, at least, that there has been no attack on the hall, about which she is obviously pleased. Thomas, though, far from being happy not to have been attacked, has been the most mulish, distracted and bitter-tempered of them all, quick to snap, even at Rufus. It is as if he is struggling to keep down an emetic, she thinks, and she cannot help wonder if he would not be happier if he could let it out.

And because they have not worked themselves to the bone, as they are used to, they all find it hard to sleep, and so the house is in constant chaos, with men and women and children on the move throughout the long and short hours. And who are they? Katherine knows most by name, and a little about each, but they are still strangers to her, taken in as tenants, their stories mostly unknown, but now they have moved in under her roof. They are friends of friends, or known to friends, or friends of people Thomas knows. She might see a shadow loom in the night, and have no idea who it really is. And they are also eating too much, using up valuable resources because they are so bored, and she thinks of the Lent to come, and then how hard Easter will be if they go on like this.

By the fourth week arguments blow up, and it is clear that John Stumps would gladly pull a knife on Jack if he but could, and soon every man, woman and child among them yearns to return to their old ways.

'Can't fucking stand it no more,' Foulmouth John says, and he just walks out of the door, leaving it open, and is gone. His father hardly looks up from his clumsy stitching of a flap-soled boot.

And that is the end of it. Thomas, still sticking to his theory that it was a rogue band of robbers, decides the danger must have passed them by.

'They must have left the county,' he says. 'We should ride to Lincoln and pay the choir to sing a *Te Deum*.'

He is only half joking, Katherine thinks. But the next morning, a Sunday, under a pale sky that might clear by midday, they saddle their horses in anxious excitement at the thought of being away from the hall, and at the thought of seeing new people, and hearing new things, and there is nothing that will stop Jack coming with them, 'just for the sight of something new'. They bring two other men, John, who was once stabbed by his priest, and Bald John, who is the father of Foulmouth John, and who looks as if he has spent the previous few nights drinking wine and has yet to go to bed, for his cheeks are slack, and the whites of his flaccid eyes are the colour of morning urine.

'What's wrong with him?' Thomas asks quietly.

She doesn't know.

It is like coming out of winter's sleep, she thinks, and when they reach the road, they are all of them hesitant, and she is overtaken by anxiety, like a mouse poking her head from her hole in spring, and she half expects – what? A cat? A band of outlaws? In the end there is nothing save the sedge-lined length of the old road, running straight, pitted and muddy, south to Lincoln, and the call of a wood pigeon.

Thomas leads the way in his best coat with Rufus on his lap, then Katherine, then Jack and the other two men. The men are armed with nocked bows, and Thomas has a sword at his hip, sheathed in red leather that is beautifully worked with tabs of what look like silver, and which she has not seen before. She cannot help wonder what the blade must be like, and where and when he acquired it, and for how much?

They ride in speculative silence for a bit. Katherine's bay pony is even-gaited and fitted with the side-saddle Thomas gave her for the year's turn: in the same beautiful red leather as his sword sheath, skilfully stitched, and padded where you would wish it to be padded; and Katherine wears the conker-brown riding boots the cordwainer made for her after taking the shape of her foot and sculpting a wooden replica, just as if she would be returning time and time again to have a hundred pairs of shoes made, and she cannot help admire the way the boots fit her ankles crossed as she rides. She is in her blue rabbit-trimmed winter cloak, too, which she had made overlarge, for precisely a moment like this, and of course, her best dress – of fine blue kersey, which she paid a woman in Lincoln to make for her. She will have to let it out again soon, she thinks.

Being with child this time has not been half as bad as the first, with Rufus, when she was half-dead with the sickness most of the time, and there are times when she feels the grip of fear that perhaps the baby is dead within her womb, but then there is that curious internal wriggle, an elbow scraped across her gut only from within, like a reordering, as the baby turns and settles, and she feels warm relief. She has already lost too many to be sure of this one.

She still thinks of Rufus's poor dead twin now and then, still-born in a field below Bamburgh Castle, but she finds herself immune to any speculation as to what the child would be doing now, had she lived. She was baptised, so that is enough, and she has been spared the scrambled life Rufus has had to endure. She does not try to imagine how it might have been with two of them.

They stop fairly often to let Rufus climb down from Thomas's saddle to collect a long brown tube of a bulrush, say, or to push aside the fence of reeds to get a closer look at some coot chicks on a mere, and each time they do, Katherine hears the bald, pouch-eyed John burp softly. But she can ignore him, for Rufus is delighted by how much the world has changed in the month or so since they were last abroad, and it is impossible not to share his pleasure at the sight of nature reborn.

They ride on, carefully keeping watch ahead, and she had hoped to try to gauge the temper of the country as they pass, to meet that needle merchant, say, with news of the south, or some pilgrims, or in fact anyone, but the roads are very quiet and they meet no one, not a soul, until at last they recognise the shape of Foulmouth John loping towards them, barefoot, with tears dried on his cheeks and an eye so black it is closed up.

'Fucking squirrel done it,' he tells them without breaking stride, and he leaves them in his wake, trying to imagine how that might be. His father bald John just shakes his head very slightly.

Further on they meet the carrier, coming warily towards them through a long straight stretch of tree-lined road. He will know what is afoot, she thinks, since he travels from Lincoln to Gains-borough and back three or four times a week. He sits in his cart, rather than walks alongside, and behind him, unusually, come three men in helmets, thick jacks, two armed with bills, the other a bow. Up close they look unsure of their own military might, and Katherine supposes they might be recruited from the Watch on one of the city gates, and are more used to leering at nuns and warming their hands over a brazier than fighting off bands of robbers.

'God give you good speed,' the carrier greets them when he recognises them, and they return the blessing, and the carrier draws up his mule. Despite his life on the move, he's a fat man, awkward in his seat, under layers of filthy russet, like a shuffling, shaggy bear that you see in poor fairs. He speaks with a strained whispery voice, and he tells them of his cargo that today includes three dun-coloured puppies in a wicker cage and a fierce-looking cockerel that hangs by his spurs from the back of the cart. He tells them business is bad, as he always does when you meet him, but that is to be expected at this time of year.

'So have you heard anything further of the attack on Thomas Burgh's house?' Katherine asks.

The man sucks his teeth.

'A bad business, mistress. A bad business. Though no one killed, praise the Lord, save a servant boy thrown from a window.'

'Is it known who did it?'

'It is well known, mistress,' he says, tipping his head. 'For the perpetrator never sought to hide his sin, unlike Eve when first she tempted Adam.'

He is that sort of man. He licks his lips and speculates on the costrel of ale on Thomas's saddle. Thomas sighs and hands it to the man, who takes it with thanks and drinks long. A strong smell emanates from the yeasty folds of his cloth.

'It was Lord Welles,' he tells them when he has wiped his lips with the back of his hand. 'Lord Welles and another gentle who goes by the name of Sir Thomas Dimmock.'

The names mean nothing to her, nor to Thomas, who looks crestfallen.

'Not – not a band of outlaws?' he asks.

The carrier laughs.

'No, no, indeed. Or not any more. The family was once attainted – after old Lord Welles was killed at Towtonfield – but our Lord Welles has regained the King's mercy, so is outlaw no longer, though how long that will last, only God above can say.' He raises his eyes heavenward. Thomas still refuses to believe it.

'But then why is he attacking Thomas Burgh?'

'Oh, they're like Cain and Abel, that sort, aren't they?' the carrier says. 'Forever at one another over this or that. Welles's lands are mostly to the south of Lincoln, and when the old King was on the throne, his was the family to whom the whole county bent its knee. Times change.'

So it seems both Katherine and Thomas were wrong. It was not some banditry, nor was it some piece of provocation: it was merely local rivalry between two gentles, a feud got out of hand. She feels warm with relief.

'Thanks be to God,' she says.

The carrier inclines his head.

'Aye,' he cautions, 'but Burgh has used his influence with King Edward . . .' He holds up the costrel and raises his eyebrows for permission.

Thomas nods. The man drinks again. His guard are shuffling their feet. The mule farts sonorously.

'Fine ale,' he says when he has caught his breath and wiped his mouth again. 'Fine ale.'

'King Edward——?'

'King Edward? Oh yes. So King Edward has taken up the cause of Burgh in this, as he might, you'd think, since Burgh is King Edward's man after all, and what use is goodlordship if it cannot be called upon? And so King Edward summoned Lord Welles and this other gentle to appear before him down in Westminster, and he has them down there still.'

So that is it? Katherine thinks. This last month spent cooped up in the hall, taut as cloth in a tenter frame, peering out over a crossbow at any noise without, and it was – for nothing? Thomas at least has the decency to look abashed.

'Well,' he says. 'Let us give thanks to God for a swift resolution then, anyway.'

'Amen to that,' the carrier agrees. 'Though there are . . .' And he holds the costrel up again, and Thomas nods again and they sit and watch him finish the ale. There was more than two pints in there, Katherine supposes.

'Though there are many who fear a wider reckoning yet. They're saying that King Edward is preparing to come up here to see for himself the temper of our county.' The carrier raises his eyebrows as he repeats the formal phrasing, and it is obvious he is quoting something he has heard said elsewhere. Katherine remembers Thomas's story of King Edward claiming that he always learned his lessons, and that he would never underestimate a threat again as he had that last summer. So it seems he may be true to his word.

'A friar told me he was coming to hang us all,' one of the guards adds.

Katherine is as surprised as Thomas.

'Why?' he asks.

'Many from around here turned out for Robin of Redesdale last summer, didn't they? Or they went over to the Earl of Warwick while King Edward was in the Northern Parts. They'll have reason to fear his coming.'

'Including this Lord Welles?'

The carrier nods.

'He was one who went over, yes.'

Katherine has a thought. It is like being stung by a nettle, sharp at first, but its warmth spreads through her.

'Did you say Welles's lands are south of Lincoln?' she asks.

'There or thereabouts. Around Tattershall in the main.'

And she finds herself nodding, because the word Tattershall rings familiar.

'Is that where the castle is?'

'The pink one?' The carrier nods. He obviously doesn't hold with it.

'And does Baron Willoughby come from near there?' Katherine presses.

The carrier smiles broadly.

'Baron Willoughby, mistress? Baron Willoughby? Why, Baron Willoughby and Lord Welles, they are one and the same, mistress. They are the same man!'

The carrier's laugh is wheezy, and Katherine can smell him even above the horses and the silent puppies in the back. He wipes each teary eye with the back of his index finger and then returns the costrel, and now the ale is gone, so too is his desire to share any further knowledge. They repeat their blessings and wish him well, and they leave him to grind his way northwards to Gainsborough, with his shuffling guard and the cockerel glaring at them as they go.

'What was all that about?' Thomas asks. 'Do you know of this Baron Willoughby?'

'Last year,' Katherine begins, 'in the summer, when you were with King Edward in Middleham, I went with Isabella to Tattershall to appeal to Baron Willoughby for the release of Jack and John and Nettie.'

Thomas remains puzzled.

'How would he have been able to help with that?' he asks.

'Because Isabella said he had the ear of the Earl of Warwick.'

'But he didn't, remember?' Thomas says. 'We had to go up there to get them out ourselves.'

'But only because he was not there,' Katherine tells him. 'Only because he was with the Earl of Warwick when we came. He was with the Earl.'

She sees it all now. Warwick induces Welles to cause an affray, knowing that this time King Edward will not make the mistake of underestimating it, and then when he comes north to show his strength, Warwick will strike elsewhere, perhaps, or cut him off from his strength in London. Yes. That is what he will do. Lure King Edward north, and interpose his own troops between him and his allies.

'But – but you heard the carrier,' Thomas says. 'It is a simple feud!'

'But Welles is Warwick's man, isn't he? Just as Riven was. A different tool for a different job, perhaps.'

'Even so. The King has both Welles and the other one in Westminster. He has them, and the matter, in hand.'

'But then – then why is King Edward coming up here to "see for himself the temper of the county"?'

'Oh, that is only a rumour,' Thomas says, but she can see him thinking hard.

'But what if it is true?'

'Well, then,' he says. 'I suppose King Edward will come and then he will hang those who have rebelled against him.'

'But what if Warwick *wants* him to do just that?'

Thomas looks to Jack and then the other men as if they might explain it to Katherine. They are dumb beasts, she thinks, and stubborn, too. Why can't they see what she means?

'Come on,' Thomas says, trying to change the topic. 'We shall be late for Mass.'

They ride on, meeting no one until the reach the Newport Arch in Lincoln, where they find the men of the Watch looking pinched and anxious. Normally they are full of cheap swagger, but today something is up. What, though?

'King Edward,' one of them mutters when she asks. 'He is coming up here from London, bringing with him a very great number of men to punish the county for all the riotous commotions of last year.'

So it is not just a rumour. Katherine hears Thomas puff out his cheeks. She resists looking at him. She wonders if the guard might ordinarily use such words as riotous commotion to describe anything? She does not think so.

'Who told you that?' she asks.

'It was a friar,' he tells them. 'Just been through. You must have missed him on the road.' He gestures down the road, as if at the man's back. They'd seen no friar.

They walk their horses into the city towards the cathedral.

'It is still only a rumour,' Thomas says.

'But a friar?' she asks. 'The same one that the carter heard it from?'

Thomas shrugs. 'Why not?' he asks.

That is true, but still, something is odd about it. She wonders why they did not see this friar themselves? There's an odd atmosphere on the close cramped streets north of the cathedral, too, as if the place is battened down in readiness for heavy winds or a rainstorm. Men and women hurry by, heads ducked, shoulders hunched, not looking up, offering no blessing, and Katherine feels they know something she and Thomas do not. Perhaps it is always like this, she thinks, and it only seems odd because she has been away from it for so long? But no. There is some extra humour in the air.

They walk past the apothecary, whose shop is boarded shut, and down into the cathedral precinct, where a small crowd is gathered on the steps of the great church. Someone is reading something out in a low voice, and the crowd stands listening quietly. They are not the usual crowd coming from Mass, Katherine thinks, and when the man has stopped reading there is only a low burble of voices, and then the knot – there must be twenty of them perhaps – begins to fray, with men and women stalking away, necks bent again, shoulders hunched as if in readiness for a beating, muttering to one another.

'What is it?' she asks.

'Wait here,' Thomas says. He swings Rufus from the saddle, takes him by the hand and together they make their way to the front of the thinning crowd where Thomas peers short-sightedly at the sheet of paper nailed to the jamb of the cathedral's west door. Katherine stays with Jack and the other two, and the horses. Jack doesn't say anything, but his eye flits about, seeking novelty and diversion, and he is bent to be off and away into the city's sloping streets. Katherine's gaze slips across the façade of the cathedral, across the precinct, past the stationers' stalls and down the hill to the pardoner's widow's house. She wonders if she is still there, still at the window in her ghostly attire, still waiting for her new husband to come to take away all those books she hated so.

Thomas returns looking serious.

'What does it say?' she asks.

'It's a summons,' he tells her. 'From someone calling himself the Great Captain of the Commons of the Shire.'

'A summons to what?'

Thomas relates what it says in the voice in which he imagines the summons was written:

'It says King Edward is coming up here with a great power and many judges who will sit and hang and draw a great number of the said commons of this county for the revolt they carried out this

41

last year before and at the time of Michaelmas, and this Great Captain of the Commons is calling on them to meet at a place called Ranby Hawe – on pain of death – to resist King Edward.'

Katherine is speechless for a moment. It is no wonder they've seen men and women stealing away looking fearful and shocked. It is treason even to suggest such a meeting, but to spell it out in a handbill like this – that is to invite a death sentence! The cathedral bells ring out and a cloud of pigeons erupt from their perches among the shit-spattered saints on the towers. The horses shy on their reins and they must gather them and soothe them, and after that they walk away, leading their nervous horses, and it seems Thomas's *Te Deum* is to be forgotten for the day.

As they walk, she thinks on the summons, and sees it for what it is. Yes, she says to herself, it is the reaction to the reaction. Another link in a chain of events. So that is why the rumour is being spread! It hardly matters now if King Edward was ever going to come here with his armies or not, because now, faced with this growing revolt, he must.

But what is the nature of the trap King Edward has been set? That is what she cannot know because she has been sealed away in Marton Hall for the last month, and even had she been free to go, where might she have gone? She would hardly have been riding around the land, spying on the dealings of the Earl of Warwick. But she can imagine them. She can imagine him hatching out the plot, blowing on its embers, getting it going.

'Does the Earl suppose he can defeat King Edward in battle?' she wonders aloud. 'Is that it?'

Thomas sighs. 'It will not come to anything like that,' he says. 'King Edward will come, and those who answer this summons will vanish like smoke in the wind, and the so-called Great Captain of the Commons will answer for his treason with his head.'

In the past, Katherine thinks, Thomas might have believed her, or taken her word on trust, but now she is pregnant, it is as if she is out of her wits.

'It is natural,' he says, trying to reassure her. 'Natural that you should worry. The child has disturbed your humours. That is it.'

She feels a spike of anger and places a hand under her belly.

'No,' she says. 'It is not that. It is that if I am right, and if the Earl of Warwick is once more making war on King Edward, then you know what will happen.'

At this Thomas looks stern, resolved. 'No,' he says. 'William Hastings will not call on me, and even if he did, I would not go. I would find some excuse. I am done with that. We – we are done with that.'

She turns to him.

'It does not matter whether you think you are done with it, Thomas. What matters is whether it is done with *you*. Whether it is done with *us*.'

Thomas stares at her without saying anything. His eyes are fierce, blazing even, but now he knows what she is thinking. He closes his eyes and pinches the bridge of his nose.

'Oh Christ,' he says. 'The ledger.'

And she needs say no more.

Yes. The ledger. It has lain buried for these last few months under the hearth in Jack's house, hidden from all the world, but still as potent as a body in the plague pit, and whenever Katherine steps across his threshold, inevitably she glances first to the hearth before she looks up again at Jack or his wife or his child. They should destroy it. Of course they should. They should take it outside and burn it. And yet they have not done so, and they have not done so because they cannot do so. They must keep it, and they must keep it for ever, because when one day it is discovered they have it, or even that once they had it – as one day it surely will be known – then one or other of the two most powerful men in all England will come calling for this ledger, and yielding it up to them will be the only thing she and Thomas may do to save their lives.

But until then, there it is, bundled tightly in its waxed linen and leather bindings, heavy as any chain, shackling them, inescapably, to the great weight of their pasts. It had first come into their possession by chance ten years ago now, and the man who had – in a way – left it to them had claimed it was of incalculable value to the right man. But when they first looked at it, they could not see why nor to whom it might be worth a penny, for it was unpromising fare: long lists of names of troops from the garrison in Rouen, in English Normandy, written on cheap paper and bound in third-grade leather. It detailed the soldiers' movements around English France, and the efforts made to supply them with armaments – mostly bows and arrows, which they could not plunder as they went – and it covered the months from spring 1440 to early autumn in 1442.

For three years its worth remained a mystery until with the help of Sir John Fakenham they had divined its secret, and hence its value, and when they had done so, they had sat back in silence and Katherine will still swear that she could see the hair on the old man's head standing on end. The simple, dangerous truth that the ledger contains is that nine months before King Edward was born in 1442, his mother Cecily was in Rouen, in the north, while his father, Richard, Duke of York, was in a place called Pontours, in distant Aquitaine, in the south, and they were separated from one another by a journey of at least six weeks.

So the Duke of York cannot be King Edward's father, and since it is from the Duke that King Edward inherits his claim to the throne of England, his claim to it is as illegitimate as he is himself. But just thinking this, Sir John had told them, was enough to have them each hanged and then drawn twice over. 'If this should get out,' he'd said, 'if it should be learned that we know of it, then we, and everyone we know, and everyone they know, will be rounded up to be split from bollocks to chops, to have our guts pulled from us and wound around a winding wheel while we watch on.'

So they had hidden the ledger from sight, and if only they had left it so, wrapped in its length of moth-eaten kersey at the bottom of an elm coffer at the foot of Sir John's bed, then it would now be just as if the thing had never existed.

But they had made a mistake: when Fortune's Wheel had turned against them, and when they were at their most desperate, they had unearthed the ledger. They had taken it north to use it to try and buy the favour of the old King – Henry of Lancaster as he is known now – who was then still holding out in one of those northern castles. With the ledger in his possession, old King Henry might have been able to persuade the nobility of England to rally to his banner once more, and help restore him to his usurped throne.

But their scheme failed, and King Henry failed, and for that they later gave thanks to God, but while they were with him in the castle, at Bamburgh, the ledger had been stolen. They had recovered it soon after, but not before Sir Ralph Grey, the castle's governor, had stumbled upon it and, though mostly drunk and incapable, had somehow discerned its secret. When the castle fell and he was captured, he had passed his knowledge of the thing on to the Earl of Warwick in the hope of a pardon for holding out against King Edward. Perhaps this might have saved him, if only he had had the ledger to go with it, but by that time Thomas had reclaimed it and spirited it away, and so Grey – still unsteady from the falling masonry that had knocked him senseless at the end of the siege – went to the block cursing his fate.

Of course the Earl of Warwick began looking for the ledger as soon as Grey was rolled in his pit, but Grey's grip on the thing had only ever been fleeting, and by then all trace of it seemed to have vanished. In addition, at that time the Earl of Warwick was still King Edward's closest ally, his bosom companion, so his search was fuelled only by the desire to suppress its secret, rather than anything more sinister; and though he recognised its threat sufficiently to enrol the help of King Edward's Chamberlain, William Hastings, in finding it, neither pressed hard, and neither had any luck, and so the matter was allowed to lie, and the ledger lay buried under the hearthstone of the new house Thomas built over it.

But a few years later, King Edward and the Earl of Warwick fell out, and the Earl began seeking both cause and manner with which to displace his ingrate protégé, and he remembered the ledger. He started searching for it again, only this time with all his mighty intent, employing Edmund Riven to break bones and burn flesh in its pursuit.

Naturally enough, though, news of his frantic search reached King Edward's Chamberlain, Lord Hastings, who had stayed loyal to King Edward, and, realising the Earl's design, he too began looking for the ledger with equal urgency. He sent a man – a cleric, he said, but with a wink – whom he called his bloodhound across the Narrow Sea, to Rouen, to try to trace the ledger's disappearance from that end.

But then, suddenly, thankfully, before Michaelmas last, King Edward and the Earl of Warwick seemed to settle their differences. They made up, and peace broke out up and down the country. And if the two men were never quite such friends as they had once been in the past, it had seemed they were at least united in the desire to keep this peace. With this in mind, Katherine and Thomas have been able to rest more easily, trusting that if the Earl of Warwick no longer seeks the ledger so pressingly as once he did, then neither does Lord Hastings.

But what if the peace does not last? Katherine now thinks. What if the attack on Burgh's house is the first move in some new war between the Earl and the King? This is the question that most pre-occupies her that afternoon as they ride back up the track to Marton Hall: what does all this mean for them?

3

'So what are you going to do?' Jack asks.

They are walking past the church, back from the butts with the other men ahead, all of them steaming like cows in the cold from the exercise.

'I don't know,' Thomas admits. 'All I've been thinking about is this.' He gestures at the hall, and the fields around them. 'Trying to get it right, so that when I get to heaven, and when I meet Sir John – God bless him – I can look him in the eye, you know, and I can shake him by the hand, just as we used to, and he'd tell me that I'd done right by him and right by those he loved.'

'And you've done so, Thomas,' Jack says. 'By God. Look at the place.'

'But it's not enough, is it, Jack? It's not enough. When Katherine killed Edmund Riven, and when we found all that money, I thought that was it, we could come back here and bide to ourselves. I thought we could make everything better, little by little, if we just stuck to it, and that if we did that none of us'd ever again find ourselves standing starving by the side of the road with only one shoe; none of us'd ever again have to go off to fight for someone in whom he did not believe, for something he didn't believe; none of us'd have our bloody arms cut off, and none of our women'd ever have to give birth to a child while they're chained to a wall.'

Jack waits. These are more words than Thomas has spoken for a good few days.

'You will say it is pride, Jack,' he goes on. 'I know, but once the Rivens were dead, and once we were all back here, then I honestly thought that so long as I was diligent, and so long as I observed God's ways in all things, then He would afford us peace.'

Jack nods, though it is not clear he completely understands. Thomas is not sure he does either.

'But now,' he goes on, 'now it seems it's not ended. We've seen those two Rivens sent to hell, and yet, if Katherine's right, and I suppose she must be, then it will still go on. More of the same. More and more. And the worst of it is that every blessing that God has given me only means I've more to lose.'

He thinks about Rufus, and about the child in Katherine's belly, and he looks at the fields and woods and the orchard and the mill, and he looks at the chimney of the hall he can see above the trees, and he thinks about the men who troop along behind him, and of Nettie and the squalling baby, and of poor crippled John Stumps, and he tries to remember the words of the Evangelist who claimed that those whom God loved, He first tested in the fire. And Thomas cannot help wonder if this latest development is God testing him further, afresh, yet again.

'When I was a lad,' Jack says, 'my mam used to tell me a story that she said was passed down from the old days, when the Danes were here, mouth to mouth on Twelfth Night and so on. Least that's what she said. It was about a man – Wolf, I think it was – who comes to live in a village terrorised by some sort of flying dragon.'

'St George,' Thomas tells him.

'No. Not him. This Wolf wasn't a Christian. Anyway. Wolf decides one day he can't go on like this, with the people he loves being snatched away and his home being set on fire every night, so he decides he must kill this dragon. So he gets his sword and shield and out he goes, and after a fight that lasts three weeks or something, he does. He kills the dragon.'

Thomas feels deflated. He had hoped Jack would have a solution.

'But the problem was,' Jack goes on, 'the problem was that this dragon, well, he had a mother, didn't he? A dragon mother who when she heard her boy was dead, came roaring out to find this Wolf, and she was much, much bigger'n her son, wasn't she? And she was really fierce, and really angry at this Wolf, and so she came for him, and this time he had to fight her for five weeks.'

Jack feels he's made his point, and they walk in silence for a short while. Thomas is not certain he has.

'Five weeks?' he asks.

'Something like that. Anyway, what I mean is that – that this Wolf is like you, isn't he? Like us. And the dragon: she's like Riven.'

'But both Rivens are dead,' Thomas tells him.

'Yes,' Jack says. 'And now there is an even bigger dragon in their place.'

'So . . . you are saying there will always be someone – a dragon – coming between us and – and peace?'

Jack nods. They walk on in silence for a moment. It is a good story, Thomas thinks, and he imagines he'd've liked to have heard it told properly.

'What happened in the end?' Thomas asks.

'Of the story? She always changed it. Sometimes the man'd win, sometimes the dragon.'

He pauses.

'That's in the nature of these tales,' he says eventually.

Thomas wonders if that's true.

Early on the next day it is decided for him, and it comes almost as a mercy: a messenger with a blob of lead fashioned in the rough shape of a bull's head pinned to his coat. He hands Thomas a sealed letter. Thomas reads it.

'Well?' Katherine asks. She has a fist on her hip and looks sceptical. She has never quite trusted William Hastings, or Thomas's devotion to him, though why, Thomas still does not know.

'Lord Hastings sends his blessing to us all and asks for me to go to Ranby Hawe to ascertain for myself and with my own eyes the temper of the King's people there. And then I am to come to him wherever he may be.'

She looks pinched to hear him say it.

'What about us?' she says. 'What will we do?'

Thomas bites his lip.

'Well, perhaps you are right?' he says after a moment. 'Perhaps there is no gang of thieves in the county?'

She cocks an eyebrow at him. After the arguments they've had.

The messenger finishes his mug of ale. He's waiting for a reply.

All three of them know Thomas must go.

Thomas takes the paper and writes a few words on the back. He has no seal of his own, and anyway, the letter is of no interest to anyone other than Hastings, and so the messenger tucks it back in his bag and clambers back up into his saddle. They watch him touch his heels to the horse's flanks and turn and go.

'I am sorry,' Thomas says. 'He – We need him, so I must do as he bids.'

She knows this. They all know that they rely on Hastings's goodlordship. Without his backing – in any court case, or in a fight – they would be prey to any passing speculator with an eye to their property or even their lives.

'Well,' Katherine says with a smile haunting her lips and eyes, 'perhaps you may do him good service? Perhaps you can tell him that I was right and that you were wrong, and that the Earl of Warwick is behind the attack on Burgh's house, and that even now he is setting King Edward a trap?'

Thomas smiles back at her. She is very clever, he thinks.

'It may come to nothing,' he says.

'With God's grace,' Katherine tells him, serious again.

When he is ready to go he takes her in his arms and plants a kiss on her mouth. He feels her arms around his waist and they hold one another, his cheek on her crown, her face pressed into the hollow of his neck, and he feels the simple comfort of her touch.

When they break apart, and he swings himself up into the saddle, and he and Jack ride in silence, Thomas thinks that it is strange God should reveal his design through a pagan tale told to a small boy, and now only half remembered, but then again, he supposes, the Lord is well known to work in curious, roundabout ways. So here he is, on a good horse, with a good man at his side and a good sword at his hip. He wears a stout padded jack under a brigandine of very dark blue linen, studded with tin-coated rivets and lined with steel, and he has his tight-fitting archer's sallet bouncing from his saddle behind. His bow and two sheaves of arrows are strapped across the horse's withers, along with a bag of his other possessions, including some parchment and an ink pot and pen-quill case so that he may write to Katherine if needs be. All he misses is the pollaxe. He wonders who holds it now? Christ, it was a fearsome thing.

Ordinarily Ranby Hawe might be hard to find. No one they

know to ask has heard of it, and so Thomas and Jack ride out in hope rather than expectation of discovering it, well laden with bread and ale, anticipating a few days in the saddle asking questions of pedlars, travelling merchants, carriers, pilgrims and friars. In the event it is easy to find, though, impossible to miss even, for the roads to the north and east of Lincoln are busy with the companies of men strung out seeking the same destination. There is a celebratory mood in the air, with many men calling out to one another, and the drumming and piping of the boys is as cheerful as on St John's in June. Thomas and Jack pull up their horses and sit forward to watch the procession.

Thomas does not now know what he hoped to find, but he sees none of the Earl of Warwick's red livery among the men.

'Ranby Hawe is five miles hence,' one horseman tells them, indicating eastwards. He is in a travelling cloak, but it cannot disguise the bulk of the thick archer's jack below, and his man rides behind, smiling vacantly as if slightly drunk and leading a mule stacked with the tell-tale rolls of arrows in their sheaths of oiled cloth and numerous long tubes that can only be bows. Behind him follow five more men, nondescript.

Thomas offers him ale from his costrel, and probes his loyalties.

'I am Guy Watkins,' the man tells him, guileless as the day is long. 'Of Langton, in this county, and I owe my service to Sir John Pyble, who in turn owes his to Sir Robert Welles. Which is why I am answering the summons.'

Thomas is confused.

'Lord Welles?' he prompts. Lord Welles was the man whom King Edward summoned to London.

'Ha!' The man laughs. 'No doubt he will be one day, but while his father lives, he remains Sir Robert.'

'And he – this son of Lord Welles – he is this – this Great Captain of the Commons?'

'In deed and thought!'

Thomas does not know what to think. He had supposed the Earl of Warwick might reveal himself as the Great Captain of the Commons, and finding this is not so, a small spark of hope is ignited in his breast: perhaps after all Warwick has nothing to do with this? Perhaps it is as the carrier said: a local feud? One family against another? Perhaps now Thomas will be allowed to turn and ride back home after all? But then – why are all these men gathering?

'May we ride with you?' Thomas asks, offering him some of his ale.

'It would be my honour,' Watkins tells them.

'We came as soon as we heard the summons,' Thomas begins his falsehood.

'You did well. We must be strong to resist King Edward in this.'

'Do you have particular reason to fear him?'

'Of course! He is coming to punish us for what we did last year. I know he has issued a general pardon, but how much is that worth when he is coming up here with such a great power of men?'

'But did you yourself go over to the Earl of Warwick last year?' Thomas persists.

'I think all in the county did,' Watkins says.

But there is a frown gathering and he's stiffened in his saddle, bristling slightly at Thomas's intrusive line of questions.

'But are we doing so now? Is the Earl behind this summons?'

'The Earl?'

'Of Warwick?'

'Why do you ask?'

'I hoped it were so,' Thomas lies.

Watkins is perplexed, and after a moment shakes his head and then they ride on in silence.

Ranby Hawe is not much more than a few houses around a cross-roads in a broad stretch of wet saltings, ordinarily nowhere anyone would wish to spend any time they need not, but today it is almost hidden under the number of men and horses thronging its narrow muddy tracks, in a gathering that is more like a fair than a muster, with the drummer boys and pipe-players competing, and loud cheers from the men, mostly older than Thomas had expected, who are standing ruddy-faced in groups, garrulously comparing horses, harness, weapons and the usual things, just as if this were any normal Shrove Tuesday.

Stalls are set up in houses and yards, and under ash-poled canvas awnings along the roadsides, selling everything a man might need, from bits of old meat to steel-ribbed gauntlets. There are the usual itinerant smiths, bowyers, stringfellows and arrow-makers hard at it, with boys and women shouting out the value and virtue of their wares in competition with similar shouts from bakers' boys and brewsters and piemen, and over everything, above the smell of horses and men and even the bitter bite of the smith's fumes, washes the smell of roasting meat.

'This should be fun,' Jack says, and he pushes his horse ahead, eager to be among crowds of men, eager to put domestic dreariness behind him and embrace the chance to throw stones at a tethered cockerel. Within moments he has ale in his hand, and has found a crowd to laugh at one of his jokes. Thomas looks at Watkins, who is also very bright-eyed. Thomas tries one more time.

'Do you know this – this Welles?'

'In passing,' Watkins admits.

'You'd point him out?'

'If I see him.'

Watkins slides off his horse and Thomas does likewise and they find a boy running a business to tether them, and then they set off, Watkins looking for a familiar face, Thomas for anything to suggest the Earl of Warwick might be behind any of this. Watkins stops to look over men's heads and shoulders at the final moments of a close-fought cock fight, which he seems to enjoy, but the adamantine mood at these things reminds Thomas of the beheadings he has seen.

'Ha! Ha!' Watkins cries as one bird is wounded and falls to its side, scuttling mad circles in the mud. 'Look at that!'

The other bird seems to hang his head in bloody shame, Thomas thinks, but half the crowd cheer, and the other half groan. Another bird is brought forward and Watkins is pulling another man's sleeve and there's a coin between his fingers and they'll obviously be here for a while.

'Where will I find Robert Welles?' Thomas shouts in Watkins's ear.

Watkins wafts a hand.

'By the crossroads perhaps,' he says. 'You'll not miss him.'

Watkins has outgrown his use, so Thomas seeks out Welles on his own. He passes men in every shade of coat. There are hundreds of badges he does not recognise, and banners too: the small square ones, suggesting knights rather than lords. But though there are plenty of men in red, they wear different devices, and Thomas can find no sign of that bear, or of the tree stump, or the club. There is nothing to say that any of these men owe their loyalty to the Earl of Warwick. Nor is there anything to suggest that these men are grimly fixated on fighting, or the coming of King Edward. Instead they are pleasure bent, enjoying the day.

He finds Robert Welles a little further on, sitting on horseback, fist on hip, a nervous boy despite his dark brigandine and fine leg plates, surrounded by a handful of his own servants and men-at-arms, dressed similarly, none of whom seem to know what they should be doing. He's so young, this Great Captain of the Commons, that Thomas can't believe he hasn't been put up to this; he looks self-conscious, and is forever touching his face, and smiling suddenly and shyly as if astonished to be the centre of attention amidst the numbers swelling before him.

Thomas watches him a while, but still can't be certain that this is the man he saw directing those soldiers – some of whom are probably here today – in the ripping apart of Burgh's house. That man seemed more resolute than this boy, who appears so young. Thomas turns his attention to the boy's retainers, who he supposes will be a handful of men with whom this Sir Robert grew up and some older, possibly wiser men of his father's generation, and mostly he's right, but there is something else that is odd: their bodies are not angled towards Robert Welles; rather all of them are turned towards another man, who is crouching, and it is only when Thomas edges forward that he sees him, trying to write something on a scrap of paper, resting on a low coffer.

Of course it is a friar. He's a Franciscan, with his face hidden under his hood and one grease-matted sleeve rolled back to reveal a muscular forearm, writing in a rough-and-ready hand that must have earned him many a stripe in the friary.

Thomas sidles closer. The friar finishes his writing and stands. He looks at the others gathered around him with an economically dismissive glance that sweeps past Thomas, flicks back to him, and then slides on. There is not much to be seen of him under the hood that hangs down and the beard that rises up to cover most of his face, but he carries himself lightly, as if he may be called to fight or fly at any moment.

'Where's Boyce?' he asks.

'Here, sir.'

Thomas is sure the friar flinches in irritation as a whip-thin man in already mud-spattered riding clothes steps forward. The friar gestures for him to come close and speaks quickly and quietly into his ear. The messenger nods, takes the folded note and secretes it in his coat, and turns to go.

Thomas steps back, easing his way through the men who've gathered behind, and he circles around, his eye on the thin back of the messenger, Boyce, who is quick into his saddle, and who turns the horse about and sets off, nudging through the fraying edge of the crowd. He is riding westwards, back towards Lincoln.

To whom is he taking the message?

Thomas hurries down the track towards the horses, but now where is Jack? Where is the idiot? Thomas cannot leave him. He searches the crowds at the stalls and the cockfights, but there is no sign of him. He curses him. They'll have to ride like madmen to catch up with Boyce now.

Thomas eventually finds Jack, inevitably in the last place he looks: at the edge of the village where it gives up its fight against the saltings and sinks back into the mud and water. He sees many of the men have drifted away from the stalls and cockfights and are lined shoulder to shoulder on a low bank, staring eastwards as if expecting the Second Coming. Thomas joins them up on a dyke above a stretch of foul mud, bordered by a looping river a hundred paces beyond. The men are ale-softened, waiting in rowdy, excited anticipation of some entertainment.

Thomas fillets the crowd for Jack, but he is not there among the spectators; then Thomas hears a shout and he turns and looks out across the muddy stretch, and there is Jack, up to his knees, waving and grinning at him from among the thirty or so men gathered in the mud beyond, each stripped to his braies and shirt, each with a great drunken smile on his face.

'Oh Christ,' Thomas murmurs.

Everyone around him is laughing in anticipation, the atmosphere ringing and bright, and a fat, older man with a beard – the only one still in his clothes – has the ball under his arm, and he is just now shouting something, and everyone's laughing at what he's saying, and then some of the men on the bank are shouting things such as 'get on with it!'

The ball is made of leather, forcefully filled with air from a smith's bellows, and the man in the beard throws it high above his head and then the naked men start running as best they can through the mud towards it as he – the bearded man – makes his awkward getaway to the safety of the dry bank where he pushes the others aside to make himself a space to turn and watch. There is a general roar of encouragement. The ball lands in the mud. The men converge. And then there is a simple, furious, grappling fist fight between all the men in the mud. There is no order to it. They just throw themselves at one another. At first there are a lot of separate fights. Men are downed in the mud and let go again to emerge blinking. The ball lies untouched on the surface of the mud for a long while, and every time any man flounders his way near it, another seems to materialise from the mud to knock him down. Other men on the bank are untying their pourpoints and hose and throwing themselves into the fray, their linens swiftly turned brown.

Thomas loses sight of Jack. Or can no longer identify him in the mud. Gradually some sort of order emerges. The ball is collected by a big man – an archer, obviously, with heaving plates of muscle in his chest and great cords of it along his arms. He has calf muscles the size of an ordinary man's head, and a head the size of one of the balls they blasted at Bamburgh Castle. He reminds Thomas uncomfortably of the giant, that servant of Edmund Riven's, but his hair under his hat is ruddy and gingerish, and his eyes – he is one of the few yet to be brought down – are lively as he tucks the ball under his arm and starts moving from right to left. Someone tries to stop him but is smashed into the mud. Two more fight themselves free of their own attackers and, coordinated, they hurl themselves at those massive legs, and then another man clambers on to his back. All three are rebuffed and the man marches on. More men discard their clothes and come running to help or hinder.

'Who the fuck is he?' Thomas's neighbour asks. 'Fucking unstoppable!'

The big man continues marching the ball towards a line of trees on a dyke that marks the end of the marsh and the beginning of some drained furlongs, but now someone is organising the other men to stop him, just as men on his own side seem to be gathering in support of him. And there are signs of organisation among the spectators too. The sounds, which have until now been mostly random bellows of rabblish support, and groans as one man seemed to have his arm broken, are now beginning to settle into regular pulses of sound, coming from the end of the stretch of fen towards which the big man is wading, still knocking all attackers aside.

Then his neighbour joins in the cry.

'A Clarence!' he bellows, hands cupped around his mouth. 'A Clarence!'

And that is what the rest of them are chanting as the big man at last kicks the ball through the mud and into the trees, with four other men clinging to him like dogs after a bear, and then he falls backwards, exhausted, into the deep mud, taking the men with him, and the crowd continue to cheer him and shout the same thing: 'A Clarence! A Clarence!'

The man next to Thomas with a ruddy drinker's face, an oft-broken nose and very blue eyes is suddenly grabbing Thomas's brigandine with both hands and his face is in Thomas's and he's roaring something, and Thomas is readying himself for a butt, when the man thrusts himself away, fists clenched, roaring still, the veins on his face like worms under his skin, and he's just celebrating the goal.

Thomas wipes the spit from his face. The whole crowd is now chanting, 'A Clarence! A Clarence!' as the big man who last kicked the ball is hauled back out of the mud and helped to his feet and has his arms held aloft in triumph, and even though there are fights still ongoing in various parts of the bog, it seems the men on the right-hand side – Jack's side – have won the game.

Jack comes wading towards Thomas. He is laughing and his eyes and teeth are unnaturally white against the mud and blood. He doesn't seem to care or understand what he's hearing and when someone offers Jack a mug of foaming ale he reaches for it, until Thomas grabs his wrist.

'Get your bloody clothes,' he says.

'But we won!'

'Get your bloody clothes! Now.'

They ride hard after the messenger, along the tracks and dykes back towards Lincoln, trying to imagine which way he might have gone, but it is hopeless. Once they reach Lincoln, he might have gone any which way, so Thomas and Jack pull up their sweating horses at an inn outside the city walls to let them rest and eat and drink.

'How many men do you suppose were there?'

'I can never tell. Thousands.'

Thomas writes Katherine a message and thinks about sending Jack back home with it and riding to find Hastings alone, but whatever else he might be, Jack is handy with a bow and two men are more than twice as good than one if there is any kind of trouble.

'Are we going to London?' Jack asks.

'Or Westminster.'

'How long will it take?'

'Three days, then however long it takes to see Lord Hastings, then three back.'

'A week?'

Thomas nods. Jack smiles at the thought.

'Be able to get some sleep away from the baby,' he says. 'And I've never been to London.'

When the horses are refreshed a little, Thomas pays a boy to take the message to Katherine, and they ride up into the city, through the gate where the Watch is much reduced, past the cathedral and down past the pardoner's house. He cannot help but study it as they go by. It is looking shabby, he thinks. Uncared for. He wonders if the man's widow still lives, and he wishes he could recall the pardoner, whom Katherine said Thomas had very much liked, and the attempt he and Katherine had made to return the ledger to the old man's widow, but that was before Towtonfield, before his memory was sent awry by the blow that has left a divot in the side of his skull from which his ordinarily dark red hair grows white. That was before they discovered the ledger's value, of course. He wonders if they could take it back now. Would that change anything?

When they are out from under Saltergate and across the river they start kicking the horses on, setting them to trot across the old road where the water still laps and there is the suspicion of a furze of new grass growth stippling its oozy surface.

Once again, Jack tells Thomas that he did not hear the men shouting for Clarence.

'You had your ears blocked with mud, you fool.'

'But were they really?'

'Yes.'

'But not for Warwick? You didn't hear any cries for Warwick?'

'No, they were the Duke of Clarence's men. Not all of them. Just the side you were playing for.'

'But they were all right.'

Thomas nods. 'Everyone's all right,' he says. He thinks it's probably true.

Jack mulls this for a while.

'And you're sure the Duke of Clarence and the Earl of Warwick are – together in this?'

Thomas isn't, but they were last year. He remembers the Duke of Clarence married the Earl of Warwick's daughter against the expressed wishes of King Edward, and he remembers the way the men at Middleham used to talk about Clarence just as if he were Warwick's plaything. So it is at least plausible Warwick is using Clarence again, using his troops against King Edward.

But William Hastings will know better. He will know how it lies.

'This is bad news for King Edward, isn't it?' Jack asks.

'I don't suppose he'll be too pleased to have his brother go against him,' Thomas agrees.

'Hmmm,' Jack says, with a point to suggest. 'And we're riding down to find him to tell him this.'

'Yes.'

'And didn't you say the last time you brought King Edward bad news, he nearly had you hanged?'

Thomas grunts.

'But remember what he said? That he always learned his lessons? I reckon he's learned that one, too, don't you?' Jack looks askance.

Thomas kicks his horse and wishes he had brought the spurs he bought in Ripon.

'We'll ride until nightfall,' he says. 'Or until the horses are done in.'

Night falls first, and they stop at an inn in a town called Sleaford, where everyone is becoming drunk and the board is covered in empty dishes, crusts, rinds and cracked bones, and afterwards they share a bed. Jack falls asleep first, still in his filthy linens, still stinking of mud, and he snores resonantly and resists being woken, and Thomas wonders at poor Nettie's life, caught between Jack and the baby.

In the morning it is Ash Wednesday, and Lent, and the air is filled with the smell of boiling herring.

'Oh Christ,' Jack murmurs.

With dry mouths and curdling stomachs, they hear Mass at St Dennis's, and kneel before a white-haired priest with foul breath to be blessed and have crosses smeared on their heads before they are sent on their way south. The land around here is endlessly flat and sodden, more lake than land, and echoingly familiar to Thomas.

'Will it be like this all the way?' Jack asks. 'Horses' hooves'll rot off before we get to London.' His face is peppered with spray from Thomas's horse.

'At least it is flat,' Thomas says. 'And at least it's not raining.'

Just then the road rises and it starts spitting. Thomas laughs. It reminds him of something. Sometime. Someone. This sort of thing is happening to him more often these days: strange lancing shafts of memory that seem to cut through time, so that he can see himself doing something like this – riding in the rain the moment after someone has said at least it is not raining. Fleeting glimpses of another life lived. Strange but lucid dreams. History opening up.

They ride all morning not saying much, and stop to feed and water the horses around noon. Thomas frets over of the safety of Katherine, and of Rufus, left alone with only John Stumps and the men from the village to keep them safe, but at least now he can be certain there is no roving band of thieves in the county, as he had once hoped, and such threats as exist, well, they have always done so, haven't they? And they will do so as long as men such as Earl of Warwick are left to breathe.

They reach Peterborough at dusk and find rooms and stables at an inn hard by the cathedral cloister, where the bantams roosting in the rafters above erupt in squawks and cackles every time the bells ring, so dawn comes early, grey, miserable, shit-pattered, with little to look forward to but another hard and hungry day in the saddle.

'Even the horses eat better than us,' Jack mumbles.

They are gone by first light and through the throng of carts and barrows edging out of the gates. On the road south toward Huntingdon the pace of traffic is steady but purposeful; there is no evidence of any shock or alarm, and all seems as it should do, on a dank first Thursday in Lent.

They don't hear the news until that evening when they are in the town of Huntingdon, some miles to the south, having ridden all day again.

'King Edward is coming with all his household men,' a leather merchant tells them. 'Bloody lucky to get past them where the road goes through that heath, just north of Waltham Abbey. Never seen so many men in all my life, I swear. Road's backed up five miles in front and behind. Chaos.'

He sells Thomas a pair of very fine gloves, and they decide they cannot go on, but must wait for King Edward to reach them.

'So it was true, that rumour of King Edward coming with a mighty power?' Jack says.

Thomas nods. Christ, he would like some proper food, he thinks. His stomach roils and cramps. He is simultaneously listless and restless and his mouth itches for ale. Once again he thinks back on what Jack said about bringing King Edward bad news. Then again, the prospect of being hanged might be preferable to another night with him snoring, and with the prospect of neither meat nor ale in the morning.

The night is just as bad as he'd anticipated, worse indeed for there being another man in the bed with them, and a dog, too. But at least there is nothing much to be done the next morning while they wait for King Edward to come, so Thomas sits in the hall of the inn and tries to keep warm and preserve energy.

King Edward's outriders arrive just after midday. They are the usual sort: hard-bitten, self-reliant men with little time for niceties. They get the innkeeper to clear everyone from every room in the inn and they requisition the stables. Thomas tells them he needs to see Lord Hastings, and has information about the rebels. They call their captain, who looks him over, and then they let him and Jack remain, for a bit anyway. An hour or so later, a herald arrives on a beautiful grey palfrey and attracts a crowd of servants in the yard. He swings his leg down and stands in the courtyard, as if waiting to be congratulated. It takes Thomas a moment to believe what he is seeing, for the man is Sir John Flood, last seen with King Edward in the Northern Parts, and a stranger to him since.

When Flood sees Thomas he beams and strides towards him.

'By all the saints, Thomas Everingham!'

He throws his arms around him and pounds Thomas's back with pleasure, and then steps back with a puckered frown.

'You are well accoutred, sir?'

He gestures at Thomas's brigandine and sword, though he himself is wonderfully dressed in a silken livery jacket quartered in the royal colours and an arrangement of fat pearls hanging from his hat, a sword at his hip, and riding boots with toes like chisels and spurs as long as a man's hand.

'I've come from Ranby Hawe,' Thomas tells him.

'Ah! You are not some rebel, are you?' Flood laughs, but there is a gleam of something new and hard in his eye.

'You know they are gathering?'

'A steward of Lord Cromwell has sent word from Tattershall Castle. He says there are as many as twenty thousand men already gathered, with as many as a hundred thousand more coming from the north. '

'A hundred thousand!'

Yet Flood remains happy and relaxed.

'We are sceptical, of course, but King Edward has already sent out his Commissions of Array and we've near enough that number promised to us, including the household troops of my lords of Warwick and of Clarence.'

'Clarence? Clarence?'

Flood is suddenly concerned. His eyes stray around the yard, at the servants, porters and ostlers.

'I know,' he says. 'I know, but he's not that bad.'

'You don't understand,' Thomas tells him. 'The men in Ranby Hawe, they were all cheering for him. Cheering for Clarence.'

Flood's expression narrows.

'No,' he says.

'Yes,' Thomas tells him. 'You cannot rely on Clarence. He is with Warwick behind Welles, I am sure of it. They put Welles up to it, to attacking Burgh's house.'

'But King Edward has pardoned Lord Welles already,' Flood points out.

'But this is Lord Welles's son – this is Sir Robert Welles. He has appointed himself Great Captain of the Commons.'

'No.'

'Yes. And he is Clarence's man. Or he has Clarence's men with him at Ranby Hawe. We were there. We saw them. We heard them shouting for him.'

Flood will not believe it.

'But you did not see the Duke of Clarence himself, did you?' he asks. 'No. Because, do you know why? Because Clarence was with King Edward. They have been together in London these past days, and Clarence even rode with us on the way here, as far as Waltham Abbey where he left the King on excellent terms, armed with those Commissions of Array so that he and my lord of Warwick are able to raise troops to help suppress this Great Captain of the Commons and his rabble.'

Thomas stops with his mouth open. He can think of nothing to say. He looks at his boot caps. At Flood's boot points. He shakes his head.

'Thomas,' Flood says, dropping his voice. 'You'd best not – best not say anything more on this. You know how King Edward hates to hear of treachery. And especially about his brother. You remember him last year? When you told him that Warwick was behind Redesdale? Did he not threaten to castrate you or something?'

'But I was right, wasn't I?' Thomas asks.

There's a moment's silence. Thomas can feel Flood looking at Jack for support, just as if Thomas were a stubborn child.

'You were, Thomas,' Flood sighs at last. 'Yes. But that was then. This is now and you are talking of King Edward's brother, for the love of God. However fond of you he may be, and I believe he is, King Edward is fonder yet of his brother, and if he hears of you talking of him this way, then this time he will have first your balls, and then your head.'

'But I am right, still,' Thomas says. 'And the King must know. If he's sent out Commissions of Array to Clarence, or Warwick, he must reverse them.'

'Thomas!' Flood says. 'If you say another word, I will have you taken away myself. I would never rest easy knowing your wife might blame me for letting you talk yourself into an untimely death. So now come, let us put Lenten restrictions aside and have wine, and I have goose pie, for we need to keep our strength up, and let us, for the love of all that is holy, talk no more of this.'

There is nothing more to be said now anyway, or not to Flood. So Thomas and Jack go with him and they talk of the past few months since last they saw one another, and it transpires that Flood is become a widower.

'Childbed fever,' he says, his face expressionless, his grief masked.

Thomas remembers Flood's wife: a beautiful girl whom they were forced to leave when they rode to find the Earl of Pembroke, days before the battle of Edgecote. Flood would not have seen her again for many months.

'She left me a strapping son,' Flood tells them, 'whom I have named Edward for King Edward.'

When they have finished the pie and drunk the wine, watched with envy by those less insouciant of the Church's prohibitions, Flood leaves to find the best bed in town, and organise the town's guildsmen and aldermen to be ready to receive the King.

'He will be here by nightfall,' Flood tells them as he is leaving the inn. 'But please, Thomas, if King Edward summons you, do not say anything about his brother. There is a reason we call him our most dread liege.'

4

'When will Father be back?' Rufus asks.

'Soon,' Katherine says. 'Soon.'

She has tried to keep the boy busy since Thomas left, and this afternoon he has dug out the handful of oak galls that he and Thomas collected before Christmas last, and now he is keen to make ink to show Thomas when he returns. So they set about grinding them with a pestle, and heating them up in a little dish over the fire, mixing the dust with soot and honey and egg white. When it is done Rufus looks very doubtful.

'Will it work?' he asks.

'We can only try,' Katherine says. They find one of Thomas's reeds, cut it afresh and then look around for a piece of paper on which to test their product. They find the message from Thomas, telling them of the Duke of Clarence, and how he has taken Jack and gone to find William Hastings in London. It says he will be back within the week, 'come what may'.

She watches Rufus for a moment as he bends over the paper, the tiny tip of his tongue between his lips as he carefully marks the unfolded sheet. He is so grave, she thinks, so studious. Does that come from her? Or from Thomas? She has so few memories of herself as a child Rufus's age. Nothing more than those of being in the priory. Dear Christ. How did she ever survive that? Remembering it now, even while sitting here by the fireside with her child next to her, warm in her own house, it still sends a shiver down her spine. Even her memories of the place have different colours: white, grey, black. The colours of ice. While of here they are red, green, golden.

The only recollection she has of her early life that is at all different from this is the glimpse she once had of a fire in a stone fireplace, and of a window glazed with coloured glass, something she recognises she must have seen before she became an oblate, for she never knowingly saw such a thing while she was cloistered. But she has returned to this memory so often it's become like a coin worn to a slip by the rub of many fingers over the years, and she wonders if it is not now a mere memory of a memory, rather than a memory itself? It is like the other one she has: of being invited to hand over a heavy purse and some letters to a kindly-faced old woman in black, after which she senses a parting, and then the gates seem to swing shut behind her, and then the Life began. She supposes she might have imagined this too; might have created it as a myth to cling to, except odd new details sometimes spring to mind when she least expects, adding to the scene. Now she thinks there was another woman in the background, sobbing, and she wonders again at Isabella's words, spoken in this very room, the summer before: whoever put Katherine in the priory must have had connections and money to pay the order to break the Church's law against oblates. So they must have been somebody. But who? This has never interested Katherine because she has always known that she would never find out who it was, and she never believed it mattered. She has refused to know, wilfully blocked her ears to Thomas's speculations, because how could it help achieve anything but further unhappiness? It is better not to care.

But now, when she looks at Rufus and sees little of Thomas in the boy save his reddish hair, she feels a creeping sense of unease. Who is he? Really? He is so slight, so sombre. He starts at any noise. He refuses to eat meat. He sometimes moves as if he is frightened of the world around him, as if he feels himself made of glass.

And what of the baby that is to come?

She shifts uncomfortably and then stitches on, passing the needle through the loose weave of linen, joining sleeve to body, finding not one whit of satisfaction in her skill. She glances over at Nettie, who slumps exhausted, asleep with her own baby at her breast. They call the baby Kate. She only ever sleeps, eats or cries. Sometimes all three at once. Nearby John Stumps sits with his eyes closed but he is chewing something slowly, like an old ram, so she knows he is awake. John Who-Was-Stabbed-by-His-Priest stands at the window, staring out at the rain, and Katherine can hear and smell John's wife and children in the buttery where they are talking quietly while they're crushing violet petals for oil.

Another stitch.

When will Thomas come back? He says a week, but she remembers him vanishing for the best part of two years after the battle of Towton. She remembers last year, when he rode to tell King Edward about Robin of Redesdale and was gone for months on end, and nearly came back not at all, since King Edward wanted him hanged for bringing unwelcome news. She wonders if he will be more circumspect this time? She prays he will not believe King Edward has learned all his lessons from last year, and that he will know to tell the news of Clarence's treachery first to William Hastings. She wishes she were there instead of Jack. She wishes he would just come home.

With Thomas gone, Katherine feels herself more than ever responsible for the safety of the other people in the hall, especially as now it is known she was right about the attack on Burgh's house being not the work of a band of robbers but some new strife inspired by the Earl of Warwick. That bloody man. Has he nothing better to do? No, she thinks. He has nothing better to do. He has all this immense power, this immense wealth, an apparatus designed for and pointed at fighting the French, but with no Frenchmen to fight, what is he to do with it? She almost laughs aloud, seeing this. It is true of all of them; yes, all of them. The dukes. The earls. The lords. They are trained to fight, and they train others to fight, and then, once they have done that, what else is there to do but fight?

Another stitch.

And she thinks which of these lords she'd prefer to come for the ledger first: the Earl of Warwick's man, whoever he may be, or William Hastings's bloodhound, whoever he may be? She thinks perhaps the former, for there is a chance, if they hand it over to him straight away, that he will not have them all killed, and they might be left to live with their consciences for what they'll have done to King Edward and William Hastings. But if it is Hastings's man, this bloodhound, then, dear God, there will be no short end to their torments.

She thinks that tomorrow she will dig the book out, up from under Nettie's floor, and she'll place it back in the coffer at the foot of her bed, the selfsame one in which Sir John kept it all those years. It will be to hand then. Yes. That is what she'll do.

She looks up from her sewing to watch Rufus a little longer, his head still bent over the paper, and she can hear the scratch of his reed; then he senses he is being looked at, and he glances up and their eyes meet, and they smile at one another, and he returns to his scratchings, and she to her stitching, and she thinks about Thomas out there, somewhere; they sit like that as the daylight dies, half listening to the baby's waking murmurings, the ticks and clicks of the fire, and the very faint moan of the wind in the chimney top.

*

The night passes slowly, but peacefully, and the next morning after prayers Katherine remembers her intent to dig up the ledger. She sends Foulmouth John for a mattock and gets him to attack the floor of Nettie's house while Nettie looks on with the baby in her arms and the baby is, for once, quiet, as if soothed by Foulmouth John's bizarre act of violence. The floor is crumbly and damp under its top layer, but the ledger, in its tight-stitched sleeve of waxed linen, has survived its months of incarceration.

When he sees what she is about, John Stumps gives her a narrow look.

'So,' he says.

He lost his second arm because of this book, and he has as much right to a say in its fate as anyone. They leave Foulmouth John to repair the damage to Nettie's floor as best he can, and they take the ledger into the hall, deserted with everyone at their tasks, and she finds a properly sharp knife to snip the stitching. She tries to keep calm, yet her fingers are trembling as she slides the thing out of its case and places it on the table.

The book is dry, and entirely unchanged, though perhaps the leather is crazed slightly, and one of the seals crumbles under her touch like an oatmeal biscuit. She opens it. The pages are crisper and louder to turn than she remembers, but the ink within is as clear – or not – as it ever was. Long lists of soldiers' names; when and where they were in France nearly thirty years ago. Taken all together, it means little or nothing, but in among it all are the details of Richard of York's absence from his wife for nearly seven months before she gave birth to her son Edward, who has since become King of England based on a claim passed down from three months this same absent, cuckolded father, this Richard of York.

'So where does it say that – that he's as he is?' John asks. Even he cannot bring himself to say that King Edward – a man whom he likes – might be a bastard. Katherine goes through the pages until she sees the little rose of York in the margin, to mark the boy's birth, and she works back from there to the entry describing the Duke of York's journey to the town of Pontours.

'There,' she says. 'That is it.'

John peers close, reverent before the word, as if before a bible that once belonged to – a saint, say.

'Just that word?' he breathes.

She nods.

'What does it say?'

'Pontours,' she says.

'Pontours,' he repeats. 'And that is enough to condemn a man? Enough to change his life? Make him not the king when he is the King?'

It does seem absurd.

'If it had been destroyed,' John starts, 'the King would still be the king?'

'Yes,' she tells him. She supposes it would.

'So why do we not destroy it now?'

She sighs.

'We could do, but then what if the next men up the track are not Thomas and Jack, but someone such as Edmund Riven, may God curse his soul, or worse, come from the Earl of Warwick? They would never believe we have hidden it and . . . well.'

She trails off with a shrug. John has been tortured before, by Edmund Riven, who burned his hand off, and even now she cannot help but glance at his right stump. She imagines he might rub it if he had a left hand to do so.

'But you don't think he can still be looking for it?' John asks.

Katherine blows out air.

'He knows it exists,' she tells him, 'and if what Thomas says about the Duke of Clarence is true, then Warwick will want it more than ever he did.'

'Why?'

'Because it proves that the Duke of Clarence should be king.'

It's hard to know how much of this John Stumps grasps.

'So what are you going to do with it?'

'I don't know. If he knows we have it, and he comes . . . well. I am not going to let him hurt any of you. I will – just give it to him.'

John Stumps is alarmed.

'And see King Edward unthroned?'

She forgets in what high esteem they hold King Edward.

'I'd rather see that than . . .' She trails off. She has a sudden image of a knife cutting Rufus's skin. 'I'd rather see that than anyone – you, or Rufus – be hurt.'

John Stumps nods. He can see that, too.

'He's been ever like a wolf, that one, hasn't he?' John says. 'The Earl of Warwick and his red-coated devils. Just circling and circling, getting closer. I'd like to send a bolt through his bloody eye, that I would.'

The means for doing this are at hand, propped against each door, and she knows how John feels. The thought that out there, at any time – in the night, even, when it falls – the men of the Earl of Warwick will circle the house like wolves.

Christ, she wishes Thomas were back.

At that moment Rufus comes and sits with them. For some reason she withdraws the ledger from him, hiding it in its sleeve as if it might contaminate him. He picks up his pot of drying ink and sniffs it. His nails are gnawed to the quick. He finds the reed and dips it in the pot. The ink is dry. He splashes a tiny drop of ale in and then strokes the reed around the bottom of the jar. Now Rufus wants for paper, so Katherine looks at the ledger, and thinks: Why not? What harm can it bring? She removes the ledger from its sleeve and opens it to find a patch of paper that is blank towards the back. She passes it to him, and he settles down to draw a dog, and a man with a stick. They are nicely done. A pigeon, maybe, too.

'Your mam says your letters are coming on, Rufus?' John asks. It is a nice thing for John to say, she knows, and her heart goes out to him, because Rufus's letters, to be truthful, are not yet good, and the boy knows it too, and he smiles and passes her the reed and asks her to show him a word. She writes 'Rufus' under his pictures.

'Your father taught me,' she tells him.

She has a very clear memory of Thomas teaching her to read. It is about ten years since, she supposes. He bought a treatise on cutting fistulae from a stationer in Westminster, and set her trying to pick out the letters in that. The writing came later, when they were together in the castle up north, and in times between.

She sits next to Rufus and opens another page at random, and tells Rufus to show her any Rs he can find. He mixes up R and P, as is easy to do.

'P for – what is that word?'

'Paris. That is a city in France.'

'Oooh, you don't want to go there, Rufus,' John says. 'Full of Frenchmen.'

Rufus smiles.

'What about that one?' she asks him, opening it on a new page. 'That has a P and an O.'

'Not Paris?'

'No,' she says. 'That is P for Pontours.'

She sees she has opened the ledger on the fatal report: the one that describes the Duke of York's absence from his wife at the very time King Edward was conceived. He tries another.

'What about another? Here.'

She opens another page and lets her finger wander through the words and letters until she finds a P.

'Pontours!' Rufus says.

'He's quick, this one,' John Stumps says.

But he's not right. It is not Pontours.

'Nearly,' she says. 'It is a place – maybe? – called Pontoise.'

John Stumps peers over.

'Looks the same to me,' he says.

She reads the full sentence aloud.

' "Sir John Cheney and ten men from Rouen to Pontoise on first day after Ascension." '

'Do all French towns sound the same?' John asks. 'Paris. Pontours. Pontoise.'

'There is Calais,' Katherine supposes.

'That is English,' John tells her.

She mumbles agreement, but her mind has detached from the conversation's flow. Something is bothering her. Paris. Pontours. Pontoise. Can those last two be different spellings of one and the same place? she wonders.

'Just a moment, Rufus,' she says and takes the ledger and folds the pages back to find the incriminating page. She checks the spelling again, holding it up to the light. It is definitely Pontours. Surely place names would be something a man must get right, especially in a ledger such as this, otherwise what is its point? She passes the book back to Rufus, still wondering, and he finds his place again.

'There is another P,' Rufus says. 'Is it Pontoise once more?'

She leans forward and looks at it, then at him.

'You tell me,' she says.

'It is' – he checks against what has gone before – 'Pontoise.'

She reads the sentence.

' "Sir John Cheney" – him again! – "and ten men of Essex to

Pontoise with four score of best arrows on fourth day after Ascension." '

That doesn't make sense. They can't have gone twice.

'What would Thomas say if he comes back to find you can read?' John Stumps asks Rufus as he watches the nub of the boy's finger travel along the dates, names and places.

'There,' Rufus says. 'Another P.'

She looks.

'That is P for Pryse. Good.'

Rufus likes Ps. He finds another.

'Pontoise?'

Again he is right, and she looks again and this sentence details another troop movement from Rouen to Pontoise, this time twenty men of Hereford, but their return is recorded, too: they are back after only three days. She turns the pages. Men are always coming and going to Pontoise. Only sometimes are they recorded as coming back, but when they are, it is often as little as a day later that they return.

'I wonder where it is?' she says to herself. 'It cannot be far from Rouen.'

Rufus has lost interest, and she is about to slide the book back into its sleeve when she remembers she must remove his name from the page; she opens it where she wrote his name and takes out her knife to cut away the paper. Already the ink has faded: it looks almost as old as the original letters below. She excises the word Rufus, and is about to do the same to the dog and the man with a stick when she hesitates. Thomas will like to see these, she thinks, so she leaves them, and she puts the ledger away.

But then she gets it back out again; her mind is slipping and racing, as if she has been given a glimpse of something like an insight, or a sign, the sense of which dangles beyond her reach, and she looks at Rufus's drawing, and that is when she sees what she's been overlooking all along.

She feels a great surge of excitement up and down her body.

'Rufus,' she says. 'Your reed. Lend me it.'

He glances up at her and then looks alarmed.

'Are you well?' he asks.

'I am,' she says. 'Oh, I am.'

She takes the reed and its pot and she finds the page in the ledger that lists the Duke of York's movements during July in the year before King Edward's birth. She looks at it for a long moment. Is this the right thing to do? How will it affect anything? She feels she is on an edge, peering down, and everything she has ever known is dizzyingly far below, and she must make a leap. She is gripped by a strange rushing sensation, the sort of feeling that might make a man claim to hear the voice of God, and she dips the reed into the ink and, careful to hold the pen upright as Thomas has instructed, she changes the word Pontours to Pontoise, twice.

When she's finished she looks up. Rufus watches her placidly.

'What are you doing?' he asks.

'I don't know,' she admits. 'I don't know.'

She feels she has lost something, something huge. A burden, yes, but also a benefit. She feels she has destroyed something. Brought it down. The sound in her ears seems to stop and she is surprised now not to hear a great crumbling noise, as if a tower of a castle were collapsing into rubble. She has breached the walls of Jericho. And yet there is nothing. Not a single thing has changed. Only those two little words.

'But what has that done?' John asks when he sees it.

'It means – it means it is no longer proof of anything.'

John thinks about this for a while.

'So if the wolves come, we may give them this in all good conscience?'

Katherine nods.

'And why did we not do it sooner?' he asks.

She stares at him, and he at her, and she feels the blood rush to her face because, of course, had they done so, he would still have at least one arm.

'I'm so sorry,' she whispers. 'I'm so sorry.'

Something wakes her in the night. She does not know what it is but, from being fast asleep, she is wide-awake, rigid. She does not move but lies there, hearing only the pulse in her ears, and Rufus snuffling in his sleep beside her.

The wind is up outside. Then she hears what must have woken her. A dog, barking in the distance. One of theirs? She cannot tell. Her heart is thrumming again; her throat's constricted and her breath hard won. She lifts back the sheets and blankets and swings her bare toes through the curtain and out over the edge of the bed.

'Mama?'

'Shhhh, go back to sleep. It is nothing.'

Katherine feels her way across to the shutter, finds the rope from months of doing the same thing every cockcrow and lifts it off its hook to let the shutter drop and a finger's width of moon-light slice through the room. She stoops to look, but from here can see only the privy and the stream where the wringing post throws a long sharp shadow in the cold blue wash of moon light. She stays there in the cold, her face pressed to the shutter, her heart racing at every imagined movement. The trees shift in the wind, the shadows sway and thin clouds scud across the moon. She feels alone and vulnerable, and the dog keeps barking.

After a long moment she lifts the shutter back and hooks the rope, and hurries across the dark to where the steps creak and the air is warmer and scented with fish from dinner.

'John?' she whispers. 'John?'

'Mistress.'

Both Johns are awake already, John Stumps because he never sleeps and John Who-Was-Stabbed-by-His-Priest because he's also heard the dog, and they move through the low light of the now uncovered fire where flames flutter on splints of hawthorn. John Stumps is at the door to the yard, his eyes very white in the gloom. John Who-Was-Stabbed-by-His-Priest is by the back door, still in his braies and shirt, crossbow in hand.

'What've you seen?' she asks.

'Nothing.'

The baby wakes and Nettie hushes her with a nipple, but now everyone else is up, fumbling to set aside children and blankets, rolling to their feet to reach for their weapons and responsibilities. Bald John joins John Stumps at the front door, John Who-Was-Stabbed-by-His-Priest and Robert From-the-Plague-Village are either side of the back door, and there is a woman or a boy or girl peering out at each window. One of the boys is stroking the two lurchers, trying to calm them, but the lurchers are all stiff-furred, straight-legged, tails-up, waiting by the door, each eyeball a dark glossy orb flecked with light.

All have shrugged on their heavy jacks and the helmets Thomas bought them, even the women, and they catch the low firelight, giving the impression each has his or her head aflame. John Stumps has even had someone buckle a sword around his waist, though how he'd ever use it in anger, let alone draw it, is a mystery known only unto God. All this is done in silence and low light. Katherine can hear everyone breathing very quickly. She's sure she can even hear their heartbeats.

'It's them, I swear,' John Stumps mutters. 'Just come on.'

His teeth are clenched around the trigger loop of the crossbow he's had whittled for himself, and he stands ready to kill the first man who comes through the door. It is what he has been dreaming of ever since he worked out that with a few modifications – leather ties and loops – he could still shoot the bow. She'd thought it strange beyond belief that killing a man was how he wanted to prove himself, but now she's glad. She hears Foulmouth John stalking up the steps to the room above, complaining that he's been woken for no good reason.

The dog is no longer barking.

This is how it always happens.

It means they are close, whoever they are.

'We just need to wait,' John Who-Was-Stabbed-by-His-Priest whispers. 'Wait for them to come into the yard, that's what Thomas said.'

They respect Thomas for having been at Towton, though none of them know he cannot recall a thing about it, or that since then he has been on the losing side in each of the three battles he has fought. She feels curiously blank about Thomas at the moment. She supposes she might have reason to be angry with him for leaving them to fend for themselves like this, but for now she only wishes he were here to help. Rufus has appeared by her side, still in his nightshirt and cap, his eye pressed to the gap at the top of the shutter. He is shivering with the cold.

'Go up,' she tells him, but he shakes his head, determined. She places a hand on his bony shoulder. After a moment, he places his on hers.

'Anyone see anything?' John Stumps asks.

No one says anything.

'Who the hell are they?' Bald John wonders. 'Only owls sup-posed to be out and about this time of night.'

He speaks in quick, swooping sentences, as does everyone in Droitwich, he tells them, and it's a good question. Who is it out there? She'd never imagined that either the Earl of Warwick or Lord Hastings's men would come for them like this, like thieves in the night. She'd imagined they would arrive on a wet morning, backed by a long line of soldiers in travelling cloaks carrying flags, winding up the road to the hall as if on official business, or in a funeral cortège, and everything would be sombre and tinged with regret at the inevitability of what was about to happen.

But then, perhaps – perhaps they *are* mere thieves in the night? Perhaps Thomas was right? Robert seems to think so.

'So Thomas was right,' he says. 'bloody thieves. We'll bloody show them.'

Once more she wishes Thomas were here. All this standing at the windows, this was his plan. His and Jack's. Fine in daylight, she thinks, not so in the dark. She lowers the shutter of her win-dow half a finger's width. From here she can see into the yard and across to the stables and beyond to Jack and Nettie's house. The yard is deep in moon shadow, its edges crisp one moment, gauzy the next as the clouds ease across the moon. Nothing else moves, but still she catches her breath when she thinks it does. They wait in silence. The fire picks up. She glances over her shoul-der to see the circle of women's faces, pinched in the light of the flames, waiting for what is to come. It is the lot of women, she thinks, to wait like this, and she remembers the time she waited with Alice in the church of St Mary's Priory, while the bell rang its alarms, and outside the walls rode Giles Riven and his foul son Edmund. She'd prayed then, little knowing just how much her life was about to change, but she does not pray now. Instead she grips the smooth length of the crossbow she's taken, all oddly balanced, and she peers out of the window, willing someone to dare to try so that she can pull the lever and send a bolt spitting across space. Compared to a longbow arrow, a crossbow bolt looks like an ugly, flightless bird, but by God it is vicious.

How long they wait no one can be sure. At one point Robert settles himself more comfortably by the back door, and someone lets out a long sigh. Katherine pinches the bridge of her nose and shakes her head. She is starting to see floating, sinking circles in the dark. Bald John's daughter brings her a mug of ale, even though Lent is begun and one for Rufus, too.

Slowly the tension seeps out of the room, and it seems to Katherine that this must have been a false alarm.

'Well—' John starts, levering out the bolt from his bow.

But just then there's scratching at the door. Everyone stiffens. The dogs are up, growling. Katherine's whole body burns; her hair crawls. John replaces the bolt. Christ! There is someone without. John Stumps fumbles with his crossbow. She can see him trying to catch the trigger loop between his teeth.

'Steady,' she urges. 'Steady.'

Though – heavens – she does not feel that herself. One of the girls puts the cover back on the fire and the room is plunged into darkness. Then Rufus gasps next to her and presses his face against the shutter, his eye to the gap.

'There's someone,' he whispers. 'By the stable door. Look.'

He points. She puts her own eye to the crack. She sees something. Someone. A length of leg. A man is waiting at the corner. Yes. He's there. Then one of the girls upstairs – Joana – hisses something. She's seen someone too. Around the back of the house. Katherine hears Foulmouth John crossing the boards above to join the girl at the window. They all look up, waiting, hoping he'll not do anything stupid, hoping that he'll wait for Katherine's signal.

Suddenly there is a rattle of a shutter falling above, and the bang of a crossbow.

'You little fucker!' Foulmouth John shouts gleefully.

Upstairs Joana screams. Her mother – Anne – abandons her post by the back window and runs up the steps to see if she is all right. They can hear Foulmouth John is laughing.

'Do it!' John Stumps growls, his teeth clamped to the leather strap. 'Do it!'

The boy by the door looks once to Katherine and, when she nods, he throws up the drawbar and yanks the door open. John Stumps jerks his head back. His crossbow twangs.

Rufus drops the shutter in front of Katherine. She lifts her bow to her cheek and pulls the lever, aiming into the darkness above that leg. The bolt snaps away. There's a cry from without. Rufus hauls the shutter back up.

'Quick! Quick! Quick!' John Stumps is growling through his clenched teeth. He wants another bolt loaded but the boy who must load his crossbow is closing the door.

Katherine engages the string to the hook on her belt, bends to puts her foot through the hoop and then straightens to cock the crossbow. Rufus places the quarrel in the slot. She is ready for the next shot. She looks around at the others. All the doors are closed and the shutters up. Everyone is reloading. No one is hurt.

'Ready?'

'Ready!'

She can hear wailing outside.

'Oh God. Oh God. Oh God.'

She hesitates.

'You little fucker!' Foulmouth John shouts from above, and his crossbow bangs again; there's a half-gasp, half-cry from outside and then silence. They hear Foulmouth John laughing again. She waits. They are all primed, ready to do it again. She glances at Rufus. He has his eye back on the shutter.

'Come on,' John Stumps growls around his strap. 'Come on.'

He's not talking to her, but to them, whoever they are, out there. The next moments are fraught. They've betrayed their strength. Given themselves away. Now they can expect the worse. Now the rest of them will come.

'Anyone see anything?'

There are grumbles of denial.

'Can't see no one,' someone mutters.

'Where in the name of Holy Mary are they?'

Time inches past. But they do not come.

'Keep watch,' Katherine tells Rufus. She climbs the steps to the bedroom. Foulmouth John stands beside the window overlooking the courtyard, shutter down, crossbow cocked. He's peering out. She joins him at his shoulder. He laughs his horrible wheeze.

'Look at that fucker,' he says.

He indicates the dead man in the yard, and before she can stop him he sends another quarrel whipping down, jerking the already dead man's head in a grim little bounce. He laughs and respans the bow. She puts her hand on his arm.

'Don't waste them,' she tells him and she crosses back to the window on the other side of the room, where Joana still peers out over the shutter.

'I think he's dead, mistress,' she says. There's another splayed corpse below, half on the track, half in the herbs. Probably shot by Bald John from the back door below.

'Have you seen any more?' Katherine asks her.

'No, mistress.'

Foulmouth John still fills the window as she goes back down the steps. The atmosphere below is strange, as if everything has been turned on its head. No one knows if they should be happy or frightened.

'I got one,' John Stumps tells her. 'I got one. Sly little fucker ducked but I still got him. Crawling on the ground, he was!'

'But how many more are there?' Bald John wonders.

No one knows. So once more they stand poised in silence with their bows cocked, sweating even in the darkness while they wait and she can hear nothing, only the wind around the chimney top and prying at the seams of the house.

Suddenly Rufus stiffens by her side.

'A light,' he says. 'Behind Nettie's house.'

Someone with a lamp.

'It will be a parlay then,' Bald John supposes.

Now she can see the glow. She listens for a shout from beyond, but nothing comes. The light grows stronger.

'Let's just give it to them,' John Stumps suggests. 'Throw it out to them?'

He means the ledger, and she thinks: Yes, let's do that. They'll take it and then they'll go, and it will be good riddance. But what about their dead? They won't leave the dead men unavenged, will they? Regret and fear sit on Katherine's chest like a weight. Why didn't they ask for the ledger before their attack? Why didn't she offer it up before they killed those men?

'Let's just – let's just wait to hear what they have to say.'

She knows exactly where the ledger is. She will throw it to them if they would but ask for it. But she hears no shouted overture, nothing to suggest men interested in talking. The lamp is brighter now, but not moving. Then her heart catches. It's not a lamp. It's a fire. They are setting Nettie's house alight. She cannot help but turn and look at Nettie.

'What?' Nettie asks.

Katherine wonders if she should tell her. Will she not try to run out there or something and get herself killed?

'The fuckers're back!' Foulmouth shouts from above. 'They're burning Jack's house down!'

Nettie gets up and brings the baby to the window where the shutter is still raised, but now there's a bar of light across her headdress and Katherine can see her eyes white in the darkness of the hall.

'Let me see,' Nettie says.

The flames have caught, and Katherine can see their reflection in Nettie's eyes. Nettie starts a low moan.

'No,' she says. 'No. No. No. No. No.'

Nettie dumps the baby on Katherine, who takes her in one arm, for she still has the loaded crossbow in the other, and she goes to the door where John Stumps can only watch helplessly as she lifts the drawbar. Bald John comes scuffling towards her.

'No, Nettie—' he begins, but Nettie ignores him. Katherine passes the baby on to Rufus, who takes her in well-practised arms.

'Nettie, wait!' she calls.

But Nettie hauls the door open and steps out into the darkness. Before she can even cross the threshold there is a twang from over the way, a crack as something hits the oak of the door, and then a wet thud, a gust of expressed breath and Nettie staggers quickly back into the hall, arms flailing.

But there's another bang from upstairs and a cry of pleasure from Foulmouth John too.

'Got 'im!' he shouts. 'I got the cunt!'

But Nettie lies on her back in the rushes at John Stumps's feet.

The boy at the door forces it closed and drops the bar. Katherine is at Nettie's side in the darkness.

'A light! Quick, for the love of God! A lamp.'

The girl — it is Joana again — lights one from the fire and brings it over and she gasps as the circle of light expands to reveal Nettie on her back, one leg bent at the knee and an arrow buried in her right cheek, just by her nose. Her eyes are open, but she lies very still and she does not speak. And she's looking up the arrow shaft's length, seemingly just a little surprised, and her hands are wavering in mid-air.

Upstairs Foulmouth John is still laughing with pleasure.

'D'you hear me?' he calls down. 'I got him? Lit up like a fucker he was!'

'Boy!' Bald John barks. 'Shut up! Shut up now!'

Katherine is surprised how little blood there is. That is good, she thinks. She touches the quarrel. It is wooden, which in part explains why it has not gone clean through Nettie's skull, but it is firmly dug in, probably in the back of Nettie's skull, Katherine thinks, and now become solidly part of her face, thrumming with her vital force. It is a miracle that she still lives.

'All is well, Nettie,' she soothes. 'All is well. We will have this out of you in moments. Joana, stay with her, hold her hand. I will fetch what I need.'

She takes the lamp and steps through the darkness to the buttery. She knows precisely what she needs and where to find it: a handful of barley seeds from the barrel, rose oil, honey and ale, and then, from a nail on the back of the door, the bag of unguents and powders she bought from the apothecary in Lincoln, including the dwale of hemlock and poppy seeds. She sends Joana up for some lengths of unused linen from the coffer in the bedchamber.

'Keep a good lookout,' she tells the others. 'Can you see any more of them?'

No one can, but everyone is distracted, heads half-turned towards Nettie.

Katherine pours the ale into a leather beaker and mixes in some of the dwale. Wine would be better but they have not seen that for weeks. She tips it, little by little, into Nettie's mouth. It is bitter and Nettie resists.

'Please, Nettie, you must,' she says.

But Nettie won't. Katherine asks Anne, Joana's mother, to help a moment. She steps out of the shadows and holds Nettie's head so that she has to drink. When the cup is empty she sets it aside. Nettie looks terrified, as well she might. How long do they have before the pain starts? Katherine wonders. Anne stays with Nettie, stroking her face.

'It is all right, Nettie. All will be well,' says Katherine. Then she turns to the others. 'Right. Now I need a jug of piss. Each of you. Do what you can. One at a time. Everyone else: keep an eye out.'

'The fire's really taking hold,' Rufus says.

There's nothing they can do about that for the moment.

Bald John goes first, untying his codpiece and urinating loudly a few feet from her, so that she can smell it over Nettie's blood. She takes the arrow shaft, stands it on the hearth and then splits it with her knife, tapping down its length. She does this three or four times until she has a clutch of long stiff slivers, which she dips in rose oil.

She cuts up some linen into pieces and when the jugful of strong-smelling urine is brought to her, she dabs the linen in and wipes Nettie's face clean with it, and then sloshes some on to the wound. Nettie flinches. Not surprising, really. There is still not too much blood, but she wishes Nettie would close her eyes, or she could put something over them.

'Can you pull it out?' Katherine asks Bald John and even in the gloom you can see the thought terrifies him. He nods, though, and gets down on his knees. He holds the quarrel by the end, but it is as if it is a stubborn weed, suddenly sprouted in Nettie's face, and there's not much of it to grip.

'Hold her head,' she tells Anne.

Bald John is sheened with sweat. He opens his mouth to say something.

'It has to be done,' she tells him.

He nods and bends over and tugs the shaft, gently at first, and then with more force. It is stubborn but suddenly it comes with a quick sucking pop. He rocks back, and it is as if Nettie is released. Katherine leans forward with the linen to staunch the blood that rises like black water in a ground spring.

But then he shows her the quarrel.

There is no head. Only the bloody black shaft.

Oh Christ.

The quarrel head is still in there.

The blood is coming very strongly now, welling up in the wound. Nettie is trying to blink it away. Katherine tries to think. What can she do? What can she do? She remembers cutting an arrowhead out of Richard Fakenham's shoulder, and out of Giles Riven's back, but this is different. This is a face. A head. Oh Christ.

From hope to this.

She is kneeling with her backside on her heels now. She places her fists on her thighs. Nettie is looking at her through one panicking eye.

'It is fine, Nettie,' she says. 'You will be fine.'

But blood still overfills the wound and the black star on her face is spreading and filling her eye so that she thrashes her head to clear it and then there's only more blood.

What to do? What to do?

Can she leave it in there? No. That will bring on the black rot. She must get it out, but how, now? She must first stop the bleeding and then she can think. She wads the urine-soaked linen into a tampon and then packs it into the wound. Blood is splashed everywhere now, all over her clothes, up to her elbows, all over Nettie, and Katherine's movements are clumsy and rushed and she is grateful that no one can see her panic. Just then Nettie starts shaking, her whole body convulsing, thrashing like a fish on a riverbank. Heels, backside, shoulders, head, banging on the floor as if she's overtaken by an evil spirit.

Katherine's never seen anything like it.

She pulls back.

There is a great wave of heat from Nettie, as if she is on fire, and then – she stops still. She lets out a great woof of air and a strangulated cry and is finally still.

'Nettie,' Katherine says. 'Nettie, wake up.'

She leans forward and places a hand on Nettie's breast. Then she unties the laces of Nettie's jack, and she rests her ear against the bloody cloth of her shift. Nothing. No sound. No heartbeat. Katherine sits back. She rests her hands on her knees. The others look at her, waiting for her to do something, waiting for her to give them hope.

But there is nothing she can do, and she can give them no hope.

She shakes her head. Her heart aches forcefully, as if it has outgrown its reserved space, and her tears come struggling up and she cannot contain a sob. She cleans her hands on the sleeves of

Nettie's jack. John Stumps snivels and wipes his nose on his stump. The other women in the hall start weeping too, but then the baby starts howling for something, and Katherine thinks the noise is such a small thing but it is also the worst thing and – dear God! They will have to feed her!

She lifts her hands and they are wet with blood, black in the light of the fire. Nettie's eye is still open. Katherine closes it, leaving dark marks on her skin. She gets to her feet. Rufus manages to soothe the baby for a moment, but it will only be for a moment. Katherine takes a candle to the buttery to find something for the baby to eat. A pap, perhaps, of bread and ale? She returns the honey, barley and the rose oil to their places and she sets about making it. She remembers doing the same with Welby's wife's child, though with him she began with milk from the goat. Kate is older, and must make do with ale until they can find her milk.

She makes a bowl of the stuff, with Nettie's blood in the lines of her hands, and takes it, still unable to speak, back to where Rufus dandles the baby in his arms. He is whispering to the child, keeping her head turned from the sight of her dead mother, as if she might understand it, and they're both lit up by the burning house, the blaze of which they can see through the crack above the shutter. She gives him the bowl of pap and he sets about trying to feed the baby. Weaning is not easy at the best of times, she knows, and now are not the best of times, but the baby is instantly quietened by the very first taste of the food. She wants more. Her little hand reaches for the wooden spoon.

It is the first good thing to happen to them, she thinks. Then she ruffles Rufus's hair and returns to the window to take up the crossbow again, and she stands keeping watch out of this window, her eyes gritty, and she tries not to think what they will have to say to Jack if he ever comes back to find any of them alive.

Flames leap from the house across the yard, buffeted by the breeze, and she can smell the thick stench of the smoking thatch and knows that it will not be long now before it will go up with a dirty dull flare that'll signal the start of the real danger, when the sparks will take wing and fly, and she thinks of the stable roof, and of the thatch above their own heads, and she remembers Sir John telling her that Giles Riven's men once set fire to the stables to get the horses to scream so that he would be caught between rescuing them and rescuing young Liz Popham. Sir John had chosen the horses, not believing what they'd do to Liz, and had later told her that this was the single worst thing he had done in his life, a choice that would haunt him to his grave.

Rufus has managed to get the whole bowl into the baby and she is sitting upright on his knee, trying to peer around him to see her mother. Rufus places his hand over the baby's eyes to spare her the sight. It is heartbreaking.

Katherine turns back to look out across the yard at the flames again, and tears fill her eyes so that she can hardly see what she is looking at, and she just wishes Thomas were here. He and Jack. They would have been able to stop Nettie opening that door. She rests her head against the jamb of the window and closes her eyes and she just wishes all this were over, one way or another.

'Why don't they come?' John Stumps asks.

'Smoking us out?' Bald John suggests.

They stand in silence, and time inches past. Katherine watches the fire burn, and occasionally her gaze sinks to the dead man in the yard, lit up now, but then it springs back up, back to the dancing shadows, and she is always surprised there is no one to be seen. She wonders how long it will be before the oak beams really start to burn, and she wonders why it is the men out there haven't already set fire to the stables or the barn and whether they will, and she is so absorbed in this that she does not perceive the light is changing until it has done so, and all at once she looks up and she sees the true darkness of the night is passed and the blackbirds and the robins are beginning to sing, and, mercifully, with the dawn comes a thin rain, falling like a benediction.

'Just before dawn's the time they'll come again,' John Stumps says. 'Thomas always says so.'

She's never heard Thomas say such a thing and, even if it is true, she wonders why he would know it anyway, but nevertheless, they gather themselves up and resume their vigilance and wait watching while the birdsong swells and the light grows and first faces then features become distinguishable. She keeps a watch on the shadows, and on the dead man in the yard. He's prone, face turned away, one arm flung out, the other wrist against the ground, elbow cocked above his back. Who is he? Where's he from?

'Never short of food, that fucker!' Foulmouth John calls down.

They wait until it is quite light before there is a subtle disengagement, as if they all recognise the task is complete and that the next stage in the process must now commence. They each of them turn to look at one another, and then, on her signal, they open the doors and the windows all at once, and then they step back and wait, each ready to shoot at anything that moves. Nothing does. The flames still burn in Nettie's house. The smell of wet ashes is strong in their noses.

After a while John Who-Was-Stabbed-by-His-Priest steps out into the yard. Then he steps back in. He grins one of those terrified grimaces: teeth clenched, eyes very round. He is sweating and red-faced. He does it again, and again, each time lingering longer and stepping further. They hear Foulmouth John shouting down at them – something lewd but indistinct – and Bald John, the boy's father, summons him and tells him to go out himself if he is so sure. The boy says something else that is also mercifully inaudible as he passes John Who-Was-Stabbed-by-His-Priest, and then he trots into the yard, just as if he'd only now been woken up after a good sleep. They watch him standing in the yard, yawning and stretching, and nothing happens.

'One of you's killed a fucking dog,' Foulmouth John calls back to them. 'Look at it, poor little fucker.'

Katherine goes out next and sees the dead dog has a bolt smack in the bony dome of its forehead, and its neck is bent at a sharp rake. John Stumps follows and stands over it, stricken, his crossbow hanging by his knees. There are tears in his eyes. 'Oh Christ,' he says.

The others come out after. Bald John lays a hand on John Stumps's shoulder.

'It was a good shot, though,' he says.

The fire in Nettie's house still burns, hissing and spluttering and spreading choking gusts of smoke and ash into the air above their heads.

'Are they all dead?' she asks, and she notes how each man makes first for the body of the man he thinks he himself killed. She is no different. She steps around that first dead body in the courtyard, and walks slowly for the side of the stables to find the man she shot at. She still has the crossbow cocked, the string straight and a quarrel in its slot, and she steps quickly around the corner, ready to shoot. There's no one there, and nothing to show there ever was. Except in the wood chips on the ground is a dark medal of blood. There's a little smear of it further on, and a bloody scrape, and then more of it – and there, in the shadows of the birches, is a presence. Her heart fills her throat. She levels her crossbow and it wavers in her shaking hands as she takes a step.

Suddenly Rufus is next to her.

'Rufus,' she says. 'Go back to Nettie.'

He ignores her.

'Is he dead?' he asks, gesturing.

'I'm not sure,' she says. 'That is why you must go back. Please, Rufus?'

The dead man has dragged himself from where he was shot, through the woodchips to the woodstack, and is sitting against the log ends with his legs straight out before him, his head hanging heavy on his chest, hands cupped over a belly punctured and stained dark with blood. From between his laced fingers sticks her quarrel.

He's dead.

Katherine straightens, relieved.

'Come, Rufus, leave him. Leave him. There's nothing we can do for him.'

Rufus is reluctant, but they return the few steps to the yard where someone has overturned the fat man, who has lost his hat in the process of being killed, and his hair is blond and shaggy, his lips full and sloppy, each arm like a suckling pig. He'd been carrying a hefty-bladed falchion, rusted, chipped and blunt.

'Fat fucker,' Foulmouth John says, giving him a kick with the side of his foot.

'Leave him,' she says. 'And all of you, bring water. We need to put this fire out.'

They start bringing buckets and jugs from the barrels that Thomas had them fill before all this started and they set up a chain, passing from one to the other, stepping around the dead body in the yard, with Bald John from Droitwich at the front, taking the buckets as they come and flinging their contents on to the flames. After just a few moments his head is slick and his clothes are wringing wet with sweat and rainwater. It takes them most of the morning to extinguish the fire, but by noon it is a steaming frame of charred oak beams, like a gallows for a mass hanging, and each man, woman and child is black with stinking wet soot. Except the baby, who cries and cries, and whom only Rufus seems to be able to soothe.

Katherine stands shoulder to shoulder with John Stumps and she looks through the gap where the doorway once was and the floor within is filled with the steaming, twisted wreckage of Jack and Nettie's life, all the sooty shards of furniture, the clothing, the bedding and everything they ever had and held dear.

'Food,' she says. 'We must all have something to eat.'

'You should wash first,' John says.

Nettie's blood has smeared all over Katherine's wet clothes and it is beginning to gum: she can smell it now. She nods and goes to the well; Bald John is there and he hauls up a big bucket for her and helps her pour it over herself. The cold is intense and painful. She makes him do it again. And again until she is sodden through but clean, and then she lifts her skirts and walks with squelching boots back to the house to strip off her apron and gown and then her kirtle and shirt and her hose, all of which are now smutted with ashes and stained pink with blood. She dresses herself again and ties her girdle around her grown waist and then she carries the sodden clothes back down the steps. Joana can wash them later.

Smoked hams are brought down from the beams of the hall, the last of yesterday's bread is broken into the thin pottage and there is the first of the March ale that they water down. When they've finished this, they turn to the bodies, dragging them from their various places of death, to lay them out on the track below the hall. When it's done, they gather to look down at the five corpses, speculating on the causes of their deaths, and the types of men they might have been while they were alive.

There is the fat blond one whom Foulmouth John killed in the yard: a thinner man – whom Katherine killed – with a lolling head, fleshy lips and strikingly large ears, 'like best back bacon,' one of the women says. The third is short, with very wide-set eyes and a down-turned mouth from which his tongue lolls. Bald John hit him, pinning him through a drinking costrel that has leaked and made the blood thin. The fourth has a scrubby white beard and wears an ancient moth-pitted hood of a style no one has seen for twenty years or more. The fifth – the one who killed Nettie and was also shot by Foulmouth John – is sunburned even in this season, with white hair and a much-broken nose. He lies on his back and, apart from the quarrel buried in his breast, he could be sleeping. He does not deserve to look so peaceful. She wishes Foulmouth would kick him.

'Who the bloody hell are they?' Robert asks. 'And what were they doing coming up on us like that?'

They do not seem an obvious band, and their clothes give little away. A bit worn perhaps, but nothing to suggest desperation, and only the bearded man looks as if he needs a wash. There is nothing obvious to unite them. John Who-Was-Stabbed-by-His-Priest has gathered their weapons in a jumble by their sides. Knives, bows, the falchion and two billhooks, one repurposed with a long handle for fighting, the other just a tool for laying hedges.

They can't be the Earl of Warwick's men, of that Katherine is certain. Bald John undoes the fat blond man's belt to tug off his flaccid purse. There are a few coins within and a set of good beads.

'They must have horses,' John Who-Was-Stabbed-by-His-Priest supposes, and they look up and around, but can see none, so he and Bald John set off down the track to see if they can find them.

'Careful, now,' one of them tells the other.

'We'd best fetch the priest,' Robert supposes. 'And the bailiff.'

Katherine feels a stab of something like panic. The bailiff? Christ. She has such pungently foul memories of the bailiff they'd called when Eelby's wife died that she has a profound distrust of anyone who goes by the title.

A moment later Bald John returns leading five poor-looking horses by their fraying reins, and John Who-Was-Stabbed-by-His-Priest brings a skinny boy, held by the ear.

'Down by the crook in the road, they were,' he says. 'Being looked after by this 'un.'

The boy is lifted off the ground, and John drops him in front of Katherine. The boy falls scrabbling in the mud, a tangle of spindly limbs. He is in a sleeveless leather jerkin, his arms like sticks and his hair scissored short. His face is so filthy that his eyes, which settle on the dead bodies, appear huge and round and white with fear.

'Who are you?' Katherine asks.

'No one,' he moans. 'No one.'

'You must have a name?'

He shakes his head. You can see every rope of muscle move below his skin. He's shivering.

'Like a fucking greyhound,' Foulmouth John sneers.

'Who are they?' Katherine indicates the dead men.

'I don't know. I don't know.'

'You must,' Katherine tells him. 'You were looking after their horses.'

The boy shakes his head once more.

'Do 'im! Let's just fucking do 'im.'

'Shut up, John,' Katherine tells him. His father belts him around the back of the head so that he staggers forward.

'So who were they?' she asks again.

The boy buries his head in his hands and begins to weep.

'I don't know,' he says. 'God's honest, I don't. They promised me goods is all. They said I'd get a house and a furlong of my own if I looked out for them!'

'But why did they come here? Why did they choose this place?'

'They said that you'd taken land what didn't belong to you. They said you was churchmen.'

'Churchmen?' Bald John scoffs. 'What do you mean "churchmen"?'

'They said you was clerical. Monks and so on what couldn't own land. Weren't allowed to.'

There's a rushing in Katherine's ears and her heart pounds in her throat.

'So they wanted to kick us out,' Foulmouth John says, 'because – because we're supposed to be fucking monks?'

The others laugh but Katherine keeps her eyes on the boy. Her mind is buzzing but no conclusions emerge, only questions: Can it be that someone knows? After all these years? Jesus God!

'What did they say about us being monks?' she asks.

Now the boy looks more frightened than ever.

'It weren't any of them,' he says, indicating the row of corpses. 'It was the other one.'

The others are suddenly quiet.

'There's another?'

'He was the leader,' the boy says. 'What told them what to do.'

'Where is he?'

The boy gestures into the distance.

'He said he would come this morning. When it was done.'

'Who is he?'

'He's a man of the law, he says.'

'What's his name?' Katherine asks.

'Mostyn,' the boy says. 'John Mostyn.'

103

5

It is evening, and Thomas and Jack are in the town's guildhall, a good-sized solar, with glazed windows and red-painted pillars and beams, together with such local dignitaries as Huntingdon can muster, many in fur-trimmed cloaks of scarlet or blue, standing in the round because King Edward is at their centre, sitting at a board, his feet outstretched so that Thomas can see the long shoes tenting the cloth below. Thomas also sees King Edward is shamelessly forgoing the privations of Lent and has a leg of cinnamon-roasted fowl in each hand. Light from the table's candles – and the grip of anger – pucker his face, softened now by recent over-indulgences.

'I only tell you what I saw, sir,' Thomas tells him again.

William Hastings is also at the board and although when he had first seen Thomas he too had embraced him, he now regards him with regret, as if the sight of him hurts his eyes. Flood stands just behind Hastings, wincing and shaking his head slightly. Behind them are more men-at-arms, just a fraction of those who have arrived throughout the day.

King Edward is still staring at Thomas.

'You are brought before me to speak of the rebels gathering under this so-called Captain of the Commons, and yet I find you speaking of my brother of Clarence? With whom I have just passed four happy days, refreshing the bonds of brotherhood, enjoying conversation with our mother, riding abroad and seeing the people of our dear city of London and in the country south of here? My lord of Clarence whom I sent on his way with a fraternal kiss and a ring pulled from my own finger here, to see his wife in the West Country, and armed with Commissions of Array to raise troops for my disposal against our enemies? My lord of Clarence from whom only yesterday I received this – this! – pleasant letter to tell me that he is making his way to Leicester, with as many men as he can muster, there to meet my cousin of Warwick? And you tell me – you come here – and stand before me, again, and tell me that you believe that he – he – my own brother – is behind this – this upstart Great Captain of the Commons of Lincolnshire? Is that it? Is that what you are telling me?'

Thomas has been here before and heard these sorts of words. Even so, he can hardly move his tongue or swallow for fear of this man and the knowledge of what he might very well have done to him. You would think he would have learned. You would think he had not been warned. But no. As soon as King Edward had overcome his delight at seeing Thomas, and had recounted for the pleasure of the assembled riders who'd come in with him the story of the night Edmund Riven was killed and Katherine cut off John Stumps's remaining arm while also delivering Nettie of her child, Thomas had blurted out what he knew: that King Edward's brother was a traitor.

'It is what I saw, sir.'

'*It is what I saw, sir. It is what I saw, sir.* By the blood of Christ, Master Everingham, if I did not hold your wife in such high esteem I would – I would hand you over to my lord of Worcester right now. You do know that?'

The Earl of Worcester – in deep blue velvets and a dark cap – is back at King Edward's other side; the candlelight throws strange emphasising shadows across his aquiline nose, and the way he turns his head to acknowledge his king with those expressionless black eyes only makes him look more like a goshawk than ever. He even has a scrap of what might be chicken liver on his knife.

King Edward tosses both chicken legs on his plate and sits back. He glares at Thomas. His eyes seem very small in so large a face, and they are calculating and shrewd, yes, but are they also cruel? Would he enjoy seeing a man hang or endure whatever cruelties the Earl of Worcester might dream up? Thomas cannot decide. He can only breathe very shallow breaths for the weight on his chest.

William Hastings leans over to whisper to King Edward, and King Edward, who in other moments might have bent his neck to hear his old friend more clearly, does not, and it is clear that Hastings is a supplicant. Hastings speaks quietly for a few moments while King Edward listens. King Edward's gaze flickers over Thomas. His lip remains curled. Silence elsewhere in the room. The air is thick. Everyone itches to know how King Edward will punish Thomas and most are thanking God they are not him, or in his place.

When Hastings finishes, he leans slowly back, his eyes on Thomas, and King Edward grunts. Hastings takes a drink from his cup and wets his lips. His expression is almost unreadable, but not quite: I have done my best, he seems to be saying, and I can do no more. Next to him King Edward drums his ringed fingers on the snowy cloth of the board.

'Is Lord Welles here yet?' he asks, angling his face so that his voice carries over his exuberantly padded shoulder to a secretary, or steward, standing behind. 'And that other one. Dimmock. Is he here?'

There is a moment's sending back and forth, during which King Edward picks up one of the chicken legs again and takes a bite, his eyes still on Thomas, until the answer comes back from a steward.

'They are expected tomorrow, my lord king.'

Again he grunts.

'Very well,' he says at length. 'I will further speak to them tomorrow. In the meantime, have this one . . . I don't know . . . incarcerated. Somewhere uncomfortable. Do you have such a place, alderman?'

The alderman, one of the men in red, nods enthusiastically. King Edward raises his eyebrows as a signal, and Thomas feels a beefy hand slide under each arm; he turns to see two men larger than he, in King Edward's livery, who walk him away back down the room to the door to the steps beyond.

That is his first interview with King Edward on the first Friday in Lent, in the tenth year of his reign.

His second takes place late the next day, when he is brought into another, smaller room in the guildhall, this time crowded only with King Edward's household men all in livery jackets or badges of allegiance. There's no fire lit, and the room smells of vinegar and sweat and resounds to the creak of leather. Lord Hastings is there, looking harassed, and John Flood too, but the centre of attention is not King Edward – he is not come yet – but two men standing with their backs to the hearth, facing the empty chair behind an unadorned table set before the window. The attention is not of an amicable nature, and there is already animosity in the air.

When Thomas is brought in Flood steps forward, nodding at the guards, who relinquish his person and step back and out through the door.

'Sleep well?' Flood asks. He knows Thomas cannot have slept

a moment, even had he been in the town's most comfortable bed. Thomas takes his sardonic smirk as a reason for cheer.

'Who are they?' he asks.

'The one on the left is Welles. The other's Dimmock.'

Thomas sees Welles look over at him, and his expression, which was anxious before, becomes more so. He's a tall, spare, elderly man, in his forties at least, with a fine fan of wrinkles around his mouth and eyebrows like horns. He does not, Thomas thinks, look entirely resolute. He looks as though he is caught up in something that is beyond his control, such as stubble burning that has spread beyond his own furlongs. Dimmock is younger and fatter in the face, and he stands turned slightly to Welles: the follower of the two. It seems Welles is going to say something to Thomas, but just as he opens his mouth, King Edward comes in and there is a flurry of caps being removed.

King Edward looks ruddy-faced, as if he's just come from exercise, and maybe he has. He sits heavily and takes the proffered mug of something and drinks. A single drip snakes down his chin and throat and when he lowers the mug with a sated gasp, he stretches his neck to allow a servant to dab at the offending snake of ale. A servant does so.

'So,' he says, addressing Welles. 'You say one thing, he says another.' He indicates Thomas.

'Who is he, sir, to contradict me?' Welles begins.

'This is my good and faithful servant, Thomas Everingham, in whom I place almost every trust.'

Welles sees he has got off to the wrong start, and recalculates his approach.

'I am certain it is a mistake, sir. Perhaps he misheard?'

'What of it, Everingham? Could you have made a mistake?'

'If I'd heard it once, sir, then I'd say perhaps, but I heard them shout for Clarence – for his grace – twenty times or more.'

King Edward turns back to Welles. He smiles.

'What do you think of that, my lord Welles?' he asks. 'Do you think Master Everingham here could have made the same mistake twenty times over?'

Welles tries another approach.

'Which of us has not done exactly that, sir?' he chuckles, citing human foibles. But he has misjudged it again. King Edward rears to his feet. He hammers his fist on the table to make the mug and jug jump and everyone in the room flinch, and he glares at Welles. Thomas feels his core turn hot and liquid, even though King Edward is not even looking at him, and suddenly no one can forget this was the man who fought all day at Towton, and who gave the orders that none, none should be spared.

'I know you have!' he bellows.

His face is purpled. Hastings cocks an alarmed eyebrow and begins to murmur something soothing. King Edward thrashes a gesture at him and Hastings slinks back. Welles too.

'And I know I have,' King Edward goes on. 'Jesus. Yes. I have made the same bloody mistake countless times! Countless times! With you and your bloody family. First your father, then you, and now your accursed bloody son. Defying my word, raising men against me, flouting my laws, and attacking my own man in Gainsborough! The fucking Sheriff of Lincoln!'

'But, sir – that attack! It was never meant in any way seriously!'

'So you keep saying! So you keep saying. But the fact of the matter is that you did attack Burgh's house!'

'But it was not meant – it was not intended—'

'It was not aimed at me? Is that it? It was not aimed at me? You attack my own man, my sheriff in the county, but it was not aimed at me?'

Welles is confused. For a moment, he seems to be searching his memory for the answer. It is as if he does not know why he did it. But then, why do it?

But King Edward is not interested in the finer points of Welles's motivation.

'Nevertheless,' he goes on, 'I still issue you with a pardon, since you seem a decent sort of chap, only when I suggest I might come up to Lincoln to see for myself how my subjects fare, this happens! A full-scale bloody rebellion!'

'But, sir! It is my son! Not me.'

'So you know of it?'

Welles and Dimmock look at one another. What they are about to say requires courage.

'We – we are the very provokers of it,' Welles says.

King Edward seems astonished. He says nothing for a moment. He turns on his chair and looks up at the glazed window through which the southern light falls.

'The very provokers of it,' he repeats, his voice low. 'You are not shielding the involvement of my brother, are you?'

'No, sir.' Dimmock finally manages to speak, his voice contrastingly high. There is a murmur of laughter in the room.

King Edward turns back to Welles.

'So your son, Sir Robert Welles . . .'

'Yes, sir.'

'He is acting so under your orders?'

'He is acting so because he is concerned for my safety, sir.'

'Your safety? Even though he must know I pardoned you this weekend last for your attack on Sir Thomas Burgh's house?'

'Yet you still keep me close, sir.'

King Edward breaks off to gaze at the window again. He holds his hand up and admires the way the window filters the light that falls on the four rows of pearls that adorn his sleeve.

'He is a good son, sir,' Dimmock adds.

King Edward nods. He has no son of his own, everyone remembers.

'And he is doing all this for your sake, not at the behest of my brother of Clarence? Not at the behest of that slithering shitsnake, my lord of Warwick? He's not raised half the fucking county against me on their behalf?'

'No, sir. It is on my behalf only, I am sure of it. He only wishes me well, and you too, sir. He only wishes you well.'

'Does he now? Does he now?' King Edward twitches his mouth in a play of thought. 'Right,' he says, coming to a decision. 'Pen, paper.'

He clicks his fingers. A jar of quills, a pot of ink and a quire of vellum are slid on to the table before him. He shoves the vellum across the board towards Welles.

'Write to him. Write to him and tell him that unless he comes before me, on bended fucking knee, within two days I will chop your bloody head off. Tell him that. His too.'

He nods at Dimmock, and Dimmock swallows, and then he and Welles look at one another and, without another word, Welles takes a pace across the room to begin writing the letter.

'Tell him,' King Edward says, 'tell him I shall be in Fothering-hay the day after this next and if I hear he has not disbanded his troops, and that he isn't on his way to beg another pardon, which I may or may not grant, then I shall be sending your head to his mother. Tell him I shall send your other parts elsewhere. Yes. A leg to Exeter. An arm to Cardiff. The usual sort of thing. The rest of you, do you know what I'll do with it? I won't even bother to do anything with it. I'll just have it chucked in the castle privy and the bloody pigs can make of it as they will. Are you getting all this down?'

Welles's letters are probably not good even at the best of times, but writing this letter on a flat surface, with an unfamiliar quill that looks small in his clumsy hand, and standing before King Edward and his household men while his life is being so explicitly threatened, his words are scarcely legible for shakes and blots of ink. Behind him Dimmock is rose-faced, and sweating like cheese rind on a hot day. King Edward smiles at him falsely.

'You trust the boy to do as his father commands?' he asks as if Welles were not there. Dimmock tugs at his shirt collar and tries to say something that does not come out.

'I'm sure it's all a misunderstanding,' King Edward reassures him over Welles's bent back, just as if all this were perfectly normal, 'and when the boy gets his father's letter, he will realise his mistake, and where his best interests lie, and he will send his men away and he will come crawling to us, and all order shall be restored.'

It is obvious King Edward thinks nothing of the sort, but Dimmock nods. He thinks he sees an escape route.

'Unless,' King Edward goes on, 'unless you think he might not know his best interests lie with me?'

Now Dimmock shakes his head. Then nods. He doesn't know the answer. His hair is glossy with sweat. Sodden with it. It is very warm in the room all of a sudden, even though there is no fire. Welles finishes the letter and King Edward reads it before passing it back to be sealed and an imprint of Welles's ring is pressed into the wax and attached. Welles steps back with an anxious glance at Dimmock. Both already look like hanged men.

'So how do we get our message to him, this son of yours?' King

Edward muses. 'Once again, it seems I must turn to my much-abused friend Master Thomas Everingham here, who seems to know the back roads of this county better than most.'

Hastings rolls his eyes with relief.

Thomas is forgiven, and has been found useful.

Thomas finds Jack in the same inn in which he'd left him the day before. He is sitting by the fire with a mug of ale, and does not see him come in, he is so busy discussing something with a group of men in loosened field armour.

'Of course,' he is telling them, 'everyone knows a harnessed man's weak spots. The face, the armpits, the elbows, the groin and the backs of the knees. Everyone thinking of going into a fight always says: Yes, yes, if I was fighting such a man, I'd stick my bill in here, or here, or there.'

He still does not see Thomas as he points out the body parts.

'But the thing is,' he goes on, 'the thing is that the man in full harness, he also knows his weak points, doesn't he? He knows you'll want to jab him in the armpit. So this is my point: he won't let you. He won't show you his armpit. He won't lift his arms like this' – he lifts them as a headsman might, showing both sweat-stained pits – 'will he? He'll come at you like this, everything covered up, and just you try to get through that—'

He sees Thomas and stands, looking furtive for moment, caught boasting about something he knows nothing of, but the admiring crowd part to let him through, watching him as he makes his way around to clasp Thomas in a hug. He laughs.

'Knew you'd be fine!'

It almost seems as if he did. Thomas tells him they have a task.

'We found them easily enough last time,' Jack supposes. 'And maybe there'll be another game of football.'

As they find their horses, a general order is given. King Edward is to leave Huntingdon this morning, and move on northwards to Fotheringhay, where he hopes to receive Lord Welles's son Robert as a penitent.

'D'you think he'll come?' Jack asks.

'What would you do?' Thomas asks. 'If King Edward told you he was going to chop your old man's head off if you did not come and beg his pardon?'

'He'd be welcome to my old man's head. Long since mouldered in the grave.'

'Try to imagine it, for the love of God.'

'Well. I would go and beg his pardon, wouldn't I? Unless . . . unless I didn't much care for the old bastard, or if I had an army at my back that I'd raised against the King, and with which I fancied I might beat him.'

'He must know he'd never beat King Edward's army. You saw them. They were pig-gelders and hedge-layers.'

'Some of them looked useful. You saw Clarence's men.'

Thomas supposes that's true.

'That's the point, though, isn't it? They're Clarence's men. What if Katherine is right, and this rabble of Robert Welles's is just a lure to bring King Edward's army up here? What if Clarence, and – God forbid – the Earl of Warwick are secretly meeting up and they're going to come up behind us with a hundred thousand men they've managed to raise while King Edward was concentrating on Welles?'

Jack looks at him blankly.

'You think too much, Thomas,' he tells him. 'All we have to do is what King Edward's asked of you. Take that letter to Robert Welles, and then we can go home to Nettie and Katherine.'

'We have to bring back any reply,' Thomas reminds him.

Jack sighs.

'Well, once we've done that.'

Thomas hopes he's right.

'All right, then,' he says. 'Let's go. Welles is supposed to be on the road west of Lincoln.'

'Do you know the way?' Jack asks.

'I don't, but John Flood does. We are taking him.'

Jack groans, because of course John Flood will know nothing of the roads, but he likes Flood, and at least it means they will have the best provisions wherever they stop, and riding with King Edward's herald in his livery is enough to make any man feel important. They meet Flood and another man, John Wilkes, who actually does seem to know the roads, at the stables of the White Hart, where they leave their own horses with King Edward's ostlers and take two fine palfreys to match the two that Flood and Wilkes take, all well saddled. Flood looks good, even in a red bonnet with a bouncing tail from the crown, and Wilkes seems quiet enough – almost invisible, in fact – and it is only when you look at him closely that you see there is something odd about him, something extra, as if he knows something no one else does, and Thomas feels that old feeling, and wonders if they might have met before he lost his wits at Towton?

'Perhaps,' Wilkes allows. 'I've been in my lord Hastings's household since before Towton. But I do not usually forget a face, and I think I should recall yours.'

He wears soft, easy travelling clothes, blue and russet, of the sort you see every day on every road, though he has a good sword around his waist, and polished boots. His forehead and cheeks are ruddy from riding in all weathers, but the rest of his face is smooth and pale, as if he always wears a bevor.

They ride fast all that day up the crowded North Road, under cool grey skies, through countryside that is more stock pond than pasture or wood, stopping only once to rest the horses, and finding nothing to eat themselves but boiled fish and greens. Thomas is constantly struck by Wilkes. Where has he met him before? The priory perhaps? Christ, he wishes Katherine were here. She would know his type instantly and even if she had not met him, she would be able to tell Thomas where he had.

They cross the river at Stamford in the early afternoon and stop at an inn beyond the church where the innkeeper knows of the movements of this Great Captain of the Commons of Lincoln.

'He's moving south from Grantham. His scouts have been in, trying to get us to yield all we have left in our storerooms on promise of payment from the Duke of Clarence.'

'The Duke of Clarence?' Flood demands. 'Are you certain?'

'Aye.'

They wonder if they ought to send one of their number back to tell King Edward this further confirmation, but they decide it will wait, and they change horses, and ride on, armed with the news that Welles's army is somewhere on the road south of Grantham, to the northeast of Melton Mowbray. They ride the rest of that afternoon, and finally see the army camp as dark is falling: a great spread of light where watch and cooking fires are lit, and something about the sight triggers in Thomas a strange sliding sense of the familiar. It is something he's seen before, and he thinks of the time he and Katherine and Rufus stumbled on the camp of Robin of Redesdale.

They approach the camp up a much-chewed trackway, expecting to be hailed by pickets at every moment. Instead of the usual tense stand-off with men who might be expected to inspect Flood's ornate livery coat so closely that their torches nearly set him alight, they find themselves almost into the camp before someone thinks to stop them.

He's a fat man with a beard down to his nipples and a hedge-layer's bill and when Flood shows him the letter for Sir Robert Welles, sealed with his father's sign, the man admits to having no letters, so they are permitted to lead their horses into the camp, past the cooking fires, through crowds of tired, bored and anxious men. Christ, Thomas thinks, these are not soldiers: they are just like any number of men he knows, only older. The camp has the atmosphere of the night before a fair rather than a soldier's camp. He feels fraudulent walking among such men wearing his jack and carrying a sword. It is as if he is somehow taking advantage of their good nature.

'Not having so much fun, are they, now?' Jack mutters.

Thomas turns and sees Wilkes seems to have shrunk back into himself, just as he did when they first met, so that an observer's eye tends to pass him by. It is an odd trick. A sort of assumed humbleness.

Welles's tent is reasonably grand, with red-painted details on the seams and a canopy under which a small fire flickers cheerfully enough. Five or six men in long boots are gathered about, wearied from their day in the saddle, watching a bent-backed old woman fuss with the contents of a pot hanging from a tripod.

Thomas thinks about when he saw Welles last, in Ranby Hawe, with that friar. Where is he now? he wonders.

'Which of you is Robert Welles?' Flood demands as they approach.

Welles raises his hand. He is still the youngest of the lot, Thomas notes, and the freshest faced, apparently unstrained by the weight of his newfound responsibilities as Great Captain of the Commons. He is sitting on a low coffer, boots turned down, brigandine open. He makes no move to get up, even when Flood tells him he is in the presence of the King, for he represents King Edward himself, and is to be treated as such. Another man tells Flood to fuck off and another supposes he must be joking.

Flood turns on him and is about to say something, and his gloved hand is not far from his sword grip when Wilkes makes a slight movement and Flood hesitates and realises, perhaps, where he is. He settles on asking the man's name.

'Sir Thomas de la Lande,' the man says, as if everyone in Christendom should be familiar with this name. Flood pulls an elaborately bemused face. Thomas likes Flood more with every passing moment.

'What do you even want?' Welles asks.

'I've a letter for you, from your father,' Thomas tells him, 'written in the presence of King Edward, signed and sealed with your father's ring. See.'

He passes him the letter, and Welles rights himself, stretches a hand for it, takes it, inspects the seal, then breaks it and, holding the square of parchment to the light of the fire, he squints at it and reads with his lips moving, mumbling the words. In this light it is hard to make out his exact expression, but Thomas is struck by just how much the boy resembles the father. His mannerisms are identical, down to the way the eyes move around, as if seeking advice from some bystander, and Thomas wonders if he is looking for that friar?

'What is it?' one of the seated men asks.

'King Edward threatens to send my father to the headsman if I do not yield,' he says, without thought of keeping this news to himself. The men are now leaning forward on their stools. Eyes are suddenly bright, faces attentive.

There is a long moment of silence as the news settles.

'We knew he would do something,' one of them says dismissively.

'But not that,' an older, bearded man with a missing tooth interjects.

'By what right can the King even threaten it?' a soft-faced, fair-haired boy asks. 'He has already issued your father a pardon! He cannot execute your father for what you have done.'

'It is a bluff!' the first man laughs. 'King Edward would never dare!'

'He is trying to frighten us. It just shows how desperate he is!' the fair-headed boy is certain.

These two men might be brothers, Thomas thinks. Both are young, tall, handsome, broad-shouldered youths, with the same large noses and fringes of blond hair that each keeps brushing back under his hat.

'We should turn on him,' the first youth suggests. 'Wheel our army on his. Imagine his ugly old face if we marched against him now!'

'We'd catch him on the road – it'd be a rout! We would avenge our father. Our fathers, I mean. We would be famed for ever as the men who avenged Towton!'

'No!' the bearded man barks. 'We must press on to Leicester. We've no chance on our own.'

Thomas sees Wilkes's eyebrow notch upwards. Leicester?

'Pshaw! You are too pessimistic, sir.'

'We must keep our pledge!'

'Our pledge did not involve the threatened execution of Lord Welles. Of Sir Robert's father. An innocent man!'

Or a pardoned one, at any rate, Thomas thinks.

He watches on as they discuss it for a moment further, and

Robert Welles says nothing. He follows the conversation, just as Thomas does, nodding slightly as if he agrees with each man as they contribute. Jesus, Thomas thinks, he will do as the last person he's met tells him. He has no idea of his own. No plan at all. Where is that friar? He was the one with the plan. Where is he? Thomas looks around. He sees that Wilkes has also slipped away.

Then Welles's men seem to recall that King Edward's herald stands listening to their babble. They become ashamed of themselves for gabbling, they now become generous and hospitable. Welles himself gets up and opens the coffer on which he's been sitting and he digs out a pie and a bottle of what looks like wine from among the jumble of cloth and plate within, and there's even a salt cellar in there, and a boot that does not look to have a partner. Another brings bread, and they are anxious to find the King's men a space to sleep for the night, and someone to rub down and feed their horses. A tent is emptied of its occupiers the other side of the watch fire, and Thomas, Jack and Flood are shown to it, and brought stale bread and pissy ale.

'The best on offer,' the servant says.

The three of them sit in the mud outside their tent on the other side of the fire, and over the meagre flames and curtain of wetwood smoke they watch Sir Robert Welles's council of war as its members continue to discuss their options.

'What would you do?' Jack asks Flood.

'Knowing King Edward's threat is serious, and knowing the extent of his army as I do, I would bend my knee. But Welles may believe King Edward is exaggerating, and perhaps he has no idea of his forces? So – he may not.'

'He's no guns, did you see?' Jack says.

Just then Wilkes appears with a roasted pigeon on a skewer.

'Where've you been?' Flood asks.

Wilkes holds up the pigeon as if this is the answer, and offers it to Flood, who hesitates, but then yields.

Nothing more is asked or said, and they share out the little bag of baked bones and it flavours their bread and ale, and they sit in silence for a moment, until someone raises their voice in the council of war on the other side of the fire, and Thomas and the others stare through the dying light, trying to gauge who is likely to win the argument.

'But he cannot hope to beat King Edward with these men?' Thomas wonders aloud. 'Surely? I mean, look at them.'

They look more like armed pilgrims than an army. There are no liveries that he recognises, and there's little order, and none of the noise Thomas associates with these sorts of camps. Where are the smiths? The bowyers? The drummer boys? No one is up to much, and you can see clumps of fat, elderly men gathered to sit and talk about the weather or the stiffness of their backs. Still, there are enough of them, Thomas thinks, and if those reports from Yorkshire are to be believed, there are a great many more yet to come.

'The bearded man still favours passing on to Leicester,' Wilkes observes, nodding at the war council.

'Isn't that where Clarence intends meeting Warwick?' Thomas asks. 'In Leicester? With all his men-at-arms?'

Flood tilts his head in assent.

'But can he really be serious?' Thomas goes on. 'Can he really be thinking of using King Edward's own men to go against King Edward? His own brother?'

'What do you think, Wilkes?' Flood says. 'You know Clarence, don't you?'

This is a surprise. They lean forward and wait for Wilkes's answer. For some reason Thomas is certain Wilkes would rather Flood had not told anyone of his connection with Clarence.

'Clarence,' he starts after a moment, 'is a puzzle. On one hand, he is the least serious man you will ever meet, for he believes that nothing he can do will ever have consequence, good or ill. But on the other he is no fool, either, so his intentions, such as they are, can only be understood with reference to which planet happens to be in the ascendant on any given day.'

'But that is true of us all,' Flood objects. 'We are all influenced by the stars.'

'I mean,' Wilkes explains, 'that Clarence is influenced by those around him, and so to divine his intentions, one must first look to the intentions of others in his vicinity, in this case: the Earl of Warwick.'

'So the question should be,' Thomas suggests, 'does the Earl of Warwick intend to use King Edward's own troops against King Edward?'

Wilkes nods. 'The Earl will use anyone against anyone,' he says. 'He's using these men here just as he is using Clarence, and this Clarence knows full well, only he chooses to ignore it.'

'But why?'

'Clarence half wishes to be made king.'

'But I thought Warwick wished to be king?' Jack says.

Thomas cannot tell if he is being a simple countryman for show.

'Well,' Wilkes says, less contemptuous than Thomas might have supposed. 'If he could he would, perhaps, but he cannot be. No man would permit it, not just in this land, but elsewhere – across the Narrow Sea in the royal houses of France and further afield too. The right of kings is self-serving, of course, and so is fiercely protected.'

'But King Edward is still king,' Thomas points out. 'Removing him would be still be removing the rightful king and replacing him with someone – in this case Clarence – who should not be king. It is the same thing: a rightful king deposed.'

'Ah,' Wilkes says, 'but what if it could be proved that King Edward ought not to be king?'

'How could that be done?' Flood asks.

And now, in the perplexed silence that follows, Thomas feels his face warming and he turns away to inspect the underside of his boot. He already knows how it might be done. Wilkes remains silent and Thomas is certain he is watching him, noting his reaction, and so after a moment, Thomas picks out a tiny pebble from the leather of his sole and tosses it on the fire. He is grateful for the falling dark.

'There are ways,' Wilkes then says. 'There are always ways.'

When Thomas looks up, he glances first at Flood, who is looking very serious, and then at Wilkes, who is, indeed, looking at Thomas. Thomas stares back. It is all he can do.

'So – I have heard rumours,' Flood is saying. 'Rumours that—'

'Rumours that should not be spoken of,' Wilkes says, breaking eye-lock with Thomas and quickly turning on Flood, shutting him up instantly. Flood nods and swallows whatever he was about to say, but he is rebuked, and there is a long period of silence.

'In the meantime,' Wilkes says, adopting a more discursive tone, 'what are we to do about our friend young Welles over there?'

There is another silence while they ponder this. If Wilkes is right about Clarence never being serious, then the same cannot be said for the Earl of Warwick, whom they know to be serious in all things, and whom they know to have a great number of men at his command, many of them well trained and well accoutred.

'So if this lot join up with the Earl of Warwick's men,' Jack starts, 'and also with Clarence's household men and his levies, and with those coming from the Northern Parts then – they will number, what? Twenty thousand? Thirty thousand? A *hundred* and thirty thousand?'

'As many as fifty,' Wilkes says.

Jack whistles.

'King Edward'd never come close to matching that number,' Flood says.

'No,' Wilkes agrees.

'So we need to ensure they do not combine,' Thomas says.

Wilkes turns on him. 'How would you do that?'

'Get the little pipsqueak to bend his bloody knee,' Jack says.

Wilkes nods. 'That might do,' he says, 'but it is merely postponing the reckoning, surely, and it leaves the threat alive. No. We need an engagement. Something decisive.'

Thomas has an idea.

'Persuade Welles to do as those two boys wish,' he says. 'Persuade him that his army can beat King Edward's without the help of Warwick, and so he should turn his army on King Edward.'

Wilkes nods, pleased.

'How, though?' he asks. 'The bearded one seems to be carrying the day.'

It seems obvious to Thomas.

'Suggest to Welles that the bearded man lacks courage. Or not to Welles. Suggest it to one of the brothers.'

Wilkes looks speculatively at Thomas, as if he is revising an estimation.

'You want to provoke a battle?' he asks.

'It is what you want, isn't it?' Thomas replies. 'King Edward's army will rout this lot as it stands. If the defeat is decisive then those from the north will want no further part of this rebellion, will they? And Clarence's men will surely waver.'

'As will Clarence himself,' Wilkes supposes.

At that moment, one of the brothers gets to his feet and steps out of the circle of light, presumably to relieve himself, and Wilkes is on his feet in an instant. He spills some ale down his chin, pats Thomas on the shoulder as he passes, and wanders vaguely around the fire, staggering slightly, feigning drunkenness, but also unerring in his pursuit of the boy.

'Bloody hell,' Jack mutters. 'He's quick.'

They sit in silence for a while, watching, waiting, until both men return. Wilkes has his hand on the boy's back, and they are laughing about something. Wilkes has removed his hat and the fire gleams on his close shaven head. They part, and Wilkes replaces his hat and comes over and sits next to Flood, and takes up his ale again and drinks more, and Thomas watches the activity on the other side of the fire as the boy whispers something in his brother's ear, and the brother turns and stares at Wilkes across the fire, and Wilkes laughs at something no one has said and raises his cup in a show of ale-softened bonhomie.

'The seed is planted,' he says, from the corner of his mouth, and there is nothing more of consequence said that night.

In the morning, the birdsong wakes Thomas as the darkness fades and the world begins to take on its daylight form. He is lying under his travel cloak, below the dirty canvas canopy of the borrowed tent, between Jack and John Flood, and beyond is Wilkes, already awake, scratching his bristling head and listening carefully.

When he sees Thomas is awake, he looks over at him, and raises his eyebrows twice.

'And sprouted,' he says, just as if there have been no ten hours of sleep since last they spoke.

When they are all awake and emerged from the tent, there is no sign of the bearded man.

'Do not ask,' Wilkes warns.

The other men in the camp are getting ready to move out, and are forming like bees around their hives as Thomas and the others set out to find Sir Robert Welles, who gives Flood a letter for the King, sealed with a similar imprint as that from his father. Thomas tries to gauge his mood, but the boy is as vague and slippery as ever. One of the two brothers is with him, though, harnessed in the scuffed and scratched plate of a man who has fallen on harder times than he might have been brought up to expect. He looks secretive, and pleased with himself.

'Sir Robert will parlay with King Edward at his castle at Fotheringhay,' the boy says. 'Where they will have much to discuss.'

'In the meantime,' Welles chips in, 'I trust in King Edward's goodness to keep my father from harm.'

Flood suggests prayer might be the most effective defence.

'So your men are disbanding?' he then asks. 'They will return to their shires?'

All turn and watch the vaguely organised churn of roughly dressed men. They seem to be gathering, rather than dispersing, but that is perhaps just an impression. Wilkes, though, looks cheerful.

They mount their horses and ride out on to the road, retracing their exact steps back towards Stamford, and throughout the countryside the bells are ringing in every parish to summon all to Mass. Wilkes, who has now fully emerged from the shadows and revealed himself as the true captain of their party, tells them they do not have time for Mass, but must ride on to find King Edward.

'Do you think it worked?' Thomas asks.

'Who can say? Welles is fickle, and might change his mind the moment we are out of sight, but the bearded man was the only one of them who spoke with any sense, and after they had accused him of cowardice, he told them he would take his men – all twenty of them! – and ride to Leicester himself alone, since he owed no allegiance to such as Welles. They wished him well of it.'

Thomas turns to look over his shoulder, imagining Welles's army traipsing along the roads after them.

'It seems wrong, though,' he says. 'To have provoked them into their destruction.'

Wilkes sighs. 'If they come,' he says, 'and there is no surety that they will, then we will have saved many lives with this piece of work, Master Everingham, may all the saints and martyrs and God above be my witnesses.'

He is so certain, he repels doubt, but Thomas cannot be sure. He feels he has engineered a fight that will see Englishmen kill Englishmen, and he knows that if it comes to pass, it will weigh heavily on his conscience.

They ride all morning, reclaiming their own horses at Stamford and riding on to find King Edward with his army at Fotheringhay. They come in over the drawbridge mid afternoon, and are shown straight to King Edward's solar where he is dining alone with William Hastings and three surprisingly rough young women, of the sort who expect sumptermen to wave at them on roadsides. Stewards and servants stand in the shadows, waiting, and there is a pork pie in the centre of the table as big as a drum. King Edward is still having nothing to do with Lent. Perhaps he never has to?

When it is known Flood has brought back Welles's reply, the women are sent from the room, and more candles are brought.

'Well?'

After a deep bow, Flood passes Robert Welles's letter to King Edward, who breaks it and reads it with a frown.

'He trusts I will not kill his father,' he tells Hastings.

'Is that all?'

'He wishes to parlay at a mutually agreed location, so long as, in advance, I issue a pardon to him and his followers for all acts of rebellion so far committed, and that I release his father and the other one.'

'What is he offering you?'

King Edward turns the parchment over, as if he may have missed something.

'Nothing,' he says. 'That's it.'

Hastings looks up and catches Wilkes's gaze. Wilkes cocks an eyebrow, Hastings nods, and after a moment Thomas, Flood and Jack are dismissed with a steward to find something to eat and drink in the kitchen. Wilkes remains.

The steward guides them down to the kitchens. It is the first time Thomas has been alone with Flood since meeting Wilkes.

'Who is he?' he asks. 'Really?'

'Wilkes? I don't know. I am not sure if that is even his name. But he's one of Lord Hastings's men of business,' Flood tells him what he already knows, then goes on: 'He was a cleric, I believe. A friar. I am not sure why he is no longer. Perhaps he strangled his abbot? Or got his abbot to strangle himself? I know he was involved with reforming the Mint, but more than that – nothing.'

Thomas nods. He is not reassured, but he is too tired from two days in the saddle to think much about it, and the next day, after a night spent in a corridor, he is up at dawn with the rest of the inhabitants of the castle to hear the news that after Mass to celebrate St Gregory's Day, King Edward and his army will move northwards, to Stamford.

Once again, Hastings requires Thomas's presence.

'Sorry, Thomas,' he says, 'but if what Wilkes says is true, you are partly responsible for the way the coming days will unfold, and so you should be here to see it done, whatever it is, good or ill. Also King Edward has issued his usual demand for your presence.'

'But my wife—'

'Can look after herself better than any man I've yet to meet, so do not try that one on me, Thomas. And look at you! Better accoutred now than ever you were when we went into battle at Mortimer's Cross, or Towton!'

Thomas only knows what he is talking about because Katherine told him what happened before those battles.

'I've not heard from her in a week,' he says. 'I had hoped there might be a message?'

'Another day or two'll make no difference, Thomas,' Hastings says.

Jack agrees, and Thomas has no choice, so he sends Katherine a message by one of Hastings's men, to ask if all is well and to tell her that with God's blessing he will be home soon, and that Jack sends his love to Nettie and the baby, trusting that the Holy Trinity hold them safe; and then he and Jack reclaim their horses, saddle them again, and clamber back up into their saddles in time to watch King Edward ride out, accompanied by his household men, the Duke of Gloucester and William Hastings. Trailing behind them are Welles and Dimmock, in pourpoints, hose and bare feet.

6

Thomas and Jack join the line of men on the road to Stamford. Both of them have been wearing the same linen for a week now, and there is nothing more Thomas would wish for than a change and a bath, but in this they are hardly alone, and as they march out the smell of unwashed bodies, leather, horse sweat and black powder is thick in the air. A drum beats and there are pipers ahead, and Jack tells him that this is what a real army looks like.

They move at the speed of the wagons carrying the guns. There are a dozen of these, not of the fearsome size that sent stones to blow apart the walls of the Bamburgh Castle, but field guns, each perhaps five paces long, mounted on two wheels, capable of sending stones and iron balls the side of a child's head at astonishing speeds and hard enough to blow through the very finest plate.

'Thanks be to God Welles has none himself,' Jack says, and he crosses himself at this, because he only has his jack, a helmet and a small buckler for defence. Not enough to face a gun. Not enough to face anyone, really. Thomas feels the luxury of his brigandine, though he wishes he had leg armour – vambraces, cuisses and sabatons – as once he had.

'It is the noise that will do for them,' Jack says, for the guns are the loudest thing imaginable. 'Like putting your head in a church bell.'

With them roll carts laden with arrows, bound in sheaves ready to be bagged up by bowmen's boys. There is bread too, and great roundels of cheese, and King Edward's men have managed to get hold of pies of dense-packed pork that must be guarded by a watch of their own, as must the ale wagons, for no one could be expected to fight without ale.

Thomas watches them all pass and Jack asks him what it is they are supposed to do if it comes to a fight.

'Lend our bows, I suppose,' Thomas says. He remembers the last battle he fought, when he and a few others – now dead – made up the entire number of bowmen fighting for the Earl of Pembroke.

Just then Wilkes appears at his shoulder. He is freshly washed and shaved, in a dark green brigandine and wonderful leg armour. He smiles but doesn't say anything, and they sit together, the three of them, watching the guns roll past. After a while he speaks.

'King Henry the Fifth had guns in France, did you know?' he starts. 'They were old-fashioned things, iron-hooped, and clumsy by comparison with these. Each took a day to load, prime and then fire, and they were so inaccurate as to be more a danger to those firing them than those being fired at. But King Henry had a master gunner who could sometimes hit what he was aiming for. One day this master gunner set up two guns side by side, and he fired them one after the other. The first brought down one tower of the town they were besieging; the second hit the other tower and the gates fell. He hit the thing he was aiming at. Twice. Twice in one day. Imagine.'

'Pretty good,' Jack admits.

'His men thought it miraculous, and he was a great favourite with the King, but in those days, we were all very suspicious of the guns, weren't we? So the others – archers and billmen and some men-at-arms and I dare say a few of the knights, too – they thought the master must be in league with the devil, so they burned him to death.'

Thomas cannot think of anything to say to that. He looks at Wilkes, and Wilkes looks steadily back at him. What is he up to? What does he know? Wilkes merely raises his eyebrows twice again, and says he must go on, and he leaves them.

'What was that about?' Jack asks.

'I think he's telling us that none of us is sacred,' Thomas says.

Jack looks at him blankly.

'What's got into you?' he asks. 'You're as mad as him.'

Thomas shrugs and shakes his head and they ride on, reaching Stamford early in the afternoon, with the first real softness of spring in the air, and they come down the slight slope to the clutch of grey stone houses on the southern bank of the river with more chance this time to look about at the still-blackened stones left over from when the northerners pillaged the place ten years earlier.

By the time Thomas and Jack are with Hastings's men at the head of the queue to cross the bridge, news comes from the other side of the town that King Edward's scouts have returned, having encountered Sir Robert Welles and his army marching towards them from the west.

'He's drawn them up a few miles to the north,' a man tells them. 'Near a place called Empringham.'

'Is he preparing to lay down his arms?' Thomas asks hopefully.

The man scoffs.

'No. They're readying to fight.'

'Oh Christ,' Thomas cannot stop himself muttering. Just then there is a small stampede of townspeople running across the bridge. They are like rats, slipping between horses and carts and bodies of men drawn up under their vintenars.

'Where are they going?'

No one knows. Thomas waits until a tall thin boy runs past; he leans out of his saddle and seizes the boy by the collar of his coat and lifts him off the ground. Jack laughs as the boy's feet continue to run.

'Wait one moment,' Thomas says, 'and tell me where you are all off to in such a hurry.'

'Come on, master! They're going to chop some heads off!'

'Who is?'

'King Edward's men! Two of them! Come on! I'll miss it!'

Thomas drops him and he scrambles away with a shouted curse and an obscene gesture.

'Welles and Dimmock?' Thomas wonders aloud, looking west along the river to the towers of the castle.

'Must be,' Jack says. 'D'you want to see?'

Thomas shakes his head. He remembers having to stand and watch Earl Rivers and John Woodville having their heads struck off. It is an unforgettable thing to see: just before it happens, the light becomes unnaturally bright, but also watery, as if the air is thickened, and everything becomes heavy and still, and the birds cease their song, and it feels as if in these final moments the spirits of those present are very closely connected just as one of them prepares to depart this realm for ever. And, in truth, this latest act of King Edward, if it is to happen, sends a chill through Thomas.

'It seems – petty,' Jack says, and Thomas agrees. They had hoped King Edward would be above what seems like murder, but though many of King Edward's soldiers remain on the road, unmoved by the appeal of the spectacle of two men going to the

block, the townspeople of Stamford, as with townspeople everywhere, flock to witness the blood being spilled.

They wait with the other men in the streets of Stamford, among
the grey-stone buildings, and Thomas sees a stationer's shop,
where the man is selling paper and pamphlets and there are one or
two books even. He cannot resist. He swings himself out of his
saddle and leaves his horse with Jack while he inspects the mer-
chandise. The stationer is young, with reddish hair like Thomas's
own, worn long and greasy under his cap, with a bobbling Adam's
apple and a way of waggling his head as he speaks.

He enquires if Thomas is looking for anything in particular.
Thomas is not. Seeing Thomas is a soldier, he recommends a copy
of a book written in what looks to Thomas like German, but is
mostly pictures of men in long pointed shoes fighting one another
with long swords and pollaxes. There is a series of three or four in
which a man in a hole fights a woman with a stone in her veil. The
man seems to win, for the woman ends up in the hole, upside
down. Thomas doesn't buy the book, but he does buy a girdle for
Katherine from the tradesman in the next shop. It is of red leather
with a silver buckle and silver medallions, including a likeness of
St Margaret, the patron saint of childbirth. He does not barter.

'What've you got?' Jack asks, watching him slide it into his saddle bag.

'A girdle for Katherine.'

'How much?'

Thomas tells him. Jack whistles.

'You're like no northerner I ever met, Thomas.'

Thomas feels a spike of shame, but then remembers how much
he is being paid by Hastings to remain with the King's army, and
thinks it is the least he can do for her. He swings up into the saddle
and they wait in silence while the shadows begin to lengthen, and

Thomas finds his lips moving in prayer. He hopes it will be too late to fight now, too late to take the field even against such an army as Welles's. He takes a drink from his costrel. It is water, as befits Lent, and he wishes he had bread. He yearns for evening, to be told it is too late to move out, and that they are camping in Stamford for the night, and that Welles and Dimmock will face their fate — whatever it is — in the morning, as is traditional.

But then they hear a sudden roar of a thousand voices, like that first distant ripple of thunder, carried on the cooling afternoon air, from the direction of the castle. Birds take flight from the mossy roof tiles above their heads and on the streets below each man cranes his neck, half expecting to see Lord Welles's or Sir Thomas Dimmock's spirit come trailing overhead like a meteor or flame-tailed comet.

Nothing happens, of course, and Thomas and Jack each hunch their shoulders, waiting for the next head to roll, and Thomas can imagine this second victim — Dimmock probably — being dragged on to the block and having his head pushed down into the blood of the first, and then — his timing perfect — the axe falls and there is the second great roar of the townspeople gathered in the castle's bailey.

'We can go now,' someone says.

'Surely it is too late?' Thomas suggests. 'It'll be sunset before you know it.'

But trumpets sound and the drumming begins, and it's obviously not. There is a smattering of switches being smacked against ox backs, the creak of weight being taken up, and the shuffling jangle of harnessed men moving out. It is late in the afternoon and the men around them are beginning to show urgency. Men are changing caps for helmets. Bows are taken from bags, swords and hammers loosened in belts. The first fully harnessed man rides by, visor up. It is still such a startling sight, more contraption than human, and the horses react to it too, as if they also know how unnatural a thing it is. Thomas wonders who among Welles's men will stop such a man? Neither of those fair-headed brothers, he feels certain.

As they follow the road northwest, he feels his heart missing beats, racing like the boy he'd picked off the ground. Christ, he thinks, this is it. Another of these bloody battles. Another fight. It is really going to happen.

'Surely it is too late in the day?' Thomas repeats.

But no. Ahead there is the usual hurry-up-and-wait confusion that always goes with these sorts of things, and word comes back that the main body of the enemy has been seen, off the road to the north, just as described, in rough chalky heathland where there are odd sinkholes that might swallow a man whole. The men are all driven like sheep off the road while the guns are brought grinding through, and then, gradually, minds are reapplied and order re-established. A wagon park is designated to the south of the road, and horse lines are decided. Trumpets blare and men shout for their lords' retainers to gather in certain spots. There are the usual flags, and the customary liveries of King Edward, and the old murrey and blue that signified his men when he was the Earl of March and then the Duke of York, and soon the fishtailed banners are unfurled and held aloft over men's heads.

Thomas sees Flood wearing King Edward's colours again. Flood looks very anxious and Thomas knows it is not fear, but regret. They both feel it. With their help, Wilkes has created this clash. They could have spoken to Welles, he's sure of it. They could have got him to bend his knee.

'Is there any chance of stopping it?' Thomas asks.

Flood shakes his head. 'The King is adamant.'

'But – Christ, you saw the boy. He's a fool. You could make him bend his knee still. Just talk to him. Get him alone. Get him away from those two idiots of his. Englishmen are about to kill and be killed, for the love of God.'

Flood acknowledges the truth of this.

'I know. I know.'

There is nothing more they can say.

'Good luck, Sir John,' Thomas says, caught by the formality of their parting.

'Master Everingham.'

They shake hands. Thomas and Jack are given Hastings's black bull on white wool livery tabards to wear over their jacks, and are told they must go with Hastings's master of bowmen, Ryder, to join the left battle. Sombre, they make their way through the crowds of anxious, milling men, and find themselves among broadly familiar types, who regard them as incomers, and they must press to find space among the ordered companies of archers. Jack is better at this kind of thing, and eventually space is made, and now Thomas can see the disposition of Welles's army facing them across the heath: they are spread out across perhaps seven hundred paces and are still about five hundred paces distant. Edward's army is spread across a broader front of perhaps a thousand paces, and among them many a lord's banner. That is a good sign for King Edward, less so for Welles. Even better for King Edward, though, must be sight of his guns taking up the forward position. The gunners have got a fire going and are getting themselves organised.

'They look more than I thought,' Jack mutters. 'And they're all in livery jackets. Must have handed them out this morning. They look more like it, don't they?'

Thomas scans the far lines. His eyesight has never been good so he cannot make out individual faces, and there are few flags. Nevertheless, he fancies he sees Welles, mounted, and perhaps, at his right- and left-hand sides, those two fair-headed boys whose impetuous natures have drawn these men here, now, to decide their fate.

'Still got no fucking guns,' an old archer mutters next to him. 'Still ain't got no fucking guns.'

They move forward to within long bowshot, and still Thomas prays that nothing will come of this. He prays that Flood will be able to parlay for peace, and that every man here can go home without having to fight. He joins the others around him as they nock their bows, though, just in case, and he pulls out his arrows, fulling the fletches, checking the shafts are straight and true. They are King Edward's arrows, not his own, which are too good for this sort of thing. Or perhaps he will save them for later, if things go very badly. He has twenty-four. Enough? You never know, do you? But there are more in reserve, and the youngsters are already milling around, their shoulders strung with gathered sheaves of shafts for when the first ration is used up. What about the wind? There is almost none, and no threat of rain, either. He cannot decide if that is good or bad.

'So now we wait,' Jack says. It is always like this. Men lick their lips, nerves stretched taut, every action exaggerated. Men laugh loudly, suddenly, or yawn until it seems their jaws must break, and there is constant movement of fiddling hands, as strings, beads, buckles, tabs and points are checked and rechecked. Thomas cranes his neck. He waits to see Flood ride across to Welles, and he prays again that there will be no fighting, and no lives lost or blood spilled.

'Welles'll never receive him now, will he?' Jack asks. 'Not now King Edward's killed his father.'

Thomas looks at Jack and realises with a falling heart that he is right, and that there's no point even hoping. Just as he is thinking this above their heads a hundred thousand starlings put on an astonishing display, creating towering twisting shapes that drift over their heads and distract the men, and there are widespread murmurs for it is an amazing, mesmerising sight; however, it seems it does not impress King Edward for just then, dispensing with the formality of sending across his heralds, he orders his guns to fire.

The sound makes the unexpectant among Hastings's bowmen cry out and clap their palms to their ears. From the guns, great belches of filthy grey smoke punch across the sloping plain, and there are dark spikes of bruised fire within the smoke as more guns erupt, one after the other, with dull crumps to compress the men's ears further. As the clouds of smoke drift, the smell of the burned black powder is pestilent in their nostrils and on their tongues, and each explosion is so loud the gunners and those nearby must open their mouths for fear something within will burst.

When the reverberating din fades, they hear the noise of the stones and balls hitting Welles's troops. First it's a thundering drum of hammer blows, then come soul-rending screams of agony, and then a great spreading bleat of alarm. It takes until the smoke clears in the windless afternoon actually to see the damage done, and when it does, the men on King Edward's side draw breath. Great cavities have been dug in the front line of Welles's army, just as if the men were reaped wheat stalks, and there is instant and fatal confusion among those who remain in the line, waiting for the next salvo.

'Nock!' Ryder shouts. Open-mouthed men remember their bows and their arrow shafts held loose between forefingers.

'Draw!'

A thousand bows rise.

'Loose!'

There's a rippling din of bowstrings. A thousand arrows leap from King Edward's line, smudging the air above and replacing the starlings, to hang a brief split of a moment in the space above and between the two lines before dropping on those beyond and below.

Before they do, another thousand shafts have followed; and before those drop, there are another thousand in the sky. On it goes until each man has used up his first ration. They have received not one shaft in return.

A bugle sounds a sharp signal.

'Cease! Cease!' Ryder shouts. 'Cease now!'

King Edward's men-at-arms are moving forward from the middle battle, rounding the guns and covering the ground quickly. They start at a determined tramp, but after a moment they are running. Ahead, among Welles's army, there is absolute chaos. After the stones and balls, the arrows have almost completed the business, and you can see Welles's troops have lost all order. They are turning and running, fighting one another to get away. The battle is lost and won in less time that it takes to say the rosary.

Around Thomas the archers are laughing and cheering and whooping with pleasure and joy. Those at the front set off running across the intervening yards; those at the back start pushing to catch up with them. They shove past Thomas and Jack. Jack is caught in two minds. He wants to follow. He wants to stay with Thomas. Thomas takes his bow and nods for him to go, and he does so with a grin, his run impeded by his limp, laughing as others stumble and fall in the rough grasses. It is just his thing, Thomas thinks, no different from the football match. The older men stay and watch the younger men run. Ryder looks at Thomas and shrugs. Thomas shrugs too.

'King's given word to spare the commons,' Ryder says.

'Well, that is what they mostly are,' Thomas tells him.

Ryder nods.

'Thought as much. No banners. Only a few horsemen. And look, they're on the move.'

They stand watching for a while, but there is nothing much to be made out above the horde of men pushing and shoving. Such horsemen as there were on Welles's side have turned and fled, as Ryder says, and as they watch about twenty of King Edward's horsemen – prickers with long lances – set off across the divide after them, and Thomas wonders how far Welles's men will get. He supposes Welles will give himself up. It is not hard to guess what fate awaits him. He wonders if the boy will have his head struck off on the same block as his father?

Thomas feels no sense of cheer, and Ryder looks glum too.

'So,' he says. 'That is that.'

And Thomas nods and they shake hands on a thing being done, and Thomas walks back through the lines. He catches a glimpse of Wilkes, ducking away, hurrying about his business, and for some reason Thomas is left remembering Jack's story about Wolf and those dragons: the first is slain, but the next, the greater, awaits.

What he cannot decide, there and then, is who that next dragon might be.

7

'We should send for the bailiff,' Bald John says.

'No,' Katherine tells him. 'If the bailiff has not already heard there has been a house burned down and six people killed, then what manner of bailiff can he be?'

She'll not tell him, of course, about the last time she had dealings with a bailiff, after Welby's wife died, and she – Katherine – faced a packed coroner's court where she was falsely and maliciously accused of the woman's murder. She'd been sent back to the mercies of St Mary's Priory, Haverhurst, for safekeeping until her trial, and it might as well have been to hell. Ever since then, any mere mention of the word bailiff sets her twitching with fear.

'Then we should wait for Jack,' Bald John goes on. 'He should be allowed to see Nettie once more.'

She would have agreed then, but that afternoon the message comes from Thomas to tell her that he and Jack will be away longer than he – though not she – had thought, and so it is that John Stumps has to agree with her, for even in this cool weather, Nettie will not keep, and so that afternoon they carry her body down from the hall, wound in her sheet, and they gather in the church to watch the priest read aloud the service for the dead. When she is anointed and blessed, they lay her in a grave that Foulmouth John and the skinny boy have sunk in the long shadow of the yew tree, and they sprinkle her with holy water and then sod, and they bury her, and all the time her baby wails piteously.

Afterwards they walk back up to the hall together, just as they have done a hundred times before, but this time everything is changed, and Nettie's inconsolable baby is on Katherine's hip, and Rufus is ahead with Joana, walking with that strange springy stride of his, stooping now and then as he is distracted by something in the grass. They pause for a moment to see the way things have changed with the absence of Jack's house.

'We can always rebuild it, I suppose,' John Stumps says. It's more or less the first thing he's said since they found he'd shot that dog during the attack. It didn't matter that it was a good shot, or that the bolt had killed the dog instantly. He'd wanted to show he could still kill a man, still make himself useful.

'Is there any point?' Katherine wonders. 'If we don't know who this Mostyn is?' Since they first heard his name a few days before, Mostyn has become like the first symptom of a canker. A black spot on a petal, a red spot on skin. How serious is it underneath? How far gone is the plant or patient? Will he pass by in the night? Or is he embedded? How many men has he, and who is supporting him? To whom does he look up and who is his good-lord? All these are unknowns that will, by the by, make themselves known, Katherine supposes, but most mysterious is how he – this Mostyn – knows that Thomas was ever a cleric?

She hefts the baby to her other hip as Kate continues her crying, and she and John Stumps look at one another over the child's head, and there is not much either can say that is not obvious to all. The baby is always grabbing at things to relieve the pain in her gums and now she catches Katherine's hand and gnaws on a knuckle and Katherine can feel the sharpness of her teeth. Perhaps a fob of leather would help? She'll see what she can find.

Rufus comes back and takes the baby, and he and one of the older girls wander off around the other side of the house, where the smell and taste of the ashes in the air don't make you want to spit. Ahead, Foulmouth is cuffing the new boy, the skinny one left over from the night of the attack. Bald John shouts at him, and Foulmouth John slinks away, and the skinny boy settles on the step, cowering like a starving dog.

'Well, at least we know it wasn't the Earl of Warwick come for the ledger,' John Stumps says, gesturing at him. 'More likely to have been sent by the Three Wise Men than by the Earl of Warwick.'

Katherine agrees. The morning after they'd been attacked, and the house burned down, they'd stood in wait till noon, tense again, crossbows spanned, waiting for this John Mostyn to make his appearance, ready to shoot him dead, but he never did come.

'But who can he be?' she'd asked the others as they waited. 'Have any of you ever heard of him?'

'He'll be some little – I don't know,' John Stumps had said. 'You've heard of it happening, haven't you? Some fucker comes up with an excuse and just – nips in there, while backs are turned, and takes the place over. Happened to Sir John, didn't it, when he was away in France that time?'

'But he said we were clerics,' Katherine had repeated herself.

'If that's true,' Bald John had supposed, 'then that'll be the last we see of him.'

But Katherine had not been so sure. She'd wondered if any of them knew that Thomas was once a canon of the Order of St Gilbert, and that he'd spent his youth in the Priory of St Mary in Haverhurst? She had supposed they might not, for why would Thomas ever have told anyone? But then how would this Mostyn know? Or was he merely using it as an excuse to get those other dead men to attack the house for him?

So they'd gone back to the shivering boy, to find him being watched over by Foulmouth John with a long knife in his hand.

'So where did you meet them?' she'd asked the boy.

'I met Johnson in the Tun,' the boy had told her. 'In London.'

The Tun is a jail in London, renowned even as far north as Lincoln.

'Johnson?'

'The big one.' He'd puffed out his cheeks to mime being fat.

'And he knew Mostyn?'

'Not very well,' the boy had said. 'No love lost between them.'

'Did they meet in the Tun, too?'

'Mostyn isn't the sort you find there,' he'd said. 'It's all night-walkers and common strumpets in the Tun.'

'So where and how did you meet Mostyn?'

'On the road,' the boy had said with a gesture of his wrist to indicate the land beyond the distant trees, the realm of elsewhere, the space of the ceaseless toing and froing of nameless men on nameless roads between nameless places.

'And did he ever say how he knew – why he thought we were clerics?' Katherine had asked.

The boy had shaken his head. Of course he wasn't interested in the whys and wherefores.

'Just said you were, like.'

He'd looked so miserable that no one, not even Foulmouth John, could wish him further harm so they kept him with them, as a witness for when the bailiff turned up, as surely he would, and the next day they'd made him bury his dead companions together, naked save their braies, behind the church, where the land is sunken and smells of sewage, and after a few careless words from the priest, they'd thrown wet mud over their upturned faces while rooks cawed in the treetops.

The rest of that day, and the next, there had been bright, thin sunshine, and an east wind in which clothes dried stiff and would have smelt of iodine if they had not stunk of the ashes that swirled up from Jack and Nettie's house. There were leaves in bud on the hawthorns and cuckoo song in the air. They heard nothing from Thomas or Jack, and still they had to keep watch for men sent by the Earl of Warwick, or for William Hastings's bloodhound, or for Mostyn, or for Wymmys to come riding back. All eyes were strained with tears for Nettie and her baby, and yet there was no time for mourning, but all had to take their turns, crossbows spanned, waiting at doors and windows, ever vigilant.

They are barely back inside the hall after burying Nettie when the bailiff finally comes, accompanied by two men with halberds. Katherine's heart beats almost out of her chest when she's told, and she thinks about running, taking to the woods until he is gone, but no, she will face him. She gathers herself and she goes down the track to meet him, to try to keep him from the house. Each pace seems to set her body burning.

He is a slim little man in elegant clothes with a tall red bonnet on his head, though his horse's ribs are as prominent as knuckles and, close by, the impression of elegance is spoiled by his nose, which is pale and boneless, as if made from a different substance than the rest of his face.

'Good day to you, mistress,' he greets her, his gaze flitting from her face to her belly, back again, and then over to the burned-out stump of Jack and Nettie's house. He removes his hat and dismounts to give her an unnerving bow. He is not so bad, Katherine thinks. He is a worm, and he provokes none of the terrors she had feared. Still, though, her body is quivering and her voice is pitched higher in her ears than ordinarily.

146

'We expected you days ago,' she tells him.

'I have been busy, mistress, with the affairs of men.'

She wishes Thomas were here to deal with this. Already she can feel sweat on her forehead.

'Well,' she starts. 'We have buried Nettie, and the five men. So we shall have to have them disinterred.'

'Oh, I have not come to see you about that matter.'

She is surprised.

'No?'

'No. In such scrambled times as these, such things – they seem to matter less. And the quality of the men . . . was not high, was it?'

She is still for a moment. He knows about the attack, and he knows about the men who carried it out. How? He laughs nervously, and something in his manner makes her call for John Stumps, who comes running. Seeing him, the bailiff laughs more nervously still at his ungainly run, for without his arms John seems more fish than man, though he still wears his sword as a badge of pride.

'So?' she asks.

'Oh,' the bailiff explains, 'I am sent here to enquire after your husband, Thomas Everingham.'

'Thomas? What of him? Why do you wish to see him?'

'Ah. Well. It is not him I wish to see, but a document I am confident he possesses.'

Her heart makes a great drop. Then picks up with a charge. Jesus! The ledger. Her ears fill with the sound of waves on shingle. She feels scorching hot, then freezing cold. She puts her hands behind her back to hide their tremble. This is Warwick's man? This?

'Tell me who you are again?' she asks.

'I am John Wymmys,' he says. 'County bailiff.'

147

This she knew. But she had heard he was connected to Thomas Burgh of Gainsborough, the man whose house Thomas saw attacked. Can he be after the ledger on Burgh's behalf? Surely not.

'What – manner of document?' John Stumps asks. He too has made the connection.

The bailiff correctly judges John not to be the sort to concern himself overly with documents.

'Oh, it is a small thing,' Wymmys says. 'But important, for it is a dispensation from the Pope in Rome.'

For a moment Katherine is lost for words. Does she laugh? Cry? Hit Wymmys? Hug John?

'A dispensation from the Pope in Rome?' John Stumps repeats. Wymmys smiles unpleasantly. His nose is sweating.

'A dispensation from what? Or for what?' Katherine asks, certain that this is a mistake that can still be cleared up. But Wymmys has the look about him now of a ferret with a rabbit in sight.

'Why, the dispensation from Thomas Everingham's vows as a canon of the Gilbertine Order,' Wymmys says. 'He cannot own property, having taken those vows, and I have checked to see if his name is on the deed to this estate, and it is, but there is no mention of the dispensation. An oversight, I am sure.'

Katherine hears that distant rushing in her ears swelling again.

'What?' she asks again, but Wymmys just smiles. John Stumps looks at her for clarification.

'Thomas?' he asks. 'He was a canon?'

She shakes her head, more to clear its clutter than to deny the accusation.

'Yes, yes,' Wymmys says. 'I heard it as a rumour first, and scarce believed it myself, but a certain man of the law courts asked me to press for information, since he claims certain enfeoffments are made on this land, and the hall there.'

He indicates. Katherine knows enough to know that an enfeoffment on the land is a bad thing, like a claim on it, though how and why such a thing might arise, she cannot say.

'I don't believe it,' John Stumps says. 'Where was he a canon then?'

'At the Priory of St Mary,' Wymmys tells them. 'In Haverhurst. Just south of Lincoln.'

'But that is burned down!' Katherine says.

'Ah!' Wymmys muses. 'So you know it?'

'I know – of it. I know it burned down.'

'Just so,' Wymmys agrees, 'but before it burned down there was one of those scandals that often devil such places, and its running was taken back by the order's Prior of All.'

Katherine finds herself mouthing the words 'Prior of All'. She has not heard them spoken aloud for ten years. Now here they are, heavy as stones. She sees that John Who-Was-Stabbed-by-His-Priest and Robert From-the-Plague-Village, and now Bald John and Foulmouth John are making their way down from the hall. She turns back to Wymmys, who is going on.

'And it so happens that I have a cousin who is a clerk in Canterbury,' he says, 'who was able to make enquiries among his peers, and he tells me that all the papers relating to that priory were gathered in Canterbury before the fire, and so are extant still.'

'What are you taking about?' John Stumps asks.

'The archive is extensive' – Wymmys ignores him – 'and well kept, and it stretches back beyond the very first years of the last King Henry's reign. Following my suggestion, my cousin's contact discovered that there was at one time a certain Thomas Everingham, of Derbyshire, taken in as a canon at the Priory of St Mary, who did abscond not merely the once, but the twice. First in the last year of King Henry's reign, and then again in the third of Edward's.'

'Who are you? Who has put you up to this?' Katherine finds herself hissing.

He throws his hands up and feigns shock. 'Mistress,' he says.

'Who is this – this lawyer?' she demands. She can see his Adam's apple bob up and down as he swallows. His hair is greasy with sweat too.

'His name is John Mostyn,' he says.

'Ha!' Katherine cries.

'He is an attorney in the law courts. And has the protection of my lord of Warwick.'

Katherine is speechless again. So this is it, she thinks. She looks around, anywhere other than at Wymmys. She feels that curious force within her, as if her body is glowing. The noise in her ears is swelling too, and she feels if she does not act she will be crushed, or she will extrude heart's blood from every pore. She reaches across John and pulls out the sword at his hip. She turns on Wymmys.

'Go!' she shouts, waving the short blade at him. 'Get away! Take your horse and your men and get off this land. Go back to your snivelling Mostyn and tell him – tell him—'

'Tell him to fuck off,' Foulmouth John jeers.

Wymmys keeps his gaze on her as he backtracks to find his horse. His two men watch on, placid as cows, careless of their master's trouble, and Katherine recognises them as the sort who are hired for the day on the understanding they'll need do nothing. Wymmys turns and scrambles up into his saddle, even his slight weight nearly pulling the poor horse over, but even up there he cannot intimidate her.

'We have a case!' he bleats. 'We have a case! We will see you at the assize!'

She raises the sword. The two men with Wymmys now start to

look anxious. That Bald John and Robert and John Who-Was-Stabbed each have a bow has not escaped their attention.

'Come, sir,' one mutters.

'Please, mistress,' the other says. 'We are away.'

And the first of them takes Wymmys's dusty horse by the reins and tugs it around and they set off, the second man giving an ironic bow, half-turned on the back of his horse. She watches them until they are lost in the line of trees on the road, and no one says anything, but when she turns back to the others, they are all watching her, waiting.

She shakes her head, returns the blade to John's scabbard and walks past them, back, alone, to the hall.

Dear God, she misses Thomas, but she dare not go out on to the road to ask for news of the world for fear any one of her potential aggressors will take advantage of her absence, or perhaps even simply take her.

And by the Blood of Christ she feels so damned weary. She sits on the bed and her shoulders and arms weigh her down.

She lets her eye fall on the ledger, still atop the coffer at the foot of her bed, yet to be hidden away within, and she thinks about how a single detail in a ledger can damn a man as a bastard, or mark him as being unable to own property. She imagines how this ledger and the one in the archive in Canterbury might be similar: dry lists of names, dates, places, each entry in a different hand in fading inks, on assorted, rough-bound papers, though she supposes a ledger of the Gilbertine must necessarily have fewer movements, and fewer arrows, and be written in a finer hand.

She laughs when she sees the irony. Here they have been with a ledger that damned one man, while somewhere else someone has a ledger damning them. It is perfect justice.

But . . . if she altered the one to render it powerless, then why not the other?

The thought makes her stiffen and sit up.

Why not? Why not?

A moment later, her shoulders are slumped again, for she knows this sort of solution is beyond her compass. It is one that requires different skills, different connections, and besides, it is probably too late for that.

But still, she imagines Thomas's name written twice in this far-off ledger, and she tries to imagine how she'd alter it. It hardly matters, though, does it? It just needs to be destroyed, for then what proof is there?

What other information about him is written there? she wonders. The name of his village? The name of his family? She supposes it must be.

And then she realises with a start that, of course, if his name is down there, and the name of his village and his family, then so too must be her own name, and the name of her village, and the name of her family.

Dear God.

She stands upright. The thought – and the strength of feeling that follows – catches her by surprise, and all the other thoughts, theories, fears and frights that have been churning in her mind – about Thomas, about Rufus, about the childbed that awaits, about the death of Nettie, and about this Mostyn and this Wymmys – they are gone, like spiders' webs in the wind, and the fatigue drops from her shoulders and she feels feverish heat radiate within her.

Somewhere in Canterbury there is information relating to her. To her parents. It was not all burned up with the priory. It was not only reposited in the black heart of the Prioress.

She forces herself to try to collect up the yarns of those earliest memories that have only ever come to her in dreams, or unexpect-edly, set off by a sight or a sound or a smell: a glazed window with coloured glass, and a stone hearth wherein a fire burns. Then a horseman in a cloak, lined with marten fur, she thinks, and a letter, a heavy purse. A transaction with an old lady in black. Then there is a gate in a stone wall. Closing. And that is it. She knows now she was the object of that bargain, and she feels nothing when she thinks about that. No rancour. No rage. It is just as it was.

She stands to look out over the gap in the shuttered window into the night, and she continues to think of the priory, forcing herself to remember the deprivation and cruelty that were so much a part of daily life it once seemed the way things ought to be. She thinks of the matt of fine scars on her back and the dull aches that grip her knees in winter, and she wonders, for the first time ever perhaps: Why? Why her? What did she do to earn such wrath, such malevolence? Was the Prioress somehow out of her wits? Or was all that malice levelled at her for some other reason, some external reason not connected with her, so much as who her parents are or were? Could that be it?

And as the night wears on Katherine becomes gripped with an odd sense of purpose that has nothing to do with Marton Hall, but elsewhere, and even if she wanted to, if she'd been permitted to, she'd never be able to sleep for the excitement that heats her body like an imbalance of the humours. She wants to go to Canterbury, to find this Prior of All and his archive, and discover who she was and why she was treated so cruelly.

The next morning, bone-tired, she sleeps unknowingly past dawn and wakes to find the light streaming through the gaps around the shutter and Rufus calling out for her in a piteous wail from the hall below.

She is off the bed and down the steps before she stops to think.

Rufus is alone down there, on the floor behind the board where he's been making more ink and he's bleating like a lamb, and she rushes over and sees he's with the baby Kate, and he is struggling with her, just as if he is fighting her.

'Rufus!'

He looks up. Tears and snot smudge his face.

'She was – she was—' he manages. 'She was coughing. Coughing.'

She's making a high-pitched crowing sound as she struggles for air, and it is the oddest and most alarming thing Katherine has ever heard. It is as if the baby is not human.

'Let me see,' she says. Kate is in the grip of spasms just as her mother was before she died, but her lips are turning a shade of blue and her eyes are about to burst from their sockets.

'She's choking,' Katherine says.

She comes around and picks up the baby. Her limbs are rigid, but she's scalding hot, and juddering. It reminds Katherine too much of her mother. She tries not to panic. This time things will be different. She lays the girl on her back. There's drool over her chin, and her lips are drawn back. The tiny little seeds of her teeth in her gums scrape Katherine's fingers as she tries to find if there's anything stuck in her mouth. She can't imagine what it might be. The cave of the baby's mouth is a hot socket around her finger but she cannot feel anything that should not be there. Everything within is stiff, though – the cheeks, the lips, the tongue – as if they all are made of something else.

The wheezing croak is setting Katherine's hair on end.

What else? She must bang her on her shoulders. She gathers the girl up and carries her to a chair where she sits and puts her on her knees, sitting up. She bangs her back. Once, twice, three times.

Between the shoulder blades. Each blow becomes successively harder. The girl bounces and flinches. Bang. Bang.

Nothing.

The lips are getting bluer. The crowing continues, but it is so weak now, barely a croak.

Christ.

She now lies the girl across her knees, face down, and she thumps her back. She prays she'll hear a clunk as whatever it is in there drops to the rushes and the girl can get some air into her.

'Please – Mother!'

She bangs again. A proper thump with the flat of her hand. Nothing. She does it with the base of her fist this time. Nothing. Again. Still nothing. She can feel the sweat in her own eyes. Oh Jesus. One more time.

Nothing. But the crowing has stopped, and with the next thump, the baby reacts not as a live thing, but as a lump of flesh. She could be hitting a slaughtered piglet! Jesus.

The girl's not breathing. She turns her over.

'Kate!' she shouts at the girl an inch from her face, as if this will help. She starts to shake her.

'Kate!'

Her face is almost all blue now, spreading from those taut lips. It is terrifying.

She turns her over on her chest again, her arms now flopping down and she thumps her back.

'It's no good, Rufus! It's no good!'

She is crying. Rufus is crying.

John Stumps comes in.

'What? What's wrong?'

'She's not breathing!'

'Bang her back!'

'What do you bloody think I'm doing?'

She bangs again. And again. It is still like hitting meat. More so.

'Oh Jesus! Something must be caught. She must have swallowed something!'

'What?'

'It doesn't matter!' She's thinking hard, fast. Air goes down a pipe. Block that and a man will suffocate. That is how men die on the gallows with the rope against their windpipe. If Kate has swallowed something that is blocking her windpipe then – what about – trying to get her to breathe below the blockage?

'We have to get her breathing again. We have to – we have to bypass it.'

'By – what?'

She does not know, but she will find out, she thinks, and now she feels she's into her stride again. Suddenly the panic is gone. She knows what to do. On the table are Rufus's drawing things, including his penknife and some reeds.

'Rufus! Get the honey from the buttery! Rose oil!'

It all comes to her. She remembers those books the physician Payne showed her while they were in Bamburgh Castle. An operation on a man's throat. That is what must be done, but by God, it must be done fast! Fast!

'John! Get some piss!'

'I have just pissed outside.'

'Oh Christ! Hold her.'

She passes her over. He gathers her in his flippers.

She lifts her skirts and holds the jug under her. It is a good thing about being with child, this constant need to piss. She fills the jug halfway and puts it on the table. She moves faster than she ever has before. She takes Rufus's penknife – a small, dark little thing with a point, a present from Thomas – and she swirls it in the urine, warms up her fingers.

'Come on, Rufus!'

He trots in with the honey. She snatches the jar from his hands. He steps back. She's no time to smile at him. She smears the knife in the honey. And drops it on the table. She takes the baby from John Stumps and lays her on her back.

She doesn't even have time to roll up her sleeves. Her hands have stopped fluttering. She is swift and purposeful and she knows what she's about to do. She takes a reed from Rufus's collection – the stiffest she can find – and swirls its thickest end in the honey, and then in the urine to remove any globs of it. She cuts it with Rufus's penknife, on the slant, making a thick nib such as no clerk would accept. Then she cuts it off further up, a short finger's length. She sets it to one side, and takes the penknife and bends with it over the baby.

'What are you doing?'

'Shhh.'

She tips the baby's chin back so that her throat is exposed and elongated. She thinks it is the most intensely vulnerable thing she has ever seen, a tiny throat. Oh God. She can't. She can't do it! She feels as Abraham must have felt. But the baby will die if she does not act, and act fast.

Bald John has come in to watch too. John Stumps tells him what's happened. He crosses himself.

'She'll be all right,' John Stumps says.

'Say a prayer,' she tells them and they start the paternoster.

'Bless me, Father, for what I am about to do,' Katherine whispers to herself and to God. 'Guide my hand and my heart. Watch over baby Kate as you would your own son, and deliver her unto us safe.'

She feels down below the chin, pinching the tiny windpipe. She feels the ripple of the baby's Adam's apple, and knows she must do it – there! She drops the blade of the knife into the infant's throat, right in the middle, just below her tiny Adam's apple, a finger's width below the soft curve of her chin. There is a slight bounce. She brings just the weight of her hand to bear and there is blood as the skin breaks, but that is fine. A little blood is fine. A little blood is fine. She presses the knife further, a whisker further, down through the tougher tube wall of the windpipe. Instantly she knows she's through. Her knife is in the empty tube of the airway. The baby coughs and splutters, and there is a bubble of air in the blood. Perfect. She has sweat in her eyes. She mops it with her sleeve. She looks at the cut. Another bubble. Right. Right. She removes the knife, and takes up the fibrous tube of the reed's end and she slides it down between the lips of the wound. The fit is tight. It is held firm.

Nothing happens. She had hoped . . . not for this.

'Guide me, God,' she mutters. 'Guide me. What now?'

She is lost. She had hoped the breathing would start but why would it?

'What's wrong?'

'She's still not breathing!'

She puts her hands on the girl's chest. It is a gesture of despair. But there is a thin whistle from the reed. She is startled. She presses down again. Another whistle.

'Sometimes, with a lamb,' Bald John says, 'you need to blow into it. Give it life.'

Katherine waits not a moment.

She purses her lips over the reed and tastes the blood. She would have thought infants' blood would taste sweet, but it is hard and coppery. She blows. Baby Kate's chest rises. Katherine takes her lips away. The chest slowly falls.

'Do it again!' Bald John encourages.

She does.

The chest rises. Falls. She is about to blow again when there is a clogged little whistle in the reed and the chest creeps up of its own choice.

Katherine's hair riffles across her scalp.

The baby is breathing through the tube. She's done it. Christ.

'Thanks be to God!' John Stumps whispers.

The baby lies there, unconscious still, but breathing. In. Out. In. Out. The little heart is going fast as a drummer boy's sticks.

She stands up.

They all look at her.

'What's she going to do with a tube in her neck all her life?' John Stumps asks.

Katherine had not thought of that. All she'd thought of was the breathing.

'I suppose – I suppose I could . . .'

She thinks: I can push whatever it is that is choking her up from below, into her mouth. She could do that. Yes. She has an idea. It is a leftover from when she cut Sir John Fakenham's fistula. She'd best do that while the baby is asleep like this.

'Rufus! Fetch a skewer.'

He hurries back with one, and after she has checked to see it is not too sharp, she swirls that through the urine. Then, after a long moment, when she's certain the baby's breathing is an established, regular suck and drawl, she grips the reed in her forefingers and tilts it down, so that it points up towards the baby's head. Instantly the child's breathing becomes strained. She twitches and heaves.

Katherine presses her down with an elbow and then slides the skewer into the reed and then through its length. She's as quick as she can be, but she does not want to cause damage, or force anything, so she slides the skewer slowly up the baby's windpipe. Sweat stings her eyes and drips from the tip of her nose. It is hard to know if she is pushing flesh out of the way or puncturing it. She moves minutely, applying gentle pressure, but with every hair's breadth she moves forward, she fears she is stabbing the baby through the roof of her mouth.

And then she feels it. A tap. Against something hard and foreign, transmitted down the length of the skewer. It is the blockage. She nudges it. It is gripped and doesn't want to yield. Christ. Could it be a tooth? Something like that? She thinks not. She turns the baby's head so that whatever the blockage is, or was, Kate does not swallow it again, and she gives it a slow pressing shunt. The blockage resists, but then yields. She feels a great rush of relief. She withdraws the skewer. She makes sure to keep the baby's head on its side, and she opens the mouth and slides her finger in, and she cannot miss it now. A hard, dark thing. She hooks it out and it spills into her palm with a lot of bloody spit. She looks at it for a long moment, and then closes her hand around it.

'Well?'

'She's alive,' Katherine tells them.

They all breathe out their own pent breath.

'What is it?' John Stumps asks, nodding at her closed hand. She tries to shake her head, to warn them off asking, but they are all peering, waiting, eyes bright. She should throw it on the fire, she knows, but it has gone out. She cannot do anything else but hold out her hand. When Rufus sees what's in it, he simply turns and runs from the house.

'Rufus!' she calls. 'Come back!'

But he's gone.

'What's got into him?' John Stumps asks.

She holds out her hand and shows him what is in the palm.

It is one of the oak galls that Rufus uses for ink.

8

Sir Robert Welles is caught the day after the battle, riding westwards along the old road towards Leicester. He has two men with him, one of the brothers from the camp and another man, and, outnumbered, they surrender without fighting. Sir Robert is brought before King Edward at Stamford Castle, to whom he admits on his knees that the Earl of Warwick and the Duke of Clarence were behind the rebellion. He tells the court that they had caused it with the specific intent of removing King Edward from the throne, and replacing him with the Duke of Clarence.

'King George?' King Edward says, trying it for sound. Men shake their heads to display their disgust at words only he is permitted even to think, let alone speak, without being hanged, drawn and quartered for the pleasure. After a moment, King Edward closes his eyes and rests his head against the back of the chair. He sighs deeply and pinches the bridge of his nose. Hastings, who knows him so well, reads the signs, steps forward and tells everyone, including Thomas and Flood, to leave the room, and they do so, in barely broken silence. A moment later Hastings has to call the guards back in to lift Welles from his knees and drag him out, too.

Thomas and Jack had returned to Stamford the night before, after the rout in the fields by Empringham, hoping to find King Edward or Hastings in the sort of mood to allow them freedom to return to Marton Hall. But by the time they had gained entrance to the solar, both King Edward and his lords had been in a different sort of mood, and those three rough girls were back, among many others, and the two were intent on celebrating their almost blood-less victory; it had been impossible to approach them, or even to hear oneself speak, for the music and the shouting and the drunken capering. Fairly soon Jack was in the same mood too, and so Thomas took a drink, even though it was Lent, and the opportunity to ask for leave to return to Katherine, for that night at least, slipped away.

The next morning they'd woken to a stream of King Edward's men coming into town from the field of battle carrying such things as they'd managed to take away with them, trying to sell them on. It was mostly livery coats, Thomas saw. Hundreds of them, and all in Clarence's colours, and for that day at least the price in Stamford for blue- or murrey-dyed sackcloth fell very low.

'They tore them off as they ran,' Flood had told Thomas as they watched on, 'so we are calling it Losecoat Field.'

As a herald, Flood had the right and duty to name the battle-field, and this joke pleased him a little, but he was disappointed, as were all those men who'd not fought on fields such as Towton, and who had hoped for some battle more worthy of the name. But the previous evening's engagement with Welles's Lincolnshire com-mons could hardly even be called a rout, since after that first salvo of gun ball and arrow shaft, the enemy had fought with their heels, and with such success that by the time King Edward's men had reached their lines, all that remained of them were the dead and wounded, piles of discarded hedging bills and, strewn in the wake of the fleeing commons, all these damning livery jackets.

'Will Lord Hastings see us now?' Thomas had asked.

Flood had been unsure.

'He is not in the best of tempers,' he'd advised them. 'And anyway King Edward will not let a single man go now.'

'Why not?'

'They've found that casket. D'you remember it? Welles was sitting on it when he would not make the proper obeisance to King Edward's herald—'

'He kept a pie in there, didn't he?' Jack had laughed.

'Some billmen found it in a bush, and Wilkes has been going through it,' Flood had gone on.

'What for? More pie?'

Flood had not smiled. He'd seemed much older that morning. He had lowered his voice.

'It was filled with letters from my lords of Warwick and Clarence, revealing the true extent of their plan to subvert the King and the country.'

Flood had held Thomas's gaze.

'But that is . . .' Then Thomas saw it. 'Wilkes's doing?'

'Yes.' Flood had nodded. 'A man of many parts. Anyway, because of it, King Edward needs men more than ever if he is to declaw either of those two. We may have scattered Welles and his rabble, but Warwick and Clarence are in Coventry, and just now making for Leicester, with more troops than we can think of raising in so short a time, and their men are not likely to run at the first sight of the black powder, are they?'

'So – so this is it? The Earl of Warwick is now out in total rebellion?'

Flood had nodded.

'This is not like last year, when no one knew what he was doing, least of all the Earl himself. This time he's really done it. And King Edward is determined that there will be no quarter. No fudge of circumstances, no slipping back to the way it was.'

Flood's fists had bunched and his jaw had hardened. He was picturing martial glory again, Thomas saw, and he resisted reminding him of the last time he'd experienced that, at the bottom of the hill at Edgecote, when he had needed to be dragged unconscious from the carnage, and Thomas had had to carry him insensible over his shoulder for a day. If Flood had been able to see what had happened to his servants – Brunt and Caldwell – who were cut down by horsemen while they tried to cross a field in the aftermath, he might not have had that faraway starlit cast in his eye.

At that moment Wilkes had appeared as if he had heard them talking about him. He had been dressed in a long brown coat, and he had nodded to them, but hardly broken stride, and was just as quickly gone, ducking purposefully through the yard and on towards the stables. Thomas has never seen Flood look anything other than sunny – except when unconscious – but as he had watched Wilkes go a cloud had fixed itself over his face.

'I confess to the hope that he's back away to France again,' he'd muttered.

'France?'

Flood had mumbled something about that being where Wilkes has been for the past few months. 'On some errand of Lord Hastings's,' he'd said, and with that he'd wandered off after some business of his own.

But then something had occurred to Thomas and for a moment it seemed the ground was turning under his feet and he might fall.

Christ. Christ!

'Jack,' he'd said. 'We need to go. Home. Back to Katherine. Back to Nettie.'

'Now?' Jack had asked. 'What about Lord Hastings? What about what Flood just said?'

'We've – we've done enough for him,' Thomas had told him. 'We need to leave.'

'What's wrong with you?' Jack had asked. 'You look – out of your wits?'

'It is Wilkes,' he'd said.

'Wilkes?'

'Wilkes is – I think – I think Wilkes is Hastings's man. The bloodhound.'

Still Jack was blank.

'The one after the ledger.'

Then Jack had seen it.

'Oh Christ Jesus, Thomas,' he'd said. 'You're right. We need to go!'

They ride that day, north along the old road through the familiar fenland again. Everyone coming south stops them for news of the engagement by Empringham, and everyone is sensible enough to seem pleased to hear King Edward's men prevailed, but probably what cheers them most is the news that there were so few of their relatives and friends killed.

The great lump of Lincoln looms on the horizon from just after noon, and when they reach the city they dismount and walk up through its streets. In late afternoon it is much quieter than the last time they were there: all battened down and shut up, with just a few people on the streets moving quickly as if expecting rain. The pardoner's widow's house looks just as it ever did.

'Something wrong with that one,' Jack says.

Thomas tells him what he knows about it, but that is little enough.

'Ask Katherine,' he goes on. 'We went there once, before Towton, and saw his collection of books. She says he must have had a hundred.'

Jack whistles.

'But the widow – she was out of her wits even then and that was ten years ago.'

'She must be dead, surely?'

Thomas tells him that every time he's been past, there's been a face at the window. 'She steps back every time she sees me.'

They look up now, just as they are approaching the house, and there's the pale disc of a face in the green glass windowpanes. It looks like a drowned woman.

Jack gasps.

'Blood of Christ,' he whispers.

'You see?' Thomas says.

Jack is about to cross himself but he blends the move into a touch of his cap as, up there in the window, the face slowly sinks back into nothingness. Jack shivers as if he were wearing a damp shirt.

'Saints, Thomas!' he breathes.

'Come on,' Thomas says, and they carry on up the street and cross the precinct between castle and cathedral. The stationers are absent, though there is a man selling oysters and golden-skinned smoked eels. They buy a half dozen of the former, and one of the latter, which Jack takes bites from, just as if it were a carrot.

'Why did you go there?' Jack asks, spitting out a chunk of bone that might have been a tooth. 'To see the widow, I mean.'

'To give her back the ledger. We thought we should since it was hers, or maybe it was to find out if she knew why it was so valuable, I can't remember, but she didn't want it.'

'Wish to heaven she had,' Jack says. 'Would've saved us a lot of trouble.'

'But that's the problem with the bloody thing,' Thomas tells him. 'So far as William Hastings is concerned, it hardly matters whether we have it now or not: it is that we had it at all, and didn't tell him, and have kept it hidden from him when we know he is looking for it.'

Jack nods.

'But who knows that you had it at all? That you know its secret?'

Thomas exhales.

'Well, she does, for one.' He indicates the house they've passed.

'But she's the only one who'd be able to link you to the pardoner who you got it off?'

Thomas thinks for a bit.

'Yes,' he says. 'No one else who knew is alive.'

'So say Hastings's bloodhound – Wilkes, if it is Wilkes – has caught scent of the ledger in France or wherever, and followed it back to your pardoner here in Lincoln, then to her in the house back there, she is – what? The last link to you?'

Thomas nods. Jack is right. It is now only her. Such a weak link.

'So you're hoping she'll die before Wilkes finds her, so she'll not be able to tell him where she saw it last?'

Thomas says nothing. He supposes that is what he had been hoping. It certainly is now that Jack has put it into words. Jack finishes the eel and throws the head and spine to one side.

'Well,' he says, wiping his fingers on his jack. 'Why don't you just – kill her?' They both know these are just words. But then Thomas thinks of Giles Riven, and then of Edmund Riven, and he supposes that is what they would have done. That is what any normal man might do, in this day and age.

'I'm not a murderer, Jack,' he says.

'No. I suppose not,' Jack admits. 'And anyway, it is not as if it's she who threatens you.'

Thomas thinks: Who does threaten me?

Wilkes.

'You want me to kill Wilkes?'

'You could try.' Jack laughs. 'I remember you trying to kill Giles Riven. Took you a few goes, that, didn't it?'

They walk on a bit and then they mount up.

'You know,' Thomas says, 'I keep half expecting to see him around every corner now, don't you? Wilkes, I mean.'

Jack nods.

'He looked to be going south, I thought,' Jack says.

Why he thinks this, he can't say, and without discussing it much further, and with their minds occupied by thoughts of home, they pick up their pace, until, as they approach Marton, Jack starts laughing again.

'Bloody hell, Thomas,' he says. 'We only went out for the afternoon and we've been away a week, nearly been all the way to London, only just avoided getting ourselves hanged, been in a football game, and won a battle!'

'Yes,' Thomas says. 'It's been good.' He is only half joking.

'Still,' Jack muses, 'it'll be good to be back. See my Nettie. That bloody baby. I've been praying to Our Lady that her teeth have come through.'

'It hasn't been so bad,' Thomas lies, and they both smile and they ride on, expecting to be welcomed with a shout at any moment, but as they come through the village there is only one woman about, carrying a basket of linen, who ducks her head when she sees them, and slips away between the houses so as not to have to confront them.

'Thought we were a couple of villains,' Jack says. 'We do look pretty rough.'

He's right about that, Thomas thinks. Their clothes are filthy and his beard has become bushy.

There is something about the silence that reminds Thomas of another time he's done this: when he's ridden back to Marton to find corpses in the fields and the place ravaged. It sends a dank feeling up his back and through his chest. Wariness replaces excitement and a moment later, as they pass the churchyard, his eye is caught by a slim cross of whitened sticks, there in the shade of the yew tree, and his heart starts a nauseating slide. Jack does not notice anything, and Thomas says nothing, and they ride on, and ahead through the fresh-leafed trees he can see there's something odd about the hall. It looks different. Its weight has changed: it seems unbalanced; and it takes him a moment to realise that the roofline is changed, and that his old house, now Jack's, is gone.

'What the—?' Jack murmurs.

They ride up to the yard and dismount. Jack draws his short, battered little sword and Thomas's hands itch to hold his pollaxe again. When they see the burned house they stop and then they run forward together.

'Nettie!'

'Katherine!'

There is movement within the house and a shutter comes down.

'It's fucking well Thomas and Jack!'

The drawbar is lifted and the door flung open and Katherine comes out. She is so pale she is almost translucent. The weight has left her face, too, and she is drawn and pinched. He feels a weight of sorrow and shame press him down.

'Katherine,' he says, 'what has happened? By all the saints! I am so sorry! I should never have—'

But her gaze slips past him and fixes on Jack.

'I'm so sorry,' she says. 'I'm so sorry.' Her voice breaks.

'Nettie?' he asks. 'My Nettie?'

She nods, and Thomas turns to Jack as the others come filing out of the hall, one by one, and Katherine moves past Thomas to take him in her arms, but he is that much bigger than her, and it looks as if she is latching on to him, and anyway, it is too early for anything like an attempt at consolation. Jack steps back.

'What happened? Where is she?'

'We were attacked.'

'The baby?'

'Is well. Not even – look.'

Rufus emerges with the baby. She is sleeping, her face squashed against his narrow shoulder. Rufus looks at his mother, and Thomas sees her shake her head slightly, and he knows something else has happened but that it will wait.

Jack does not know where to begin, which questions to ask. He knocks his cap from his head and holds a clump of his greasy black hair.

'Oh good Christ,' he says. 'Oh good Christ.'

When they've told Jack everything, or almost everything, they have to stop him finding and killing the boy who'd been looking after the horses.

'What made them do it?' he keeps demanding. 'Who told them that? Why? Why?'

No one has any answers for him so they sit and watch him drink strong March ale until he can hardly stand to relieve himself. He eats nothing. He just drinks until there is no more of the ale, and Thomas sends Foulmouth John to fetch more from a woman in the village, and it is not until it has long been dark, and Jack is lying unconscious by the fireside, snoring like a tree saw, and all the others have gone to bed, that Thomas and Katherine can look one another in the eye.

'I am sorry,' Thomas begins.

She swats aside his apology.

'We missed you, is all,' she says.

'I know,' he says. 'I – We . . . well. We missed you.'

It is pathetic.

'Hmmm,' she says, nodding. 'We got your messages. About the King?'

Anything she hears now will only make things worse.

'I should never have left,' he says. 'And I'm sorry for it.'

'Well,' she says, 'it is not me you should say sorry to, is it?'

He opens his mouth and shuts it again. She's right, of course.

The fire is low. He should put the cover on it and they should go to bed, but he can smell the burning house in his nostrils, the bitter stench of failure, and however tired he is, he knows there will be no rest for either of them when they are like this.

'The Earl of Warwick is in open rebellion,' he tells her, imagining for a moment this will change the subject.

'Is he?' she asks, her voice flat.

'Yes,' Thomas goes on. 'King Edward is pursuing him and the Duke of Clarence back to Coventry.'

'I am surprised you are not with them? With King Edward, I mean, and William Hastings, no doubt.'

'I came back to be back with you.'

She murmurs something and looks away.

'Katherine,' he says. 'I am sorry. Sorry for leaving you, and for being so long.'

'As I say—'

'No. I am saying sorry to you. I will do what I can to expiate my guilt as to Jack, but that is between him and me. What I need to apologise for is for leaving you, and for Mostyn.'

Now he has said something she did not expect to hear. She rounds on him.

'Mostyn? Why do you need to apologise for him?'

'Because it was me. I told him. I told him I used to be an ecclesiastic.'

Katherine stares at him, her eyes lost in the shadows of her cheekbones. She is absolutely still for a moment.

'You did – that?' she asks.

He nods.

'Mostyn is – was? – Burgh's man of business,' he tells her. 'I dealt with him when I bought those acres in January. It was a stupid thing to do. I knew it as I said it. I told him I'd been in a priory, which was why my letters were finer than his when we were signing the contracts. It was all I said. I never expected him to – to follow it up. To find out who I was. But I should have known. I should have said something.'

Katherine closes her eyes and nods minutely, as if she'd always supposed something like this might happen. That knowledge of their past would leak out into the world. Perhaps she is right? Perhaps it was inevitable, and they had – he had – become distracted by the here and now, and they'd been looking one way when the real enemy lay in another?

'Well,' she says after a long moment. 'At least now we know who he is. This Mostyn. And where to find him. '

There is a long silence. Thomas knows she means more than she says, that she means for Thomas to kill Mostyn. But he thinks of his words with Jack, earlier that day. *I am no murderer*. She reads his mind perfectly.

'He killed Nettie,' she says. 'If he did not shoot the bolt that took her, he sent the men to do it.'

Thomas says nothing. He has conspired to kill a man – men – before, but he has never succeeded in doing so unless provoked beyond tolerance. Even in battle – at Edgecote when he had the chance to pick and choose his targets – he felt sick with the responsibility of killing this man, say, and not that man. That power – of life and death – made him bilious with guilty shame, but now he sees that too many men and women have suffered for his squeamishness. He looks at John Stumps. He would still have an arm if Thomas had been able to bring himself to kill Edmund Riven when he should have.

So now he knows what he must do.

'I will do it,' he says. 'I will go and find him. Tomorrow. At first light. He will still be at Burgh's house. Or someone there will know his whereabouts.'

She nods, sombre in the gloom.

'Don't take Jack,' she tells him.

'Why not?'

'Because he will kill Mostyn.'

Thomas opens his mouth to suggest that surely that might be a good thing, but then sees what she means: if Jack kills Mostyn, then he will be the murderer, and he will take the blame for – and pay the price for – something Thomas must do alone.

'The bailiff,' Katherine says. 'He told us Mostyn was able to count on the Earl of Warwick for his goodlordship?'

'Well,' Thomas says. 'The Earl of Warwick is in no position to help him this time.'

She nods again.

'Well, that is something,' she says. 'But what about you? What about us? If you have left William Hastings's service——?'

Thomas knows what she means. Now he has no lord. No one to protect him from the importunities of men such as Mostyn, who might come at them bearing writs and so on, or men such as Riven, who will come at them with pollaxes and flaming arrows. Anyone could now come and muscle them from Marton Hall and no man in the land would lift a finger to help. By leaving Hastings's side without his permission, and risking his goodlordship, Thomas has thrown the estate into jeopardy again.

'Hastings will understand,' he says.

'Will he? That you felt you needed to come home, just at the moment when he needed you most, perhaps, because you were worried his agent might be closing in on the one thing he seeks above all else, and which you have kept hidden from him for the last ten years?'

'But if you'd seen Wilkes at work, you would have done the same! He – he is terrifying. You should have seen how he made the boy – Robert Welles – he moved him just as if he were a child's puppet, from one moment taking his men to meet the Earl of War-wick at Leicester, to the next when they were taking the field against King Edward. He said that it would save lives that way, and I believe him, but then, afterwards, everyone was talking of a coffer found on the battlefield that was filled with many marvel-lous papers implicating the Earl of Warwick and the Duke of Clarence in the rising. The thing is, no one ever saw these papers, but I saw what had been in that coffer before the battle – at Robert Welles's camp. It was the usual stuff that such men take with them when they go to war: silver plate and a salt cellar, some linens and woollens, an apple his wife had given him.'

Katherine raises one eyebrow. 'You think neither Warwick nor Clarence had anything to do with it?'

'I don't know,' Thomas admits. 'Would they really have writ-ten letters to Welles, telling him they planned to remove King Edward? And you should have seen Welles! He was a boy. You'd hardly write to tell him a thing. Certainly not that you planned treason!'

'But what about the attack on Burgh's house? What was that?'

Thomas tries to think. There is something that sticks in his mind: some oddity.

'I don't know,' he admits again. 'But I am certain that it wasn't the Earl of Warwick's doing.'

'But Welles's father – the old man who lost his head – didn't he admit responsibility for the attack?'

Thomas tells her about the interview between King Edward and Welles, and how Welles had been confused, as if he genuinely could not remember why he'd attacked Burgh's house in the first place.

'And the attack – it was not very committed. The men – Welles's men – they just let Burgh's people go. Mostyn included, may God take him, and they ran off with their arms full of stuff and there was not one single arrow loosed.'

'So what are you saying?'

Thomas holds up his hands.

'Perhaps,' he begins, 'perhaps you are right in what you said about it not being a real attack? Perhaps it was a token, but instead of a lure, as you thought, it was intended as an excuse? To give King Edward a reason to come up here with his soldiers?'

As he speaks he knows he sounds out of his wits. Katherine nods slowly.

'Yes,' she says, 'and remember when we rode to Lincoln, the gate Watch were talking of a friar who had stirred them up? Told them that King Edward was coming with an army of men to hang every man who had risen in rebellion the year before?'

'You don't think that could have been Wilkes himself?'

Katherine shrugs. Now Thomas thinks on it, Wilkes made himself very absent while they were in Robert Welles's camp. He had stood back, hadn't he? In the shadows, as if he did not want to be recognised.

'By God, you may be right,' he says. 'I remember: his forehead and nose were wind-burned, but his jaw was pale, as if he had just been shaved after a long journey.'

He strokes his own beard, tugging into a near point on his chin. It seems fantastical that a man might do that.

'But why would he do all that?' Katherine asks.

'To lure the Earl of Warwick out into the open,' Thomas suggests. 'At a time of King Edward's choosing, rather than the Earl of Warwick's. So that he might get his revenge for the indignities of last year.'

There is a long silence while they think about this. Jack snores on. John Stumps is likewise asleep in his corner, as are Bald John and his son Foulmouth John; and the skinny new boy, whom Jack will kill if he gets the chance, has somehow crept back in, and is lying curled in a ball at the join between Foulmouth's and his father's mattress. He's like a houseleek, Thomas thinks, or a mushroom.

'I begin to see now why you came home,' Katherine says.

9

The weight of his promise to kill Mostyn lies heavily on Thomas that night, gnawing at him. He lies awake and thinks about the look on Mostyn's face as he showed Thomas out of the room. The man had been exultant. It must have been the same as Thomas's expression when he'd heard Katherine's story of the mule in the mine in the woods beyond Hexham, loaded with enough money to buy Marton in the first place. He thinks about Jack, lying down there by the fire's embers, gripped with hate for his loss, and he thinks about it being his fault that Nettie is dead, and he thinks about murdering Mostyn, and he cannot sleep.

What will it be like to kill him? he wonders. He knows that had he been there that night when those men attacked the hall, and had Mostyn been there, he would not have hesitated. He would have happily smashed his face with a hammer, stabbed him in the guts time and time again. But now? Even with the heat such thoughts brew up in him, he knows he will find it hard to stride into Mostyn's room and yank the man from behind his desk and plunge his sword into his chest. It is not merely the thought of the hot blood, and the noise of gasping and gagging, and the rolling eyes. Nor is it the stench of blood and shit. It is the unholy thickening of the air that happens when a soul passes in violent affray, when it clogs your mouth and fills up your nose, and to breathe it in is to drink in the sin of it, to take it into your body knowing it will stain your soul black until it is your time to go.

Katherine shoves him awake when the dawn is already a pink band above the still-closed shutter. He swings his feet from the bed and hurriedly dresses with his back to her. He does not want her to see him. His hands are shaking and though he is starving, he knows he will not be able to eat.

By the time he has said his prayers and is down the stairs, the light is grey and Jack is gone. John Stumps sits hunched at the board, scowling at the fire. He eats like a dog when he is alone, and there's a scrag of chewed bread on a plate and a bowl of watery ale left over from the night before him. He is morbidly ashamed of himself, eating thus, and he can hardly raise his eyes to meet Thomas's.

'He's gone,' he says, nodding to the space Jack has left empty. 'While it was still dark.'

Christ.

Thomas finds his horse brushed and well tended by Foulmouth John and the skinny boy, who Thomas is interested to see has two black eyes and a gash across the bridge of his broken nose; there's blood on his shirt, too.

'Jack done it,' Foulmouth John says.

The skinny boy says nothing, but keeps his head down and goes on brushing the flank of Thomas's horse. He seems almost sorrowful, Thomas thinks, and Foulmouth John is outraged on the boy's behalf. Thomas hefts his saddle over and eases it on to the horse and when they've fixed the strap and reins, he ties on his bow and then clambers up.

There are two routes worth taking to Gainsborough. Jack will have taken the most direct, but Thomas knows that will still be flooded, so he swings down through the village and on to the north road. He has been this way before, of course, many times, most recently with Jack himself, when they were riding that first time to see Mostyn. In spring it is easier going, soft and gritty under his horse's hooves, though he has no time to stop and appreciate the greening. He looks for tussocks and hoof prints in the damp sod. It is turned here and there, pocked by holes and small lifted curves of dark soil. Ahead on the track is a long scatter of horseshit. He stops above it and he can smell it, so it is fresh. He kicks on.

What will he say to Jack when he sees him? He doesn't know how he will persuade him to stand aside and let him kill Mostyn. Is there a way with a man like Jack? In the mood he will be in? Probably not. He thinks he will have to get past him. Overtake him. Get there first and kill Mostyn before Jack comes blundering in with no thought for the future.

He almost gags at the prospect. He wishes he had forced himself to have something to eat. When he cuts off the road and reaches the first trees in the orchard where they'd seen the grafter back in January, he is splattered with mud, and sweating heavily. His sword thumps against his heel, a constant reminder of what must be done, of what he must do.

With this in mind, he hardly gives a thought for the other thing Katherine told him the night before: the cache of documents in Canterbury. He accepts it exists, and can see it perfectly – a deep stone shelf like an alcove, piled high with rolls of paper and skin. He probably wrote a few of the letters there himself, he supposes, but the thought is distant, detached, or set aside at least, because he is riding to Gainsborough to kill a man, not to Canterbury to go through an archive looking for traces of Katherine's past. That will have to wait, he thinks, however Katherine feels about it.

He plods through the orchard, following the track, feeling some relief. He stops to look at the house from the brow of the slope. The scaffolding he'd seen pulled down is back up and there is a small camp of tents beyond, from which the smoke of more than one cooking fire rises. The Flemish bricklayers must be back, Thomas supposes. He sees the gates to the house are swung open and there is a small crowd of men milling in the yard. A couple of servants, a man in a long leather apron and a boy leading a horse. Two men come from the camp, oddly dressed. They must be Flems, back for the summer. One of them carries a bucket of something heavy. They are ignored as they walk past, and one after the other they swing up on to the ash-pole scaffolding and make their way along planks at well over head height towards a spot where the walls of the house are still half built, and where a pile of pink bricks awaits.

Thomas rides down the slope, dismounts and walks past the gate, the horse between him and the distracted watchman. He expects a shout at any moment, but nothing comes. The grass is sodden and there are the tracks of many men and horses, coming and going. He walks on towards the camp. He passes a broad woman in a blue woollen cloak, a bonnet of the same and some grey fur wrapped around her shoulders. He touches his cap to her, but does not break stride, and she more or less does the same. He stops in a spot between sightlines, and he fiddles with the saddle while he studies the back of the house, and in particular the window of the room wherein he met John Mostyn.

He is in luck.

There is scaffolding both above and below the window, but no one is on it. He walks his horse to the hedge at the back of the house and ties him to a post. Then he eases through the gap between the willowy shrubs and walks confidently towards the ladder that is propped against the lowest run of scaffold. He climbs it swiftly to the first level of planks, and then the second. He follows the planks along, ducking swiftly past two windows that are already glazed with new panes and then he is at Mostyn's window.

Odd. A pane is missing and the lead bent, as if it has perhaps been forced.

Christ.

Jack.

He peers through the aperture into the room.

There is nothing there.

No desk. No chairs. And certainly no Mostyn. Instead, against this near side, there is an oak coffer on which sits a jug and a dish and some fabric Thomas knows instantly must belong to a woman. He turns to the left. Perhaps Mostyn has gone to a different room? Then he hears the shout.

'Oi!'

Thomas straightens. It is the watchman. He's standing foursquare and pugnacious as a mastiff on the grass below, amid the makings of a herb garden. He has his glaive with him. Thomas gives him a wave. Thanks be to God he had not drawn his own sword.

'God give you good day, sir,' he calls down, his voice wavering but settling into a carefree tone by the last word.

'What in His Holy Name are you doing up there, sir?' the watchman barks.

'I was hoping – I was hoping to give my old friend' – he tries to think of the man's Christian name – 'John Mostyn a fright! Nothing more. Is he in?'

The watchman looks up him as if he is chewing a wasp.

'I remember you,' he says after a moment. 'You came here the day Welles and his men attacked.'

Thomas groans inwardly. A witness.

'No,' he says. 'Though I heard about it. A sorrowful business. I was glad to hear there was so little blood spilled.'

'Aye,' the watchman agrees, evidently still not sure about Thomas. 'They were merciful in the end, though they set the works back.'

There is a pause. Thomas shuffles back along the planks to the first of the ladders.

'Is he here?' he asks.

'Who?'

'Mostyn.'

'Mostyn? No. He has left the household.'

Thomas concentrates on coming down the ladder safely. When he is on the ground he approaches the watchman.

'Left? But where has he gone? Do you know?'

The watchman regards him suspiciously through small eyes.

'Do you know,' he says, 'you are the second fellow who's been around here asking for him today?'

Thomas hides his lack of surprise. Jack, he thinks.

'I see. Well. John Mostyn is a popular man. Where's he gone, can you tell me?'

'Aye. He has set himself up in town. Wonder why he did not tell you himself?'

'Busy, I expect,' Thomas says.

'Ha!' the watchman scoffs. 'He told us he no longer wished to advise Sir Thomas Burgh, and that he wished to make himself town recorder, but was there ever a lawyer happy to hold but one position when two were on offer?'

Thomas laughs obediently.

'Lawyers, eh?'

'Aye. I think he had taken frit after the attack. Even though no harm was done to him or his, he became chary thereafter, and was constantly worrying about being attacked again.'

Thomas frowns.

'And have you been attacked?'

'No.' The watchman smirks.

In the end it is easy enough to get directions and, according to the watchman, Mostyn's chambers are hardly any distance.

'Did you by any chance tell all this to the other man asking after him? The one from this morning?'

'I did and all,' the watchman confirms. 'He seemed a good Christian sort of fellow.'

'Oh?'

It is hard to think of Jack being in a 'good Christian' sort of mood. Thomas bids the watchman goodbye. He mounts up and rides on into town, following the man's instructions, and as he rides he prays to God he will not find Jack has beaten him to Mostyn, and already killed the man already killed Mostyn, for then not only will he have done so when Thomas should have done the deed, he will have left a trail of witnesses in his wake who will swear under oath that he was asking after the murdered man the very morning he was murdered. Not even the good offices of William Hastings – even supposing they were on offer – would be able to exonerate him of the crime then.

And then it occurs to him that he has done the same, only he has made the greater mistake of leaving a witness – the watchman – who knows exactly who he is, even if he cannot recall his name. And now as Thomas leads his horse below the church, he sees he is only making things worse for himself, because now the town is really coming awake, and people are getting about their business. Men and women are coming from the church, and everyone greets one another but they stare at him as he passes, for he is a stranger, unknown in his down-turned cap and spattered riding boots, and he supposes that his travelling cloak is not so long that it hides his sword well enough. Each man who sees him is a witness, likely to be summoned to any inquest, and they'll be able to condemn him with ease, and that means only the gallows.

He must stop Jack killing Mostyn. That is all he can do.

Mostyn's new chambers are on a road that leads northeastward from All Saints – a humble enough street for a man who wishes to set himself up as town recorder, Thomas thinks – but the watchman had no idea which of the houses is Mostyn's and Thomas dare not ask, for fear of leaving more witnesses, so he saunters as well as he is able, studying the façades for any clue. A stout woman in green is dusting the front of one of them with a goose's wing, and she stops to watch him walk past. He touches his cap in salute, but feels her see right through him. Christ, he thinks, now everyone has seen me coming and going.

He continues. The houses become steadily newer the further on he walks, and at the end, shored up above a stretch of land still given over to teasels, another one is being built, though the carpenters are yet to arrive. There's a boy, though, perhaps some sort of nightwatchman, keeping an eye on the piles of timber staves.

Thomas risks asking him.

'The lawyer's is the third house, down there.'

Thomas retraces his steps, keeping watch for Jack's horse, and when he can't see it, he becomes hopeful. Perhaps Jack too has hesitated? Perhaps fear or caution has got the better of him? Perhaps he is drunk in an inn?

Thomas nods again to the stout woman with the goose wing and, head lowered, walks very deliberately past the third house on the left, studying it over his horse's withers. Then he sees it.

Oh Christ.

The door. It's broken in. Was it like that when he passed first? He cannot say. He didn't notice it; that is certain. He looks around for Jack again. There's no sign of him.

Should he walk on? Or should he at least see what has happened inside? He walks to the next house, its beams red with flaking paint, and on to the next. Then he turns the corner and finds another house with a rough-hewed post jammed under the overhang, as if it might slump. He ties his horse and walks quietly back to Mostyn's road. He is thrumming with anxiety, and now it is as if he is granted some extra sense. He sees deep imprints in the grainy mud underfoot: hoof, wheel, heel and toe. To the side of the door's frame is a long gash of pale, fresh, splintered wood where the lock or bar has been broken away.

Thomas hesitates. He can see no one. He pushes the door open. He smells it straight away. The unmistakable grip in the back of his throat, as if his body knows he ought not to be breathing it in: blood. He stands still within the door frame for a long moment, listening. Nothing. In the gloom he sees only a few square feet of spread rushes, the sides of a much-abused coffer on which lies the flattened circle of a cap, and there's a bundle of feathers, bound, that will make good pens.

'Hello?' he calls.

There's a sudden movement. A soft scurry. A careful tap of something. Thomas's skin crawls and his heart jumps. He holds his breath and eases his sword from its scabbard. A blade such as this is a comfort in every situation.

'Jack?' he calls again.

Silence.

'For the love of Christ, Jack. It's me.'

There's a stealthy creak from the boards of one of the upstairs rooms. Thomas steps into the gloom and heels the door shut behind him. It is gloomy and close in the hall, which opens on one side into a buttery and on the other a solar with a fire. Thomas glances into the buttery. He steps back.

The body lies against the wall in a twist of rumpled skirts, like a big roll of canvas that armies use in the field, her ankles crossed, boot soles facing him. One arm is thrown out and there's a broken pot on the other side of the room with a few dried lentils scattered among the shards. She's dead, he knows, but can Jack have killed her? Thomas swallows and takes a long sideways step into the room. The woman's linen apron is pulled up over her face, by accident or design, and there is blood all over it, still wet. Thomas takes his sword and with its tip he tugs away the linen. He inhales quickly, swaps hands, and makes the sign of the cross. She's a solid woman, round-faced, with blood all over her breast and a small, glistening gash in the cloth over her heart. Thomas stares at her a moment. Who would have thought such a small cut could end a life, and leak so much blood? He bends. The gore is not only still wet. It is still warm.

He straightens again.

There's a noise above. A slow muffled slide, the grind of something hard against something else that's hard.

He steps back out of the room into the hall solar. A board, three stools, a blackened pot and a tripod, a few cooking implements and air that smells of onions. A tendril of smoke still rises from the mound of ashes in the centre of the room, but the sticks are burned through the core, and no one's touched it since first thing. There are steps up to the upper floor. At the top is a door, closed.

'Jack?'

His voice sounds small in the larger space. He puts a foot on the step. There is a sharp bang in the room upstairs, and a flurry of action that suddenly stops. He hears something else. A thud maybe. From elsewhere. He swallows. He takes the stairs steadily one by one, everything in him telling him to turn back. To run. His hair prickles.

'Mostyn?'

He reaches the second-to-top step and pushes the door open, again with the tip of the sword. He glimpses a window-lit interior before a draught closes the door. The wash of cooler air also smells of blood. Thomas pushes the door open again. The window shutter is dropped, the lifting rope bumping in the breeze that blows through. He steps up the last step and into the room.

It's empty. Or almost empty. Mostyn is spreadeagled on the bed, fully dressed save for his boots. He's in yellow felted hose, dark green pourpoint and there is a hole in his sock from which his big toe sticks. He's dead. There is a particularly shocking stillness about a corpse, even one so recently dead as Mostyn. His pourpoint is a sodden, glistening mess, but through it you can see the rippled lips of the cut in the cloth and the flesh opened in just the same way as the woman's down the steps. His eyes are clenched, and his mouth is folded in a tight flap, as if he has just tasted something sour. But apart from the fact that he is dead, and he lies on a stain of blood, he looks almost unmolested. His purse is not even opened, and on his belt his two knives stiffen their sheaths. The room is in more disarray, though: boxes of papers have been thrown about and the contents lie scattered like bones on every surface – the bed, the floor, in the thrown-back coffer lid, in the gulley under the writing board. There are drifts of them uncurled against the walls, as if they've been discarded.

Thomas takes a step forward to look more closely at Mostyn's body. The blood is still very fresh in the wound, winking as if it were still flowing, and Thomas would swear he can feel the heat of the body still, warm as a fire. He steps back. The board creaks under his foot. He turns and looks at the open window. It is small, of course, but too small? He sticks his head out. Below is a herb garden with fresh-dug beds and, under the window, twelve feet down, two deep indents of heels in the earth among a patch of flattened pea shoots.

Beyond a rough line of sedge at the end of the garden the land gives way to ploughed furlongs and then a fringe of alder trees. There're a couple of men ploughing with donkey and ox, but no sign of anyone running, or them behaving as if they've seen anyone running. Thomas cranes his neck. There. Just as he stretches furthest, he sees a man go dipping around a corner. Russet coat, black hat. Heavy set? Maybe. But – Jack? He is not sure. In truth, it did not look like Jack.

But then . . .

He turns back to Mostyn.

'Christ, Jack,' he says aloud. 'What have you done?'

Why? Would he run? Why would he do it like this? Why would he kill the servant or whoever she was down in the buttery?

He slides his sword into its scabbard with an oily click and picks up the nearest tube of paper. It is some deed or other with its chunky disc of wax. It is what they all are, mostly. Here is a letter from someone Thomas has never heard of, dabbed with a thumbprint of blood. And here is another, likewise smirched.

Jack must have started looking at the papers after he'd killed Mostyn, but why?

At that moment he hears a crash on the door from below. He jumps in the air and scrabbles for his sword handle again. The door to the road is hammered back against the wall.

'Mostyn!' a man shouts. 'Where are you, Mostyn?'

There is another crash. Pottery breaks. Something splinters.

'Where are you, Mostyn you bastard?'

Thomas recognises the voice. Jack. He opens the door and steps out. Jack is coming up the steps with his dagger drawn.

'Jack!' Thomas shouts.

Jack stops below, staring up. He is sodden through and covered with wet mud and weeds as if he has swum here. In the gloom his eyes seem to roll.

'Thomas,' he says. 'What? What?'

They stare at one another.

'What have you done, Jack?'

'Nothing. I've done nothing. I just – I've done nothing.'

'Then why've you come back?' Thomas demands.

'What d'you mean? I've not come back. I've come to kill Mostyn!'

'He's already dead,' Thomas tells him.

'What? You killed him?'

Thomas shakes his head.

'I came to stop you, Jack. I thought you were going to kill him.'

'I am. I bloody well am.'

Thomas steps back into the room. Jack follows him in and looks down at Mostyn for a long moment.

'No! No. No,' he murmurs.

Jack is no dissembler. This is as much a surprise to him as it was to Thomas. He looks at Thomas.

'Why? Why did you do it?'

'I found him like this. It was someone else. Look. They jumped out of the window when they heard me come in.'

He tries to show Jack the view through the window, so he can see the dents in the ground where someone has jumped, but Jack is not interested. He stands there, sodden and stinking of mud and water, with mill-weed specks all over his coat. His boots leak water. He is breathing heavily.

'Why are you so wet?' Thomas asks.

'Bloody road was flooded,' Jack answers without taking his eyes off the corpse.

So he came the wrong way to Gainsborough. That is why Thomas did not catch him.

'But if you didn't kill him, who did?' Jack asks.

'Someone was up here when I came in. Whoever killed him, and the woman downstairs. I thought it was you, so I called out. I thought you were up here. They must have heard me, and jumped from the window.'

'Did you see them?'

Thomas shakes his head.

'We'd best be gone, Jack,' Thomas tells him. 'We've let just about everyone know we're here, and we must be gone before they raise the hue and cry.'

'I don't care.'

'Come on, Jack. There's no point in this. He's dead.'

Jack nods but does not take his gaze off Mostyn. While they've been standing here, Mostyn's expression has softened; his mouth is slightly open to form a sort of beak. Jack walks around to look at him very closely.

'I hope you burn in hell, you black-souled bastard,' he says.

'Come on,' Thomas tells him. 'Where did you leave your horse?'

'By the church,' Jack tells him. 'Didn't want everyone seeing me.'

'No. Well. Let's be gone then, shall we?'

They leave dead Mostyn without another glance and clatter back down the steps. The door to the road is still open, throwing a rectangle of grey light into the hall. Beyond is the road. Thomas looks out. There's no one out there the way they want to go, south back into town, but the woman with the goose's wing is standing further up the road, talking to a man with a mule. She has her back to them. There's nothing for it. Thomas leads the way, pulling the door to behind them, and they walk back towards the church, their shoulders hunched, heads bent.

'So if it wasn't you, then who?' Jack asks.

'Bloody hell, Jack, I don't know. I was so sure it was you. I rode here to try to stop you.'

'So you were one of them who'd been to Burgh's house to find him?'

'You did that too?'

Jack nods.

'I asked the watchman,' he says. 'He said two men had been asking after him already that day and that he should charge a fee.'

'I was the second,' Thomas says. 'I thought you'd been the first.'

'But who was the first? We should ask the watchman, shouldn't we? Tell him what we've found?'

'We could do. But then – Christ. Remember what Katherine says about inquests?'

Jack nods. They know the story about the inquest into the death of Welby's wife and how the jury was packed, so Katherine had been accused of murder when all she'd done was save a child's life. Whenever anyone mentions the word bailiff, or inquest, or coroner, they must spit. And any dealings with the law will be especially dangerous since Thomas and Jack know so few people in Gainsborough – indeed, no one other than the watchman – who might vouch for them in any inquest. If they were to be accused, Thomas thinks, then the only thing that would save them from being hanged for Mostyn's murder would be the goodlordship of someone with powerful levers, someone such as Lord Hastings.

When he thinks what he's given up, Thomas suppresses a shiver.

'Let's just get out of here,' he says.

PART TWO

Marton Hall, Marton, County of Lincoln, Before Lady Day, 1470

10

It is mid March. The elder trees are in full leaf now, and the ground is beginning to dry. Katherine spends the hours with Thomas, up in the top pasture, where they keep the ewes that have still not lambed. She's no match in strength for the sheep, especially in her condition, but she's able to calm them, and she wonders if they can tell that she too is approaching her time? Probably not. But lambing is more or less the only thing she takes any pleasure in at the moment, because doing any work on the estate now seems only for the benefit of those who would seek to take it from her, one way or another.

'What will you do when he comes?' she asks Thomas. She means the bailiff, that serpent with the waxen nose.

Thomas stops what he's doing and looks up. A thin wind is blowing.

'I could always try to kill him too?'

He is only half joking. She does not suppose it would be wise to kill the bailiff, though God knows she would if she could.

'He'll come with twenty men this time,' she says.

'We don't even know if the bodies have been found yet,' Thomas tells her.

'I could ride into Gainsborough to hear word?' she asks, forcing the question.

He shakes his head. 'Not like that,' he says, indicating her belly.

'I am not so far gone,' she tells him. She thinks she might be five months pregnant.

'I was waiting for that carrier to come by,' Thomas tells her. 'He'll know, for the price of some ale, and there will be no need to risk it.'

She nods and he returns to the sheep, checking their feet. He has barely slept since he came back from Gainsborough. He's been lying awake, trying to work out who murdered Mostyn and his servant. He had even asked her in the night if she thought Jack might have done it, and be playing a strange game on him.

'You should have seen how wet he was,' he'd told her. 'As if he'd been washing the mud of the garden from his clothes. And he came in just a few moments after whoever murdered them jumped from the window.'

But Katherine knows Jack is not like that, and that his desire for revenge was as forceful and direct as a bull at a gate. Since he's been back he has carried the baby Kate around with him wherever he has been, only passing her over to relieve himself. He even eats with her on his lap. She sometimes catches him staring at the wound on the baby's throat, his rough fingers prising away her linens to look at it. She can't tell if he's happy or sad about what happened, but at least the girl is alive, and at least she has stopped crying all the time. It was as if she needed the cutting, Katherine thinks, although surely to God that cannot be true.

'But they must have found the bodies by now,' she tells Thomas. 'You said yourself his door was broken in, and he has neighbours who will wonder where he is. The woman – may God assoil her – she will be missed by her family, surely?'

Thomas nods.

'Then where is he? Why haven't they come for me? For Jack?'

'But you said the watchman was not sure he recognised you. And you had your beard?'

Thomas nods and stares at the road. He's shaved it off now, and cut his hair, and he is washed and dressed for the fields, not the road, in short boots, russet hose, a much-stained green jacket and a dark felted cap, brim turned up around his head. He looks every inch the farmer, not the soldier.

'And the town is always busy with the ferry,' she tells him. 'People coming and going, passing through, dressed for the road, dressed for God knows what. No one looks at anyone they don't know for fear of inviting trouble. And, Thomas, I do not like to say it, but you do not look the sort of man anyone in their wits would wish to cross.'

It is she who first sees the sly-eyed carrier, not Thomas. It is the following day, while she and one of the girls, Joana, are out on their own together, gathering ransoms on the track's verge. With this exact possibility in mind, Katherine has taken the precaution of bringing a large costrel of ale, and the carrier, this time accompanied by only one guard, since the temper of the county is calmer, pulls his mule up and greets her with a toe-to-top inspection, just as if she is there to entrap men such as him. When he recognises her, he focuses his leer on Joana at her side.

Katherine asks for news of Gainsborough and waits for him to ask for the ale. He does so, and she obliges. When he has drunk deep, he relishes telling her that there have been not one but three murders in the town, just in this last week, and each of them more gruesome than the last. Katherine imagines this news will terrify Joana, but it is the reverse: the girl demands to hear the details with an almost unchristian delight.

The first is a baby found drowned in the town ditch.

'A baby?'

'Though that is not so unusual.'

The second and third, though, are Mostyn and his servant, a woman with no children, who used to be a common strumpet, admittedly, which Mostyn did not know when he took her on.

'Do they know who did it?' Joana asks.

'It was Jews,' the carrier says, stretching the word into a whistling sigh.

'*Jews?*' Katherine says. 'There have been no Jews in England since . . .' She stops, uncertain.

The carrier touches his nose and winks at her as if they both know the truth, but must say this for form's sake.

'So you say,' he says. 'It's what they'd have you believe.'

Joana is round-eyed with delicious fear. Katherine opens her mouth to tell her not to listen to a word the carrier says, and that there are no Jews in England, so it cannot have been Jews, but then she hesitates. It suits her, of course, that the townspeople are blaming the Jews, and were the Jews not famous for using Christian blood in their rituals? She has visited the shrine of Little St Hugh in Lincoln, seen the crowds there on his day in July, and now, despite herself, she feels a damp shiver of unease at the thought there might be Jews in the county.

'How do they know it is – it is Jews?' she asks.

'A man was asking after the victim,' the carrier is saying, wiping his mouth. 'Before the murder. And he was ever so dark and saturnine.'

Saturnine is a word Katherine's never heard before, but its similarities to another word are impossible to ignore. Still, it is the other word that interests her most.

'Dark?'

'As the night. With a black hat and a hooked nose, like this.' He gestures.

'A foreigner?'

'I should say so, yes, wouldn't you?'

She can almost not stop herself smiling. That does not sound like Thomas at all, or Jack.

'Whatever did he do to them?' Joana asks.

'Divers things that would make your hair curl, missy,' the carrier tells her.

Joana shudders with pleasure. They are of a pair, these two.

'And what does the bailiff say?' Katherine asks.

The carrier shrugs.

'He has been busy elsewhere, and besides, he can do nothing. It is reckoned the Jew arrived by boat in the night, and left the very day he committed the deed, by means of the same. He will be back in his own godforsaken country by now.'

'So there is nothing? Nothing he can do?'

'Not at the moment, anyhow,' the carrier tells her more seriously. 'No one has time for chasing Jews when the Earl of Warwick is at bay.'

'At bay?'

Katherine presses him on this and after another long suck on the costrel he tells her the Earl of Warwick and the Duke of Clarence are refusing King Edward's summons, and that as a consequence King Edward is taking his army up north in pursuit of them.

'They will come to him though, one way or the other,' is his opinion, 'but in the meantime it is causing some consternation among the seamstresses of the county, I can tell you, for they are having to stitch and unpick and then stitch afresh many a livery coat as their lord's allegiance switches back and forth twice in as many weeks.'

The carrier laughs. His teeth are flared and brown, his tongue mossy, and he returns the empty costrel and leaves them with an unstifled burp.

They return to the ransoms.

'Jews!' Joana breathes.

Katherine starts laughing, and can't stop. Tears streak her cheeks.

'What's wrong, mistress?'

Katherine waves away her concerns.

'Jews!' she says, and then: 'Come. Let's get back and tell Thomas.'

'Whyever do you think the Jews chose to kill such a man as him?' Joana asks, and no one has a good answer.

'Handy, though, eh?' John Stumps mutters.

The skinny boy, who had seen Thomas and Jack ride out, and whose nose has healed without a kink and who is now permitted to sleep in the same bed as Foulmouth John, keeps silent, and, watching him at dinnertimes scooping soup into his already full mouth, Katherine has come to respect his knack for self-preservation.

On Sunday at Mass, the second in Lent, the priest confirms the murders in Gainsborough were the work of Jews, and he warns his congregation to be ever vigilant because the Godless stalk the land, and he reminds them who were responsible for Christ's killing, and the death of Little St Hugh, and Katherine can see from the expression on his face that Thomas feels he has much to be thankful for.

'Can the townsfolk really be right, though?' he asks. 'Can it really have been Jews?'

They are replacing the fences down by the sties, a job that must be done at this time of year, when the wood is still supple enough to weave. Jack is hammering in posts with a mallet while Thomas splits poles with a hatchet. The thinner poles she can weave through the posts, but the thicker ones she must leave to the men.

She does not care if it was the Jews who killed Mostyn or not, only that it's as if they'd been granted their prayers, without ever having had to pray in the first instance.

'But if you'd seen the dead bodies,' Thomas goes on. 'Each one of them, stabbed, just so, both in the same place: just here. It was nothing like you'd imagine Jews to do.'

She has no idea what kind of things he imagines Jews to do, but did they not torture Little St Hugh to death and then try to bury him?

'Perhaps your coming stopped them?'

'There was only one of them, I am certain, and if I did stop them, I didn't stop them from doing anything other than examining all his papers.'

'Whyever would Jews examine his papers?'

'Exactly. Why?' He lets out a long sigh. Jack reminds them that he is glad Mostyn is dead, but he wishes he had been the one to kill him.

Just then the skinny boy arrives from the coppice wood with more posts for the fence. Jack is holding the mallet, and he eyes the boy, wondering if killing him would make him feel better, but he satisfies himself with snatching a post from his arms and setting it in the hole he's dug, ready to drive it in.

'Hold it for me,' he tells the boy. The boy does so.

'But why?' Thomas asks again. 'Why would they do it?'

'Who knows?' Jack replies again, raising the mallet above his head. 'But I wish I'd done it myself.' He smacks it down on the post top. Smack. The skinny boy flinches. His hands will be broken if Jack misses. John Stumps, enjoying the thin sunshine on his face and watching from nearby, laughs.

'Well,' Thomas says, 'God or the devil, I don't know, but I give them my thanks anyway.'

It sounds as if he thinks everything will be all right.

Jack swings the mallet. Smack.

'But remember the bailiff?' Katherine cautions. 'Remember Wymmys? He still believes you are ecclesiastic. And you can't rely on the Jews to kill him.'

Smack.

'No, damn them.' Thomas sighs. 'But Wymmys looks to the Earl of Warwick for goodlordship, doesn't he? And while the Earl is estranged from King Edward, there's nothing he can do against me.'

That is true, Katherine supposes. She watches the skinny boy gripping the post with both his eyes shut. Jack brings the mallet down again. Smack.

'But only so long as the Earl is estranged from King Edward,' she says, 'and how long will that be? Even after last year, when King Edward was his prisoner, it was only a matter of weeks before all was back to normal. And even then, we are safe only so long as Wymmys thinks you have the goodlordship of William Hastings.'

Thomas nods and pulls a particular face, and splits a pole with a single cut.

'What is it?' she asks.

'I sent word to Lord Hastings,' he tells her after a while. 'I sent it with the carrier. He's always been reliable in the past, but . . .' He tails off.

'But you've heard no answer?'

He shakes his head. He selects a new pole to split and stands it on its end.

'It has only been a week,' he says. 'And who knows where he is?'

'What did you say?' she asks.

He chops another pole and starts the split.

'That I was sorry. That I had to see you, my wife. I thought he would understand. That he would sympathise. He was there when you nearly died with the last child.'

Katherine feels cold all the way down her spine. Jack looks up at Thomas as if he is mad. Even the skinny boy looks unsettled.

'You did not tell him that there was something wrong with me?' Katherine asks Thomas. 'You did not tell him there was some kind of a fright with the child?'

He looks up but cannot hold her eye. 'I told him the midwife had summoned me.'

'Oh, Thomas!' She feels breathless. Everyone knows if you ever use an illness as an excuse for something, as sure as night follows day you will be struck with that illness.

'It was all I could think of,' he says. 'All that I believed he'd understand. I could not tell him – I could not tell him the truth.'

'But what of this Wilkes?' John Stumps asks. 'You come tearing home in a hurry, casting aside Lord Hastings's goodlordship just when you need it most and then – nothing.'

What John Stumps says is true. It's been a week since Thomas has returned and they've heard nothing of Wilkes, only of Mostyn.

Thomas and Jack look at one another.

'Perhaps – perhaps he had other business to attend to?' Thomas admits.

Katherine can see he feels foolish.

'Did you really think he was coming here to find the ledger?' John Stumps goes on. 'But why would Lord Hastings be interested in the ledger when he has the Earl of Warwick on the run?'

'He'd know that the Earl would be after it now more than ever,' Thomas says, angry now.

'And why is that?' John Stumps presses, trying to make some point.

'Because,' Thomas enunciates very clearly, 'the ledger proves that King Edward is a bastard, and that the Duke of Clarence is the rightful king.'

'Shhhhh! For the love of God!' Jack hisses.

They all look around. The skinny boy stands holding a post, stone still.

'Go away,' Jack tells him. 'Go and help them.' He nods at the others who are weeding the pea crop, a hundred feet away.

The skinny boy slinks away.

'Christ,' Thomas says. 'I'm sorry.'

'Anyway,' John Stumps says, equally chastened. 'It doesn't now.'

Thomas stops.

'What do you mean?'

'Oh God!' Katherine blurts. She stiffens and claps her hands to her face. With everything that had happened since, she'd set the ledger to the back of her mind, and because she has acquired the habit of secrecy, of never mentioning the thing unless she has to, she has not even told Thomas what she has done.

'What is wrong?' Thomas demands.

'Thomas,' she begins, and the whole thing sounds so stupid she barely knows where to start, but she must. She owes an explanation to Jack, too, who's suffered for that book as much as any of them.

Both men stop working to listen to her, and she wishes she could just show them, so they'd understand, and she can hear her voice becoming higher-pitched as she tells them about Rufus's ink, about Pontoise and Pontours, and when she's done, no one says a word. Thomas gathers up the tools – the mallet and the hatchet – and starts back towards the hall. It is hard to read his expression.

When she catches him up, he has already brought the ledger down from the coffer in the bedchamber, and is at the table in the hall, sliding it out of its covering. His hands are still muddy, and for some reason she takes this as a good sign. It is her turn to be silent now, and she watches him bend his head over the alterations, studying them with his poor eyes, and she cannot help but wonder again if it was wise to alter the text. She is thinking of what to say, of ways to excuse herself, when Jack comes in, carrying the baby.

Thomas looks up at him and starts laughing. It is a slow sibilant chug to begin with, which grows until it becomes a cough, and he cannot stop himself. Tears pour from his eyes and he rocks back and forth. He slaps his chest with one hand and the ledger with the other.

'Oh Christ,' he breathes. 'Oh Christ. After all that. Oh Christ.'

Rufus comes in from the pea field and stares at him, huge black eyes blinking in the semi-dark.

'Sorry,' Thomas says, waving through his laughter. 'Sorry.'

He recovers and he sits there for a long while, drumming his nails on the book's covers.

'It was Rufus's ink that did it,' Katherine tells him.

The boy smiles his hesitant smile.

'If only you'd made ink years ago, eh, Rufus?' Thomas asks. 'We could've handed this over, and – and how different everything would be.'

It is an interesting point.

'You'd still have one arm, at least,' Jack tells John Stumps.

It is supposed to be a joke, and John Stumps opens his mouth, perhaps to make some remark about Nettie giving birth in chains, though he stops himself in time, but still the mood becomes sombre. Thomas stands and looks down at it lying on the table. It seems to have lost all its power.

'By Christ.'

Bitter-sweet. Rueful. Katherine wonders what he really thinks about what she's done. This book – this ledger – it has been with them for so long, influencing their course in so many of the things they've done and had done to them, and now, thanks to a quick alteration, it has reverted from having the same power as a saint's bone, say, to a simple, ugly lump of paper and leather.

The various marks it has acquired – the great divot is just the largest example – serve as a reminder of their progress through life since they were left it, in a manner of speaking, by the pardoner. She remembers their first fumbling attempts to understand its value, after they had snipped through its canvas covering on the walkways at the top of the castle outside Calais, when they were so young; and then how Thomas slept on it, and took it with him everywhere, even on to the field at Towton, and how the man who'd looted it brought it to her and tried to pay her with it to treat him, even though there was nothing she could do for him. She remembers the day the book's secret made itself apparent. She remembers Sir John's terror when he realised what that secret was, and how it might be used to their advantage, or disadvantage, right there in the yard. She remembers taking it up to Bamburgh to try to sell it to old King Henry and his allies, and then how it was stolen, only to turn up in the possession of Ralph Grey, who, despite being a sot, recognised it for what it was, only to be knocked senseless the moment he revealed himself. Then she remembers a darker time, when Edmund Riven sought it, and took Jack and Nettie and poor John Stumps in his efforts to find it.

And now here it is, sitting on the table in the hall, and it seems to have lost some of its weight and power.

'But you still have to show it to Warwick,' Jack says. 'We still have to let him know it's got no value, or he'll still send someone like Riven to burn the rest of the place down.'

That is a point. The ledger is only declawed when it is known to be declawed.

'But we cannot take it to him now, can we, surely?' Katherine asks. She feels panicked at the thought. 'We don't even know where he is.'

Thomas shakes his head. 'We can only wait,' he says. 'We can only wait for him to come.'

But in the next week, when they are collecting the quarterly rents after Lady Day, they hear from the miller that in the aftermath of the scattering of the Great Commons at Losecoat Field, instead of obeying King Edward's summons to his side, the Earl of Warwick and the Duke of Clarence have taken to their heels, and are running with their families and just a very few hundred men, first north, then west, then finally south, towards Bristol.

'All over the realm, and no one can say for why,' the miller tells them.

'But by Our Lady,' Jack laughs later when they are home, 'it is typical that just when we finally want Warwick to come for the ledger, he can't.'

Katherine sees the irony, but surely the Earl will yield to King Edward at some point, and once peace is achieved, he will resume his behindwards scheming, and come for it by and by.

In the meantime, though, the threat looms from elsewhere.

'So it is just Hastings's bloodhound we need fear for now, is it?' John Stumps barks. 'Him with the powers of the Holy Spirit, may God forgive me, able to move heaven and earth just as he pleases.'

Thomas looks uncertain, and that night, in her second sleep, Katherine is tormented by vivid dreams of this Wilkes, her mind's eye seeing him as a stocky man with powerful hunched shoulders, heavy black eyebrows and a nose like a goshawk. He sits on a perch and watches, and then bunches to strike, and she wakes with a yammering heart. In the morning she puts her dreams down to excessive heat from the child in her womb, and she forgets them.

11

Two weeks pass. Nothing happens. Mostyn's murder seems to have been forgotten, and there is no sighting of Wilkes. Katherine talks to Thomas of going to Canterbury, and of somehow gaining access to the archive of records. He agrees, but he is distracted, perhaps put off by the difficulty in doing so, perhaps by something else, and she finds it odd to think that it is now she who is pushing to find out who her family is, whereas once it was he, though he cannot remember doing so.

Then it is Palm Sunday and John Who-Was-Stabbed-by-His-Priest is chosen to dress as John the Baptist, with a flowing beard of sheep's wool and an eight-foot cross, and he leads them around the parish with the priest bearing the monstrance behind.

Afterwards, Katherine stands back and watches the others throw discs of unleavened bread at one another, and she thinks of Thomas's description of the football match, and especially so when Foulmouth John nearly breaks Robert's arm in retaliation for his hitting the skinny boy in the face with a piece of bread. Then, when they are eating a late dinner of smoked haddock and the saved and clean pieces of bread, the priest tells them he has further news of the Earl of Warwick and the Duke of Clarence: not only have they refused to bend their knee to King Edward, as everyone thought they must, they have evaded King Edward and made their way from Bristol southwards to seize some ships in the port of Plymouth in the west of the country, and they have taken to the seas just before they were caught, trusting more in God's mercy than King Edward's.

'And the Duke of Clarence's wife is expected to be in childbed right soon, too,' he tells them.

Katherine can hardly believe it. She has seen Warwick's power: his great castles – in Warwick itself, and in Middleham – and she knows there were others besides, all over the country. She's seen the Earl's men in their red coats, how they had seemed to course through the country's roads like its lifeblood. Sir John Fakenham had been fond of the idea of Fortune's Wheel, she remembers, but this was too quick a turn, surely? From exaltation to catastrophe in but a moment.

'Where do you suppose he will have gone?' Jack asks.

'Calais,' she tells them, suddenly certain it cannot be over for such a man as the Earl of Warwick. 'He has always been strong there.'

She is the only one among them who remembers being in Calais when the Earl and King Edward – then the Earl of March – were exiled there, nearly ten years ago now. She remembers how together the two men had gathered a small army of exiled York adherents and invaded England, claiming they were coming to rid old King Henry of his corrupt advisers, and how that was, to begin with, all they wanted to do. But after a while they had to change their tactics and, eventually, King Edward took the throne.

'If he tried it once, he will do so again,' she warns.

'But he did try, didn't he?' Jack supposes. 'With the Duke of Clarence and this latest rebellion?'

She thinks about Thomas's theory of how Wilkes tricked Welles and made him tip the Earl of Warwick into over-hasty action, so that he snatched at the opportunity and scotched it.

'But they always said he was fucking good with his men,' Foulmouth John is telling them all. 'Gave them stuff and that. Ale whenever they pleased. And he had a feast once where he roasted a thousand beeves and gave every man as much meat as he could carry on the point of his dagger. Imagine that! I'd've brought one of them two-handed swords. Put a whole ox on it and walked off and we'd've lived on beef and liver till the end of our days.'

He is smiling at the skinny boy. There is something sweet about it.

And so they enter the last week of Lent with the storeroom almost bare, and this is the time of year that everyone is usually shortest-tempered, but in the days that follow, the mood in Marton Hall is odd, unreal, shifting and impermanent.

'It is as if we have lived all our lives in the Earl of Warwick's shadow, isn't it?' Thomas says. 'He's been like an oak tree over a house, always providing shelter and wood and acorns for the pigs, but also always threatening to fall on it and destroy it, and kill everyone inside. And now he's gone and there's sunshine and air where there used to be shadow, and it catches you by surprise.'

'It'll take some getting used to,' Jack agrees.

Slowly, though, the realisation seeps into their bones that the Earl of Warwick is gone, and the weight of the uncertainty and fear that had been pressing down on them, like the heavy limbs of Thomas's louring oak tree, is replaced with an astonishing lightness of heart that Katherine can barely contain. It is as if they have been labouring up a hill for the last ten years, pushing a cart before them, and now they have reached the hill's crest, and the cart rolls under its own weight, and everything she does now is a pleasure, for she feels as if it is for their benefit, for their future, and for Rufus and this unborn child in her womb.

'But Warwick's not dead,' she has to keep telling herself. 'He's not gone completely.'

And she becomes feverish for news of him, though for a long while there is none. It is as if he has vanished off the face of the earth, which perhaps he has, though they all must know it is merely the fitful nature of tidings. Still, though, the longer the silence goes on, the more convinced they become that perhaps he is lost at sea, which is, God knows, hardly uncommon.

'Plenty of men get drowned,' Jack reminds them.

But it cannot last, and in the week that follows Eastertide, late this year, when cherry blossom has replaced hawthorn and the first swallows are seen overhead they learn from a man who heard it from a grey friar for whom he could vouch that the Earl of Warwick had sailed along the coast from Plymouth and attempted to seize some ships from a port in the south of the country. This time the sailors were ready for him, though, and they fought him off and even managed to capture some of his own sailors. Each man's eyes go round when they hear that the Earl of Worcester – at the mention of whom Thomas cannot suppress a groan – that the Earl of Worcester had these traitors hanged on the quayside and then impaled on stakes.

'Spikes up their backsides, so they are pinned there still in all probability.'

'Crucified Christ,' Jack mutters. 'What kind of Englishman does that?'

But that's not the point of the story, Katherine thinks. The point is that the Earl of Warwick is alive, and that he is still at liberty with a fleet of ships, and so she reminds them how popular he is among the men of Kent, who hold him dear for keeping the seas free of pirates, and who will help him if he needs put in. And of course there is still Calais.

Then there comes another period of time in which they hear nothing from the outside world, no news at all, and that is spent finishing the ploughing and harrowing the fields. It is back-breaking work, since the oxen are new this year, and not yet used to working in pairs or following the donkey, so they need much muscular attention. Katherine watches the men – particularly Thomas – throw themselves into the work with a strange zeal that at first she thinks is similar to the manner in which she takes joy in her work, making cheese and butter and combing through the garden to separate the useful from the useless. But after a while she sees he is not doing it out of pleasure but from a desire to exhaust himself, so that he does not have to think about Wymmys, whom she imagines working away in the dark, like some pale-fleshed maggot feeding on carrion; or about Wilkes, whom she imagines as the sort of man they employ to strangle women at crossroads; or about Lord Hastings, whom she knows to possess a ruthless streak wider than the River Trent.

She goes out to the field with the pretence of taking him one of the straw hats and she asks him if he has decided what to do about the three men. He scratches his bristling chin and looks wary. He is not such a fool as to think her question casual.

'What can I do?' he asks.

She thinks about this.

'Perhaps go and see Hastings?'

'And leave you here if Wymmys comes? Or, God forbid, Wilkes?'

He has a point.

'Besides,' he says, 'Hastings will have been busy chasing the Earl of Warwick all over the country. That is why he has not sent word.'

Thomas goes back to the oxen, but that evening he makes the

men finish their work early, and he takes them to the butts behind the church in the village, and when they come back two hours later they are red-faced, and stinking, and Thomas looks worried enough so that they are up and at it again the next morning, groaning about their stiff muscles. This goes on all week, and into the next, until finally Thomas seems happier and it is only then, of course, in the third week after Easter, that word comes from Lord Hastings.

A single messenger on a good horse arrives from his master, who is in York and the Northern Parts, where King Edward still has not been able to exert total authority, despite reinstating Percy as Earl of Northumberland.

'Whatever happened to the old one? To Lord Montagu?' Thomas asks.

The messenger shrugs. 'Given some lands in Devon, I believe.'

He takes another mug of ale and then splashes water over his sunburned face while the horse drinks from the trough. They all have cause to think of Lord Montagu in their different ways, because it was his men who shot the arrow through Jack's leg, and it was his men who chased them from the fields of Hedgeley and Hexham.

'Montagu is the Earl of Warwick's brother, of course,' the messenger goes on, 'and so not likely to be foremost in King Edward's mind when it comes to favours.'

He speaks absently as he rummages in his bag to find the square of paper for Thomas. Katherine watches while Thomas breaks it open and reads.

'But Montagu was always loyal to King Edward,' Katherine says, her eyes never leaving Thomas. 'Even last year he did not join the insurrection.'

'Well,' the messengers supposes, 'after what his brother is up to, Montagu is lucky to be given anything.'

Thomas finishes the message and looks solemn; she sees a

flicker in his eye. It's something bad. He shakes his head minutely. Whatever it is will have to wait until the messenger is gone.

'You have news of the Earl of Warwick?' she asks the messenger instead.

He looks slyly about him, as if about to impart an indiscretion that will be overheard; then he talks quietly and seriously, telling them what they want to know: that when Warwick and Clarence approached Calais in their little fleet, the guns and bombards in the fort that guards the harbour fired on them, and a great chain of iron links was raised up across the harbour mouth, so they could progress no further.

'But what of the Duchess?' Katherine asks. 'We heard she was with child.'

The messenger, seeing both Katherine's concern and swollen belly, is hesitant. 'It is feared that she lost the child, mistress,' he says, 'while her husband's ship was stood off at sea.'

Katherine feels the sun go behind a cloud. It is as if sorrow is a cold shroud placed over her shoulders. The poor woman, she thinks. Poor woman. Thomas places a hand on her arm.

'All will be well,' he soothes. 'We will make an offering to St Margaret, and you still have your girdle?'

She smiles as well as she's able, but says nothing of her supposition that the Duchess of Clarence may have had a girdle, too, and probably paid a hundred priests to pray to St Margaret. Thomas is doing his best, but when it comes to childing, it is a journey every woman must take alone, and it is dismaying to hear news that one of their number has not reached the far shore, and that a life has ended in a hasty baptism and a shroud-wrapped corpse dropped with a small splash into the sea.

'So where has he gone?' Katherine forces herself to ask the carrier, just as if that did not matter.

'Oh, it is thought he is sheltering with the King of France,' he says. 'Or maybe the Duke of Brittany, though I do not know for sure.'

'Lord Hastings always said Warwick was too close to the French King,' Thomas adds, pleased to be on firmer ground.

'Well, there you are then,' the messenger says, now anxious to be off. He asks if Thomas has an answer for Lord Hastings that he might give another messenger riding north should he meet one, or take himself when he returns there in a few days' time. Thomas has none for the moment, and the man swings back up into his saddle and leaves them to expectant silence.

'Well?' Katherine demands.

'Lord Hastings is coming himself,' Thomas says. 'To Lincoln on his way south.'

'To Lincoln? Why?' Jack asks. 'What's he want in Lincoln?'

'He doesn't say. But he comes with Master Wilkes.'

'Oh Christ.'

'When?'

'As soon as he is able.'

They slowly absorb what is threatened.

'How does he sound?' Katherine asks.

Thomas frowns.

'Do you know,' he says, 'I don't think he even knew I'd gone?'

'So you need not have made that excuse as to my health?'

He shakes his head.

'I'm sorry,' he says, and he is, she can tell. 'But at least we still have his goodlordship.'

'Yes,' she says. 'There is that.'

And it is true: they are, for now, tethered in the world's order, made safe from the buffeting winds of men such as Wymmys.

*

216

Which is as well, for Wymmys returns as promised, sometime in the middle of the following week, the second before Ascension, when the bees are swarming. He comes hobbling up the track on his halt mare in rusting breast- and back plates he has borrowed from someone and a sallet that sits on his head like a fire cover, but this time he has fifteen men to back him up. Most of them are, like him, poorly armed, though, with bills, and blades made by clumsy smiths. Only one has a longbow, and that unnocked. Some of them Thomas recognises from the Watch at Gainsborough, and when he sees them, his mouth goes dry. Have they come about Mostyn? Or this dispensation from the Pope?

'We should fucking kill him now,' is Foulmouth John's view, but Thomas gestures to restrain him.

'Let's just see what he has to say,' Thomas tells him. 'Besides, you can't just go killing bailiffs.'

'I'm not even sure he is a bailiff,' Foulmouth John says. 'Look at him. Mad, capering fucker.'

Thomas has summoned all the men, and the boys, too, though not the skinny boy, who seems to have gone missing, which is perhaps why Foulmouth John is so foul-tempered. One or two of Wymmys's men are alert to the fact that though they are not outnumbered, they are very exposed sitting up in the saddle. The sensible ones dismount, and stand very close to their horses.

Thomas finds Wymmys just as Katherine described: it seems as if he has taken everything he wears from a number of recently dead men and that waxen nose of his is beaded with sweat, like a cooking egg, as if he is very ill. Nevertheless, there is something almost impressive about him, Thomas thinks, because he is so obviously frightened and is overcoming his fear.

'Are you Thomas Everingham?' Wymmys asks, still from his saddle, his voice reedy with anxiety.

Thomas tells him he is and he wishes God give him a good day.

'Aha, I hope He shall. Yes. I hope He shall. But I am afraid He will not give you such a good day.'

'No? Even though He is all mighty?'

'Well, He moves in mysterious ways, as is well known, and sometimes it must suit Him not to give someone – any fellow, say – a day that is not so good as the day of another fellow.'

Thomas supposes this to be true.

Wymmys wants his horse to stand like some stallion, but it is not that sort of horse, and Wymmys's helmet keeps tipping forward over his eyes, so that he must hold it in place. Thomas, who like most men does not enjoy being spoken to by anyone on a horse, or down the length of their nose, wonders whether he might just pull him from his saddle and threaten him with a fist. Surely that would solve it?

He starts to talk about the dispensation Thomas must surely have, when Thomas interrupts him to ask how he thinks he knows all this.

'It is as I told your – wife,' Wymmys says, with just enough of a hesitation on the word wife to cast doubt on its truth. 'All the records of the Priory of St Mary at Haverhurst are gathered in Canterbury, and there is named within one Thomas Everingham, a canon of the Order of St Gilbert, of Derbyshire.'

'It is a common enough name.'

'But your accent,' Wymmys says. 'It is of the north?'

'Which is where most men called Thomas Everingham come from.'

Wymmys smiles.

'Well, that is for the courts to decide,' he says.

Thomas is puzzled. Has Wymmys found some new lord to lend weight to his case?

'Well,' he says, 'I wish you luck with that.'

Wymmys looks sly.

'I think that I shall not need mere luck. Not when I have the King's blessing.'

Thomas stops.

'The King's blessing?'

His thoughts churn and grind. Can Wymmys really have King Edward's blessing? If so then they may as well clear their possessions now.

'In his trust of me as his officer of the law.'

Relief sweeps through Thomas.

'Oh. The office of bailiff?'

Wymmys nods.

'It is all I shall need,' he says.

'But I can count on the goodlordship of Lord Hastings. He is Lord Chamberlain.'

'Ah! But do you? Do you have his goodlordship?'

Wymmys seems to know something Thomas doesn't.

'I do,' Thomas tells him.

Now Wymmys is puzzled.

'But—?' he says, and he starts looking around, at Jack and at Bald John, and at Robert and John Who-Was-Stabbed-by-His-Priest, but he is looking beyond them. Then he reverts to Thomas. 'But you have lost it. It is well known,' he blusters. 'You left his side before he permitted it, and – and – you told him she was sick.' He points to Katherine.

Thomas is alarmed again. How does Wymmys know such a thing?

'Where did you hear that rubbish?' Katherine calls over. She is laughing. Not wholly convincingly, but Wymmys appears fooled.

'I also have the backing of the Earl of Warwick,' he tells them.

219

Now Thomas laughs. He is on safer ground with this.

'A fat lot of good that will do you,' he says.

'He will soon mend fences with King Edward,' Wymmys tells him, 'and be back in his accustomed position by the King's right side, and from there—'

'He'll do all this from France?' Thomas asks.

'France?'

'You do not know, do you?'

Wymmys has no idea about Warwick's failed entry to Calais. He shifts in his saddle as Thomas tells him. His whole body turns as if it wants to be elsewhere.

'I don't believe it,' he forces himself to say. 'Everyone knows the Earl of Warwick is well loved in Calais.'

Thomas shrugs.

'Well,' he says, 'it seems King Edward is loved more.'

Wymmys bites his lip and gestures to his men.

'I have fifteen,' he says hopefully.

Thomas laughs. Even Wymmys can see his men are underpowered. They are mostly old men or young boys with bills and pikes and short swords that are of no use against arrows loosed from fifty paces. Those still in their saddles sit looking straight ahead, clinging to the shreds of their dignity, aware they are being studied and found wanting.

'No,' Thomas tells Wymmys. 'If you want to evict me from what is legally mine, then you will have to bring an awful lot more men than this.'

Wymmys cannot deny it.

'Very well,' he says. 'Very well.'

He gives one last long look about the place, as if for someone or something, and then pulls his weary horse around. His better men climb into their saddles.

'I shall do that, Brother Thomas,' he says. 'Yes. I shall do that, and when I do – it will be you slinking away like this.'

Later, when Wymmys has gone and they are alone, Katherine brings up Canterbury again.

'It is odd,' she begins, 'the power of words in a book. There in the coffer is the ledger with details of King Edward's father, damning the boy as a bastard, and down in Canterbury there is a record to show you were once a canon in the Order of St Gilbert.'

'Yes,' he says warily. 'And you of course. Your name.'

'Yes,' she says.

He feels resistant to her wish, but he does not know why. Perhaps it is because the last time he had any dealings with the Order of Gilbert he ended up locked in a stable.

'Perhaps that is something for the future?' he asks. 'When times are less scrambled?'

She supposes he is right, but then she reminds him that Mostyn is dead; Wymmys has been sent packing; the Earl of Warwick is in exile across the Narrow Sea; and they may rely now on Lord Hastings's goodlordship once again.

'So it is as quiet as it is ever likely to be,' she tells him.

'There is still Wilkes,' he says. 'He will be here soon.'

'But when?'

Thomas cannot say, of course. But for the moment she is silenced. He rolls over and tries to find sleep, but he can feel her still awake, taut and preoccupied by something that won't let her drop off.

'What if we make the journey after the baby is born? After you are churched? We might go then.'

He wonders how long that will be. A good while. Two months? Three? Anything might happen in the meantime.

She murmurs some agreement.

'Well,' she says, 'perhaps that is best.'

But she still will not sleep. He can feel her mind spinning.

'What is it?' he asks.

'Still Wilkes,' she says.

'There is nothing we can do about him now,' he says.

'No,' she agrees, 'but the thing is that we want him to find the ledger now, don't we? Now we want him to find it before he finds us.'

'We've been through all this before,' Thomas reminds her. 'We can't let Hastings get hold of it, because he'd destroy it without telling anyone about it, and so if Warwick sends someone for it, as one day he surely will, now that he has the Duke of Clarence on his side, we'll have nothing to give him, and he'll torture us all to death!'

'But . . .' Katherine starts, and he can almost feel her mind whirring, 'now that the ledger is harmless, now that it no longer proves King Edward is a bastard, then surely, if he had it, Hastings would let everyone know – I mean specifically the Earl of Warwick, of course, mostly – that it no longer proved what they once thought it did?'

There is silence while Thomas thinks about this. He turns to face her.

'I suppose he might,' he says. 'If he had it. But he doesn't.'

'But that's it!' she says. 'We have to get it to Hastings! We have to let your man Wilkes find it.'

'But – how?'

'Last year Hastings told us his man – Wilkes, if you are right – was working back along the list of people who had it, from whoever stole it from the garrison in Rouen to whoever sold it to the pardoner, yes?'

222

'Well, yes.'

'So we need to interrupt the chain. We need to break it somewhere, and place the amended ledger where Wilkes will find it. Once he's found it, he will look no further down the chain, will he? Because – because why would he? He has what he wants, and more besides, since it proves the rumours are without foundation.'

They can hear the barn owl calling outside. Some people think they are unlucky birds, owls, but Thomas finds the noise strangely comforting.

'But how will we do that?' he asks.

'We must give it back to the pardoner,' she tells him.

'But the pardoner is dead,' Thomas reminds her.

'Yes,' she says. 'But his widow is not.'

12

Jack will come with them, it is decided, and they are on the road early the next morning, while it is still cold, ready to intercept the sly-eyed carrier on his way to Lincoln, this time with a cargo of broadcloth, two falcons in a wicker cage and a leaking barrel of bad-smelling wetfish.

'Are you sure about this?' Thomas asks Katherine.

'The child is two months away,' she reminds him. 'I will be fine.'

She still moves comfortably and, hidden under her travelling cloak, it is not obvious she is so many months with child, but the sly-eyed carrier knows they'd not be stopping him and asking him for a ride unless they needed to, so the starting price is already pitched high. Then he tells them that since there is only so much room on his creaking cart, he must yield his place and walk, and so that will add a bit more, for his labour, and then he tells them that he is already fretful that he will miss the weekly market, and him walking – he is a slow walker, he reminds them – will mean he is now guaranteed to miss it . . .

Thomas counts out the coins without a quibble, watched by Katherine, and Jack, who shakes his head in wonder, and the carrier taps his mule with his switch and they set off, grinding slowly along the track south. The carrier sniffs constantly, despite the season, and sighs breathily with the effort of walking, and Thomas, already impatient enough, rides on ahead for a few moments, and then stops to let them catch him up.

Spring is giving away to summer now, in mid May, and shade is deep. Crowfoot fills the meres and there are turtle doves calling from among the flowering candles of a horse chestnut above.

'Got it, have you?' Jack checks.

Thomas pats the ledger, slung over his back just as it once always was. It is a comforting weight.

'Will you miss it?' he asks.

'Miss it?' Thomas wonders. 'No, not really. There was a time when it was . . . when it kept us going – the thought of its value anyway – but there have been times too when . . . well, I've wished I'd never set eyes on the bloody thing.'

Jack nods. Him too, of course.

'Jack—' Thomas begins, but Jack holds up a hand. He has heard it before, a hundred times already, and Thomas can apologise no longer.

'I'll just be glad when it's gone,' he says.

'Amen,' Thomas says. 'Amen to that.'

'Got any ale?' the carrier asks when he catches up. 'You usually have ale.'

His piggy little eyes search their saddle bags.

'Shame,' he says. 'For I've heard some interesting tidings of the Earl of Warwick? You usually like to hear about him, don't you, mistress?'

Thomas is tempted but Katherine remains steely.

'We'll soon be in Lincoln,' she says, 'and besides, we've already paid you more money than you'd earn in any normal week.'

The carrier tells them to suit themselves, which they do in pent-up silence while he continues his sweaty huffing and puffing. In the end he cracks, and tells them his news. It is exactly what

Hastings's messenger told them, with the added nugget that the Earl of Warwick's little fleet has attacked some Burgundian merchantmen before sheltering in a river mouth near the town of Honfleur. None of them have heard of Honfleur so they are glad they did not give up any ale to learn it.

They've made this journey countless times, in countless states varying from elation to trepidation, but this time it feels very different. This time it feels as significant in its way as any birth, or death, because it is perhaps a bit of both. It is the end of something, and the beginning of something else. Thomas knows that when he rides back this way again, this afternoon, he will be a different man, with different prospects and a different relationship to the world. He supposes he will ride lighter, easier, higher. Less encumbered, maybe, but also less accoutred, since he will no longer have the ledger, and the weight of responsibility that comes with it. When he thinks about it he feels joy, but it is not untainted by loss.

They soon see the spire of the cathedral – 'The tallest in Christendom, let me remind you, mistress' – and are at the gate just as the bell for sext sounds, and the usual cloud of pigeons is sent flying.

'You'd think they'd be used to it by now,' Jack says.

At the Newport Gate the Watch are back up to strength and refilled with their usual bullies' swagger. Thomas, Katherine and Jack leave the carrier to his business and they walk under the arch and along the road past the apothecary towards the cathedral precinct where the traders are busy selling things off cheap prior to packing up their stalls, and the gutters are filled with brown cabbage leaves and pearly pink offal, and the blue stones are stained with butchers' waste and God knows what else.

The news from across the Narrow Sea is on most minds, and the mood among the townspeople is uncertain. Some are pleased to have heard of the Earl of Warwick's difficulties, and are happy to say so, but other voices are raised in regret, and there is sorrow that the Duke's child – a boy, it turns out – died in such circumstances, and there is widespread sympathy for the Duchess.

They stop at the top of the hill and look down towards the pardoner's widow's house. Thomas feels a great pang of anxiety.

'Are you sure this will work?' he asks.

Katherine nods. She looks determined.

'If the widow is unchanged,' she says, 'and the books are still there as they were, then yes, I am certain of it.'

'What will you say?' Jack asks.

'Thomas is going to ask if he can buy one of her books,' she tells Jack. 'He found one he admired. A psalter from somewhere. Utrecht, I think.'

This is their plan.

'I – I have not enough money to buy such a thing,' he tells her.

'She need not know that,' Katherine says.

Jack stops at the top of the hill, before they come into view of that jettied storey, and he wishes them luck. Thomas feels they ought not to need it, since all they are doing is tricking an old widow, but he is unaccountably nervous about this now. Perhaps it is the thought of parting with the ledger? He has spent ten years guarding it, keeping it hidden, nurturing it almost, so that it has become something more valuable to him than any mere object. Perhaps it is also because he is relying on Katherine, and on her memory of the last time they came here together? She told him the women – both the servant, and the mistress – were astonishing and peculiar, and she is relying on nothing having changed since then.

He shakes Jack's hand for some reason, and then he and Katherine walk down the hill, angling towards the house. Time and neglect have softened its lines. Roof tiles have slipped and new weeds sprout from cracks in the green-tinged daub, but somehow you know it is still inhabited. Thomas's mouth is dry and his limbs are heavy, and he finds himself dawdling, pretending to be waiting to see if the widow appears at her window. My God, he thinks. Is this it? Is this the solution to the problem that has plagued them for ten years? It feels suspiciously easy, suspiciously obvious, even slightly cowardly. To foist the thing on an old woman. But what if she does not know that she has it? What then? No blame can attach to her, surely. If Wilkes finds — *when* Wilkes finds it, he can't blame her for possessing it.

'Come on,' he says, more to himself than to Katherine.

She nods, takes a deep breath and wraps the travelling cloak around her, and they cross the road with only a quick stolen glance up into the window where last he saw the widow, and walk up the steps to knock on the door.

A moment later the door is opened by a round-faced maid, broad-hipped and about thirty years of age, who steps back, and it is just as if they are expected.

'Is Mistress Daud within?' Thomas asks.

The girl says nothing; she only bends her knees slightly and then steps further back to admit them.

Thomas crosses the threshold. The house smells of autumn in the woods. Christ! He does remember being here! He remembers it. That smell! And the dust and the cobwebs festooning every-thing. And the books! Yes. At least a hundred of them. They are through there! A psalter from Utrecht! A Life of Julius Caesar! He remembers. He remembers.

He feels Katherine push him forward towards the room.

'Shall we wait in here for Mistress Daud?' Katherine asks, indi-cating the darkened room.

'Oh yes,' the woman says, her voice all breathy. 'I will let her know you have come again.'

She smiles at them knowingly, as if they are all three in on some curious scheme together, and she starts to climb the steps up to the solar, looking neither left nor right, but straight ahead, still with that faint smile on her face. Thomas crosses the rush-strewn hall to the other doorway through which is the room with the books, shrouded and gloomy.

'It is just the same as last time we were here,' Thomas tells Katherine. She looks at him, surprised.

'You remember it?'

'I do. Yes.'

She blows air out of her nose. There is no time to discuss this. But Thomas's mind reels and spins.

'Come on,' she says. 'Quickly.'

The smell in the room with the books is sharper still – of mice, and of paper and leather and wood turning to dust – but it is otherwise just as it was, and here are the books, piled up on trestles, of all shapes and sizes, laid out and piled up, and covering everything is a thick layer of grey fibrous dust, tracked over by a thousand paws and speckled with mouse shit.

'Should have brought a cat,' Thomas says.

He slides his bag around and digs out the ledger. With fumbling fingers he takes it from its cover. It is best it is done quickly. He approaches a pile of the books that is topped by a large, badly damaged psalter. Katherine comes to his side. She lifts two of them, holding them up from below, and Thomas places the ledger on the book below. She replaces the books so that they cover the ledger and hide it completely, and they step back into the middle of the room. Thomas lets out his breath. He is about to look again at the other books, and then back at the ledger to see that it looks undisturbed, or to see it for one last time, when he realises the light in the room has changed and there is a shape filling the doorway.

The widow.

Has she seen what they've done?

He is about to open his mouth to offer a conventional greeting when something makes him stop. The widow's eyes are round, and – expressionless. They do not register what she sees. For a moment he thinks she may be blind. But no. She is an idiot.

He breathes a plume of relief.

Widow Daud walks into the centre of the room. She smells strongly of urine, and they have to step aside to let her take the space and she stands there, breathing loudly through her mouth as if she cannot stand the smell of herself. She is in a dress the colour of sage leaves in winter, the hem of which is faded and fraying with age. No one says anything for a moment. Thomas slides the empty bag around so that it hangs across his back.

She looks at Katherine, and when she speaks, her voice is as whispery as two dry palms crossed.

'Have you come from him?'

'Him?' Katherine asks.

'I have been waiting. So long. He said he would send word for me.'

'Who said they would send word for you?' Katherine asks.

'He said he would come. He said he would send a litter covered in cloth of gold, carried by four fine palfreys, each whiter than the next, and a retinue of forty Knights of the Garter, and that there would be a wedding banquet that would last a twelvemonth or more.'

'Who? Who said this?'

But it is too late. When she sees they are not sent by the man for whom she waits, her face falls. Tears wink in her eyes and then ooze like oil to splash her dusty cheeks, and she clutches herself and starts keening a wavering, high-pitched note, a lament as tuneless as wind in a crook.

The maid appears in the doorway.

'You'd best go,' she says.

Thomas and Katherine nod and begin their retreat, circling around the widow who stands there still, ignoring them as they pass, and Thomas feels the beginnings of a smile lifting his lips, and he thinks they've done it, they've secreted the ledger where it will be found, and it will never come back to them, and he begins to think warm thoughts about the poor widow, when suddenly she stops her crying and turns on Katherine, now with one clear eye. She extends a finger, pointing at Katherine's face.

'You,' she says. 'You are hiding something.'

Katherine steps back. The widow steps after her.

'You are hiding something. But what? What are you hiding?'

Katherine cowers and turns her cheek. The widow extends both hands towards her face. Her papery hands are blotched and snaked with veins. Then she drops them and opens Katherine's cloak. Katherine tries to hide herself. But the widow gasps when she sees her belly, and then once more her face folds into an expression of terrible, distraught sorrow. She mews and sobs and tears come rolling down her cheeks again.

But then her expression changes suddenly, as if a cloth has passed over her face, and it hardens from sorrow to bitterest spite. Her fingers become like talons and she pulls them back, as though she might suddenly plunge them into Katherine and rip out the baby. Thomas steps between them and moves Katherine aside.

The widow takes a pace backwards.

'I curse you!' she hisses. 'I curse you!'

Katherine rears away as if bitten.

'What? Why?'

'I damn you! I damn your child! I pray you wither before you are brought to term. I pray your bones melt and the child becomes a stone in your womb! I pray he is born a beast, with horns and a tail!'

Katherine is aghast. She pulls herself further back, and grasps her cloak together at the throat, but she cannot seem to tear her gaze from the now drooling madwoman. It takes Thomas a moment to react, and he takes Katherine's shoulders and turns her away, into him.

'Come!' he snaps. 'She is out of her wits. She knows not what she says. Come. Come on! Don't listen.'

The maid returns, running.

'You'd best go,' she says again.

'Be gone!' the widow calls. 'Be gone, you whore, to whelp your monster in a ditch!'

The maid slaps her mistress. Thomas gathers Katherine up and guides her out into the fresh air and the sunshine.

'Oh Christ, Katherine,' he says. 'She means nothing. She is out of her wits. Come. All is well. All is well.'

He guides her quickly up the street, away from the house, and she trips and stumbles and he must support her, but she says nothing, and all the joy of accomplishment is turned to ash in his mouth.

By the time they reach the brow of the hill and are among the crowds in the cathedral precinct, Katherine has recovered herself.

'It is done,' she says. 'It is done, and that is all that matters.'

He hopes she feels that way, but she is shaking as if she has a

fever, and her whole body is stiff. It is done. It is done, yes. But —
at what cost?

They find Jack waiting anxiously with the horses.

'What happened?'

'A misunderstanding,' is all Thomas will say.

'But it worked?'

Thomas nods. He can't say any more.

They pay another carrier to take Katherine, and the trip back is
quicker, with Katherine able to sit atop a sarpler of finest wool
bound for Gainsborough and thence Hull, to be shipped to
Calais, the man tells them with a tap of his nose to indicate no such
thing. He says little and asks less and they are back at Marton
before the swifts have risen into the night. Katherine goes straight
to bed.

'I'd expected that to be more fun,' Jack admits when they are
currying the horses. Thomas grunts. He tells Jack what happened.
Jack crosses himself.

They both know how bad this is. A curse before childing. There
can be nothing worse, really.

'Damn her,' Thomas says. 'Damn her. I've a mind to ride
back — and — and kill her.'

Jack says nothing. He does not think that will help. Nor does
Thomas.

'Christ, Jack, what am I going to do?'

'Nettie always swore that jet was the answer.'

'Jet?'

'You wrap a pebble of it in a cloth that is blessed by a priest, or
a bishop is better, and you wear it around your belly when you are
in childbed.'

It will need more than that, Thomas thinks, and now he feels worse because Jack has not tried to encourage him by telling him that at least they've got rid of the ledger, and saved themselves a visit from Wilkes. It means Jack thinks it is bad, too.

It is the second week before the Ascension, in the middle of May, 1470.

13

In the next week, Katherine starts to double in size, and she is able to do less and less. She watches them all go off into the fields at the dawn of each day, and then she slowly moves through the garden, weeding in among the skirrets and the fat hens to remove the stray dead nettles and corn cockles. Or now that the lambing season has ended, she helps Anne and Joana milk the sheep for the cheese, and she spends long afternoons on her feet in the dairy with them, listening to their chatter, helping them churn the butter while the netted cheeses drip down on them from the rafters above. She helps Anne with the ale, too, and then she helps cook supper until the others come back again, sunburned and tired, for a dinner of eggs and herbs from the garden. John Stumps is always about, a dark frustrated little presence, and Thomas has given them a hunting horn that they can use to summon help if needed.

Haymaking begins. The weather stays fair, and it is a good crop this year, the best anyone in the village can recall. This bodes well for the coming winter, when they will be able to keep more of the pigs and sheep alive for longer, and so have fresh meat just when they need it most. Then the sheep shearing begins. The work is harder still than haymaking, and the men return exhausted and stinking at the end of long days, and they don't even have that many sheep to shear. It is good to get it over and done with early though, because the fleece are better at this time of year, and because the next month, July, will be the one without bread.

And still no one comes. They hear news of the Earl of War-wick: he is still at large, his fleet still sheltering in some estuary in France, as Hastings's messenger said.

'He must have some aim?' Thomas says.

'I expect he is aiming to mend fences with King Edward,' Jack says.

Jack has found a woman – Jane – from haymaking to come and look after the baby Kate, and neither Anne nor Joana bothers to resist speculating on the nature of their growing relationship.

And then, when it is done, at last, Lord Hastings comes. It is in the middle of July, just after the octave of the Visitation of Our Lady, when Katherine carries her belly so far before her she can hardly encompass it with her arms. First a troop of his outriders comes trotting up the track, perhaps twenty of them, riding ahead to forewarn them of his coming. Katherine sends Joana to blow on the horn, and she tries, but, red-faced and round-cheeked, she manages to coax only a parp from it, and they are still trying to get more out of it when the men draw up before them, all beautifully dressed in Hastings's bull's-head livery, carrying his standard and mounted on horses of the best sort.

'May I, mistress?' the man who leads them asks, so Joana passes him the horn and he holds it to his lips and sounds a rippling sum-mons. He slides from his saddle, returns the horn and introduces himself. 'John Wilkes, mistress.'

Katherine's heart stops.

Wilkes smiles at her.

'Ah. Your husband has mentioned me, I see?'

Now her mouth is dry.

'Yes,' she says. 'He has.'

She feels very vulnerable, caught out alone without Thomas's protection, but Wilkes is entirely affable, and though obviously alert he hardly seems the menace Thomas and Jack have described – but then again, there is something about him that makes her believe he is only showing a tiny part of himself.

'I was sorry to hear of your scare,' he tells her. He holds up a piece of paper on which she recognises Thomas's hand. The message he sent Hastings. 'But I see all is well now, and so I was right not to pass this on to Lord Hastings. I thought he did not need to know, and there is no sense tempting fate, is there?'

He returns the message with another smile. My God, she thinks, Thomas and Jack are right: he is – extraordinary.

'Thank you,' she murmurs, and she puts it in her sleeve. The message doesn't even look as if it has been unfolded.

'So this is Marton Hall,' he says, looking past her at the buildings, and at John Stumps and Joana. 'It is very pleasing to the eye. I am not surprised Master Everingham cherishes his time here. And with you too, of course, mistress.'

Katherine finds herself blushing.

'Though you have had a fire?'

She nods. She doesn't know what to tell him.

'Will you take ale, sir? We have some made fresh.'

He does, with pleasure. She finds herself awkward with him, though she does not know why. Something about the way he looks as if he knows what she is about to say, as if he can almost see through things and possibly into the future. She must keep reminding herself that the ledger is not on the property now, and she has no need for fear of its discovery. But good God it is hard.

'What are you doing in these – these parts?' she asks.

'We have come down from beyond York,' he tells her, 'where there's been more of the usual trouble.'

'Not again? I thought that with the Earl of Warwick over the sea . . . ?'

'It is a cousin of his, another one this time: Fitzhugh. It is not much to worry about, but after last year, and what happened here, King Edward is taking any rebellion very seriously. My lord Hastings has tried to use his influence with Fitzhugh, since their wives are sisters, but . . .' He shrugs to suggest that this was worth a try, though it has come to nothing. 'Anyway,' he goes on, 'other events have become more pressing, and we are bound for London, but not before – not before I complete a few tasks up here.'

Wilkes smiles. He means to suggest she knows what he means, and that it is something of which they both know he cannot speak.

'In Lincoln?' she probes.

He says nothing, but stares at her, still maintaining that smile. She feels she has fluttered slightly too close to the flame.

'Has anything else been heard of the Earl of Warwick?' she asks, changing the subject.

'There have been developments,' he admits.

'Such as?'

'Oh, it is all rumours. But look, here comes your husband, and here, too, my lord Hastings.'

The two men arrive together: one summoned from the fields by the horn, hurrying, accompanied by a handful of men in ordinary workaday clothes clutching bills and bows; the other from the road at the head of a small party of very finely turned-out horsemen.

She does not know what to expect from Hastings. He has always been a puzzle. How much does he know about her? How many of her secrets has he guessed? She first met him in Calais when, disguised as Kit, she'd borrowed his knife to remove an arrow from Richard Fakenham's shoulder. The next time, still as Kit, he'd saved her from being hanged for looting an apple when she deserted from the Earl of Warwick's army outside Canterbury, and he stood witness to Thomas clipping her ear with red-hot blacksmith's clippers.

After that, he'd met her when she was pretending to be Lady Margaret Cornford, and during that dark time, his constant knowing smile had half enraged her, half cheered her. It had been as if he had been laughing up his sleeve at her pretence, and in doing so, showed her that her pretence had not placed her beyond redemption.

Since then they have encountered one another fairly often, she always as Thomas's wife, whom he might call Goodwife Everingham, but whom he chooses to honour with the title mistress, and she still does not know what he knows about her, or who he thinks she really is, but it is surely telling that in all that time he has never asked as to the whereabouts of the boy they used to call Kit.

Now she is standing before him, and Lord Hastings is as polite as he ever was, swinging his fine booted leg from the fine saddle on his fine horse and removing his fine hat to show his fine receding hair before taking her in his arms and kissing her on her mouth.

Then he turns to Thomas and he is no less genial, even embracing him, and congratulating him on the happy news of the coming child; then he turns back to her and asks after her health, and tells her he will pray for her, and he asks them to let him know when the child is to be christened so that he may send a gift, and in the background she is conscious of the faint smile that floats on Wilkes's face.

Thomas asks after Lord Hastings's own health and he says it is rude, given what has happened in the last few months, and he confirms that there has been some trouble in the Northern Parts, but he is pleased to be riding back to London on some business to do with minting coins, among other things, but Master Wilkes had some businesses to attend to in Gainsborough and Lincoln, so they have come by this road, and stopped by, as he said he might, and if they will adjure it, just as he used to when Sir John Fakenham was alive, and just as he did for Sir John's Month's Mind to see how goes their occupation of the old man's hall.

They look around at one another, smiling. Hastings rubs his gloved fingers together. He has a fine emerald ring on one, and two golden loops on another. Katherine cannot help speculate on their worth. Probably as much as Marton itself.

'You came through Gainsborough?' Katherine asks.

'Yes. Yes. Wilkes has some business with Thomas Burgh.'

Wilkes coughs. Hastings glances at him, frowns and then changes the subject.

'Are you strong enough to walk, Mistress Everingham?' he asks. 'To show me the property again? To show me such improvements as you've made?'

Despite herself, she laughs. She has always found his interest in their land endearing. He tells them again that he is looking for ideas, and he has great hopes of building a place of his own, which he says will be a castle, but more comfortable. He is not quite certain how it will be, but he knows how it will not be.

'Not like Bamburgh! Do you remember that place? Ooof. No.' He mimes a shiver.

They walk through the garden where Anne and Joana are still at work with the weeds, and they bob as he passes and he smiles at them and asks how they do, and Katherine walks with her hands pressed into the small of her back, almost breathless with the effort, and she does not think she can keep going like this for very much longer.

'Is there somewhere we might sit, Master Everingham?' he asks. 'I believe Mistress Everingham is in need of rest.'

'Thank you, sir,' she pants.

They return to sit in the yard on the logs that serve as stools, where Sir John Fakenham used to sit on summers' days in the past and play chess, and, not wishing to put them to any undue trouble, Hastings has one of his servants bring wine in pewter cups and very fine white bread.

'It is better to eat here than in any inn or abbey,' he tells them, 'where one cannot choose the company.'

Hastings eats just as if he were in camp and while they do so, but before they come to the meat of the reason for his visit, he brings specific tidings of the Earl of Warwick.

'After Rivers saw him off in Southampton, he went on to Calais, as we knew he might, but that old fraud Lord Wenlock raised the chain across the harbour and fired the bombards from Risban, driving his ships off and out to sea. So then he went south, and now his fleet – not a big one – is anchored off Honfleur, where he's living off piracy and trying to blackmail France.'

'Can you not send King Edward's ships to attack him?' Thomas asks.

'He has France's protection, for the moment. He was always very close with that bloody spider Louis, if you recall?'

Katherine smiles again. Hastings always credits everyone with far more knowledge than they might ordinarily have, as if Thomas knows the first thing about how well the King of France got on with the Earl of Warwick. Nevertheless, Thomas has become quite pink with the flattery.

'In this he is at odds with Edward – his grace the King – and most Englishmen,' Hastings goes on, 'who rightly hate the French, of course, and who favour an alliance with my lord of Burgundy and his Flemish weavers who do so love our good English wool.'

Again Thomas nods as if he knew this.

'So you might think that in opting for help from France, my lord of Warwick has made a mistake and is not likely to be welcomed back in England any time,' Hastings says. 'But . . .'

'But?'

'But Wilkes has just returned from Normandy, from Honfleur itself, off which my lord of Warwick's fleet is, for the time being, anchored.'

She cannot help herself glancing at Wilkes.

'I thought he was up in York?'

Hastings laughs.

'He gets around quickly, that is true.'

They all look over at Wilkes, who is listening to Jack tell him something – archery, by Jack's miming – but she can see he's not paying Jack much attention and instead is watching not Hastings, as she might have thought, but Rufus, who is sitting with his pens and ink in the bright sunshine, scraping clean a shapeless piece of vellum Thomas has given him.

'And', Hastings is saying, 'he has brought back a rumour that he – France – has set in motion a plan that will unite the cause of Warwick with that of Lancaster.'

It takes a moment for this to sink in.

'What? Warwick with Lancaster? Warwick with old King Henry?'

'Well,' Hastings says. 'Not exactly with him. With his queen. With Margaret of Anjou, and her son, Edward, whom we describe as being of Westminster, since that is where he was born, though Lord knows where he was conceived.'

Hastings is making a joke neither Thomas nor Katherine pretend to understand. She cannot yet believe what he had said. The Earl of Warwick and Margaret of Anjou? 'But they are – sworn enemies?' she says. 'How can they—?'

Hastings holds up his jewelled hand. 'I know,' he says. 'It beggars belief.'

'But when you think of the damage they have inflicted on one another. All those – those battles. And all those men killed! And it is just – forgotten?'

'Well, it is yet just a rumour,' Hastings tells them. 'But Wilkes says Queen Margaret has left her father's castle in the east and is making her way to Picardy, where the Earl awaits.'

'They mean to raise an army? To come back?'

'And more besides, if what Wilkes says is right.'

'What was Wilkes doing in Normandy?' Katherine asks before she can stop herself.

Hastings again glances over at Wilkes, almost, she thinks, as if seeking his permission, before he tells them, his voice hushed:

'He was there to find out what my lord of Warwick is up to, naturally, but he was also there on that other matter. The ledger we were talking about last year, before the business with that one-eyed sodomite Edmund Riven, up in Middleham?'

Katherine looks over at Wilkes now, very obviously.

'He knows about it?' she asks.

Hastings nods.

'He is the man – the man I believe I called my bloodhound. Do you remember? I told you about him last year. That he has been tracing the ledger's disappearance from Rouen back to its reappearance over here.'

'Has he had any luck?' Thomas asks.

Hastings smiles.

'Well, we have had a new name come up,' he says. He leans back, and neither she nor Thomas can breathe.

'Who?' Thomas asks. His voice is thick and wooden. So this is it, she thinks. Her hands are shaking and her heart is thundering.

But Hastings does not look confrontational. He sits quite calmly, eating some dried fruit, washing it down with something from his cup, and he could be talking over a matter of interest with some old friends.

'Well, I cannot say for certain,' he says, 'but Wilkes has arrived at the name slightly arse about face, and by what sounds suspiciously like luck, because instead of finding the man who sold it on from whoever stole it from the garrison in Rouen, he's found a man who was trying to buy it in the hope of selling it on to the old King of France. He's a pardoner's sundriesman in Paris, the sort who trades in the finger bones of saints and the teeth of martyrs and so on, who heard that an Englishman – a pardoner, presumably – had it for sale, along with what he called a horn-cheeked crossbow he claimed belonged to the French witch Joan. The only problem is that this was ten years ago, and the sundriesman did not remember his name, and did not buy either the bow or the book, because the pardoner never turned up with the goods.

'But the sundriesman did remember that this pardoner – our pardoner – suffered the King's Evil, if you would believe it? And part of the bargain they'd struck was that he would be granted the right to receive the touch of King Charles, who was then King of France.'

'But why would he go all the way to France when we have a king of our own?' Thomas asks. He is either genuinely caught up in the story, or he has greater powers of pretence than she has ever credited.

Hastings laughs.

'Our question exactly! Why? So we reasoned that he must have tried old King Henry first, but perhaps that failed? So Wilkes has been going through the old court records of the old King, in

Westminster. There were quite a few years missing from the records, though, and there were also quite a few years when the old King was not up to the job of touching anyone, let alone a diseased pardoner. But one name did come up. A man named John Daud, of the county of Lincoln.'

'Lincoln?'

'That is all we knew. So Wilkes turned his attention to Church records, and the obvious place to start was with the cathedral. And lucky he did because just after Christmastide, in the year 1460, a certain John Daud, of the city of Lincoln, paid for the bells to be rung a hundred times a day to ensure the success of a trip he was making to France.'

Katherine can think of nothing to say. Nor can Thomas. Just the thought of that cunning, and how thorough Wilkes must be, makes Katherine feel naked.

Hastings smiles.

'I told you he was a genius.'

'But have you – where is he now? Is he still alive?'

'Ah. No. We think not.'

'So . . . ?'

Hastings holds up a finger.

'But wait,' he says. 'Last year we took in an old stationer – this was when we thought whoever had bought the ledger must have been in that business, you see? – also from Lincoln, who told us all he knew about the book-buying trade, its main dealers and so on. It led us nowhere, apparently, but Wilkes's men kept a record of what was said, and now, now that we have the name Daud, we went back to the record, and discovered that there was a dealer by the name of Daud, too, who was both a pardoner and a book-dealer, and though our stationer thought he might be dead, he told us that his widow is still alive – or she was then – and that she never dispersed his collection of books, which he had kept pristine.'

Thomas frowns.

'So what are you hoping for?'

Hastings sits back. He looks less triumphant now, more rueful.

'A clue as to who Daud sold it to instead of the French sun-driesman, I suppose. If that's what happened. But I don't know, Thomas, to tell you the truth. Wilkes suggests that if he kept his collection pristine, he would have kept a record of everything he bought and sold. Such men do, I understand. God and Profit and all that. But we shall see. We are on our way there now to see if we can speak to his widow, and to see what joy we may extract from either her or his records.'

Katherine's mouth is very dry. Thomas is likewise silent.

Hastings sighs and goes on. 'I don't hold out much hope,' he says, 'but I've spent more than five years searching for it, and even though it has now become of little or no interest to the Earl of Warwick, I'd still like to get my hands on it. See it destroyed or—'

'What?' Thomas interjects. 'Why is the Earl of Warwick no longer interested in it?'

'Oh, I don't suppose he's given up on it entirely,' Hastings says. 'He'd still give his left arm for it, but perhaps not his right.'

But Katherine feels a flush of warmth. A realisation.

'It's because – because he is making overtures to the old Queen and old King Henry, isn't it? It means he has abandoned the Duke of Clarence's claim to the throne, so the ledger is now only of interest to him if he wished to contest the right to the dukedom of York, which he does not.'

Hastings starts to chuckle.

'You are altogether too quick, Mistress Everingham! I have always said so, have I not, Thomas? Too quick! Too quick!'

Thomas smiles uncomprehendingly, then he sees it.

'So Warwick has abandoned The House of York entirely?'

Hastings nods.

'Well,' he says, 'that is one way to see it. I think of it as The House of York having abandoned Warwick.'

'I suppose it makes things clearer,' Thomas says.

Hastings agrees.

'There is no backsliding now,' he says. 'Especially if what Wilkes says is true: that the French King Louis is trying to persuade the Queen Margaret to let her son marry Warwick's daughter.'

The thought is too odd to keep in your head. Warwick's daughter marry King Henry's son? No. No. It is just . . . No.

'I thought she was married to the Duke of Clarence?' Thomas asks.

'The other daughter,' Hastings says. 'The younger one.' He takes a drink. 'Either way,' he muses, 'I should not like to be in old Warwick's shoes now. Nor Clarence's really, in all honesty.'

'What chance has he of – of uniting their forces?' she asks.

'Uniting Warwick and Lancaster? Who knows? Warwick has a great power of his own, of course, and there are still many who would side with old King Henry against King Edward, but then again Warwick has done them such damage in the past.' He laughs ruefully. 'Still, it may not come to pass. Queen Margaret was ever a law unto herself and it may be that she will demand too high a price of Warwick, or it may be that Warwick will come to his senses and seek the King's grace again.'

There is some sense that the conversational part of the exchange is over, and she sees Wilkes get up from where he has been watching Rufus draw. Hastings flits his gaze his way, and recalls the reason for his visit.

'But, Thomas,' he begins, 'as you know, I have just come down from the Northern Parts where there is the usual trouble, this time among adherents of Lord Fitzhugh, who, as it happens, is married to Alice, who is the sister both of my wife, and none other than Richard Neville, Earl of Warwick. Now I am not saying he is a fool or a dupe, or easily led, but – Dear God! Mistress Everingham! Are you all right?'

There is a sudden scalding heat from between Katherine's legs, and what feels like boiling water soaks through her braies and down her calves. She jumps to her feet.

'Anne!' Thomas calls. 'Anne!'

The baby takes two days to come. Katherine feels her hip bones being unknit, being forced apart and into different shapes, her flesh being stretched so that her fibres part, and her skin splitting with a pain that is needle sharp. Anne is there, able to follow instructions as she gasps and pants and pushes to get the baby out.

The men wait downstairs.

Night, dawn, day, dusk: all are as one in the shuttered room, in the shrouded bed where Sir John breathed his last. In between the contractions she stares at the beams and the daub where it is cracked and she hears the mice and vermin within and she thinks if she lives, she will move the bed to a different position and fill a new mattress with meadowsweet and so on.

She hears the priest downstairs on the second day, when she is too tired to drink ale, and the pain has gone on so long, and Jack has sent in a small disc of jet that belonged to Nettie and Anne has said all the prayers to St Margaret as she can, and is now so tired herself she can almost sleep through Katherine's cries, which she tries to muffle so as not to alarm Rufus. Katherine does not know if the priest is there for her, or for the baby, should it ever come.

Then she thinks that there is no one present able to judge better than her if she is going to live or die, and so she determines that she will live, and that the priest is there to baptise the baby.

And so it proves. On the evening of the second day, she finally gives birth. She watches Anne's eyes widen in amazement through her own tear-filled clenched lids as finally the pressure-pain is relieved below and there is just a rush of sliding flesh through her nethers. Anne takes up the slippery, basted thing and looks into its face and she looks anxious, helpless, and Katherine's heart is crushed in a powerful grip of misery. The baby is stillborn.

But then there is a limited cough. A tiny thing, strong within its own terms, and Anne starts to half laugh, half weep as the child's limbs flail, and then there is a piercing cry of rage.

'A girl!' Anne says. 'A girl.'

Katherine can only gesture with her fingers. She wants to feel the child's weight on her. She wants comfort with contact. She cannot wait for Anne to clean her up.

'Wrap her in linen,' she whispers, and Anne does so, a quick, practised fold, and she places the parcel on Katherine's breast. It is almost no weight. Less than a plucked chicken. A rabbit. Katherine's arms feel heavier than the baby. She picks them up and places them over the child, and the child's face is blue and livid, squished and smeared with blood and mucus, and her eyes do not open but she is alive, and vital, and hers, and Katherine is filled with golden yellow summer's warmth.

In this haze of happiness she instructs Anne in the cutting of the cord, which is taken to be burned in the fire below, and in the disposal of the sheets and straw and the other mess, and then hot water is brought up by Joana and the baby shouts and bawls and her face softens while she is being washed.

By the time Anne is finished and the baby is carefully swaddled, and the shutters are let down and the summer air billows through, Katherine is asleep. When she wakes, except for a persistent ache, she has almost forgotten the pain of the last couple of days, and she wants Thomas and Rufus to see this astonishing, miraculous thing she has produced.

The men gather in the courtyard outside and shoot an arrow into the sky to signify the child's escape from the womb to life, and then they come stumping up the steps to see them both. Thomas is quick but careful to come across the room to embrace her, and he is happy to see the girl whom they will call Alice, but Rufus stands back and watches, and when she sees his face, immobile as ever, she feels as if her heart were being squeezed in someone's palm. He does not want to hold the baby, or touch anything. He is too frightened

'Rufus, my love, come.'

The men stand aside to let the boy approach the bed. He is pale with anxiety. He shakes his head and keeps his hands by his side.

'Come on, Rufus,' Thomas says.

He is more brusque than he would be if he had been there the night of the oak gall. She beckons Rufus closer and shows him his sister's face. It is impossible not to smile at such a thing. He lifts his hand to stroke her cheek with the back of his finger. She can almost feel his bones melting. She moves to place the baby in his arms and when he takes her, his tears fall thick and fast. She finds tears in her own eyes too. Rufus mumbles to the girl. Some sort of promise of his own. She does not intrude. After a while he gives up the baby, but remains sitting next to her with one haunch on the side of her bed, watching, keeping close guard. She squeezes his pale hand.

Thomas has found her a gold ring in which is set a tiny red pebble of jasper.

'I bought it from a man in Lincoln,' he tells her.

'Tell me you haggled,' she says.

He shakes his head.

'Of course not.'

'And?'

'And all the widow's books are taken away by order of the Lord Chamberlain!'

She smiles.

'So he has found it?'

'He must have. He must have. You heard how thorough he is? He will have checked every book himself.'

She feels her eyes closing and a great smile spreading, and she sinks into the depths of the bed.

'Praise Jesus,' she says.

'No, praise you,' Thomas says.

Even as she is talking her eyes are closing, and she feels herself sliding into delicious sleep, only to be woken what seems a moment later with Anne and Thomas holding the squalling baby.

'She's hungry,' they say.

And this is how it is for a month. Thomas and Rufus bring Alice to her and she feeds her while they relate the happenings downstairs, what they have been doing in the furlongs and woods, and so on, and what news they have heard from afar.

'The Earl of Warwick is still in France,' Thomas tells her.

'But what about Queen Margaret?'

'She is still there as far as I know.'

'And have their son and daughter married yet?'

He doesn't know, but he finds out the next day.

'Not yet,' he says.

And she is silent for a bit, trying to think about that.

'So what next?'

'They say Warwick is trying to raise an army of Frenchmen to come and take the throne on behalf of old King Henry.'

'An army of Frenchmen?'

And Thomas shrugs as if to agree with her. It is a mad thought.

The next day he comes back with news that there is still rebellion in the north, and she asks after the new Earl of Northumberland – 'What is he doing about it?' – and Thomas tells her he has heard nothing of him doing anything; then she asks about Lord Montagu and whether Thomas thinks King Edward was right to deprive him of the earldom of Northumberland, which was all he ever wanted, wasn't it? And if Edward was right to give him not much in return, despite his loyalty, and surely he is a force in the north?

'You remember his men at Hexham? In their red coats? They were proper soldiers.'

When Thomas agrees she turns back to Alice, who tugs away at her nipple; and when she finishes, and goes slack, her dark eyes remain fixed on Katherine's as if the girl is trying to fix her image in her mind, and Katherine smiles down at her daughter and thinks: Well, there it is, and I do not care too much about what goes on in the Northern Parts.

Time passes. She hears them go out in the morning and she hears Nettie's Kate crying and Anne walking her up and down in the yard below her window soothing her, and Anne sings a simple little song to a tune that worms its way into Katherine's ear, and after a while she becomes so bored she gets up and walks about her room, creeping so as not to wake Alice, who lies in a cot that Thomas has fashioned with aspen planks and clinched nails, and that now sits on the coffer wherein they used to keep the ledger. Sometimes Anne or Joana or Thomas will take Alice, so that Katherine may rest peacefully, and when this happens, Katherine likes it for a bit but then finds she wants the girl back in her room, or on her breast.

When she hears the men come back, she is almost be able to feel how tired they are, and how sore they are from their days in the baking sun, and occasionally there is more news, depending on whom they have met that day, and Thomas brings it up and it is usually wearyingly familiar: there is still trouble in the Northern Parts, or there is new trouble in the Northern Parts, but once there comes the intelligence that King Edward is going up to suppress it himself, because in fact she was right and it seems he trusts neither this new Earl of Northumberland, nor the newly demoted Lord Montagu, to suppress it for him.

'So he has gone himself?' she asks, to make certain. And Thomas nods and reminds her of that thing that King Edward once said about learning lessons.

'I don't suppose the King wants another Robin of Redesdale on his hands,' he says. 'If he is ever captured again, there'll not be too much hunting or any fine dinners this time.'

He adds as an afterthought that while he is up north, King Edward has entrusted his wife, Elizabeth – who is pregnant, it turns out – to the safety of the Tower in London. Katherine asks him where he gets his news now, and he tells her messengers are riding up and down the road all the time. It is as if the whole country is getting ready for something.

But at Marton Hall they must prepare too, and it is easy to forget the affairs of men in far-off places, for it is now the second week before the Assumption, in early August, when the sun seems at its hottest, and she hears the men sharpening the sickles and she doesn't envy them the coming days, for she knows from bitter experience the toll that harvesting wheat extracts.

Then, when that is done, within the week she hears them

sharpening the scythes for harvesting the rye, and then the barley, and then the oats, and again she does not envy them, for a scythe too brings its own particular pain. Then it is the pea crop that must be brought in and stored out of reach of mice and rats on a bed of hawthorn branches in the loft above the malthouse.

And then, finally, it is the Sunday of her churching, the end of Thomas's gander month, when he has had to act as husband and wife, mother and father, and Katherine is so impatient to be out in the sunshine that she is up before anyone and downstairs and tottering about on weak legs with Alice wrapped and tied to her, and the girl is so incredibly hot! Everyone knows it is her special day, and everyone makes particular efforts to clean themselves and wear their best clothes, and all faces turn to her and she shows them Alice and everyone is so smitten with the little pink bun and they are so kind to her, and she is so pleased to see them and to be out of that room. The sun is shining as they walk together down the track and into the cool shade of the little church where they stand and wait outside while she makes her confession, telling the priest that she has not confessed for some time, and then at Mass Thomas stands next to her so that he is touching her and he is in his best hose, new, with a broadcloth jacket and a hat with a pearl or something on the crown, and she feels so full of emotion, so over-brimming with it, that she doesn't know from one moment to the next if she should laugh or cry. And Rufus is there too and he looks happier than she has seen him, and he keeps a hold of his sister's little foot.

Afterwards they go back up to the hall where there is white bread, beef pottage, tongue in butter, an eel they've smoked that is as long as an arm, and an omelette made of no fewer than eighteen eggs, enforced with strips of smoked bacon. There is a little wine and some good strong ale, and they sit outside in the August sunshine, and they eat and drink and then Rufus plays a tune on his pipes to which Jack and Jane dance a curious jig and everyone claps and Alice is not disturbed, and during it all Katherine occasionally presses her nose to the fluff of hair that covers her girl's scalp and smells the new-born baby smell.

Thomas drinks too much ale and tells her how much he loves her, and how the future will be filled with nothing but rosy happiness for they have their son and their daughter and one another, and all their monsters are vanquished one way or another, do you see? And she laughs, and kisses him, though she is less pleased when he snores all through the night and first wakes and then keeps awake the baby.

On it goes as the weeks of late summer pass, and Katherine helps where she can, but she is still so weak, and Alice needs her more than do the fields. So she passes long stretches of the day feeding the baby, which she does not recall ever doing with Rufus, with only Anne for company. But at last everything is brought in and dried, pickled, smoked or salted against the winter to come, and when it is done, when the storerooms are packed and the lofts are groaning, there is a moment when she sits in the shade, and she sees the boughs of the apple tree are heavy with ripening fruit, and she thinks to herself, yes, this is as it should be.

She even starts to think again about going to Canterbury again. To find out who her parents are.

And that is the day that Thomas comes back from the mill looking perturbed.

'King Edward has scattered the rebels in the north,' he tells her. 'He's sent Fitzhugh packing for Scotland.'

'That's good,' she says.

'Yes,' he says. 'But Warwick and Clarence have landed with an army of Frenchmen in the southwest.'

14

They are back in the butts, all the men, including Foulmouth John, but not the skinny boy, who has vanished, and Thomas is making them shoot and run, shoot and run. They do not enjoy it, because no man enjoys shooting in a jack and a sallet all day, but they are good at it now. They've had a few days at this, and together the six of them can lay down 150-odd arrows in a patch of grass no bigger than a stock fisherman's net, two hundred paces away, in less time than it takes to say the paternoster. More than that, when they are on the rove, each man can drop his arrow within two paces of marks that they could hardly have made out earlier in the year.

'Fucking invincible, we are!' Foulmouth John says. 'When the Earl of Warwick's men arrive, we'll fucking show them.'

But Thomas knows there are only six of them, and six is not enough because this time when Wymmys comes, at first light, a few days later, he comes on a new horse, in new plate that fits him, and at the head of a column of more than fifty men in pale livery, each with a big yellow device on his chest.

'Who the fuck are they?' breathes Foulmouth John.

The household is gathered in the courtyard after prayers.

'Someone's retained men,' Thomas knows, but not whose.

'They're King Edward's,' Jack says. 'Look, they're wearing that streaming-sun sign.'

Thomas cannot tell. Then Katherine is at his shoulder.

'No,' she says, 'it is a star.'

'A star? Who is that? Anyone know?'

There are shrugs all around.

'There's no point trying to fight them,' Jacks says. 'Just look at 'em.'

Each of the horsemen carries a lance or a spear, a bill or a poll-axe resting in his stirrup, and they are all well harnessed, in plate and with sallets. Worse, though, in a way, is the sight of five friars riding along with the soldiers, halfway along the column, wrapped in cloaks against the first fine mists of the season, but unmistakable all the same. At the very back of the line are Wymmys's original fifteen, one of them on Wymmys's old horse. It's the skinny boy, of course.

'So that's who told him about Hastings.'

'The fucker,' Foulmouth John says.

'I'd best go and see what he wants,' Thomas says, though they can all guess. Thomas's heart has risen to make his throat ache, and he is trembling. It is not fear, but bitter, bitter disappointment. He puts on his coat and goes out to meet Wymmys, who has reined in his horse at the head of the track and is waiting.

Jack comes with him.

'I told you I'd be back, Brother Thomas,' Wymmys says.

The mist seems to cling to his nose, beading on it. Thomas ignores him and instead addresses the soldier at his side.

'Who are you?' Thomas asks.

'This is Sir John Brougham,' Wymmys says.

Brougham nods. He's a lean-faced older man, with a level gaze from blue eyes that look as if they'd not even be startled by the crack of doom.

'God give you good day, sir,' Thomas says. 'I do not recognise your livery?'

'It is a molet argent with streamers charged with another molet azure,' he says, holding the badge out with one eyebrow cocked. 'I am retained by John de Vere, my lord the Earl of Oxford.'

Thomas has heard of the Earl of Oxford, but he is not local, so it is only in the same way he has heard of any of these sorts of men. He tries to remember whose side he is usually on. Or has most recently been on.

'The Earl of Oxford? And he – he has more influence with King Edward than does Lord Hastings? The Lord Chamberlain?' Thomas asks. He is checking, really, since he has no clue. Perhaps influence is irrelevant anyway, when you are but six men, four women and two babies facing fifty armed men.

'Ah.' Wymmys smiles. 'That depends on which king you are talking about.'

Even apart from Brougham and the men at his back, Wymmys obviously has another advantage.

'Which other king is there?' Thomas asks.

Wymmys snickers.

'Last time I was here,' he says, 'you took some pleasure in showing me that the intelligence – such as it was – on which I was relying was out of date, do you remember?'

'I do. You suggested my lord of Hastings was no longer my goodlord, and yet, oddly, he has this last month stood godfather for my daughter.'

Despite himself Wymmys is impressed.

'Well, you are to be congratulated, brother. There can be very few canons of the Order of St Gilbert able to claim such a connection.'

'None, I would imagine,' Thomas agrees.

'Hmmm! And yet! And yet!'

'Get on with it, Wymmys,' Brougham barks.

'You also gave me an excellent piece of advice,' Wymmys tells

Thomas. 'Which I've followed, as you see.' He gestures to the men behind him. Thomas glances at them. He is given blank, bored stares, the stares of men on duty.

'To bring more men?'

'Exactly. My lord of Oxford has done me the honour of providing me with these men—'

'To come and harass an innocent man out of his property?'

'To enforce the long-neglected law of the land.'

'But you can't do anything while King Edward is still on the throne.'

'Ah, but that's just it. It is as I was saying. He's not, you see? The Earl of Warwick is even now back in the country, and the whole of the west has gone over to him, and Kent too. And London will at any day, and within a week we will have the rightful king on the throne!'

Thomas has the sensation of everything sliding: not just Wymmys, but the horses, the men, the trees, the buildings. Everything is moving downwards and to the right, as if the earth were tipping over like a chessboard and they, its pieces, were sliding off.

'So my lord Hastings', Wymmys goes on, 'has very much more to be doing than fussing around making sure you are housed with a roof over your head and a fire to warm your hands. He must look to his own skin.'

Thomas looks around for Katherine. Jack comes down to stand by his side.

Brougham speaks again.

'Listen,' he says, half to Thomas, half to Wymmys. 'My lord of Oxford has – for reasons of his own – sent us well out of our way to assist you in this matter, bailiff, but we must be in Leicester by sunset tomorrow, and the sooner we start the better for all, so I am not interested in hearing you two bicker over the rights and wrongs of this. Get on with what you must do, and do it as humbly as you may.' He turns to Thomas. 'You, sir, must see that we outnumber you many times, and you must know that we know you have women and children in your hall, so if you do not wish to endanger them, then for the love of all that is holy put yourself in this man's care and be done with it.'

'Can we first ask the priest?' Wymmys asks, gesturing to the men Thomas had assumed were friars. 'To make certain.'

Brougham flaps a hand from his pommel. Very well.

Wymmys has something else planned.

'Why?' Thomas asks. 'What are they even doing here?'

'To see if you are indeed Thomas Everingham.'

'I am Thomas Everingham. That is not the point here.'

'Give me strength,' Brougham mutters.

But Wymmys is gesturing at one of the friars who is craning his head to peer at Thomas, and is getting off his horse to come and have a look. He's in a black cloak. He is not precisely familiar, and Thomas has not seen his face yet, but suddenly and without a fleck of doubt he knows who it is, and it is as if the last seven or eight years have not passed.

'Brother Barnaby!' Thomas cannot help himself.

And Wymmys shouts with a high-pitched laugh.

'The fool is condemned out of his own mouth!'

The man staring at Thomas is Brother Barnaby. Thomas has not seen him since he left the Priory at Haverhurst so many years earlier, still out of his wits, and in such fraught circumstances that he can hardly remember them. Part of him wants to hug the man; part of him wants to kill him.

Brother Barnaby shakes his head slowly. He has aged. He looks mortified.

'I am sorry, Brother Thomas,' he says. 'I would have said it was not you, as God above, and all the angels, saints and martyrs too, will witness. I would have lied.'

'So you are a canon?' the officer asks. 'You don't look like one.'

'I was a canon, but – I am no longer.'

Wymmys makes a dismissive noise.

'You still made your vow, Brother Thomas, and unless you can provide the dispensation from the Vatican then you are occupying this land by no right. More than that, you are absconded from your priory, an apostate, as is proved by Father Barnaby here, who used to be your prior.'

Thomas has many questions for Father Barnaby, but they will have to wait for another time.

'So what, Wymmys? What is it you want?'

Wymmys seems to think it is obvious.

'Your pretence of ownership of these lands is an offence against God's Church,' he says. 'Isn't that right, Father Barnaby?'

Father Barnaby reluctantly nods his grey head.

'And you only bring shame on the Order of St Gilbert,' Wymmys goes on, 'with your roving about these acres just as if you owned them.'

'I do own them.'

'No you do not. You can't. And anyway, that is not the point. The point is that you must return to orders.'

'I'll do nothing of the sort,' Thomas tells him.

Wymmys smiles.

'Sir John? Would you explain?'

Brougham leans forward in his saddle.

'My lord of Oxford has asked me to assist this – this man in any way I can,' he says. 'And I am to evict you and ensure you return to orders, willingly or not.'

Wymmys smiles, but Brougham goes on.

'Now I don't exactly know who you are, master' – he looks Thomas in the eye – 'but you seem to me a good man, and there is something I do not like about this scheme, so what I propose is that we meet halfway.'

'Halfway?'

'You are free to go, but go you must.'

'Go?'

'Aye, from here.'

'Never,' Jack says.

Brougham cocks an eyebrow again.

'Carter,' he calls over his shoulder. 'Shoot this man.'

Carter has a crossbow, braced, and he thumbs a quarrel into the gutter.

'No,' Thomas says. 'No!'

He stands between Jack and this Carter, who looks the sort who might be a good shot, and who might happily send a quarrel through anyone who annoys him, or his captain.

'But, sir—' Wymmys starts.

'Shut up, bailiff,' Brougham says. 'Carter, if the bailiff says another word, shoot his leg.'

Wymmys closes his mouth.

'So what will you do?' Brougham asks, turning to Thomas.

Thomas can hardly think.

'Let me – let me talk to – let me tell my wife,' he says.

'She'll want to know,' Brougham agrees.

Thomas turns.

'Come on, Jack,' he says.

Everyone is still gathered watching in the courtyard, by the burned-out ruins of Nettie and Jack's house. Thomas feels a stone in his throat. He has not felt so like crying since he was eleven years old and his brother killed his dog. There are actual tears in his eyes when he meets Katherine's gaze. Her face is a mask of frozen watchfulness. She knows.

'We must – pack up and go,' he tells them all. 'Leave Marton.'

'No!' one of them cries.

'Why?' another asks.

Thomas hardly trusts himself to speak.

'I – I cannot own this land,' he says. 'What the bailiff says is true. I am – I was a canon of an order, and I made vows to forgo all claim to property.'

'And all sorts of other things too.' Foulmouth John laughs. 'Not going to put Rufus and Alice back up Mistress Everingham, are they?'

His father bats the back of his head.

'So – I do not know what is to happen to us all, but I must leave or face a return to orders.'

'You're an apostate?'

Thomas nods.

'I am.'

Anne sobs suddenly.

'Always too good to last,' she says.

'It will be all right, Mam,' Joana tells her, but tears already brim in her eyes.

Katherine says nothing. A type of white-hot fury emanates from her.

'No,' she says. 'No.'

And she starts to move towards the soldiers, her gaze locked on Wymmys, and Thomas has seen this before. He knows there is no way this can end well.

'Katherine,' he says. He takes her shoulder. She shrugs him off with a quick twist. He sees she already has her knife out.

'No,' he says, and he catches her wrist. She tries to surge past him but he has two or three times her strength and he towers over her.

'No,' he says. 'It will only make it much worse. Much worse.'

She is scorching to the touch, her humours unbalanced. He pushes her back. The knife falls with a dull clatter on the stones at their feet. He shuffles her back into the courtyard. Then he holds her in his arms so that she cannot move but still she struggles.

'It is not for ever,' he says. 'It is not for ever. We will find Hastings and we will be back. We will be back. I promise you. I swear on everything I hold dear. I swear on my life, on your life, on Rufus's life and on Alice's life. I will bring you back here. I will. I will.'

And – dear Christ! – he means it! Only there is nothing he can do to effect it now. Nothing. Nothing. He feels her taking long, dragging breaths. She is calming herself.

'It will be all right, my love,' he says. 'We will be back in no time. No time at all.'

Everyone watches to see what Katherine will do. He feels her slowly unbend and it is as if the heat is going out of her.

'Where shall we go?' she asks very quietly. It is almost as if she believes him.

'North,' he says, 'to find William Hastings.'

He feels her nod.

'What will we do when we find him?'

He shrugs.

'He will lend us men – if not for my sake, or yours, then for Sir John's memory. He loved the old man.'

'But if what Wymmys says is true? About Warwick taking London? It is the end of King Edward.'

'No. No. He still has men loyal to him. He still has the Earl of Northumberland. He still has Montagu.'

'What about us?' Anne asks. 'Are we to come north with you?'

The thought terrifies her. Thomas tells them they can if they want, but it would be better if they go back to their families in their villages. He tells them he will give them such money as he can afford, and they must take as much food as they can carry.

'Wymmys cannot stop us doing that,' he tells them.

There is a long silence. They troop back into the hall and the air within is dusty, as if the fire's not drawing, and the others look on, shafts of watery light splashing their faces, their clothes. One of the lurchers whimpers. There are more tears, and the next hour passes slowly and miserably. Thomas takes Katherine up the steps to the bedchamber and he takes out from that coffer his brigandine, the spurs he bought in Ripon, the gloves he bought in Huntingdon and the archers' sallet. He straps the sword in its beautiful red sheath around his waist.

He watches Katherine throw a few things on top: children's linens; a few of her own clothes that come to hand. She hardly cares. He thought she would be angry and anything he says will only make it worse. He folds the blanket over their few possessions and he waits, watching her. She is shaking her head very slightly, a sort of quivering. She keeps gesturing, both hands outspread as if to say something is absurd, and starting but not finishing sentences. Through the window he can see Brougham is impatient to be gone, but he seems to blame Wymmys for any delay, and Wymmys is having to placate him. There is no sign of Father Barnaby. Thomas hopes he has gone.

When they come down Jack is there with his baby, and something to say.

Thomas already knows what it is.

'You must stay with her, Jack,' he says. 'We'll not be gone long.'

Jack nods.

'I swore I'd never leave her again,' he says.

'Of course,' Thomas says.

'I'll take John Stumps,' Jack tells him. 'Couldn't manage without him.'

John Stumps tells him to fuck off, but Thomas knows he is grateful. The thought of a long ride with no arms and an uncertain end is too much for him. Thomas tells them to take the oxen, and come back for the sheep, the pigs, the geese as soon as they've found somewhere to keep them. He tells them to load up with as much food as they can carry.

'Anything else too,' he says. He gestures at the furniture in the room: the board and stools, the shelves for their plate, the few pieces of plate themselves.

Jack looks stern.

'You don't think you're coming back?'

'No,' Thomas says. 'We will be back.'

'But not for a bit?'

Thomas shrugs and turns to help Anne and Joana and the others load misshapen sacks on to the backs of the oxen. Cheeses. Grain. The butter churn. The malt rake. Pans, the tripod, knives, spoons. These will be of use. The women are crying. Foulmouth John is repeating the same word over and over again.

At length they are ready, gathered in the courtyard, as if waiting a blessing, or a speech, and they look to Thomas to provide.

'Marton is our home,' he tells them. 'It will always be our home. Christ, have we not suffered before? You, Jack? Do you remember the tower in Middleham? John? We have been in worst binds than this, and we have always come back and we will do again. We will find William Hastings, and we will return and take the place back and make it ours once more, better even, so touch nothing, harm nothing, break nothing. It was ours, is ours and will be ours again. So let's go, past that grinning devil Wymmys, with our heads held high, because our enemies may have the whip hand now, but by God we will have it again soon, and we will return to drive the bastards out. We may not be gentlemen, but let's show them we aren't crawling peasants ready to commit ourselves to the ditch. Let us go out as a force! As people to be reckoned with.'

He takes heart himself, or convinces himself he does, and some of the easier to persuade seem to draw some strength from his words – they've perhaps never heard a man speak for so long outside of Mass – but Katherine is still as sharp and disapproving as a hawk. Nevertheless, he nods the signal to ride out, and those with horses climb up on to them, while those without follow with the oxen and the donkey, which Bald John clips with his switch. They roll towards Wymmys and Brougham, who watches them come and then tugs on his reins and leads his horse off the track to let them past. His men do likewise, and so, eventually, must Wymmys. He does not look to be enjoying his triumph as much as perhaps he had hoped.

Brougham nods to Thomas as they pass.

'I don't want to see you again,' he says. 'If you come back, I'll have to come back, and if I have to come back, then I'll have to have you killed you. D'you understand?'

Thomas nods. He understands Brougham doesn't want to have to come back, that is all. He looks at the star on the man's livery coat, and he thinks he will remember it, not because he has any hatred of this man, or of Carter his obedient archer, but because he hopes that one day he may make the Earl of Oxford regret his supporting of Wymmys, whom surely he can hardly know, and regret his depriving men and their families of homes, just for some shabby and no doubt negligible advantage.

They walk down the track, watched by Oxford's men. Some look regretful, some impatient, most bored and contemptuous. They are young men, Thomas supposes, harnessed, on good horses, with swords. Of course they look down on everyone.

As they pass Wymmys's men, the skinny boy comes forward into the teeth of Foulmouth John's ranting – 'Fucking little shit-weasel' and 'I'll cut you from bollocks to chops!' he yells. The skinny boy is sobbing fat, desolate tears.

'I am sorry,' he bleats. 'I am so sorry. They made me.'

Thomas thinks it might be the first time he's heard the boy speak.

'But I didn't tell about you murdering the lawyer in Gainsborough. I didn't tell them that.'

It doesn't much matter now if he did or didn't do it, or if Jack did or didn't do it. A suggestion like this, Thomas knows, and they could both be hanging by noon tomorrow. Thomas can only nod, and kick on.

John Stumps growls at Wymmys's men, but they take heart from the presence of Brougham's men and laugh and jeer.

'You touch anything,' he says, 'you break anything, and I'll fucking kill you myself.'

'What with, your fucking teeth?'

At the end of the track they reach the village and they pass through. Anne and Joana will stop here. Thomas says goodbye and kisses them and then Katherine does the same, but with a wiry ferocity. Thomas gives them money.

'We will be home by Advent,' he tells them.

Everyone's crying again.

They mount up and ride on, and when they reach the road, they stop again, and he says goodbye to Jack and Jane, who has become his wife, and to the baby Kate, and the scene at the village is repeated.

'God go with you,' he tells them. 'And I will let you know when we are back.'

There are more tears.

Eventually it is just the four of them. Thomas has Rufus on his lap; Katherine carries Alice. They stop at the crook in the road, from where they can look through the dying sedge across the pasture that is too damp to really serve for anything other than ducks, to Marton. They can see Brougham's men turning in the track, getting ready to leave. Wymmys is still there with his men. They are dismounted, and looking in all the buildings, for stuff to steal perhaps, or places to live. Wymmys is walking about, on his own, as if he is startled by the size and ease of his victory.

Thomas watches him for a long moment, and feels a cold wet wind blowing through him. The first of the autumn, perhaps. It gives him an idea. He swings his leg off his horse and unties his travel coat and brigandine and passes them up to Rufus. Then he unstraps his bow and takes it out of its linen sleeve.

'What are you doing?' Katherine asks.

'What I should have done long ago.'

He nocks the bow, bending it around his buttock to slip the string over, and then carefully chooses a single perfect arrow.

'Wait here,' he says.

He walks twenty paces into the sodden pasture and stops. He watches Wymmys for a moment. He is perhaps 250 paces away, about the size of Thomas's thumbnail, and he's moving erratically, this way and that. It might be a sort of jig, Thomas thinks, of triumph or of ownership, or of incredulity. It is hard to say from here. The arrow is a broadhead, a hunting arrow, really, since who keeps war arrows at home unless they are King Edward? And the feathers are all three grey, well cut and tied with red thread. It's a good arrow, subtly chested.

Thomas takes his stance, and he is in clear ground. There's a breeze at his back, which will help. He nocks the arrow on the string, and then looks over at Wymmys. He is still there, just below the window of the bedchamber. It is as if he is inspecting the property, looking up into the eaves, for marten nests, perhaps. He has his hand on his head. It is as if he still can't believe his luck, and is saying to himself 'wait till Mother sees this'. Then he turns and stalks back along the length of the house towards the yard and his own horse. Something – God? Fate? – makes him turn and look over the pasture towards Thomas. He sees Thomas, standing out there, and he must know who and what he is, but again he can't quite believe it. He covers his brow against the sun's soft glare and peers.

Thomas draws. He feels the pinch between his shoulder blades and he knows even before he looses that this one will hit its target. He might as well not bother to watch. But he does. He sees the arrow shrink to become an almost dainty flit, hanging at the top of its arch for what always seems an improbably long moment, and then regather pace on its descent. He sees Wymmys unmoving, perhaps unable to believe what is happening, or perhaps knowing all too well, and perhaps also believing that there is something inevitable about this. Whatever it is he does not move and Thomas stands poised, the bow still alive in his left hand, as the arrow knocks the distant figure to the ground.

'Ha!'

Katherine has walked up to stand behind him.

Thomas puts his arm around her shoulders and she puts hers around his waist and they walk back together to the road where Rufus waits with Alice and the horses. Once he has unnocked his bow and slid it back in its sleeve, Thomas helps Katherine up into her saddle, and then passes up Alice, who is restive now, and will need feeding soon, and then he helps Rufus up, and he is about to swing up into the saddle after him when he stops and looks down the road ahead, at the tunnel of elm trees through which they must pass to start this journey, the space he will look back on when he has taken his thousandth step, when he has found William Hastings, and which mark the beginning of his descent into whatever hell this will be.

He takes one last look at Marton, at Wymmys's men who are running like chickens, and he is satisfied none of them are thinking yet of revenge, and then he swings up into the saddle.

'Come on, then,' he says. 'Let's go and find Lord Hastings, shall we?'

15

They stay in an inn that night where the innkeeper cannot pronounce his Rs and he suggests that men are crying out for a change and if the Earl of 'Wowick' can bring it to them, then no one can blame them for wanting it so. The beds are unnaturally cold, as if they've been cursed, and there is an owl in the rafters somewhere that makes bloodcurdling noises that keep Rufus awake though not Alice.

The place they are in does not really have a name, and they leave it after prayers and ride through wide-open flat country, silvered by acres of monastic stock ponds guarded by men in conical huts who have no news, but point them the way to Doncaster where the bells are ringing out for Michaelmas. Thomas tries not to think about what he would be doing in Marton this very moment.

They stay that night in Doncaster.

'Best place for news,' the innkeeper tells them. 'Everyone must pass through Doncaster.'

He charges them for a whole room and then tries to make them share the bed with an apprentice feather merchant who has never drunk wine before but does so tonight because his master is doing right well out of all this.

'All what?' Thomas asks.

'Everyone is after fletchings. Everyone. Feathers weigh more than gold, my master always says, and even Lord Montagu has placed an order, secretly like, so that King Edward does not learn his business.'

'Why would – why would King Edward learn his business?'

But the boy is asleep at the board before he's made much sense of himself and in the morning he's still there, unable to speak and stinking of vomit. Thomas goes to see to the horses. He is beginning to think waiting is pointless, and that they ought to push straight on to York, but the ostler shows him that his horse is slightly lame in the rear leg.

'Carrying too much, master. You don't want to overload a horse like this. Give it a few days and he'll be right as rain.'

So they are to be stuck in Doncaster. Thomas hopes the innkeeper is right, and that everyone comes through the town eventually.

'Oh yes,' the ostler says. 'We get 'em all. Two days ago I got a fellow on his way to join Montagu; yesterday I got a fellow who said he was getting out of it.'

'Why?'

'Oh, didn't want to join Montagu in going over to Warwick. Said he remembered King Edward with kindness, and never liked old King Henry all that much anyway.'

Thomas feels disappointment like a punch in the stomach. He leaves the man grumbling about something and goes to find Katherine, who's trying keep Rufus occupied while she feeds Alice.

'Montagu has deserted King Edward,' he tells her. He feels sick.

'We always said he would,' she says, 'when King Edward gave away his title.'

It is true, but it doesn't help. They sit in silence for a bit. Thomas tries to think what it might mean, Montagu finally going over to his brother Warwick. He wishes he could speak to Flood or

Wilkes, who would know how many men such and such had, and in what condition the road to York was, and how King Edward will react when turned upon by his own subjects – again.

'What will we do now?' Katherine asks. 'If King Edward can't help us?'

Thomas doesn't know. He had placed all his hopes on Hastings, and without King Edward, Hastings is powerless. The full horror of his predicament unfolds before him and all he can do is refuse to believe it.

'But Montagu was always loyal,' he says. 'Even last year.'

'He was the Earl of Northumberland last year.'

'Perhaps we should ride to York,' he says. 'Perhaps there will be better news there?'

She nods.

They leave before noon, ignoring the ostler's advice, and take the road for Pontefract, but a few miles out of the town, the innkeeper is proved right. Everyone must come through Doncaster. The first they see of King Edward is a body of his men on the road, riding towards them with purpose.

'Are there any flags?' he asks Katherine.

'I can't make anything out.'

'We'd best get off the road,' he says and they ride into some poplars whose leaves are on the turn. The riders approach and sweep by, moving heads down at an efficient trot. They are King Edward's men, Thomas sees, about ten of them, carrying his standard, but they are in dirt-smutted riding cloaks, and they look ragged and tense, their horses sweat-flecked and tired.

Thomas and Katherine exchange a look. Oh Christ, he thinks, she's right: we can't rely on King Edward for help.

'Will King Edward come now?' Rufus asks.

'Yes,' Thomas tells him, and they wait under the trees and a few moments later they see the road from the north filling with men and horses. There are many more flags above this body but there's something about the shape of them – perhaps the way the flags are carried – that lets you know this isn't an army advancing on their enemy, but rather one in retreat.

Please God, Thomas prays, let this not be the King.

But it is, and with his arrival, their hopes finally die. To begin with come more heralds but their finery can only be glimpsed under travelling cloaks, for they are grimly hunched over their horses' withers, and they ride at that same efficient trot, with much on their minds. Thomas recognises Flood and nudges his horse forward, but Flood doesn't hear his greeting, and is gone by the time Thomas reaches the roadside. Behind them come a mob of men likewise cloaked and on good horses, and Thomas recognises one or two of them from the night he spent in Fotheringhay.

Then comes Edward, King of England, all in blue above his riding boots, with a fur-lined cloak that ripples as if the creatures who provided their skins were still alive, and there is a feather in his cap, but while that looks spritely, he looks mutinous, ashamed, humiliated, and as if he might kill the next man to cross him.

'Dear Christ,' Thomas breathes, because he recognises a beaten man.

'Hastings!' Katherine says, pointing.

Hastings rides with Wilkes, a little further behind. He is fraught but not thunderous, Thomas would say, and unlike King Edward he is at least paying attention to what is around him. When he sees Thomas waiting at the roadside, he cocks his head in surprise.

'Thomas!' he says. 'Master Everingham!'

'Sir,' Thomas says. 'Lord Hastings.'

Wilkes nods his greeting from under the brow of his black cap, and Thomas is somehow reassured by his presence. He is almost unrecognisable in a russet coat such as a farmer might wear, and low brown boots. Hastings cuts across him to greet Thomas. Wilkes pulls up too.

'Great God above,' Hastings says with a tired smile. 'It is good to see you. And you too, Mistress Everingham! When last we saw you, you were in childbed, and I give thanks to God that you are up and about, and with such pleasant reward for your labour.'

He even greets Rufus by name, and this meeting might be happy happenstance, were it not for the men gathering behind.

'Come on, William!' a man behind calls. Others are trying to get past. They are all in various threads of finery, but it is clear they have travelled some way, and have yet further to go, and they are already worn ragged.

Hastings nudges his horse into the long grass of the verge.

'So you've heard of our plight?' he asks Thomas, and Thomas nods.

'Something,' he admits. He is suddenly distracted by the sight of the end of the column: he can already see it. There can't even be three hundred of them.

'Is this it?' he cannot help himself asking. 'There are no men following on?'

Hastings sighs and shakes his head.

'They cleared off when they heard Montagu was coming after us with his power from the north, and that bloody old Warwick was coming up from the south. They didn't want to be caught between. On one hand you can hardly blame them, but on the other, I do.'

There is an awkward moment while they watch the men ride by.

'So you have come to join us, Master Everingham?' Wilkes

asks, even though he clearly knows the answer. 'You have come to share our hardship in our hour of need?'

Thomas opens and shuts his mouth. Hastings's laugh is rueful.

'Ah! There was some service you hoped I might do for you? Well. Ride with us, Thomas, and you too, Mistress Everingham, if you've a mind, and tell us how once we might have helped.'

Thomas tells them the bare bones of his story.

'*Jesu Christe*,' Hastings murmurs, looking at him askance when he brings it to an abrupt end. 'A cleric?'

Thomas can only shrug.

'With a very fine hand,' Wilkes adds.

'And how did you come to – to be in Calais?' Hastings wonders, but you can see him setting the answer aside to ponder properly at leisure, over a bottle perhaps, and around a fire.

'It is a long story, sir,' Thomas says.

'And I look forward to hearing it,' Hastings says, 'but perhaps now it is time I caught up with King Edward, if I am to help divert his wrath from the good people of Doncaster.'

'Where are we going?' Thomas asks Wilkes when Hastings has gone on ahead.

'Anywhere that is away from Lord Montagu,' Wilkes tells him.

'And who – who are we?'

'We are down to those who cannot hope for terms with the Earl of Warwick, or the old Queen,' Wilkes tells him. 'We are a merry band of brothers, or brothers-in-law, at any rate. Lord Say is with us, and my lord of Worcester too.'

Wilkes is telling him something, but Thomas doesn't know what, and so says nothing. He feels a little coolness ripple down his spine. The Earl of Worcester was the man who questioned him last year about the ledger. He was also the man who impaled the sailors on the dock at Southampton.

'But where are we going really, Wilkes?'

'Norfolk,' he tells them. 'He is our last hope, for the moment.'

They ride on, back through the gatehouse into Doncaster, where the people have turned out to see the King come, but the atmosphere is very uncertain. They stand and watch and at any moment they might throw flowers, coins, rotten cabbages, offal, anything. There is some relief among King Edward's men when they've left, taking the road to Gainsborough, where the little army crosses the river by the ferry and here again word spreads quickly, and the townspeople come out to watch King Edward pass in almost total silence.

They sleep that night at Thomas Burgh's new hall, though he himself is not there, and nor, Thomas is pleased to see, is the watchman. Various men come and go through the night and Wilkes, who has changed from his dowdy garb into a very fine green brigandine and lustrous hunting boots, is forever bustling about the place, organising horses for men and messages, and by morning the news is confirmed as the worst it could be.

Thomas and Katherine seek out William Hastings, who is brisk.

'Warwick has brought the whole country out in favour of the old King,' he tells them. 'And if we are taken, we cannot hope for the same deal as last time. No more pleasant hunting in Middleham.'

'What about the Duke of Norfolk?'

Hastings pulls a face.

'We can but try,' he says. It is all frustratingly vague. They set out eastwards, anyway, following a road that winds through gentle wolds until the trees become steadily scrubbier and the land flattens and it is as if it rushes to the horizon. The soil turns to slop beneath their horses' hooves, and they ride amid heaving rush banks where a punt is more use than a horse, where the gulls shriek, and the air smells of corruption and fish guts. It all feels familiar to Thomas, the way the east wind cuts your face and pulls your clothes.

'Christ,' Hastings says. 'Are you sure this is the way?'

They come to a dark steep-sided river that snakes through the mud, and there seems no point in crossing it, for there is nothing but more mud on the other side. So they backtrack to where the trees grow and follow a winding path south. King Edward rides before them with his head sunk on his chest. Thomas wonders if they have not lost quite a few men overnight.

'Down to about a hundred, I'd say,' Wilkes agrees.

They ride all that day, following paths that link them to fords over silt-thick rivers through the black mud. At one point they come to a village where they find a child standing by a dead pony, and a dog that barks at them, and here they must take turns in a small ferry across a fast-running river and the boys on the oars tell them there is all sorts going on.

'Men riding this way and that,' one of them says, and he goes on to describe the star that the men wore on their livery. The Earl of Oxford. Thomas wonders if it is Brougham. The boys say there are many hundreds besides, in all liveries.

At this news, more men melt away from King Edward's party, and by the time they have crossed the river, they are down to about seventy men.

'Intimate,' is how Wilkes describes it.

'Select,' Hastings concedes.

They ask the boatman what lies south. After a long pause he says:

'Lynn.'

'Lynn?'

'Aye. South. Across the Wash, though. Dangerous. Less you know what you're doing. Where you're going. Tides and that.'

279

Thomas sees King Edward and Hastings consult with the Earl of Worcester, whose gaze is yet to seek him out, and with a few of the other lords. They look anxious, harried, scared even, and some men – ten or more perhaps – take their leave, but what choice do King Edward and his closest advisers have? They cannot go back, or westwards for fear of Montagu, so southwards to the Wash and Lynn it is.

Thomas wonders if they should abandon King Edward too, but for what?

'Dry land?' Katherine says.

She has a point.

But they press on with Hastings, and Hastings seems pleased.

'We'll come through this, Mistress Everingham, and I am sure the Duke of Norfolk will have new linen for Alice. In fact, it shall be my priority to see it done. Wilkes will remind me.'

Wilkes smiles his enigmatic little smile.

The land is now very wet and fissured with streams that slow and divert them, and they often come to dead ends and must retrace their steps. It takes all afternoon, and it is only getting muddier and wetter with each stride, until at last they are in a shimmering mud flat that stretches as far as the eye can see.

'The Wash,' someone says.

'We must stop,' another says. 'My horse is done in.'

'But we can't stop here,' one of them says. 'Look: the tide's coming in.'

They all look around. There is nowhere dry, as where to rest the horses.

'There will be something, surely? Over there.' The man points. 'There' is on the horizon, many miles hence but what choice do they have?

'I hope my lord of Norfolk has baths for us all,' one man says.

They have been slipping in and out of the mud and the water all day, picking their way through deep sloughs of stinking salty ooze. The mud stinks and seagulls shriek. The way is getting wetter, the mud sloppier, and they are beginning to sink deeper. They dismount to spare the horses. Every step is an effort. One of the horses goes down and they cannot get it up. It is panicking and lashing out. A man nocks his bow, and then an arrow, and he passes it to the mud-covered horse's owner to shoot. It is a waste of an arrow, but it is better than seeing such an animal drown in mud.

'Sorry,' his owner says, standing apart, tears in his pale-lashed eyes.

On they go. They are knee-deep now. The water shimmers as it moves and rises. The evening is undeniable now.

'What about over there?' Katherine says. She has always had good eyes, Katherine, and she has seen some kind of hut, or shack, on the gentlest rise of an islet. They surge towards it, dragging their horses.

Another one goes down, its owner wailing with pity.

Then it is a man. He slips and splashes in the dark water, and his harness takes him down with only a murky swirl in the oily waters to mark his passing.

Everyone stops.

'Can anyone swim?'

None can.

After a while King Edward crosses himself. The others do likewise. They turn and wade on through the churning slop until at length they are at the island, mud up to their thighs, the horses really suffering, and it is only now they see they've made a mistake. There are two islands, and the hut – perhaps an eel-trapper's – is on the second island, across a swiftly growing sea. They cannot cross. They see the eel farmer or whatever he is has pulled up his boats – two punts, one larger than the other – on to the shore under his shack, by which is a huge pile of eel traps. Smoke drifts from the seams of the hut.

They shout for the man to come out. There are only the screams of the gulls in response. They shout again.

At last the eel-trapper comes out. He has a boy with him. He is startled and suspicious, and Thomas hopes he does not have a bow with which to chase them away, though of course he must, somewhere.

He shouts to asks what they want. The man the others call Chamberlain tells him. No one is very hopeful this will work, but no one has an alternative solution. Eventually the eel farmer agrees to come over with his boy and ferry them to his island, where at least it is dry. He unties his punt and pushes off with a pole, and Thomas is taken by strange swirling memories that make him shiver with fear.

The eel farmer stares from his boat as it noses through the slop. 'Gentles,' he says, and Thomas cannot guess if he is noting them as such, or addressing them, but Hastings now steps forward past King Edward, who is standing with his fists balled on his hips, staring at a subject who for now is richer than him. Hastings greets the man respectfully and explains their need to cross this inland sea, and their need of shelter. He indicates the hut.

'There is not nearly room enough for you,' the eel farmer tells them. His life does not require the exchange of many words, Thomas supposes, and he is hard to understand.

'That needn't matter,' Hastings says, 'so long as we are out of the actual water.' He lifts a boot from the mud that pours brown water from its seam.

They spend the time until it is finally too dark to see ferrying King Edward and the others across to the island, but they must leave the horses amid much fretting as to their hooves and general health on this low island. The punts are surprisingly large, but sit low in the water because they are for carrying eel traps and rushes, not men.

When they are on the island itself, Thomas sees how small the hut is. It is made with only two or perhaps three people in mind, with a broad step around it, like a jetty, and inside he sees that perhaps a hundred gold-skinned eels hang from its rafters slowly turning in smoke rising from the smouldering fire below. The whole hut is a smokery, he sees, and this is where the man sleeps. Christ, what a life. No wonder he has no wife. He looks at him again, closely, and he even looks like an eel, with a broad slash of a downturned mouth and – can it be? – sharp teeth. His skin is smoked too, though it has not turned the beautiful gold of the eels.

King Edward and the nobles sleep within, packed in alongside the eel farmer and his boy while the rest of them sleep on the rough boards of the jetty outside. Thomas sees the whole building is made from driftwood, taken from wrecked ships perhaps, and lashed together with oddments of rope, likewise sourced.

He helps Katherine over with Alice, while he carries Rufus. Katherine falls asleep that night with Alice wrapped in her travelling cloak, in Thomas's arms, while Rufus leans against him as if he were a tree. He is grateful to be so tired his mind does not continue churning through the events of the last few days, and they wake shivering at dawn. As the mist lifts none of them have ever seen a sunrise like it and they stand and gape and they take it as proof of the power of the Almighty.

As the light grows, though, and the others emerge from the hut, they see what has happened: the sea has retreated beyond the horizon and they are surrounded by a sea of foul grey mud that stretches as far as the eye can see.

'Christ!' is all King Edward can say when he sees it and the others just stand in a line and stare out southwards across the sea of mud. Alice is shrieking with the need to change her linen, and Katherine tries to clean her in a bucket of chilly brackish water, which only makes her scream the more.

'Do you think he will take us to the shore when the sea comes in?' Hastings wonders. 'His boats are – not really sea-worthy?'

The eel-trapper is sitting eating – something – in his punt, a little way off. He is shaken, perhaps, by having so many people invade his island, and perhaps by having seen the man appointed by God to rule over the country taking a shit from the end of his jetty.

Thomas asks him what the distant band of land that crowns that horizon is.

'Castle Rising,' he says.

'Castle Rising!' Hastings says. 'I have hunted there. My God. We are so close and yet . . .' He looks around him. 'This is like exile. Standing up to our nethers in tidal waters, waiting for a lift.'

'Master,' Thomas calls to the eel man, 'when the tide is in, would you take us there? In your boats?'

The eel-trapper is alarmed.

'How could I manage that? I have only two, and there is only the boy and me. And you are fifty, say, with horses.'

'Forty,' Hastings calls. 'And we would give you our horses.'

'No we bloody wouldn't,' one of them snarls.

'Shut up, Say,' King Edward tells him. 'You can have them all.'

'What would I want with so many horses?'

'Each one is worth more than – than anything and everything you can see from here.'

The eel man takes his time to think.

'It'll not be easy,' he says.

'No,' Hastings says. 'But think of the profit. A day's work. It will set you up for life and beyond.'

'I don't know.'

They all know to be quiet now. Thomas watches the man's eyes widen as he calculates the profit.

'I'll do it,' he says. 'I want the saddles too, though.'

King Edward wafts his hand. It is done. If the eel man can get the horses off the island, and to a market, before they die, he will be wealthy beyond his wildest imaginings, but the men are naturally reluctant to lose their horses.

'Can we not just ride out?' one asks. 'There must be a causeway. I heard there was a causeway. Where is the causeway?'

The eel-trapper looks at this one – again, it is Lord Say – and tells him there is a causeway, about five bowshots that way. He is welcome to try to get there, but ought to know that once he is caught in the mud, there is no way to save him from drowning in it.

'So we are stuck here? Until when?'

'The tide comes in.'

'How long will that be?'

'Noon, I'd say.'

King Edward goes down to the muddy rim and faces the sea. He holds his arms aloft and shouts at the sea, ordering it to come in. He has forgotten the name of the Danish King who tried to stop it doing just that, though, and has to explain it to Lord Say, so his joke is not so funny as it might have been.

'Cnut,' Wilkes murmurs. Hastings laughs.

'I heard that,' Say says.

Wilkes says nothing.

One of the others wonders that King Edward can make a joke at a time like this, 'when everything is in ruins'.

The morning wears on. The mist rises so that there is a band of something else between the clouds and the horizon. Gulls call. Everyone is cold and wet and hungry.

'Have an eel,' someone says.

'Not exactly moreish, are they?' a man they call Rivers volunteers.

The brooding King returns to the mud's edge in silence, and every man there descends into gloom, staring at the mud between his feet. The hobbled horses shiver and snort on the far island. They must be starving, Thomas thinks, and they look done in.

At last, when it might or might not be noon, the gorges in the mud start to fill and the surface seems to liquefy and unset and then at last the nose of the punt lifts from the bed. King Edward goes in the first boat, with Worcester, Hastings, Say and four others. Others in another boat. Between the eel farmer in his punt and his boy in his, they can take fifteen. Each trip takes as long as a sung Mass, well over an hour. At last Thomas and Katherine carry Rufus and Alice aboard the boy's boat with Wilkes and two or three others, one of whom tells him he is an alchemist, of all the things they need right now. Thomas volunteers to relieve the boy of his punting, and so he stands up there on the back and is assailed by strange sensations and looks to Katherine for confirmation that he has done this before. She is asleep.

They do not appear to be making much progress as they meander across the choppy brew of the shallow water, roughly southward, but after a while ships' masts can be seen ahead, and then their hulls. Merchants' cogs and carracks, gathered against unseen quays, or slipping from the shore out to sea, or coming in from the east with sails dropped.

'A channel,' the alchemist says as if he has divined a secret.

Thomas thinks he might be simple, but then the boy tells them they ought not get caught in the channel's current or it will take them out to sea to drown.

Alice wakes with a cry and Katherine tries to feed her and the alchemist makes some comments about transformation of one body to another, and he tries not to look as she arranges herself, and at last they come in to the port of Lynn, where the bulbous merchantmen are tethered to the stone and wood staithes, being loaded and unloaded by hurrying porters and swinging cranes. Once they have found a place to land, they are greeted with some concern by the porters on the stone-built quayside, who sense a profit to be made from sodden, mud-stained gentles coming in on eel-trappers' punts. Soon sodden silks are swapped for dry russets.

The eel man is there, and tells them it has already taken them too long, and the tide is on the turn, and that if they want to get out of the harbour before noon the next day then they'd best find a boat and pay its captain to set his sails now.

'What about the others?' Hastings gestures at the island.

'Too late for them tonight,' the eel man says. 'Have to bring 'em over tomorrow.'

'But you've another three hours before the tide goes out,' Thomas reminds him.

'I can't leave my horses there, can I?'

'A man has to look after his investments,' Wilkes agrees, and the thought of those ten lords left out there for another night obviously pleases him. It means the King's party is down to barely thirty now. He'd not even have gone hawking with so few men in the past.

They thank the eel man, and wish him and his boy luck, and they watch them push off, out across the wind-dimpled waters, rich beyond imagination, if they can only get the horses to land.

Hastings has found a boat willing to give them passage: a hulk, with a single mast that has been oft-repaired, and an Easterling for a master who is as lean as a blade and speaks in a strong accent that no Englishmen could ever understand.

'It is the best we could find,' Hastings tells Thomas. The other shipmasters are busy, either loading or unloading their cargoes, or overseeing repairs or haggling with a sailmaker, or their ships are already full of sarplers of sheep wool or broadcloths they are taking down to Calais or across to the ports of Flanders. None are in a hurry to set sail.

'They say there are pirates,' Rivers says, 'and a fleet from the Hanse who do not love our King Edward.'

The Easterling master is taking wool and cloth over to somewhere no one quite catches, but he has agreed to fit a few of them aboard, so long as it is understood that quarters are tight, and that the money needs to be good. It is. Some coins are dug out from somewhere, but they are not enough, and at length men must twist rings off their fingers.

'A man must make a living,' the master says with a shrug.

Thomas sees that Katherine is hollowed out with all this, but she tells him it is Alice who is not well; her linen was filled with something green this morning, she says, and its smell was fishy.

'Should we take a crossing? With her so ill?'

They look around.

'What else can we do? What else is there?'

They walk down the staithe together, to where the gangplank is lowered. The master is up by the tiller of his boat, gesturing for them to hurry so that he can catch the ebbing tide. They climb aboard, Thomas carrying Rufus, and they find the master has provided them with food, though they must pay for it, of course.

It is a small ship, with a crew of five, and its open hold is packed with huge sausages in skins of waxed linen under layers of tarred canvas that the master is taking back to a place that he calls Damme. King Edward knows of it, and approves. Meanwhile the townsmen and -women have come out to see the sight of King Edward quitting his realm and at first there is much confusion, incredulity and surprise on the dockside, but that gives way to some grumbled complaints and even jeering. It is only the presence of Earl Rivers, of whom this crowd seems to know, that keeps things from being thrown and the situation deteriorating into the sort of violence that leaves men with no fingers or noses.

It is decided that the Earl of Worcester will not come with them, but will ride with two of the other men to his properties in Huntingdon to see if he might raise troops, perhaps, and so their number dwindles further.

'Thanks be to God,' Thomas says.

Wilkes gives him a small smile. It is hard to tell what he's thinking, but it's definitely something.

The boat is untied, heavy ropes thrown aboard and coiled and then the crew push off with poles, and a boat full of oarsmen takes them out into the main channel of current-slicked brown water, where the ship's yard is raised and the sailors clamber along it to drop the sail. It hangs limply for a good long while, and then fattens with a ruffling thump, and the ship quickens underfoot.

The land begins to slide by, and soon the flat shoulders of sand and scrub on either side part further, and they beat out across the darkening sea. Every man gathers at the stern with the master at his tiller, and they watch England slip behind and there is silence on board, save for the piteous wail of Alice in Katherine's arms, and soon that noise is lost among the slap of the waves against the hull and the grinding creak that the various ropes and stays give off as they plunge through the roughening sea.

When England is gone beyond the horizon, men turn and find such corners as there are to be found in a boat, in which to sleep as best they can. King Edward offers Katherine his cloak and she is reluctant to take it for it is incomparably fine, and she knows she will ruin it, but he smiles and says the sumptuary laws do not apply at sea, and so after a moment she accepts it on Rufus's and Alice's behalf.

'You must return it though,' he says with a smile, 'for it is all I own. All that's left of my kingdom.'

16

Katherine wakes to a cold grey world, full of foul smells. Alice is still asleep, thanks be to God, having exhausted herself crying in the night, and she lies crooked in Katherine's arm, and for a long while Katherine dare not risk moving, despite the pain that grips her shoulder and her back from lying on the wooden deck and holding her all night.

'Thomas,' she whispers, but she cannot see him and he doesn't hear her. She can feel someone – Rufus? – pressing into her back, and she can feel him snoring, even if she cannot hear him above the slap and bang and gurgle of the sea just the other side of the planks. She looks up. The sail above still bulges with the trapped wind, and the ship feels to be surging ahead. Above is a perfect gauze of grey autumn sky. She closes her eyes, and longs to return to her dreams until this nightmare is over, but God does not grant her this release, and so, when she can stand it no longer, she levers herself upright, her numb arms still enfolding the baby as best she can and she leaves Rufus in the King's wonderful cloak, and she takes a few staggering steps to find relief and Thomas.

When she has managed the ladder up on to the aft deck, the sea below is heaving, grey-green and endlessly turbulent. Banks of mist shroud any horizon. Thomas is sitting with Wilkes and the alchemist, likewise called Thomas, at the stern of the boat, next to the master, who has been awake all night. The alchemist is telling

Thomas something and Thomas is nodding. When he sees her he comes to help. She makes her way over to him and he offers her his place next to the alchemist, and then volunteers to take the baby because she needs to relieve herself.

When she is back, Alice is awake, blinking and quiet, and Thomas smiles up at her as if he has some wonderful skill with babies, but then Alice starts crying again, and he looks up at her differently, and she thinks: It is always on me, isn't it? But that is the way God intended it, as a punishment for Eve's sin, and so she takes the baby and rearranges her dress and tries to feed Alice, who again will not latch on, even while she is sitting there, and the alchemist loses his thread and they sit in silence a moment, before Thomas tells her they are still running east on a good wind, and there is bread and ale for breakfast.

'It is good to see we are not alone,' she says, 'even out here.'

They do not understand her until she points to the ships that lie well to the south, about five of them, sails up. A moment later the watch sees them and shouts something in his odd Easterling tongue. The master swears and an argument ensues between him and the mate, who, Katherine guesses, wishes to drop his sail and come to terms with the boats, but the master, who knows he will only collect the rest of his fare if he can land King Edward and his men, is adamant and he leans on the tiller so that they describe a curve in the water and veer away from the approaching fleet, which numbers perhaps eight now.

'Who are they?' Thomas asks Hastings, who has joined them.

'A fleet from the Hanse.'

'What do they want with us?'

'They may not want anything with us,' Hastings suggests, 'but if they know King Edward is aboard, and they might well, then they will be very eager to lay their hands on him. He has been . . .

inconsiderate, shall we say, as to their persons and goods in the Steelyard.'

Is there anyone King Edward has not riled? Katherine wonders. She looks down at the rank of faces leaning over the gunwale of the ship, staring south, and there is King Edward, his cheeks mottled by the wind, his hair wet with salt spray. She wonders what she would make of him if she did not know he was King Edward. She would be impressed, she supposes, were she a man. And that is the odd thing. How has it come to this? How have so many Englishmen turned against him? What has he done, or not done, to alienate them so?

The cog is not fast. They can hear its bow battering against the waves at the front and the crew keep looking at the mast to see if it will hold the press of the sail, and then back to the Hanse fleet that now numbers perhaps eleven and is settling in behind, as if following their wake, predatory, like hunting dogs.

'We are now heading northeast,' the alchemist tells them as if this matters.

'If we can get into Burgundian waters, we should be – we should be all right,' Hastings supposes.

'Will they have cannon?' Thomas asks.

'No,' Hastings says. 'No cannon.'

The first shot is a tiny crack in the distance, a little puff of smoke that is snatched away from the bow of the leading ship behind. They do not even see where the ball goes.

The master laughs grimly and says something he thinks funny.

'He says it cost them a florin!' the mate translates.

The wind is good and strong and the boats batter their way through waters that are the colour of split flint, and only the fleet of the Hanse gives any sense of scale to what they see.

Men are arguing about which direction they are sailing in,

though. The wind is taking them north; they want to go east, to make landfall near Bruges, where they hope to attract the help of Duke Charles of Burgundy, who is married to King Edward's sister.

'We will have a long walk to find him if we continue north,' Lord Say calls.

'That is if the Duke will even see us,' Hastings adds.

King Edward raises his wet eyebrows a few times.

'He'll come around,' he shouts. 'My sister is persuasive, you know, and if Warwick aligns himself with France, then Duke Charles will do all he can to upset his shitty little apple cart. He'll give us five hundred *écus* a month, and all the rabbit we care to eat!'

Lord Say does not look impressed.

There is another gunshot, slightly louder. All heads turn.

'They are gaining.'

'Or they have a bigger gun,' Wilkes observes.

Then there is a shout from the snub-nosed bow.

'Land,' the master calls with a tight smile.

'But where is it?'

No one knows. They gather at the bow to see if they recognise anything. To Katherine's eye it looks just like the place they have left.

'Have we not done a circle in the night?' she asks.

Alice is crying again. Constant on off, on off. The men look perturbed so Katherine takes her away and tries to feed her but she still will not take the nipple. Katherine can feel the girl's fists pushing her away, and her screams rack her whole body, and everything is stiff, from her toes to her tongue. Christ. What is wrong with her? Katherine lays her down on the cloak and tries to change her linen. Her backside and legs are very red, and the linen is stained bright brown, if that is a colour, and the smell is still of fish. It looks more like snot, though, than baby shit.

What does it mean? Katherine asks herself. She doesn't know, but it cannot be good.

Thomas comes down, hesitant and awkward, as if this has nothing to do with him and he might not be welcome. She shows him the linens. He takes them and washes them in a bucket and when he returns he has some goose fat from the mate.

'It is what he uses on his face,' he says.

Katherine wipes it on Alice's bottom and legs and she howls piteously. Thomas removes his jacket, his pourpoint and then his shirt, just as if he were getting into bed, but then he puts his pourpoint and jacket back on and cuts his shirt into strips and they re-dress Alice with that. When the girl is clothed again, Katherine picks her up and sees the white fur of King Edward's cloak is stained. She shrugs. Thomas shrugs.

Alice quietens after a while.

Rufus sits next to them this whole time, with his knees by his chin, watching, but now he is distracted by something in the shadows that's probably a rat. Overhead the wind is strong now, and the sail is bowed and the mast creaks where two pieces join and are bound around with rope. They do not talk about what they will do when they land. What is the point?

Hastings looks down and tilts his head to ask if there is anything he can do. Where is his wife? Katherine wonders. Where are all their wives? Their children? All safe at home, she supposes, even the Queen who is in the Tower, though she did hear King Edward say she would take herself to sanctuary. At least they have homes to leave their wives in. What has she? Nothing.

From somewhere, Hastings has produced an apple for Rufus, and he climbs down and hands it to him apologetically.

'Best I can do,' he says. 'We'll soon make land. Or be taken by those bastards. Either way, something will occur.'

Thomas gets up and takes the baby from Katherine, just to give her some time perhaps, and he tucks her under his arm and clambers up to the aft rail. Men make room for him. The baby is shrieking in bleats. He tucks her under his jacket and hushes her and the men sort of offer her comfort by patting her and she can hear them murmuring half-hearted advice.

Katherine could weep.

After a while, though, she asks Rufus if he'd like to go up and watch what is happening. He bobs his head and then comes with her up the ladder and along to stand next to the men. The deck is greasy. She has the cloak folded over her arms, hiding the stain.

The Hanse boats are much closer now, but so is the green stripe of land. It is just like Lynn, more to even than before but it vanishes into the wide, wide sea to the north. The master tells the mate something, and the mate tells them that since this boat is shallow, and the Hanse boats are probably not, then he will make for a channel at the southern end of the island.

'That is an island?'

'Yes.'

'He knows these waters,' the mate says, but he too sounds doubtful. The master waves away their doubts, but it seems they are heading straight for land; a pointed triangular dune of piled sand. They will be beached. The master moves the tiller over and the boat yaws and loses some of its way, but that is the risk of cutting this line.

'You have no bows?' the mate asks them.

They look at him as if he is mad. Of course they have no bows.

'Englishmen without their bows,' he says as if wonders will never cease.

There is another gunshot. And now they see the ball – perhaps the size of her fist, Katherine supposes, that slushes through the heaving waters behind. Again the master laughs. But then the bigger gun goes off and the ball thrums overhead. The master stops laughing and swears and they all shrink an inch or two and concentrate on prayers that will speed the ship towards those shallow dimpled waters, and the channel the master promised.

'He is mad,' Lord Say announces.

And Katherine sees each man look for something to hold on to when the moment of impact comes.

'Drop the sail,' Hastings mutters. 'For the love of God.'

But at the very last minute, sure enough, there is a channel, hidden behind the pyramid of sand, which turns out to be a smaller island.

'Ha!' Lord Say says, as if he knew it was so, and he claps the master on the shoulder. The master does not like being touched and spits something the meaning of which no one misunderstands.

The channel is very narrow, though, and they are cutting it very fine, she cannot help think. The mate runs to the bow and pushes aside those gathered there. He shouts back instructions and the master adjusts their line. Then he glances over his shoulder at the Hanse ships, which are still coming on, gaining very quickly now, so that they can see the men fussing around the barrel of the gun in the first boat's bow.

'Come on,' Say mutters.

King Edward stretches out a soothing hand.

At that moment it seems the ugly little ship is taken by the hand of God, for she moves unnaturally under them, as if cupped from below. The master shouts an instruction, the two crewmen drop the yard and the boat is suddenly no more than a stick in a stream, flowing in, shooting quickly past that first island and into a channel between two more stretches of sand piled in dunes. The master whips his head around to see – and there! The leading boat in the Hanse fleet has headed up; its bow swings around to the north and the others behind swing away too.

The master roars with pleasure and shakes his fists. 'You milk-sops! You cowards! You square headed-bastards!'

And then they are thrown jolting sideways, and every man is knocked off his feet.

They've run aground.

PART THREE

Den Haag, Holland,
Before Advent, 1470

17

They have been in The Hague for nearly two months now, living mostly all together in the upper rooms of a brick-built house belonging to a gentle whose name none can pronounce to his satisfaction, but whom they call Groot-hoose, and whose servants provide them with a few green logs, lots of rabbits – already skinned and gutted – very bitter beer and very dark bread. All day, each day, they have sat in their quarters, waiting for something to happen, and nothing has, and there is nothing they can do to make it happen, and with each day, as Advent has approached, it has grown ever colder and so now, with Christmastide next week, the earth rings like iron and the wind that comes in off the sea is sharp enough to flay your skin.

'*Dank u*,' Thomas says to the woman behind the stall, and he pays for his bread with a tiny coin. She is not noticeably grateful. In fact they are becoming resentful, these Flemings, of having so many ragged Englishmen with not much money and very little to do wandering the streets in their threadbare clothes, not precisely begging but making everyone feel uncomfortable with what they have. And it will only get worse the longer it goes on and the colder it gets, that they all know.

Thomas hurries back with the bread that is still warm, pressing it to him under his frowsy coat, all the way back to the grand house where they are encouraged not to use the front door unless they

301

are with King Edward, and he stamps up the back steps in his rough-hewn clogs and in through the door where the servants watch him as if he is somehow unchristian.

Katherine is in one of the upper chambers where there is a chimney hearth, but wood for the fire is scarce and so they rarely manage a fire, and must instead rely on heat rising from the floor below, where the state rooms are, and where there is a fire all the time. It is there that King Edward sleeps with Lord Hastings and often has two beautiful women from the town who are there to warm their bed at night, but are only ever seen in the coming and the going.

'How is he?' Thomas asks.

'He does fair enough,' she says.

She is mopping Rufus's sticky brow with rose water to keep him cool and there are sweet-smelling herbs strewn about the place, but still, the room smells terrible: of human shit from a very sickly body.

'Will he be able to eat anything?' Thomas asks. 'I have bread – here – and I can get soup.'

Katherine sits back on her haunches and sighs.

'It goes straight through him,' she says.

'Ale then?'

'He finds it so bitter.'

Thomas frowns.

'But if he is thirsty enough?'

'Perhaps,' she says.

She looks terrible, he thinks. Her dress, once her best, is puckered with repairs, her face has lost all its accustomed flesh, and the whites of her eyeballs are the colour of old bone. Her hands, too, have become like talons, and her neck might snap with the weight of her head it is so thin. He puts his hand on her shoulder. He can feel her bones. She places her hand over his, her fingers icy, and she tries to smile, but she is so tired.

'You should eat something,' he says.

'Yes,' she says, and she picks at the bread with those bony fingers.

'I will get soup for dinner,' he tells her.

She nods. She does not take her eyes off Rufus, who seems peaceful enough, though his skin has a waxy sheen.

'There is no news from anywhere,' he says.

Again she nods. Thomas sits on a stool and tries some of the bread. It is dense, but it has plenty of salt in it, and he does not mind it as the others seem to, or the bitter beer.

'I wish we still had the King's cloak,' Thomas says, seeing her shiver.

She says it is not so bad. At least Rufus is warm. But it will get worse in February, that is what they all say. They say if you think it is bad now, wait until February.

He tells her he will go again and see if he can't find some drift-wood on the sea's shore today.

'Don't get wet,' Katherine says.

He tells her he won't.

Rufus moans in his sleep and they both tense, but then he seems to subside, and they ease.

'Do you think it will ever end?' she asks.

'It has to, some time.'

She looks sceptical.

'They say Duke Charles will call King Edward to Bruges,' Thomas tells her, 'and then things will get better.'

'Yes,' she says, but her voice and conviction are hollow and they lapse into silence again.

Later that day Thomas leaves Katherine sleeping, and he walks out of the little town and over the ridge to the broad strip of beach. Here the snow is gone, and the wind is strong and cold off the sea, filled with mineral sea spray and fine sand that scours the skin and stings the eyes. He walks down to the line of the curling waves and follows the dark wet sand until he finds a branch of wood stripped clean, like deer antlers, caught in the surf, and he drags it out and a little way up the beach. Then he stops and turns and, after a moment, he sits there next to the branch and stares out across the sea to where he imagines England to be.

When they first came to this place, whatever thoughts he'd had of what they'd left behind were overshadowed, and almost incidental, and for a long time afterwards he had felt nothing. A blankness. He was in a silent realm wherein there were no feelings save the sensation of passing time, and nor were there any colours but those washed-out shades of goose-feather grey, bleached bone white. He felt muffled, and he recognised it was sent for the protection of his own wits, and he gave thanks to the Lord.

Since then, though, as the days have become weeks, and now months, something has returned, some distant tingling, but it is not welcome, for now with each passing dawn, with each passing dusk, he feels the world's disintegration, its erosion, the sense that everything everywhere is breaking apart, fragmenting at the edges into tiny particles that blow away in the wind as cold ash does from an old fire.

Katherine says it is desolation. She says that it is the absence of hope. She says it must be endured unto death, and that there is almost nothing profitable to say about it.

But she is not quite right about that, Thomas thinks, for news of England reaches them occasionally, through the man they call Groot-hoose, of the Earl of Warwick falling on his knees before the old King Henry to beg forgiveness for past sins, and then leading King Henry from the Tower in London to St Paul's. He'd been got up in a blue velvet cape, though it was said the rest of him had not been cared for as well as a king might expect.

'They say he needed a wash,' Groot-hoose had said reproachfully.

But why could he not wash himself? Thomas had wondered. Is he become simple again? Either way, Henry was not expected to, or expecting to, rule the country and the Earl of Warwick was governing it through him as he had once hoped to govern through King Edward that summer when he had him in Middleham. And meanwhile the old King's wife, Queen Margaret, is in France, waiting to cross the Narrow Sea and resume her place by her husband's side. The prospect of how she would get on with the Earl of Warwick is the only thing that makes any of King Edward's threadbare circle smile.

Otherwise there was nothing else to smile about, except, perhaps, the charms of those two ladies from the province of Holland, but those smiles were reserved for King Edward and Hastings, while the others have to use their imaginations. Earl Rivers spends time writing verse that he will show no one, and the alchemist spends his time digging around in the sand, looking for something he says will help him with his search for some stone or other.

And every day King Edward's letters to the Duke of Burgundy go evaded, unanswered, for despite Edward's claim on him – the Duke is married to his sister – the Duke is too afeared to be seen to help his brother-in-law of York lest it provoke an invasion from Warwick and England, whom the Flems dread above all persons and things.

'Duke Charles is having built a fort on an island in Veere with a gate they are calling the Warwick Gate,' Groot-hoose has told them with an anxious laugh.

Duke Charles has let it be known that his alliance is with the King of England, whosoever that may be, and that he is happy with whomsoever the English want as their king, and is he not, after all, related to King Henry through his mother?

But King Edward is not without hope. Something will change, because something has to. And it is well known that the Earl of Warwick, in order to secure the King of France's help in reconciling with the Lancastrians and their Queen Margaret of Anjou, has promised an alliance with France against the Duke of Burgundy, whom the King of France wants, above all things, to drive from his lands.

Hastings has suggested that were the Earl of Warwick to ally with the King of France in an attack on Burgundian lands, then it would make perfect sense for the Duke of Burgundy to finally meet King Edward, and give him the money, the men and the ships he needs to return to England to unseat Warwick and reclaim his kingdom.

But so far nothing has happened.

At length Thomas gets up from the sand and he starts to drag his treetop home to the house of Groot-hoose. He thinks the wood is not too damp, and that if he is careful, and nurtures the flame, it might give them enough heat through the night so that when they wake in the morning, they will be able to wash in the bucket without needing to break the ice.

He arrives at the house just as it is getting dark, and King Edward's chambers are lit with candles and a fire, and there is music of a cheerful kind. Thomas stands without, looking at the glazed windows where shadows pass. He thinks of those two Dutchwomen.

He looks up to his chamber above, where he sees the disc of Katherine's face looking down at him. The glass is too thick to determine her expression, but he knows what it is. He continues around the back and up the steps with the wood, and he carries it up to Katherine and Rufus.

There are only three of them now. Alice died not too long after they landed. They had no name for what was wrong with her, and it would not have mattered if they had. He and Katherine and a priest buried her in the yard of a small church on the island of Texel, and King Edward and Hastings and all the others came to stand with them and the rain washed the tears from Thomas's cheeks.

That had been the first day of winter.

'How is he?' Thomas asks as he enters the room.

'He does fair enough,' she says, and she mops the boy's forehead again as they settle down and wait for the night to pass.

The music that Thomas heard that evening was being played in a rare celebration of good news: the Duke of Burgundy has ordered the Hanse towns to cease trading with France and England. It does not mean much, put like that, Thomas thinks, but Hastings tells him it is the start of things.

'We will have money, soon,' he says.

Thomas doesn't believe him, but he is proved wrong, for the money does come.

'Twenty thousand pounds!' Hastings shouts. 'Twenty thousand blessed pounds! Do you know what this means?'

Thomas shakes his head. He is so used to disappointment that he thinks it could mean Hastings and King Edward might find themselves another Dutchwoman to make it three.

But Hastings is adamant.

'It means we will be back home, Thomas. Think of that! Home!'

Thomas thinks of Marton Hall.

'Yes, well,' Hastings says. 'There is plenty to do, that I will not deny. But none of it will happen while we are rotting here. I know you have had your sorrows, but you now must gather yourself up, and do the Lord's work.'

He goes on to remind Thomas that the Lord is testing him, and that his time in Purgatory will be as a moment in summer, and that he is become the Lord's instrument of vengeance on earth.

The next day he sees Hastings in new hose, pourpoint and jacket. It is the same with King Edward, who has regained some of his regal polish.

'Wilkes writes to say the King will meet the Duke of Burgundy tomorrow,' Hastings announces, 'and we are to move to Bruges!'

'Bruges,' Thomas repeats. He has always wished to go to Bruges, to see the bookbinders, the illuminators, the press that they say is there that will save the monks their lifetime of labour. He had always imagined his visit in better times, though, with money in his purse and time at his disposal. Instead he is still living on burned scraps and handouts from Hastings, who still does not really seem to accept that Thomas has nothing beyond that which he is given, and that his remaining child is sick, his wife worn through.

Hastings finds them a cart on which to travel; they are wrapped in blankets and there is even a feather-stuffed quilted jacket to put around Rufus, who is shrunk and wizened with his illness so that he looks ever more like a little old man, and he smiles when he is settled in it, and remains carefully cheerful, smiling tolerantly when he is awake and not in pain from whatever it is that seems to be eating him up.

'He just needs rest,' Katherine says.

She is reduced to skin and bone with the worry and the constant caring, her skin like parchment. If Rufus dies, Thomas knows the boy will take Katherine with him to the grave.

They roll the few miles eastward from the hard little town on the sea, inland, the never-ceasing wind at their backs, in the week after the Epiphany, to Bruges, and to the upper floors of another, even finer, house of Groot-hoose. It starts to snow when they arrive but Groot-hoose's servants are numerous and bustling, and they are helped up to their chamber, a broadly square room, with glazed windows on two sides, where a fire is already lit and the bed is aired and there are sweet herbs in the mattress and among the rushes on the floor. Thomas places Rufus in bed, his body merely a burning hot wisp, and he stares at him for a long moment, and he thinks that is it. It has been too much for him.

Despite Katherine's feeble protests, he sends the servant, Nik-laas, who can speak sailor's English, to get a physician from the Hospital of St John.

'All the other gentlemen have sent for girls,' Niklaas tells them.

The physician comes and he speaks no English but his alarm at Rufus's condition is obvious. He takes samples of the boy's urine and consults an almanac; then he sends out for herbs that he crumbles and steeps in wine, for powders that he grinds finer yet before stirring into curiously sharp-smelling liquids which he then warms in a copper dish on the embers of the fire. He binds these together to make pastes, draughts and poultices. He says prayers. He anoints with oils blessed by various bishops. He takes blood from between Rufus's second and third fingers. He calls for white bread and ale from a particular brewster that Niklaas tells Thomas and Katherine has beneficial yeasts.

Outside it is snowing, bitter little dots and dashes of ice that swirl in the wind and sting your face like sand, and underfoot it settles in a thin shell across the town. The canals freeze. No one ventures abroad save Thomas, who walks through the clean-swept streets, crossing hump-backed bridges under which swans and ducks huddle. It is utterly silent and the sky is a perfect scrim of grey glimpsed between tall houses that seem like gully depths. In this way Bruges reveals its restrained beauty in glimpses.

The days are short and even the bells in St Saviour's are muffled in the cold. The crisis comes during their second week, and the physician stays for it, kneeling alongside Thomas and Katherine, and by the end of it, he too is dish-eyed with fatigue, his beaky little face sharpened further still, down on his black-hosed knees praying for divine intercession.

'Your boy – his soul – it is in the Lord's hands,' Niklaas translates.

A priest is called; a taper is lit and placed in Rufus's fingers. Hastings insists on silence in the house, and King Edward sends up nightcaps of ginger syrup.

Thomas goes down on his knees with the rest of them and prays using the God-given formulas. He prays to the saints and martyrs for intercession on Rufus's behalf, and he prays to the spirits of the dead for their help also: Nettie, Alice, Sir John Fakenham and his son Richard, too, though he hardly knew him. He prays for intercession to those men he cannot remember, but about whom Katherine has spoken: Walter, and Geoffrey and Dafydd and his brother Owen.

And as he enunciates this list of the dead, as their numbered souls parade before him, it is as if he passes out of the state of heart-blindness, out of that distant muffled time of grief after Alice's death, and his thoughts become clear, his sight sharpens, his hearing returns, and he sees he is asking them to intercede for his son, and that they are asking him to do something in return. He knows that the time has come. He must do their bidding.

He must now, simply, avenge them.

This is the bargain that is struck here while he is on his knees in this upper room of Groot-hoose's house in Bruges: if Rufus lives, Thomas will dedicate his life to the destruction and death of Richard Neville, Earl of Warwick.

It is about then that the physician starts to look up from his prayers not for the boy's death, but for signs of some improvement.

And so it happens.

Rufus comes back from the brink.

He will live.

After two days they open the shutters and let in the light.

After three Rufus is drinking the ale and food does not pass through him as if through a pipe. He takes in some of its goodness before it is shat out. Light returns to his eye. Colour to his cheek. His flesh will reacquire its youthful spring.

The physician laughs and says something Niklaas translates.

'He says he is stubborn, your boy. He says he refuses to die. Refuses to lie down. He is like you, he thinks.'

Thomas shakes his head.

'That is his mother,' he says.

After four days, Thomas ventures out to find the snow is melted and the town is filled with Englishmen. Big, rough, desperate Englishmen. Swaggering bands of them, all armed, most with bits and pieces of harness that look scavenged, or grabbed on the way out, or handed down, or the only piece they'd been left with after a run-in with men keen to take it from them. They carry swords or rough pole weapons and they seem to think it will be soon, whatever it is.

Thomas goes to find Hastings, who, when he sees him, thinks his son must have died. Both their eyes become glassy with tears when Thomas tells him the boy is spared.

'For great things, Thomas, I feel certain of it.'

'When are we to return to England?'

'Money is coming in steadily,' Hastings says, 'from the provinces here, and from Calais, and from the aldermen of London. We have ships, too, moored in Flushing, and men are gathering in the streets, did you see?'

Thomas nods.

'It will not be long,' Hastings says. 'We will miss you.'

'Miss me?'

'I had not thought you would come? With Mistress Everingham being so ill, and your boy?'

'No,' Thomas says. 'I will be with you. And Mistress – Mistress Everingham. We will come. We have nothing here.'

He does not add that he has nothing there either. But Hastings is pleased.

'I did not want to force it, Thomas. But you will have to spend the next months in the butts.' Hastings pats Thomas's shoulder, which is no longer as bulky as it was, for lack of food and lack of time spent drawing his bow.

'I do not wish to be considered as an archer any more,' Thomas tells him. He does not know why he says this; it is not something he had planned. But he has been an archer before, and there is nothing to be gained from it if you wish to find a man and try to kill him.

'A man-at-arms?'

'I wondered if I might – take up a lance?'

Hastings smiles.

'A lance? Have you a horse?'

Thomas shakes his head.

'Well, we must find you one,' Hastings says, but he pauses and looks Thomas in the eye. 'But, Thomas,' he says. 'It is not a simple thing, taking up a lance. Have you ever ridden a horse at a man? Have you ever held a lance? Run someone through with it?'

Thomas admits that he has not.

'These men,' Hastings goes on, 'they practise doing it in the tiltyard. And besides, we need archers. We are short of good men such as you. Please. You can lead them when we have recruited them. You can be a master of bowmen and show the vintenars what is to be done.'

Thomas understands what Hastings is offering. A fixed position. Income. He knows that most men are puzzled by his – and Katherine's – station for he wears no badge, no emblem of any guild or craft, and there is nothing to give away his position in the social scale; he is not obviously this or that. Just who is he? No one really knows, and he can see how unsettling this is to most men. Were he to join Hastings's retinue as a master of archers, then he would have some heft in life.

Thomas thanks Hastings, but that is not his plan. He needs to close with the enemy, not just send arrow shafts into the sky in the hope they will kill a distant man in plate.

Hastings seems to understand and the next day a servant brings Thomas some money for his purse and a pair of very stiff sabatons in black painted steel that come to a nice point over Thomas's toes.

'It is a start,' he tells Katherine.

When it is at last the appointed day, he still cannot believe it, but they leave Bruges by the St Katherine Gate through large crowds, and King Edward does not board his barge but walks so that people may admire him, and there is no one finer with a crowd of so many people. He is so tall and strapping, and these last few months have chiselled any complacency from his face, so that he looks everyone's idea of the perfect warrior king, and women, particularly, throw short-stemmed flowers at him.

They walk along the canal to another of the beautiful brick-built cities that proliferate in these parts and at their approach various townsmen and clerics come out to meet King Edward, and they offer him the town cross to kneel before in veneration while they sprinkle him with holy water, and then he is taken to Mass where the *Te Deum* is sung while his men cluster in the church precincts, but Thomas goes in search of an armourer, only to find the town has only one, and he is sold out of everything he has ever made, and is sitting at his table dead-eyed, massaging the palms of his hands.

On his way back, nearer the church, are the stationers' stalls, far finer than any he has seen in England, and so Thomas stops to look at their wares. He knows King Edward has been buying many beautiful books in Bruges, exquisitely illuminated volumes of Josephus and Livy, and on the Trojan Wars and the life of Alexander, and though these here in Damme are not so astonishing as those, there is still much at which to marvel.

But he wants to buy something for Katherine, and he knows she is less impressed by the appearance of a book than by what it has to say for itself. By what it can tell her. He imagines a book such as a physician might consult, of the sort that Master Payne had in Bamburgh, and there are some wonderfully authoritative-looking texts. One – badly faded now – has a chart of what the various colours of urine might mean; another how to bore a hole in a man's head for reasons that make no sense to him, but might to her. All these, though, are too expensive, and he remembers how she prefers unbound pages, which she says seem more mutable, more in the way of a proposal than a laying down of the law. There are some, in a wooden box, but those he looks at first are to do with jurisprudence, something that will be of no interest to her.

The bells in the church ring out above his head to mark the end of the service, and the pigeons take to the sky in a flurry of beating wings when Thomas finally finds something that is not on Church law: it is what looks like a poem, copied out in an old-fashioned hand, with the title which he translates as being *On the Nature of Things* by a Latin named Lucretius. It is cheap enough so Thomas buys it and he folds it into his purse and hurries back to join Katherine and Rufus, who are sitting at the back of the bed of the cart with colour in both their cheeks, and eyes that are white. He gives her the poem and she looks at it closely.

'Latin,' she says.

'You understand enough.'

She supposes she does. She reads a few lines aloud – about a goddess placing romantic love in every creature then alive so that they are smitten with the urge to reproduce – and looks up and raises her eyebrows.

'Well.' He shrugs. 'I suppose it must start somewhere.'

She goes back to it and reads on and he is content to walk behind, thinking now of how to find pieces of plate that will be of more use than sabatons. Perhaps he could swap them with someone? Thomas looks around at the clustered Englishmen, exiles tramping along behind them in the hope of a return, and he detects uneasiness, an anxiety that he does not think comes from fear of danger, but rather a fear of failure. They come from all over England, and they are perhaps of the lower order of landowner: men like himself who once had a few acres, but have them no more.

King Edward takes to a barge, and they follow him along the canal path to the big sea docks opposite Flushing, where the ships wait to take them to England, and many more men are gathered behind the levees in their linen tents. There are three hundred gunners sent by the Duke of Burgundy from parts of these Low

Countries, too, in tight-fitting helmets, smutted with soot and their clothes singed in parts from their morning's practice.

It takes another week before all the men that are likely to come do so, though, and when they do, there are not enough ships assembled to take them over the sea, so these must be found, hired and brought to Flushing. When they are ready, Rufus counts thirty-six ships in all, of very varying size, perhaps just enough to take fifteen hundred men. He tells Thomas that only one or two seem very fine, and Thomas thinks that if they could, they should board one of these two, perhaps with King Edward or with the Duke of Gloucester, who has the look of a man to be trusted to know what to do and do it, in almost any given situation.

At length the ships are made ready and the troops are loaded aboard. Two ships are set aside for horses, and those that cannot fit are left behind to be sold, and every man must carry all his belongings up the gangplank, or get his servants to do it for him. Much materiel is left behind, to be sent on later, perhaps, or left in payment of debts accrued.

Thomas and Katherine and Rufus are encumbered only with those bits and pieces of Thomas's armour, and Hastings intervenes to allocate Thomas – or, really, Katherine and Rufus – space below deck on King Edward's ship, the *Antony*. The two women from The Hague come to wish King Edward farewell and he is pleased, because just then the wind drops, and so, with nothing to do but wait on board their ships in case it should suddenly change, he invites them to cross the gangplank.

'Almost as if he'd arranged it,' a man mutters.

They wait nine days on board until the wind picks up. Conditions could descend into the hellish, but are carefully controlled. The master of the *Antony* tells them that they are to treat his ship as if it were a church, so there is no littering and no despoiling and no defaulting (as the King puts it) on deck, save by his two dogs, after whom he appoints a man to clear up. Rufus sleeps wrapped up in his down jacket, and Katherine earns money stitching new badges for the men who wish for the badge of a sunburst, to remind them of the time they fought at Mortimer's Cross, a little over ten years ago now.

One man refuses to pay for her work, saying it looks like beams of light streaming not from a sun, but a star, such as the Earl of Oxford's emblem. She tells him she does not have a good pair of scissors to cut the cloth, and that he still owes her his money. The man relents and pays the price before a fight breaks out.

At last the wind changes, and there is a great cheer from among the men, though not from the King's women who are suddenly put off, and not from the merchants that have been clustering around the dock, who see their market vanishing across the grey-green waters under a press of sail bowed by an easterly wind.

As they set off, Thomas finds himself standing with Katherine on the stern deck, near the master, watching the Low Countries slip away off the horizon, and he feels a tremendous weight of sorrow, and realises that Katherine does too, as they leave the body of their daughter buried there, across the sea, in that hard frozen ground. He puts his arm around her shoulder and squeezes her tight. There is nothing to say. They are companions in this grief, and it is best unspoken.

18

'No fleet to chase us today,' Hastings says.

He joins Thomas and Katherine as they stand in the stern of the boat, with Rufus peering over the rail back at the low tongue of Flanders that dissolves into the mist behind them.

Thomas asks where the English fleet is.

'South of Brittany,' he tells them, just as if he had arranged it himself. 'Miles from here.'

'What are they doing there?' Katherine asks. It is the first time she has shown any interest in anything beyond Rufus for many a month.

Hastings pulls an odd face and drops his voice, as if imparting a nugget of unfavourable news.

'They are waiting to escort Margaret of Anjou and her son across the Narrow Sea,' he says.

'So they are coming?'

'Yes,' Hastings says. 'It makes it easier for us if they delay, though. If we can come to grips with Warwick before he joins forces with the Queen and her army – well. You can see that might make it a bit easier.'

'She has an army?'

'She will do, when she lands.' He looks regretful, as if he himself were guilty of an oversight.

*

They sail all through the night and the next morning, blessed with a favourable wind at last, and when the slim profile of England appears on the horizon everyone cheers, even the Flemings. When they are still a little off the shore, they drop anchor and ride at ease while it is decided what to do. Eventually a smaller boat with rust-red sails is manned and sent ahead.

'To enquire as to the disposition of the people,' Hastings explains. He shoots his eyebrows up and down a couple of times.

After an hour or so the boat is rowed back with a glum-looking crew.

King Edward's messenger swings aboard the rope ladder and makes his way to the King's cabin with his news, but everybody guesses what it is because he orders the boat pulled out of the water, and swung back on to the deck.

A little later the master emerges to talk to his mate, who issues orders to the sailors, and all the other ships follow on the northerly course, sailing into the late afternoon.

'Not very friendly,' Hastings murmurs. He looks shaken. 'Bloody Warwick. He has all our friends under lock and key, and all others are made to pay surety against aiding us. By Christ, he is a busy little bastard.'

He spits over the ship's edge. The waters are swill brown and unlovely.

One of Chamberlain's men comes to the deck.

'They are spring-heeled,' he says. 'We will have a job finding anywhere to land that is not crawling with the Earl of Oxford's men.'

Thomas thinks of Brougham. He looked an efficient sort.

His eye is caught by some dense cloud building in the east. The sea is picking up, and the wind too, whipping the foam off the top of the churning swell and sending the *Antony* bobbing.

The master tells Hastings there is going to be some rough weather.

'Best batten down,' he says.

They sail northwards, along the coastline, across the great yawn in the land wherein Thomas imagines that eel-trapper lives, with that simple boy of his, on their desolate island. The wind is strong now, and waves boom against the bobbing boats, their spray drenching the men on the deck. The master and his crew have waxed linen coats. Thomas goes down the ladder to the hold where the air is thick with smells, new and old, and it is dark and not even that dry. He finds Katherine and Rufus cramped at an angle. Seawater beads the joins between the planks and they look frightened, as well they might.

He stays with them, crouched there, foul water slopping between the ship's ribs with each roll and turn, and a priest begins chanting the rosary and men join in, murmuring the responses until the morning, when they emerge to find themselves utterly alone at sea. The storm is rumbling now, a deep, low-pitched grinding as if from below the earth's surface. The waves are like rolling marble dunes, the wind still shrieks in the shrouds and the sails are reefed right down.

'Where are the others?' Rufus asks.

No one says a thing. Some are scouring the horizon for signs of other ships, others for signs of wreckage or dead men. King Edward is there on the aft deck. He stares out to sea, shattered, ruined, as bad as he was when they left the country. Hastings, too, looks tense. You can see his jaw muscles clenching with anxiety. Can it end like this? Is this what God wished? That his fleet be scattered? That his men – including his brother Richard – be drowned?

There is nothing anyone can say, save the alchemist, who now claims he can predict the future.

'I knew this would happen,' he says.

'Shut up,' someone advises.

King Edward mutters something and Hastings comes over.

'Where is that priest?'

The priest comes, but you can see in his face that he knows this is beyond him. He can no more explain it than he might the rising of the sun, or the death of babies. But King Edward looks to him for answers. Why has God forsaken him?

The priest, florid, settling into roundness, rubs his forehead with dirty fingers. You can almost smell his wine-laden sweat. The boat heels. King Edward staggers.

There's a shout from the crow's nest. Land is seen to the west.

King Edward glances over. That is something, at least. Then another shout. A boat. Two boats. Three. They are in all directions, but heading westward too, to that dark sliver of land. The priest is forgotten and the master tweaks the tiller. There is nothing to do but limp towards the land, and see what or where it is. After a while they see the crooked spire of a church, and the *Antony*'s master comes to a conclusion.

'It is Ravenspur,' he tells them. 'Not much of a place.'

'But we can dock?'

'If you want.'

They do. Every man, woman and child wants to be off this boat, and the wind seems to be gathering force again. So they make for Ravenspur, driven by the freshening wind across the estuary of the River Humber to its northern bank. They might have been able to sail up the river a bit, to Hull, the master says, if the tide were in their favour, but it is not, and by now no man wishes to be at sea a moment longer, so they make for the spire in the hope there will be a dock on to which they might disembark without drowning.

The other ships follow them across the estuary, about ten of them now, but there is still no sign of King Edward's brother, nor of Earl Rivers and his men.

'Take me back to Bruges,' the alchemist says when they are docked and he steps off the gangplank on to dryish land. He collects up a fistful of the oozing gritty mud and tastes it for something and then spits it out. Thomas tries to imagine ever finding a soil that you wouldn't spit out.

The rain comes down, fierce and cold, and they huddle there, bent-backed, while Hastings and King Edward look about them. It is decided to send a party of fore-riders first to Hull, to see if the gates there are open to King Edward, and in the meantime to find somewhere to shelter for the night, and so eventually they march off, a line of straggling refugees rather than a conquering army, up a muddy road, towards that hipped church spire.

The village is deserted save for an elderly woman out of her wits, left there to die by the looks of things, and they find shelter in the church that night, sodden and miserable; and because the crypt is flooded up to the top steps, and coffin lids bang on the joists of the nave, they think the souls of the departed are returned to haunt them.

King Edward demands the alchemist make them manna, and ale, and the fat priest suggests that such work is best left to God and there follows a pointless argument that dwindles into careless silence.

After a while the alchemist speaks.

'Do you know who landed in Ravenspur also?' he asks.

No one does. He thinks this proves his point that manna might be something man should try to make, if he could, because he says it helps if you know your history. Hastings is about to tell him to be quiet, but then the alchemist tells them that King Henry IV landed in Ravenspur when he came back from the exile into which King Edward's cousin had sent him.

'And look what he achieved!' the alchemist says.

'What?' someone asks. 'He was a usurping bastard!'

'Well,' the alchemist says. 'He was not a bastard, but yes, I agree, he was a usurper.'

King Edward is listening intently now as the alchemist goes on to remind them that the first Lancastrian king, Henry Boling-broke, Edward's great enemy's grandfather, had likewise landed here, taking advantage of King Richard II's absence in Ireland to return from exile to claim – he had said – only what was his by right: the duchy of Lancaster, which King Richard had illegally taken from him. With such modest aims, no one had thought to stop him, and it was only later, when he had seized power and put King Richard in the dungeons of Pontefract Castle, that they realised he was, in fact, already king.

'By which time it was too late to raise any objection,' he goes on, but by now everyone has stopped listening.

In the morning there are more of King Edward's ships standing off Ravenspur, and by the afternoon, with the storm abated, there are more yet. There is still no sign of King Edward's brother or of Earl Rivers, but then they turn up in the afternoon with their full complement of men, and with their arrival there is a general rise in the temper of the makeshift camp. The sun even comes out for a moment, a little glimpse in the otherwise flat grey skies of March, and as the evening falls, the only ship that has not yet come ashore is one of those carrying the horses.

While they are eating, the fore-riders return from Hull with bad news. The mayor and aldermen will not open the gates to Edward and his band. Worse, they have seen men gathering to block his path.

'The country has been turned against you, sir,' their captain tells King Edward.

And it is true. None of the locals have come out in favour of King Edward, or yet tried to join his little army, and without the men to join him, King Edward stands no chance in taking back the crown, so that night, their second in the church of the nameless little village, there is a council of all King Edward's advisers while everyone else waits outside in the dark.

When it is over, Hastings emerges.

'His grace the King – that is his grace the Duke of York – is intent only on reclaiming his right to his duchy,' he says. 'It was his father's before him, and it only reverted to the Crown while he was king, and since he is no longer the king, and has no intention to be so – so that is all our ambition's summit. Yes?'

Men nod and murmur yes in the dawn but they see this for what it is: desperation. Clinging on. And it is further decided that instead of taking to the boats again, which will look too much like a retreat, they will march not southwards to London, but north-wards, to York, where King Edward is supposedly held in some affection and which is, after all, the seat of his duchy.

That evening Thomas manages to buy a pair of matching greaves cheap from a man who looks as if he believes – or hopes – he will not be called upon to need them. They sit nicely on Thomas's sabatons and he stares at his feet, and flexes his toes. Katherine looks up from the pamphlet he bought her, in which she has had her nose for the last weeks, and nods. She knows what he is doing, he feels sure.

'How is it?' he asks.

'Mars is lying with his head in Venus's lap,' she tells him. 'He is suffering from a "never-healing wound of love".'

Thomas laughs.

'Stop that,' someone calls.

The next morning they set off towards the town of Beverley and they reach it late in the afternoon, and they refresh themselves in the narrow streets, the Flemings in particular terrifying the black and grey friars and their natural prey the pilgrims that cluster in the shadow of the great minster. While they are drinking the town dry, horses are bought and wagons with teams of oxen for their equipment, and Hastings ensures Katherine has a pony at least, and then says that Thomas must have one too, and what is found for him is a foul-tempered white stallion that snaps at all he sees and should have been put down long ago.

Then a hide merchant comes from York to tell them that there are two large groups of men – archers in the main – setting themselves up on the York road; there, they say, to stop King Henry's great rebel Edward of March reaching the town. The hide merchant is taken to King Edward who, recognising perhaps that with so few archers of their own they would never prevail against such an ambush, decides they must go around the block, and reach York by way of a dogleg.

They leave Beverley on the north road, though some wish to stay in the town for it is already late and the weather is still very uncertain, and sure enough they have been on the road for no more than an hour before it begins to rain very heavily, dunning on their hats and travelling capes, rusting their harness, turning their jacks to lead.

'We must find shelter!' someone bleats.

Ahead, across a ford, is a village with a church tower of modest ambition, but surely it will do? They turn towards it and find it before the village: a priory, walled in with grey stone walls, and there is something horribly familiar about their closed-off, secretive nature that makes Thomas instantly alert and uncomfortable.

It is like Haverhurst, he thinks and he tells Katherine and she too nods.

'What is the name of this place?' she asks.

'Watton,' he says. 'Watton.'

And he sees her gasp.

19

Watton.

The name alone makes Katherine's stomach churn.

It is where the nun in the Prioress's story came from, the last one Katherine ever heard her tell before she ran. The nun – the sister of Watton – had been an oblate at the priory here, but she had fornicated with a lay brother, and conceived a child. When the other nuns found out, they manacled her wrists to a wall and chained her ankles to a yew log that was hung out of a window, and then when she lost the baby they forced her to castrate the man with whom she had fornicated.

Even in the drizzle, or maybe particularly in the drizzle, the evil, the repression, the bizarre twisted cruelty of the place just seeps out of its stones like mist rising in the sun after rain. It infects things like a poisonous miasma, and she is half minded to clamp her hand over Rufus's face and take him away so that he does not breathe it in.

But it is more than that.

It is something that Katherine's friend Liz had asked her two years before, when they were walking north to Middleham Castle, to take the ledger to the Earl of Warwick. Katherine had told her the story of the nun: 'Where did you hear that?' And Katherine had told her about the Prioress, and about how she had told the story to stir up the sisters against Katherine when she had been seen with Thomas in the cloister at Haverhurst. Liz had said the woman was a bitch but she had been interested in the Prioress, mainly because she thought she might be the only way Katherine would ever find out how she had ended up as an oblate in the priory. Liz had said that a story like the nun of Watton was the sort of story people told only locally, and that Watton was most likely the place the Prioress would call home.

Could this really be the Prioress's home? Katherine wonders. Could this be the hearth to which she returned after her expulsion from the priory at Haverhurst? Could she be here now – somewhere in there village perhaps? Or would they have let her remain a sister? Might she, in fact, be in this priory right now?

Katherine rides with the reins slack between her thumbs, peering around, starting at anything, and she feels overcome with a swimming dizziness. Some things seem further than they are, some closer. Everything is at once so familiar, yet never before seen, every detail recognised but jarred just slightly out of kilter: the jumble of roofs above their grey stone walls, the fields, fishponds, orchards, sties and granges. There is the malthouse, the tilery, the water mill and, upstream, behind the sisters' cloister under some new-budding elms, the grassless patch around three winding posts where there will be steps down into the river in which the sisters stand knee-deep in all weathers to wash the clothes of the community, as Katherine herself once had to do for all those winter months.

And yes, even now, even in this quickly picking-up rain, there is a sister out there up to her thighs in the river's rain-dimpled water, and Katherine can hear that wet slap of her beetle against a pile of sodden linens. It makes her feel exhausted just to hear it, and there is a familiar bone-deep weariness in the rhythm of this woman's beating. Crack. Crack. Crack. It's as if she has been doing this all her life, and knows she'll be doing it for the rest of it too, which, Katherine thinks, may well be the case.

The column of men are spread out on the road behind, seeking the shelter of the trees but looking for all the world as if they are trying to conceal themselves. When the fore-riders hammer on the priory gate, rather than it swinging open, the bell in the tower is jerked into urgent summons, and she imagines the sisters gathering on their side of the nave, praying for delivery, one way or perhaps the other. She feels their nerves, their fright. She can almost smell their fear.

And still the woman in the water beats on. Crack. Crack. Crack.

Will they be let in? King Edward and Gloucester and the other gentles, perhaps, but why would anyone let more than a thousand men in anywhere? And even if they were let in, she will not be. She will have to spend the night with the sisters. And this she will not do.

She turns to Thomas, who she notes is now wearing leg armour up to his hips, and she suggests they find their own shelter for the night.

'There'll be a hay barn,' she says, though at this time of year it will be nearly empty. He nods. They kick their horses on, past the crowd at the gatehouse where the Prior will be panicking, and there sure enough are the lay brothers' granges, and the postern gates for both cloisters, each locked and barred no doubt, and across a narrow bridge over the river are the sties and the goose pens. A pair of mottled oxen glare at them as if the rain were their idea.

The bell stops its ringing and in the silence Katherine can still hear it: crack. Crack. Crack.

The hay barn is cavernous for being largely empty, and once they hobble their horses, and once Thomas has carefully removed his leg armour, they sit and watch the rain falling on the black slate roofs of the priory through the open barn doors; and then Rufus sneezes and they both become alarmed for him, but he seems fine, so they break some bread and sip at their costrels of ale. They are in silent contemplation of their pasts when perhaps fifty soot-stained Burgundian gunners come and join them with their wagon of guns and powder. They are friendly enough – they rub Rufus's hair – and they smell of saltpetre and, soon, of bean soup, which they warm over a fire made of a bit of wood they break off from the barn wall.

As night falls Katherine goes to relieve herself in the river, and sees the sister has finally taken in her washing.

That night she dreams a variant of that same old dream, the one in which she is an infant being left at the almonry door with the old Prioress, and the dream makes perfect sense, of course, because it is cobbled together with the suggestions people have made about the scene since, which she has sewn together in her mind and which obscure the truth of that original dream. So there is a letter with a seal on it, big as a slice of apple, and there is the old Prioress reading the letter and there she is bobbing a bow to whoever is leaving the abandoned younger version of herself, and it all seems very clear.

By morning the dream is muddled and already half-forgotten, and when the barn doors are pushed open, it is cold and grey outside, but the rain has stopped and the bell in the tower is ringing and there is a lay brother with fresh baked maslin and a barrel of ale for the Burgundians that they do not seem to appreciate.

Crack. Crack. Crack.

The woman is already at work.

They are ready to ride on to York before it is fully light, and the

Burgundians load up their wagon and roll it out on to the road. Katherine and Thomas follow on behind. Rufus is on her lap.

She feels almost queasy with the feeling of a lost opportunity. She knows she must make an enquiry, but of whom and about whom? She cannot merely go to the sisters' almoner and explain what she wants and why. They would first take her as an apostate, and if that did not work, for here is her child, they would then seize her for the murder of Sister Joan, whom in another lifetime she pressed down on a shard of glass so hard that blood came out of her mouth.

They ride past the front gate, which hangs open, and three or four black-cassocked brothers stand watch in the courtyard, silver-haired, senior, and when they see Katherine is a woman they turn their faces away. She almost makes one of those gestures that she's seen men make, and she wonders what Liz would have had to say to them.

Crack. Crack. Crack.

They ride down the road, and she still feels jittery with nerves. Something is happening. A door is closing; an opportunity is being lost.

Crack. Crack. Crack.

She stops.

'Thomas,' she says. 'Wait here for me. Don't come unless I call.'

And she pulls her pony around and sets it trotting back up the road, and then off, down to the riverbank where the woman is at work. Katherine does not dismount, because, by now, she knows. She pulls up by the winding posts and sees at the river's bank there are three baskets of linen and a bucket of ash soap.

Rufus is restless on her lap.

'What are we doing?' he asks.

But before Katherine can answer the woman looks up over her wet shoulder, with the beetle raised to pound the pile of linen on the rock before her. Although Katherine already knows who she is, she cannot prepare for this, and when their eyes meet, she cannot help but look away, just as she had done all her young life. Even then the woman's gaze had been so hate-filled that to meet it was to be sullied, violated – and also to be complicit in that violation.

Now she stands in the water with her skirts bunched, the beetle held high, in the same pose you might catch someone splitting a log, and she is unmoving. Katherine takes a deep breath, feels Rufus's warmth and looks at her. Her limbs are tingling and there is a painful lump in her throat, but her eyes are not misting over and she feels her strength. They stare at one another. Again, after all these years, so much has changed, and they both know it. This time it is the Prioress who looks away.

Crack.

'So,' the Prioress says. 'You've come. I always knew you would.'

Katherine is confused. All her life, it seems, has led to this and now she does not know what to say, or where to begin.

Crack.

She had often imagined killing the Prioress. She had believed that she should, and so would. She did not know how it would be done, and had always assumed God would guide her hand. But now she looks at this woman, who has withered in the years since last she saw her, and she wonders where is God's guidance? She feels not one jolt of impulse to get off her horse and wade out into the river and kill her.

Crack.

'Why?' Katherine asks.

'Why what?'

'Why were you so – why did you beat me? Why did you treat me so badly?'

Crack.

'I treated you the same as anyone else,' the Prioress says.

'That is not true.'

'Yes it is. You always thought you were special. A chosen one. Better than everyone else. You haven't changed.'

'What about all the beatings? The starvings?'

'You still think you should have been allowed to get away with all them things you did? On account of thinking yourself better than the rest of us?'

'Better? You think I thought I was better than you, so you beat me? You locked me up! You made me take your shit out to the river!'

Crack.

'You made me do the washing for six months because you thought I believed myself better than you?'

Crack.

'That your boy now, is it?' the woman asks. 'Does he know his mother's a murderer?'

Katherine regrets Rufus's presence now, but she is pleased that the Prioress has registered him, has seen that she at least has found something in her life.

'A murderer?' Katherine repeats. 'I'm no murderer. I killed a woman who attacked me, and so as to save her baby I shortened the life of another who was going to die anyway. But what about you? All those women you locked in the Priory? Alice? Whom you suffocated under a bolster? Their blood is on your hands, and you know it, and however long you stand out here in this river, its waters shall not wash them clean.'

Crack.

'But as for me,' Katherine goes on, 'I forgive you all you did to me. I may not have forgotten it, but I have forgiven it, every foul little deed.'

'You came so far out of your way to tell me that?'

'Do you know how far out of my way I came? From the track there. To here.'

'Well, nothing is stopping you going back that way, is there?'

Crack.

Katherine tugs on the rein in her left hand. 'No,' she says. 'You are good at that, by the way. Praise where praise is due. You have a nice easy action. It should stand you in good stead over the next twenty years.'

Crack.

She turns her pony and she begins to ride away. She expects to hear the crack of the beetle but the Prioress has stopped her washing.

'Don't you want to know who you are?' she calls after her.

But Katherine has raised the back of her hand, and she has ridden on. She does not need the Prioress to tell her who she is, and so the woman has lost the last shred of power she ever had over her and so, for that moment at least, Katherine feels a deep sense of calm.

She rides past Thomas, who is sitting on his horse, waiting, his head cocked to one side, his eyes flattened.

'Who was that?' he asks.

'One of the sisters,' Katherine tells him.

She sees he has his leg armour on again, and that he has somehow acquired knee joints with pieces that stick out like an Irishman's ears. He watches her closely as she rides by.

20

The column winds its slow way along, up and over a ridge of hills where they get their first glimpse of distant York, and Katherine is grateful to be mounted when those around her are wearing through boot leather. Soon, though, they come to a slow stop. The fore-riders have returned from York with a man she is told is Thomas Conyers the Recorder of the City, which sounds important enough.

The recorder tells Edward that he must not even approach York for fear he will be attacked and all he had hoped for would be lost to him; hearing this, Edward is disconsolate, and he stands at the side of the track muttering to Hastings. Conyers stands a little apart with his body shaped in a position designed to persuade them all that he has nothing to gain by all this, and perhaps that is so, but the name Conyers is hardly trusted among Edward's ranks and surely not by Edward himself.

But, really, what else can they do? They cannot go back to Hull; they cannot go across the sea, and nor can they go north to Scotland. They can only carry on to York. Edward sets his jaw. Conyers and his advice are put aside, and they press on through the luscious green-grassed farmland where sheep outnumber men by perhaps a hundred to one.

Eventually Thomas comes back to her. He is subdued, serious, disturbed by what he has seen.

'Is the whole country going to be against King Edward?' she asks.

He shrugs and doesn't answer, and Katherine sees his boots are wet from the rain and already the rust is hazing that fine leg armour.

Before they reach York they are met by a small troop of horsemen. Their leaders bear more encouraging news – that Edward will be permitted within the city gates, but only as the Duke of York – and with only a small party, not his army, which must wait on the fields hereabouts. After a hurried conference with Hastings and Gloucester, King Edward agrees to their terms. Hastings sends for Thomas again and when he refuses to come with them on account of Katherine and Rufus, the only two in their entire party who are not in any way men, or soldiers, Hastings assigns Katherine two men – one fat, called John Pentecost, another thin, his son, also called John Pentecost – and so Thomas has no excuse. He rides out with Hastings, who has given him a very fine livery tabard, and Katherine and Rufus watch them move off up the road behind the first troop of horsemen.

Father Pentecost barks orders, while Son Pentecost scurries about organising bread, ale, pottage and a portion of a tent so that she and Rufus will have somewhere to sleep for the night, but in the gloaming Thomas returns. He is more cheerful, and tells them they are all to be allowed to pass through York this night.

'You should have seen the King,' he says. 'The mayor and aldermen made him address the townspeople from the steps of the minster. He told them – you will never believe it – he told them that not only does he not want to recover the throne, he told them he never wanted to be king, ever, and it was the Earl of Warwick who made him.'

Katherine laughs.

'He even ended by shouting "A King Henry!" and "A Prince Edward!" and he waved an ostrich feather in the air!'

'Why?' she asks.

'Because that is the livery symbol of Prince Edward, King Henry's son, isn't it? The one they hate, and the one whom Hastings says is devoted to the sin of Onan.'

Katherine has not heard of Onan.

'Never mind,' Thomas says. She will come back to that later, she thinks.

'So are we on the move then, sir?' Father Pentecost asks, vaguely plaintive, as if what has happened in York is only important in so far as it affects him and his labours, and this change of plan is somehow Thomas's fault.

'Yes,' Thomas tells him. 'To York. Or through it at any rate.'

They find space in the same inn where she once shared a room with Liz and, once they have overseen the stabling of the horses and ensured that Rufus is fed, she walks up those steps to the bedchamber and is briefly immersed in memories of the woman who once saved her, then led her on, and then betrayed her. But Liz does not dally long in her mind, because she returns to the Prioress, and she feels a lurch of fear, and then incredulity; as her fingers trace the fringes of that weave of scars that covers her back she thinks of the woman condemned to wash linen for the rest of her life, all day, every day. Is that penance enough? Perhaps. Perhaps something will carry her off before she is too old to carry on. And that will be that.

She thinks again of the manuscript that Thomas bought her. In it the man Lucretius argued that there is no soul, only matter that can be made and unmade, recycled, turned over, and that this earth is all there is for humankind. A man should not live his life with the afterlife in mind, Lucretius wrote, but should accept that everything – every single thing – is transitory, and it should be enjoyed for what it is, not given some extra significance.

She sleeps deeply, dreamlessly, and the next morning they are up before dawn, and after Mass they set out, every man in harness now, and the laughter that accompanied King Edward's cajoling of the people of York is replaced by tension and even fear.

'We are coming towards Pontefract,' Thomas tells her.

'Who is at Pontefract?'

He looks embarrassed to say it.

'Lord Montagu.'

'Oh Christ,' she says. 'Him.'

Thomas nods.

'Won't he attack us as he did last year, when he drove King Edward out?'

'Maybe,' Thomas says, 'but that was when King Edward was the king. This time he is merely the Duke of York. And Montagu – well. You remember him? He always – well, almost always – did the right thing. He has no reason – or right – to attack the King – the Duke that is. The Duke of York.'

'He'd be mad not to,' is Katherine's first thought.

'Yes,' Thomas agrees.

But astonishingly Montagu sits on his hands, and the Duke of York's rag-tag little force moves down through the old places: through Tadcaster – near Towton, where they stop to pray for the many men who met their end and the Duke of Gloucester vows to build a chantry chapel, should God smile on their enterprise – and then to Sandal Castle, where they stop at an ugly little town filled with what Hastings calls inbreds, where King Edward's father and brother met their end, and Mass is said.

And all this while Lord Montagu, now Marquess of Montagu, sits in his castle, and no one can be sure why, or what he plans to do now.

'It is a trap,' Father Pentecost says. 'He is waiting until we are past and then he will come out and we will be caught between his army, the Earl of Warwick's army and the Queen's army.'

But this thought is too dreadful to contemplate, and wishful thinking is all they have to keep them going.

'No,' someone says. 'He fears King Edward too much to fight him.'

'He fears if he attacks us,' another replies, 'then the Earl of Northumberland will attack him from behind.'

'He has not enough men.'

But other questions occur too: Where is the Earl of Warwick?

Coventry is the answer to that one. Hastings tells them he is recruiting men and colluding with King Edward's brother, George, Duke of Clarence.

But the other question is: Why are men not joining Edward, either as Duke of York or king?

'They cannot understand it,' Thomas tells her, talking of Edward and Hastings. 'But surely they can see people are sick of all this? Look around you, and you will see people who have lost fathers and brothers and sons – for what reason? So that one man may be on the throne in the stead of another. But how does this affect them? Not a whit. They care about – about the harvest. The price of wool. That sort of thing. It is not a case of lacking the stomach for fighting. It is a case of lacking the interest in it.'

She agrees with him, though neither Pentecost does.

'You have to do what your goodlord says,' the son tells him. 'You know that. And sometimes it is to do this sort of thing, and other times it is other sorts of things.'

But when they reach Doncaster, nearly a thousand men prove Thomas wrong, and in Leicester there are a further three thousand waiting, among them Sir John Flood, the perfect knight, whose second wife has recently died in childbed, but who has already remarried.

'She is even more beautiful than the last,' he says, as if talking of a horse.

Katherine notices that Thomas has somewhere on the way acquired some steel gauntlets, and he sits on his horse bending and straightening his fingers, marvelling at the gloves' articulation.

South of Leicester and Katherine is aware that now the ragged band who landed in Ravenspur has changed into an army, with banners of a rough sort and, thanks be to God, women now, and even children, who follow in a great straggling tail behind their men. Katherine becomes absorbed into it, and listens to their grumbles about thin shoe leather, the price of ale, ash in the bread, the pointlessness of all this wandering. Rumour and gossip sift up and back down the line, and she sees Thomas only when they stop for the night, when he is able to tell her they are on their way to Coventry to find the Earl of Warwick, who is readying the town for a siege.

'A siege? At least we will not have to ride all day.'

Thomas agrees but wonders what it would be like to be in a fixed camp with ten thousand people trying to find food and having to shit in the bushes. Besides he does not think King Edward has the patience to lay a siege.

'Hastings says he is caught between wanting to bite the Earl of Warwick, and wanting to move on to London, where King Henry is, and where his own wife and son are, and where he can secure the backing of the aldermen and so on,' he tells her.

News of Edward's newborn son had come to them while they

were in The Hague. It had been the day after they'd buried Alice, and Katherine had lain with her face turned to the wall and listened to them celebrating downstairs. Thomas and Rufus had huddled with her and they all three wept bitter tears while the music played on.

It was that night they promised on the blessed memory of their dead daughter Alice that they would be done with this, for ever. They would return to Marton and they would never leave again, for any man, for any cause, for any quarrel.

And now here they are, close to that end.

The King – he has reclaimed that title now – decides he must winkle Warwick out of his fastness before he may move on London, so he takes them south, but only a little way, to the town of Warwick's father-in-law, Warwick, and once again they find themselves under the austere walls of the great castle. The townsmen are surprisingly friendly, having little time for their earl despite his generosity, but they are reserved in their offers of hospitality, and King Edward must force himself upon them. His little-but-growing army camps in the fields beyond the river, and already by the third day food supplies are drying up and sanitation has become hazardous to health. Each day King Edward sends heralds to Coventry to challenge the Earl of Warwick to emerge and fight, but the Earl, and his men, whom they guess to number perhaps six thousand, remain stubbornly behind the walls of Coventry, and will not come out for war or peace.

'Everyone knows he's a coward,' Father Pentecost says. 'It is why no one will fight for him until they see he has killed his horse or sent it away.'

'But he may be waiting for allies,' Thomas points out, obviously having been told this. 'The Earl's brother Montagu is coming perhaps, and King Edward's brother Clarence too. And there is

Queen Margaret, don't forget. She may have already set sail from France.'

Father Pentecost is not convinced, but only because he does not want to be. The thought of the Earl of Warwick's army, the Duke of Clarence's army, Lord Montagu's army and the old Queen's army coming together brings everyone out in a sweat. Katherine can see them resisting the urge to cross themselves. And she sees why King Edward is so keen to try to isolate Warwick. But what can King Edward do if the Earl of Warwick refuses to come out and fight, and then Montagu and Clarence bring their armies behind King Edward's? Despite all these new men, and the Flemish gunners, she sees their predicament is as precarious as ever it was.

After the third fruitless day in the fields outside the castle, it is heard that the Duke of Clarence is moving quickly towards them from the west with his army. No one knows how many men he has, but King Edward decides he must meet him before he can meet up with the Earl of Warwick, so they pack up their makeshift camp with some relief, and they march southward through a cold morning, and Katherine sees the Flemish gunners at prayer to their various saints that it will not rain. They follow a broad drovers' track, covered with old sheep shit, grass nibbled flat by the flocks as they've passed through, and the countryside is lush and well tended

Thomas is distracted trying to work out how to tie some vambraces on to his forearms while he is riding his horse. Katherine wonders at him. What is he trying to do?

There is some confusion ahead. They are stopping and there are trumpets being blown and those long fishtailed banners are being raised again. She wonders where they have been kept in King Edward's absence. She thinks if she'd been responsible for driving him into exile, she would have made sure all the trappings of his kingship were destroyed, or taken apart and remade as other lords' banners.

But now the army is trying to organise itself. They are on a heath and bright whorls of bracken are crushed under their feet as the men take leave of the women and rush to find their lord's station. Thomas is to fight alongside Hastings, not as an archer, since he has not picked up a bow in six months, but as a man-at-arms.

'I'll see him safe,' Flood tells her. 'It is the least I can do.'

Flood has on fine harness that Katherine knows must have cost him a fortune, and carries a heavy length of steel fitted with a collar of sharpened flanges that he can use as a hammer.

'From the dowry,' he says, rapping the breastplate with his metal-capped fingers.

Katherine says goodbye to Thomas just as they always have in the past: with a tight squeeze of the hands, a kiss on the lips and a blessing in God's name, which Thomas tells her he will not need but is very pleased to have. Then he tells her to be careful and keep herself and Rufus safe. She looks into his eyes. She does not think he will unnecessarily place himself in harm's way. He has no interest in this fight and he has no companions in the fray, save Hastings himself, and Flood, for whom to fight. She gives his upper arm another squeeze and finds he has plate there too. He is at least, she thinks, taking care of himself. He puts on his helmet and buckles it at the chin. Then he turns and goes off with Flood, and the two Pentecosts, to fight King Edward's brother.

She walks with Rufus and Father Pentecost's wife, whose name she never learns for they both call her 'Mother', and none of them – not even she herself – see the need to introduce her to anyone by any other name. They follow a hunters' track up the side of the heath and join the rest of the women and children and priests and old men, and they can now see the Duke of Clarence's army as it fans out into the usual three blocks at the far end of the heath. It seems slightly smaller than King Edward's, but there is not much in it and perhaps Clarence has more archers, and the wind is slightly with him. He does not have the Flemings, of course, and so long as it does not rain that will be an advantage to King Edward. Even so, though, she does not know who will win in a duel between gunners and archers.

There follows a lull. Mother Pentecost retrieves some knitting needles from her bag and sets to work on a piece of green-dyed yarn. Katherine sees Clarence's camp followers are taking up their position on the other side of the field opposite, and it is as if they are here to watch a tourney. After a while, there are more trumpets. She has no idea what they signal and nor does Mother Pentecost. Then there is the usual exchange of heralds. Two parties of men in surcoats ride out from both sets of lines to meet in the middle, there to see if the bloodshed can be avoided, and to agree the name of the battle for future purposes.

The heralds do not get off their horses but seem to reach their decision quickly. They shake hands with little or no need for negotiation, and each party rides back to their own lines. They look optimistic, she thinks. Yet more trumpets are blown when their news is communicated to the two generals, and then further riders emerge from each set of lines, more of them this time, and all in harness, but their visors are raised, and there is an unwarlike spring to the way they carry themselves. The two parties ride out towards one another, aiming to meet in the middle, just as the heralds had done.

Katherine recognises King Edward in his plate; the smaller

figure is his brother Gloucester and there is also William Hastings. Five or six others ride behind. The lines of men behind them wait in almost total silence. Every eye is fixed on these men, who come together in a small crowd, and then one of them stands and swings his leg off his horse; he drops to the ground and stands there for a moment, and then he falls to his knees. Katherine cannot hear the words, but there is an audible release of tension and of held breath all across the field as King Edward comes down off his horse and lifts the kneeling man and they embrace; and then the other men climb down from their saddles and they all shake hands or kiss, and around the field there is a rippling roar as every man and woman and child – save the Flemish gunners, who are anxious to prove their worth – starts cheering for King Edward and for Clarence and for the House of York.

'No fighting today, then,' Mother Pentecost says, putting her needles away. 'I knew they wouldn't.'

And so they turn north again; the three brothers – King Edward, George, Duke of Clarence, and Richard, Duke of Gloucester – are reunited, and no harm is done. Their army is much enlarged by men wearing badges of the white rose of York on their livery coats.

More attempts are made to lure the Earl of Warwick out of Coventry, but having seen his long-anticipated ally desert him, no one imagines he will be any more likely to come out and take the field, and even though King Edward offers him terms, he cannot now accept them, for while King Edward was meeting Clarence, Warwick was joined by his enemies of early days, die-hard men of Lancaster, who will not now allow him the possibility of surrendering his person and position. The Earl is fenced into a corner, and so King Edward must come to a decision: to continue here, where food and fodder are growing short, in the hope of enticing Warwick out of Coventry with the promise of peace or battle? Or leave him there, a hostile army at his rear, and make his way to London?

Eventually it is decided that moving to London is the best option. The Earl of Warwick's brother, the Archbishop of York, has assumed control of the city, and is every day parading old King Henry around to show the populace that he is fit and well and that he lends his backing to the Earl of Warwick, and that Edward, late King of England, is a great rebel and a traitor. More than that, Edward's sympathisers send messages to say that it is being put about that Queen Margaret will land from France any moment, and with her will come a huge army that will finally put paid to the ambitions of the House of York.

So they march, as fast as they can bear it, along that wearyingly familiar road built by the ancients, and Katherine thinks again of Lucretius and his manuscript and she sees that perhaps there is something in what he says; all those lives lost and souls condemned, and what remains of them all? These stones, which are themselves being rubbed away by the ceaseless wear of foot, hoof and wheel. She thinks she herself must have been responsible for more than her fair share of it.

They stop the first night in Daventry, and the next morning it is Palm Sunday. King Edward and all his gentles take the time to join the townsmen and -women as they process through the streets to Holy Cross Church behind a smith who carries a large wooden cross and wears the sheep's fleece beard in mimicry of John the Baptist emerging from the wilderness.

She thinks of John Who-Was-Stabbed-by-His-Priest, and wonders where he is this year, and whether Mass will be heard at

Marton, and she supposes it must be, and life will have gone on without them.

At Mass there occurs the first of two miracles. The wooden shuttering of a shrine, placed there for the period of Lent to cover an image of St Anne, suddenly breaks open with a startling crack that all in the church hear, revealing to King Edward the image of the mother of Mary. It is a heavenly reminder, he tells them afterwards, to fulfil a promise he had made on bended knee while in Flanders that he would venerate her if she would intercede on his behalf and return to him his kingdom.

Afterwards, the miracle is widely interpreted as a sign that God is once again on the side of the sons of York, and when they march out of the little town, each man is fronded with greenery or flowers, and anyone who can snatches up a loaf of unleavened bread and tucks it in to his or her jacket, and they march with a bounce in their step.

Two days later they are in London, still with that bounce as the citizens come out cheering for King Edward as Bishopsgate is opened for him and they process under its arch, certain at least of ale and somewhere to sleep in a bed for the night.

Thomas and Katherine return to the Bull, the very inn in which they first stayed with Sir John before the old Duke of York tried to have himself crowned in that distant summer more than ten years ago, but later in the afternoon Thomas is sent for by Hastings, and so she takes Rufus down to the river to see the ships and the bridge, and the mad chaos that she hopes will interest him.

'Can we not go home?' he asks.

'Soon,' she says, realising he is frightened by it. 'Soon.'

And she takes him back to the inn, where he is content to sit and feed tiny bits of a greasy pie the innkeeper swears is pelican to an astonishingly large and fierce tabby cat.

Later than evening there occurs the second miracle, though it is of a smaller, more private nature: Thomas returns, having escorted the Archbishop of York from St Paul's to the Tower, and among the Archbishop's small retinue is the man who had disarmed him of his pollaxe at Olney the previous summer. He has it still, gripped in his gloved hands. So Thomas takes it back, and now look: here it is, in Thomas's hands again, the selfsame weapon he had first taken from the giant, then left with Walter, then recovered from Giles Riven, and with which he had finally killed him.

He holds it out and stares at Katherine, God-struck.

'Thomas,' she says, 'in the name of God, what is it that you are going to do?'

21

'Stupid time to set off,' Father Pentecost says.

And there seems to be no one who'll disagree, for four o'clock on Easter Saturday in April is a strange time for an army of ten thousand to be taking to the road, but it is what they are doing anyway. They have been in Smithfield for four days and in that time their numbers have doubled, with men flocking to the city to support King Edward against his great rebel, and this morning King Edward's scouts came in with the news that the Earl of Warwick, now with Lord Montagu and his northerners, is approaching London down the St Albans Road.

'He means to catch our king at Mass,' is one theory, and Flood says it is the gamble of a desperate man.

'It is all going wrong for him,' he says. 'The Duke of Clarence is now with us, and Warwick's late-found Lancastrian allies have abandoned him to go west, to wait for Queen Margaret's fleet to come. So if he doesn't have London in his power, or old King Henry, with which to bargain against his future, then – well, you can imagine how it will go between those two parties.'

Put like that, you might almost feel sorrow for the Earl of Warwick, for the fix he is in, if not for the fact he has been the man with the poker who has these last five years been goosing the country's embers to set sparks flying and flames raging, and for why? For his own personal gain, when he needs no more of anything, but for the desire of it. It is as abhorrent to most men as it is to Thomas, surely?

Flood is not so sure and, listening to him, Thomas is given a sense of the curious pressures that weigh upon men of that class, who must run just to stand still.

'You can never simply be satisfied with what you have, Thomas, because otherwise someone else will try to take it from you. You must scheme to find a better lord at all times, someone more powerful to whom to hitch your cart. You must be on the alert for your own lord's failings and fadings. You must watch your neighbour, and his lord too, to make sure he is not elbowing ahead of you in the race.

'And then there is marriage, and sons and daughters to think of, and to whom you should yoke yourself through them. None of it is easy, Thomas. I envy you your ease, your lack of care, your lack of responsibility. You have nothing that weighs on your mind.'

Thomas does not tell him of the things that do weigh on his mind, and they clomp on up the road that will take them to St Albans, side by side, Flood riding with one fist balled on his metal-plated hip. They are all in harness, helmets strapped to saddles, and the men carry only such weapons as they will need. The archers are loaded with three or four linen bags apiece, Flood has his flanged pole and Thomas his pollaxe. Behind them come their wagons, next the Flems with their handguns, and then the big guns, pulled by teams of oxen, and finally there are some women and a few priests. Old King Henry is there, too, brought from the Tower and closely guarded by some of King Edward's old retainers. Katherine has not come. She will not risk exposing Rufus to any more harrowing sights, and she remains in the Bull, waiting news, she says, like a lord's lady.

King Edward's army is already formed in its battles and proceeds up the road that cuts through the pens and furlongs, past the little village houses and the old churches with thick columns and round arches their forefathers built centuries ago. King Edward's youngest brother the Duke of Gloucester is leading the column, while King Edward himself holds the middle ward, with his other brother the Duke of Clarence kept close by, just in case. Finally Lord Hastings takes up the rear, with whom Thomas and Flood ride in their livery jackets.

Thomas has full harness now, from the tips of his sabatons to the crown of his new sallet, which has a visor. It is not the finest plate anyone has ever seen – Flood calls it ammunition armour – and nor does he have a squire of his own to help him put it on, but Flood has lent him his boy, and it is reassuring, thrilling even. And with the familiar heft of the pollaxe across the back of his saddle, he feels wholly complete and his mind unclouded with any of his usual doubts.

'You should spend as much time as you can with the visor down,' Flood's boy tells him. 'All the others, they've had them since they were boys, and are used to them, but you? Well, you are not.'

So Thomas lowers the visor but then raises it a moment later. It is too close, too disorientating, and with it up, he is able to ride and watch the men around him as they deal with their nerves. There is a great deal of the jittery excitement that precedes fighting, when men behave in uncharacteristic fashions. Some jabber and laugh loudly. Others go very quiet. Others constantly pray, their lips never still. Others seek reassurance from those unwilling to give it. And of course everyone fiddles with something: rosaries, bowstrings, knives, swords, helmet straps, armour points.

'Will we ride all night?' he asks Flood. This surely cannot be a good idea. Already it is getting dark, and the mass of men before them seems to suck up the light, like some long black animal moving noisily along the road. The drummer boys have given up with their sticks and the trumpets are used only to send signals up and down the line. They walk for two hours, past churches where bells are ringing the Angelus, and those who have yet to cover their fires come out to watch them pass. They've stopped their cheering by the time Thomas passes them, but the people seem broadly in their favour, and he supposes at least they must be pleased that King Edward's army is passing their property rather than fighting over it.

When they are past, Thomas imagines the householders will turn and shut their doors and that will be that: Ten thousand men will have marched by, some of them to their deaths.

They come to a small town which they are told is Barnet, and Hastings and some of his household men are gathered in the fields beyond, by a fire they've got going. They are all in harness, and their horses are being taken away by grooms to a camp being made ready for the wagons and the baggage and so on in a field beyond the village.

There is the distant boom of a gun. Thomas and Flood look at one another, a quick glance, but the other men ignore it. It has obviously been going on for some time.

'Our fore-riders have met Warwick's,' Hastings tells them. 'They chased them back up on to the high ground, and say that is where the rest of the army is camped, up there behind a hedge or something. King Edward is determined we'll fight them tomorrow, so we are going to move up on them tonight.'

'Do we know their disposition?' Flood asks.

'They are across the road ahead. They did not have banners flying, or if they did, it was too dark to see. But one of their

fore-riders was in my lord of Oxford's livery, so it is to be assumed
Oxford is there with Warwick, of course, and Montagu, and Exeter. Warwick will probably take the middle ward, but King Edward
has given us the left flank, so we could be up against Montagu, or
Oxford. We shall see. Remind the archers particularly of Oxford's
livery: a star with streaming tails, on white.'

There is nodding, and then another thud of another distant
gunshot.

'Field piece,' one of Hastings's captains says. 'About a mile
away.'

'Must be theirs,' another agrees. He is a tall, flinty looking fellow –
even his face is sinewy – and everyone defers to his knowledge.

A man comes for their horses, and when Thomas hands him the
reins he feels as if he is passing over the last thing tethering him to
normal life. There is no going back now. He is committed to this.
He is Hastings's man and he must stand and fight.

'We will move up in formation, keeping to the left of the road,'
Hastings goes on, pointing his plated finger into the darkness
beyond the fire's light. 'So fill your bottles and empty your blad-
ders. It will be a long cold night for it, but King Edward is
determined, and we have known worse.'

The men begin drifting away, but Hastings remembers one last
thing.

'King Edward says we are to give no quarter,' he tells them,
'and there will be no heralds in the morning.'

The men now shake hands and wish one another God's blessings for the morning, and they turn and are swallowed up by the
darkness to attend to their own retinues among Hastings's larger
retinue. Thomas and Flood wait on Hastings. He is anxious, far
nervier in the shell of his harness than Thomas has ever seen him
before, taut as a bowstring.

'Right,' he says. 'Right. Well. Let us go.'

And they turn and leave the warmth and light of the fire and they make their way into the dark, where the men are just the pale ghosts of their livery coats. There are perhaps ten of them, all in their harness. It feels very odd being part of a group such as this.

There is another gunshot.

'Does Warwick know we are here?' Flood asks.

What do you think? Thomas almost says.

There is a quick second gunshot.

'I mean that we are *here*?' Flood clarifies.

They keep on walking until they see the rest of Hastings's men waiting for them.

'Stand back for Lord Hastings,' someone murmurs and the men part to let him through. They are silent as he passes, though if that is because they have been told to be so or not, Thomas does not know. In place of removing their hats to offer him respect, they touch their helmets. One of Hastings's captains guides them to their position in the front of the battle and then, when they are sure all the men are in place, the order is given in a murmur to move up through the field, dressing to the right, which keeps to the ditch at the side of the St Albans road.

The guns have stopped firing, and the men are relieved.

'Come on then,' Hastings says, and the command is passed along, and the whole of his battle, about four thousand men, starts to move up through the darkness, each man placing his hand on the shoulder of the man ahead. They are on rough heathland, and Thomas supposes if he were here on his own he would be smelling cows, sheep, pigs, but he can only smell himself and the vinegar he's used to clean his plate, and the smell of his arming jacket. It occurs to him that it is so dark it would not matter if he lowered the visor of his helmet, but he does not do so because he finds it hard to breathe. He clutches the livery tabard of the man in front of him and they shuffle up the rise like this for half an hour perhaps, creeping forward until the order is disseminated that they should stop.

'This is it,' Flood says. 'Christ, already I need a piss.'

This is not easily accomplished in harness, in the dark, in a crowd, but Flood manages it. While he is pissing there is a startlingly loud gunshot, a stab of flame in the darkness, and a moment later there is a ruction above as the gunshot passes overhead.

'Christ!' Flood hisses.

And he is not alone.

The enemy are less than 150 paces away. There is another gunshot, further along their lines to the right, a little tongue of flame and a distant throb of a roughly shaped stone. Then there is another. Each time the night is lit with a gloomy orange flash in which Thomas can make out the lines of Hastings's men, all crouching down now as if the ball will come ploughing into them at any moment.

'Should we go back?' someone whispers.

He is told to keep quiet.

Another gunshot. Thomas wishes he had a bow now. He could silence the guns quite simply, he thinks, and would that be so unchristian, given that they are shooting at him?

'They don't know we're here,' Flood whispers and Thomas sees that he is right, and is glad he said nothing earlier. Warwick's gunners think they are much further away down the field, and are sending their balls well over their heads. When this is understood delight communicates itself among the men, for however risky this is – and they would never have dared the manoeuvre had they known what they were really being asked to do – and however uncomfortable the night ahead will be, they understand that come the morning they will have a sudden and unanswerable advantage.

The first inkling of disaster comes just before dawn. A gun a hundred paces to their left fires a shot fizzing into the darkness. This is a gun that has not fired before, and it wakes Thomas, who has become used to the other guns. He wonders why they are firing so far over that way, but soon something else concerns him, and he does not think about that gun and why it might be there, even when it fires again. For it is apparent now as the light swells that their world is smothered in a mist that is as thick as fleece. His harness is beaded with dew and everything is soggy. He puts his helmet on and wakes Flood, who is likewise temporarily bemused.

'What in the name of God?'

'Shhhhh.'

They can see perhaps ten paces. No further. He will never see Warwick's banner in all this. It is hopeless. But then he remembers God's purpose and he knows that he will.

The guns on the ridge are still firing but the snort of flame from their barrels is now a diffused flash of yellow in the darkness, as if fired behind a veil. One fires very near them, then one to their right, over King Edward's ward, and then that one booms away to their left-hand side, well beyond their own left flank.

Trumpets sound muffled along the lines.

The men stand groggily to, and there is much suppressed chatter about the mist. Thomas is thinking about the gun to their left when another booms down that way.

Suddenly orders are hissed and men hurriedly strap on their helmets. Hastings's archers are nocking their bows and shaking out their arrows, stabbing them in the ground, and Thomas cannot help but feel envy for their ease and purpose. They stretch their backs and warm their bows with half-pulls. Around him men are making their own last-minute preparations, helping one another tighten straps they cannot reach themselves, tucking in loose points, straightening strips of steel that have become overlapped.

Then, before it is yet completely light, there is a huge ripple of gunfire from their own lines on their right. Many heavy booms, and then the shorter sprinklings of the smaller guns of the Flemings, and soon you can smell saltpetre mixing in the mist, and the coming day seems to take a step back towards the past night.

There is a bellowed order, and a huge roar, as loud as the sea on shingle, as the archers start their barrage, shooting flat, up the hill, bowstrings popping, into the men they know to be above. Under the noise though, Thomas can hear a low hum and it takes him a moment to realise that the men around him have begun their prayers, because they know what will happen next. He sees they have all lowered their visors and are standing bent slightly forward, with their arms pressed to their sides trying to shrink themselves into the shadows of their helmets as any moment they expect the shafts from Warwick's archers to come thudding down on them.

But, like his gunners, Warwick's archers don't quite know how close King Edward's men are, and the arrows they loose are shot too far and land behind the lines, there for grateful boys to collect later in the fields in which they have already stamped the grass flat.

'Thanks be to God!' someone shouts, but now Warwick's guns really open up, all of them, all down the line, from left to right, and they are all still too high, but some of them are too far to the left, and it is about now that it starts to become clear where King

Edward's night-time manoeuvre has placed his battle. Not only are they too close, they are too far to the right. Hastings's battle is not facing Warwick's right wing as was hoped, but its centre, and Warwick's right wing is to their left.

They are in effect already flanked.

As soon as whoever it is they are facing realises this, Thomas thinks, he will send his men surging down the hill to attack them from their exposed left, from two, perhaps three sides at once. It is the first unfolding of a catastrophe no man can believe will happen to him: that his life will end in ignominy because of a silly mistake. But that is what is happening, and as the trumpets sound the general advance, those men in Warwick's right flank will find themselves unopposed as they come forward off the high ground, and everyone can see that this is when the enemy will see what's happened, and they'll swing to their left, and come straight into the side and rear of Hastings's battle.

In these circumstances it would be insane for Hastings to advance, but not to do so will leave King Edward's battle open to the selfsame fate. Hastings sends a man running to tell King Edward, for in this mist he perhaps cannot know, but nothing can stop it, and so Hastings turns to his men and then lifts his visor. He sends a short look to the closest men about him that Thomas takes to be part apology, part resignation, part determination to sell his soul dear.

'We must get through their line,' Hastings tells them. 'This is our only chance or we – It is our only chance.'

Men nod. Hastings turns, lowers his visor, raises his hammer, looks along the line left and right, then drops it, and they start up the slope through the mist.

Thomas lowers his own visor and is instantly plunged into a dark world where all he can see are two broad slots of the ground before him, a few pairs of well-harnessed legs, and a lower back. He sees his own arms carrying the pollaxe. He has to lift his head right back to see anything else. He can hear his own pulse and his own breathing is already making the helmet muggy. He is instantly thirsty. They move up the field through long wet grass. He cannot see the enemy but after a moment there is a great rippling crash ahead and much shouting; the men before him stop and the din intensifies and in his helmet it is hard to tell where the noise is coming from. Then something glances against his visor and his ears and even teeth ring.

Contact is made.

There is a compression. A great force on his body. Men push from behind and back from ahead. Thomas lifts his axe, points its poll forward, and pushes and shoves at glimpses of men, but he is shielded from contact by the steel shoulders of those in front. He is rapped on the helmet again. He flinches but there's no space to fall. He looks around for someone who may have aimed something at him and is about to do it again with fatal consequences, but he sees nothing save sliding plates of steel, blades, pick points and shafts swinging, never still, a great sea of men in harness, smashing at one another.

Christ, he thinks, this is hell. He cannot see a thing. He cannot hear a thing. It is all a tight-pressing hell. He does not know if he should be swinging or stabbing or stepping back, and he cannot get to the enemy to make any difference. His breathing is far too quick and he feels a band tightening about his chest. His feet slip. Again he's buoyed along. Christ. He cannot stand it. He cannot stand it. He must breathe. He must. He frees his arm and batters the visor up and out of the way. His face is open now, but at least he can breathe, and at least he can see.

Around him men are jabbing at one another, but the two sides are evenly matched, and the lines are held in place. It will take something special – or someone special – or a mistake, to break through this. Thomas sees Flood, and a little to his right is Hastings, with a small gold globe on the top of his helmet, and he is swinging away manfully, short restricted hacks, trying to move forward and drive a wedge into the enemy.

Thomas gets his first glimpse of them: a long fishtailed banner, held above the field of bobbing helmets and the forest of bills to his left. He almost laughs: it is the Earl of Oxford's flaming white star. He thinks of himself up against Brougham and those men last seen on the track below Marton. Christ, he thinks, they were not bad men, and now here we are trying to kill one another.

But everyone around him knows it can't last, and it starts about now, on the left, with a new noise. Oxford's men have found the space before them unoccupied, and they have swung around to find someone to fight, and are now coming in at Hastings's ward from two sides. They have turned his flank. There is nothing Hastings's men can do now save run and die, or fight and die.

At that moment, the man in front of Thomas, one of Hastings's men, is caught with a billhook in the groin and he is hooked off balance so that he crashes back into Thomas, and his killer comes forward. Thomas has seen men like this before: an open-faced sallet, a padded jack, a breastplate and chains on his shoulders, his face set in a ferocious grimace. He is caught up in this, elated at catching and killing a man in plate, and he lunges at Thomas's face.

But Thomas is fresh to the fight.

The billhook is two hands' length of hammered iron, a spear with a cutting blade such as you might use for hedge trimming on one edge and a hook on the other. It is almost ideal for tight spaces such as this, but it is not as good as the pollaxe. Thomas catches the thin iron of the bill in the angle between pick and shaft and twists it aside so that the thrust is diverted. Then he slides the axe down on to the man's fingers and turns them to boneless pulp. The man drops the bill with a howling scream. Thomas could now just thrust the point into his face, but another man – better harnessed – comes at Thomas and he knocks aside Thomas's hammer and drives him back with tangled jabs.

But there is something else, behind him, to the left. A great swirling movement in the mist, more shouting than fighting. Hastings's men are flanked, and they know it, and they are throwing down their weapons and turning to run, and Oxford's men are filled with fresh heart and fresh ferocity, and as they come down the slope they beat and batter those who try to remain, scattering and killing them. Even those immune to the panic, those who know that they will die if they try to run, end up doing so, and they are hacked down from behind.

The disintegration spreads through Hastings's battle, taking each man like a plague: your neighbour goes, so do you. Hastings's men are rubbing off in numbers now, and fleeing, and are being killed as Oxford's men bear in on them from the west. Thomas fights off jabs and hammer blows and tries to inflict some damage himself and already his arms, unaccustomed to such work, ring with pain and fatigue, but Oxford's men press in on them, and they all must give ground. If any orders are being shouted, Thomas cannot hear them, but in fact the thousands of men in King Edward's army come together to act as a single organism, as if they are following those unheard orders, and the line begins a slow turn along its length as King Edward's right-hand battle, under the Duke of Gloucester, must overlap Warwick's left flank on the opposite flank, to the east, on the other side of the road.

There is a chance, if they can just hold on.

But Hastings's battle shreds, its shape disintegrating into tatters, as more men turn and flee. Mortal dread makes anyone thrice as strong as usual, and they tear at one another to get past. That is why the prickers – the men at the back, there to stop this sort of thing – are always armed with lances, and are always the most experienced sort of men who'd not mind stabbing anyone.

Only those around Hastings himself remain, pressed up now against King Edward's men in the centre battle, and the others – hundreds, certainly – now lie dead or are crouched wounded in the field or have run or hobbled back towards the village, or even to London beyond. They will have gone back through the horse lines and the little baggage camp, spreading panic as they pass, and all Oxford's men need do now is to press their attack into Hastings's flank. All Oxford needs do is bring some horsemen into the field and the day is his.

As Thomas is thinking this he sees horses looming out of the mist to his left, and even above the crash of weapons and the shouts of the men he can feel their weight through his boot soles. There may be cries of despair among Hastings's few remaining troops but, as with the orders, they go unheard.

Men cant around, and a great lurch goes through the ranks as the horses come on, huge shapes as big as boats, thundering unstoppable through the mist, and Thomas thinks that this is it. This is how he will die. After everything. He turns to face the horsemen, along the field to his left, though he must still fend off the cuts and the thrusts of the footmen, but that is easier, less wearying, than trying to attack them.

But the horses are going too fast. They are not turning on Hastings's flank. No. They are riding past. They are – can it be? They are going after the remnants of Hastings's men. They're going after the easy targets, after the men they can ride down, men whose backs they can skewer, men they can smash with their hammers just as they smash turnips training in the tilt yard! They are after the baggage train perhaps, or the horse lines!

And then, at that moment, Thomas sees the reserves from the rear of King Edward's battle come surging forward to augment Hastings's ward, and there is the beginning of a reversal, of the pushing back at Oxford's levies, who must be thinking that they are fighting while others are profiting and so they take steps back. This gives everyone in Hastings's livery encouragement and for the first time since the two sides met, Thomas takes two steps forward, over a man face down, and he drives the pollaxe at someone with the intent of not just knocking his bill away but of killing him and moving on to the next.

There are shouts for King Edward he can hear now, and the blare of a bugle for Hastings, and suddenly every man knows this is not lost yet, and they start to drive Oxford's troops back up the slope, tripping them backwards over the bodies of men lying scattered in the blood-slick grass. But there are not enough of them to reclaim the lost ground, and soon the advance falters. Thomas can imagine Oxford must be frantically gathering those gone in search of easy plunder, trying to get them back on the field. His captains – Brougham? – and prickers will be out after those horsemen – or perhaps the horsemen were the prickers? – and they will be battering at them with the flats of their swords, threatening eternal damnation and excruciating deaths for their families just to get the men to give up their lust for gain, to drop their pilfered mugs of stolen ale and return to the field.

But Montagu's men are still ahead of them. And Warwick's men too. They have not broken in pursuit of Hastings's men, and now they are filing across from the centre, and they are well trained and with their added weight Hastings's gain is made temporary, and now even King Edward's line is buckling, pivoting. And so Thomas, who started the day facing north up the road, up the slope, now finds himself facing west, with the road under his heels. He thinks for a moment the men he can see are Warwick's, but then he snatches sight of a badge that is more like a bird than a bear, and he knows they are Montagu's, but it does not matter, for he and those who have remained with Lord Hastings are driven back. The faint glow of the sun is behind him, and it turns the mist before him billowing white, beautifully soft, when underneath it is all hard steel edges and ribbed points that tear and gash at flesh and ring against plate.

At last they move back up on to the road, forced there by weight of Montagu's red-coated numbers. They hold the high ground at the top of the ditch for a moment, but then the man on Thomas's left goes down clutching his face and kicking, and Thomas is isolated, and the man who killed him – in impenetrable plate with a slit like a frog's mouth across the dome of his head – comes for him with a hammer, and Thomas knows he is no match for this man and the three other billmen who are jabbing and cutting at him with their long bills, aiming for his eyes. He slams the visor down with his wrist, and though now he is as if in a hole, he lashes out, and catches something.

But then there is an odd cry to the south, from the way of Barnet, and though Thomas can hardly hear it, there is a curious ripple that communicates itself up and down Warwick's line, and Montagu's men falter a hesitating moment. And perhaps they believe this has been too easy, and that Hastings's capitulation was a trap, for out of the mist down to the south comes a division of King Edward's men, their banners displaying the golden sunburst.

The men about to kill Thomas take steps back, uncertain now. They cannot see how many of King Edward's men there are because of the mist, but they know they are over-committed and that they are now being flanked themselves, and unless they can withdraw, it is they who are the dead men.

But they are good soldiers, and well trained by Montagu, and he has his archers with him still, behind the lines, and they turn on the newly arrived King's men and it is possible to see a smudge of arrows as they loose volleys down the length of the road at them. Thomas knows King Edward's men must attack as quickly as they can now or they will be cut to pieces before they even reach Montagu's men.

And they do. They charge forward. And as they do, King Edward comes to his left flank, and he gives courage to all those around him, and frightens all those who oppose him, so that he creates bulges in the lines. They attack back across the road with him, and Thomas goes too, though his glove is filled with blood and his head is ringing and he is hardly able to lift the pollaxe, because he knows this is another hinge on which the battle turns.

He can almost feel the impact of this second army of King Edward's. It hits Montagu's men and sends them staggering. And then – it is chaos. No one knows what is happening, because these are not King Edward's men. These are Oxford's men, returned, rounded up and brought back on to the field by men such as Brougham, only to be turned on by and shot at by Montagu's men. And now they are fighting against one another and every man seems to be shouting about treachery and traitors.

And for a moment Thomas is able to stop fighting and just watch as the man who'd so nearly killed him a moment earlier is brought down on his back by three of Oxford's levies. One of them puts his foot on the helmet while the other forces his bill blade into that frog's mouth and pushes down with all his weight while the disarmed and dying man waves helpless arms.

And here is Flood, alive, with his visor up. He has lost his mace and found a short falchion and he is laughing with incredulous delight.

'Look! Look!' He gestures. 'They think – they must think Oxford is the King! That his starburst is our sunburst!'

And he's right! Above the men whom Thomas thought belonged to King Edward is the banner of the Earl of Oxford. It is clear now, but too late. Each man in Warwick's line suspects his neighbour of treachery. Old Lancastrians have turned on old Yorkists, and old Yorkists are fighting back. And as they turn on one another, and as the sun rises, King Edward's men, from having been on the verge of extinction, now surge forward to fight anyone who will stand to fight them, and they attack Warwick's men as they are fighting against Oxford's, or against Exeter's, or against Montagu's.

Horses are brought up from Barnet, now back in King Edward's hands after Oxford's men are chased away, and so begins the last act of the battle: the chasing and killing of those whom God has abandoned. And the release of terror brings with it a sort of murderous, destructive rage: the desire to hit, stab, crush, bite, stamp, gouge, break, break and break again. You can see it: suddenly blood becomes something in which to wallow, in which to dress yourself, to anoint your hands and face and hair. To dig so deep into the mire is the only way to block out the terror, and the horror of what you've been through.

'But where is Warwick?' Thomas shouts.

Someone points a bloody blade, and a whole crowd of men go churning forward and Thomas goes with them. A fully harnessed man on the ground raises a rondel dagger to try to stop him passing or to fend him off, and Thomas swings the axe, his hands loosening on the shaft the exact moment it punctures the smooth dome of the man's helmet. But he's not alone. Five or six others descend on the man on the ground, stabbing and punching at his joints, at the glimpses of soft cloth at the back of the knee, under the arm, the groin, the eyes. Thomas wrenches at his pollaxe to extract the pick.

Hastings's men are surging forward, competing now with King Edward's men, and the Duke of Gloucester's, as they batter their way up the slope, and through the hedge and along the road. Wounded men are murdered where they are found, and the dead are now only obstacles in the way of whom they really seek: the Earl of Warwick.

But Thomas is too slow. He does not see it done, and afterwards, when it is over, or there is nothing useful he might do, he walks with Sir John Flood and two other men up to see the body where it lies by the fork in the road to St Albans. The bells are ringing for Easter Day. Flood is limping, and blood drips from Thomas's numb right hand. The mist is lifting, and there is a strange atmosphere among the small crowd gathered about.

No one is talking, and it is as if all the men know they are witnessing something they will never forget, the sort of thing they will tell their grandchildren. There are a few bodies lying around, men tossed aside, their best bits and pieces already taken, ignored now, but the Earl lies apart, as if even in death, even having been stripped down to his braies, he remains greater than any man, even those left alive.

Thomas goes over to him.

He lies on his back. His body, still muscular despite his age, is mottled blue-green with bruising across the chest, and the wheals under his chin where they have pulled his helmet off by force are purple. Otherwise he does not look to be wounded sufficiently to kill him, but Thomas knows what will have happened and sees his head lies on a pillow of his own blood. They would have held him down while someone pulled his helmet off, and they would have stoved in the back of his head. Then they would have stripped him of everything until someone with some authority over them would have stopped them removing his linen braies, for dignity's sake. And then, realising what they've done, they would have stolen away, so as not to be blamed for his death. Because even though he was the enemy, King Edward will value this earl many times more than he will value them, however valiantly they may have fought for him and his cause.

Thomas looks down and thinks about the Earl of Warwick, whom he has sworn to kill, and he thinks about how the Earl has manipulated so many lives, bringing some up, plunging some down. He has been greedy, generous, loyal only to his own ambition, a constant menace to the peace and happiness of the realm, to the peace and happiness of men such as Thomas Everingham, and now he is a mere lump of cooling meat from which the soul has fled.

Thomas turns and leaves him, and he feels as if he is leaving part of himself there, for like all of them here he has been caught up in the Earl's schemes for what seems like all his life.

He finds Flood afterwards, sitting nearby on a dead horse so as to claim the saddle for his own. He has found some bread.

'Lucky,' he says, gesturing to the field. 'Weren't we?'

'God-blessed,' Thomas tells him.

Flood laughs.

'I suppose so.' He looks terrible.

By now the morning mist has risen, leaving the field clear all the way down to Barnet. It is a dismal sight. There are perhaps as many as two thousand bodies heaped and scattered in a circle where the two – in the end three or four – armies enacted their dance on the road, and there are many more scattered around. The smell of blood and eviscerations and shit coats your tongue. The guns are abandoned, and the Flems are sitting apart in a group of their own, looking after their own dead, which number quite highly since they are lightly armoured and their fire gives them away to enemy bowmen. There are priests and friars, gravediggers, looters. The whole village is out, sifting through the damp field for what they may find, wrenching cloth and plate and weapons from the dead, and from one another. Small fights still break out. Two men kill another man who'd been lying on his back and kicking his bootless feet in the air. A woman is trying on a jack for size, and is delighted, though perhaps she has not seen the stain on the back?

'They killed Montagu, too,' Flood says through a mouthful of food. 'King Edward is said to be angry, but it could not be helped, I suppose.'

Thomas nods.

'Though it's murder, really, isn't it?' Flood goes on. 'No one should be able to do it. I mean, afterwards like that.' He gestures at the crowd around Warwick's corpse.

Again Thomas nods. But he is not thinking of how Warwick and Montagu met their ends. He is thinking of the Prioress, and how she met hers. When she saw him ride down into the river, she knew who he was, and what he had come for, and in a way it was as if she'd been expecting him. She had quoted a line that he recognised:

' "And I looked," ' she'd said, ' "and, behold, a pale horse, and he that sits on him is named Death." '

Thomas had said nothing. He had not thought how he was going to kill her. He only knew he must. She'd backed away from him, into deeper waters, and she had told him everything he wanted to know – everything she knew – about Katherine, and how she had come to the priory at Haverhurst.

And then he had climbed out of his saddle and he was waist deep in the freezing waters, and the Prioress had let her beetle float away and she had crossed herself, and he had walked towards her, and she let him, and then he had grasped her by the throat and pushed her back into the water and he held her under. She had not resisted at first, but as she started to drown she had fought back as anyone might, and though she was strong, she was not as strong as he, and he had held her under until she stopped struggling, and then he held her under longer still while he said the paternoster. And the Ave Maria. And when he had been certain of it, he had let her go, and the current turned her, and she eased away downstream.

Thomas had watched a while; then he had led his horse back to the bank and he had climbed back up into the saddle and ridden away, wet from the waist down, back to find Katherine.

PART FOUR

London,
After Easter, 1471

22

They are in the shadow of St Paul's when Hastings's bloodhound, John Wilkes, returns to London with the news that Queen Margaret's fleet has landed in Dorset. It is Tuesday, two days after the battle outside Barnet, and for the first time this year there is proper warmth in the sun's rays and the rising scent of summer to come.

Thomas moves wearily and warily today, Katherine notes, and he seems suddenly much older, with the stiffened limbs and slow movements of a grandfather. She shouldn't be surprised, she supposes. His body is a patchwork of interlocking bruises, of grazes, cuts and lacerations. It is as if he has been pummelled by washing beetles, or been caught under an ox and harrow. He also seems distant, preoccupied, and she supposes it is not only the body that is wounded in such a confrontation.

Sir John Flood is here with some of his men in Hastings's livery to see if it is true that King Edward has laid out the bodies of the Earl of Warwick and his brother Montagu on the paving stones before the cathedral steps for all to see.

'Proof that they are dead,' Flood tells her, 'and are never to return to terrify you again.'

'Or proof they are no longer worth following,' Katherine says, and he admits this with a look.

There is a big crowd, but the atmosphere is not festive. King Edward has had the *Te Deum* sung in the cathedral, of course, but there is no wine in any fountain, and there is none of the wild elation one might imagine would run riot after such a victory.

'It is because we were fighting Englishmen,' is Flood's opinion. 'And because it's Montagu, too, I suppose.'

If the Earl of Warwick and King Edward had parted ways over the last ten years, it is well known that King Edward still valued Lord Montagu and mourns his loss above all others. But the already muted atmosphere changes when Wilkes's news starts to circulate. It is the thought of a Frenchwoman leading a French army, paid for by the French King, into England.

And there is also her son, the Prince.

'King Edward hates the very idea of the Prince, though,' Flood tells them. 'Dear God, I have never seen him hate anyone so much, even the late Lord Somerset who cut his father's head off after Wakefield. He has offered a hundred pounds to the man who brings him the Prince, dead or alive.'

'And there will be no quarter. None at all.'

They consider this. So soon after what they have seen at Barnet the thought seems to horrify Thomas.

'Do you know the Queen and the Prince landed on the very day Warwick was killed?' Flood goes on.

'Will his death come to her as good news, or bad news?' Katherine wonders.

'She will have wanted Warwick's men,' Flood supposes, 'but they would have come to blows in the end, wouldn't they?'

'And without those men, will she just go back to France?' Thomas asks. He sounds hopeful.

'Well,' Flood says, 'without those men, and now that King Edward holds London, and has old King Henry is back in the

Tower, her only real hope lies in Wales, where Jasper Tudor is raising an army . . .'

Now Thomas turns on Flood.

'Jasper who?' he demands.

'Jasper Tudor,' Flood repeats. 'The Earl of Pembroke. If she can join him, then—'

'What are Tudor's livery colours?' Thomas asks. Again, he's very insistent.

'Green and white. I think. Maybe with a dragon. He's Welsh, so . . .' Flood's shrug implies it hardly matters, and Thomas says no more. But he is thinking hard, and not really listening as Flood goes on: 'And then if she can move up Cheshire and the Northern Parts, where as you know they are always keen to rise in rebellion against more or less anything and anyone, well, together they might number twenty thousand. Imagine that. Twenty thousand. That is almost as large as was gathered at Towton, wasn't it? And there is no way King Edward could resist that, even if he is the luckiest commander alive.'

The crowd begin to disperse, hurrying home to spread the word about this new business in the west.

Katherine and Thomas walk back through the city with Rufus towards the Bull in Bishopsgate. She had hoped they would return to Marton, but she knows they can't. Not yet. Not until this is over. She thinks of that story of Jack's about the hero fighting the monster's mother. She wonders where Jack is now? She half expects to see him come loping along, bow in hand, a comforting figure. But Thomas looks serious. They both know he cannot weasel out of his obligations to Lord Hastings a second time.

'Then at least we will have his support,' he says, 'and we will be left alone to – to live our lives. We won't be called upon to do any of this again.' He holds up the clotted scab on his hand.

'So you are the hero in Jack's story, are you?' Katherine asks. 'And the next monster is the Queen? And once she is beaten, there is no one?'

'Of course not,' he says. 'But once she's beaten, then yes. There will be no more monsters, or mothers of monsters – unless there is the son, and he is with her, isn't he?'

'So Wilkes says.'

'Well, once he is beaten, then no. There are no more monsters to come.' He says this as if he is sure of it.

They stop to let some of the Duke of Gloucester's men by.

'Perhaps you are right,' she says.

The summons comes a day later. Hastings commands all the retainers he can muster to come to Windsor to join King Edward, from where they will move west to find Margaret's army before she can cross the River Severn, which is what cuts her off from Wales and Jasper Tudor's rebels.

'You will come with us, this time?' Thomas asks when he sees Katherine packing her few things into a saddle bag.

'I will,' she says. 'It was bad enough watching you go out the other day when we knew you were only going ten miles. This time you will be across the country. And William Hastings would have asked me himself, I'm sure of it, save he is so chastened by what happened at Barnet that he is keeping himself to himself, have you noticed?'

'What happened at Barnet wasn't his fault,' Thomas says, 'and in the end perhaps it was for the best?'

Katherine and Rufus travel in a cart laid on by Hastings, and Flood tells everyone that he has seen Katherine deliver a baby with one hand while removing a man's arm with the other, and as the stories of her skill become shorter, so her fame spreads wider, and even before they leave the city everyone with a complaint comes to the cart to ask if she has a cure for this or that – dropsy, say, or a goitre – and Hastings sends a fat purse of coins to buy what she can by way of medicines and anything else she thinks she might need. She is joined by Mother Pentecost, who is now a widow and childless since both her men were killed at Barnet, though only the son's body has been found, and it is possible the father is still running, though all doubt it, since he was so fat.

Katherine thinks about what Thomas said, and wonders how that can be considered for the best?

They roll out of Windsor on the day after St George's Day in bright sunshine, along that great drovers' road westward, following the valley of the River Thames, first to Reading where they camp on its banks beyond the abbey, and then to a town called Abingdon, following the shimmering water of the river on their right. Reports come in from scouts that the Queen is moving southwards, and eastwards, to Kent, but King Edward refuses to believe them, and others doubt the rumour as well.

So they press on, leaving the river, and cutting due west. They aim to cut Queen Margaret off before she reaches Gloucester, which has the lowest bridge over the Severn. When they pitch camp outside Cirencester, they have been walking five days, and it is there they hear King Edward is right, and that Queen Margaret has moved her army – rumoured now to number many thousands – northwards, to a place called Bath.

'We should move to Gloucester,' Flood says, 'or down to Berkeley, and then we will have her corked in the corner. It is like chess, Mistress Everingham, and King Edward is a master at it.'

Katherine wonders if that is true when next they do not move westwards to Gloucester, nor to Berkeley, but southward to a place called Malmesbury, having heard the Queen has moved her army away from Bath, westwards to Bristol.

'They are running scared,' Flood says, forgetting his earlier words, and ignoring the rumour that runs through the camp that in Bristol the Queen will collect ordnance and many more men, and that King Edward has lost his chance to stop Queen Margaret reaching Wales.

Everyone is already tired and worn through. They have travelled seventy-five miles in a week, in good heat, carrying their weapons, their food, their tents, and they have been wearing out shoe leather, wheel iron, axle-oak and oxen.

Early the next morning, though, a scout rides into camp bellowing that the Queen is coming. He rides to King Edward and is shown into his presence, even though he is at prayer, and a moment later the trumpets are sounding and every man is snatching up his weapons, having squires strap on his plate, and running to the banner of his lord, leaving the women to pack up the camp and follow on as best they can.

It is now that Wilkes of all men comes sidling up to Katherine, and to begin with she thinks he might have some illness of which he is ashamed, and she is surprised for she did not have him down as that sort of man. Instead he asks her a favour.

'I have no family of my own, Mistress Everingham. Neither wife nor child. No son to carry on the Wilkes name, as it were, which is perhaps just as it should be, given my wandering and wondering nature, but that is not to say I have nothing of any value to pass on when I am called to heaven's gate.'

'Go on,' she says. She is more amused by Wilkes than scared of him, as Thomas is.

He now pulls out of his bag a thick wallet of papers and he

looks at her speculatively, as if making sure she is the right person to whom he should be entrusting whatever it is he's got there.

'If I should be killed in the coming days, Mistress Everingham, can I ask you a favour? To pass these on to Lord Hastings? I am his man of business, as you know, and should I be killed, leaving no heir, he must therefore become my man of business, and there are, within, one or two bequests in which he will find an interest.'

'You trust me, Master Wilkes?'

'Above all men, Mistress Everingham.'

She thinks he really means this. He offers her the package, which she takes and puts with the rest of her things. He watches closely, his dark eyes lively but clouded by anxiety.

'There,' she says. 'It is safe.'

He smiles at her.

'Thank you, mistress. I pray God you will not need to perform the service.'

'I am certain I shall not.'

He is about to go but turns.

'May I ask you one last thing?'

Her heart gives a curious clench.

'Certainly.'

'You will believe me superstitious, but may I ask you to swear to God that should I die, you will perform the task, no matter what?'

'As God above is my witness, I swear I shall pass these papers to Lord Hastings, with own hand, if you do not return alive.'

'Thank you, Mistress Everingham. A great weight off my mind.'

Katherine joins the others as they set off, moving west again, following the tracks of their men through the morning's heat until they see King Edward's army is gathered at the top of a hill. Consternation arises. Why have they stopped? They are not arrayed to fight, and yet . . . The camp followers wind their way up the hill, walking to save the oxen to find the mood sombre.

King Edward has been outwitted. Queen Margaret and her army were never here as was hoped and predicted, but have slipped away northwards, towards Gloucester and the crossing of the Severn, as had been earlier forecast. Even Flood is dismayed. King Edward takes it badly, but he does not chase after them and for that his army is relieved. Instead he starts drinking wine early and that night there is shouting from his tent, and the army gathers to witness it, an audience of orange, fire-lit faces. But before dawn a messenger comes riding up the hill despite the dangers of the dark to say that the Queen's army is already on the move, trying to steal a second march on them.

This time King Edward does not allow it. Trumpets are blown, drums are beaten and, as the sun appears, the army rolls off in battle order, winding its weary way back northwards, keeping to the chalky high ground. Riders are sent on ahead to warn the people of Gloucester that Queen Margaret is coming, and that they are to close their gates to her army and deny her everything. King Edward is coming, they are to tell the mayor, and relief is at hand.

'Good luck to them,' Flood says as they ride out. He wanted to be one of those chosen, but Hastings and his men do not ride high in King Edward's estimation at the moment, even though anyone might have run in their position at Barnet.

'But Exeter's men didn't,' one of King Edward's men says. 'And they were flanked by Gloucester on the other side.'

'That was different,' Flood points out.

They move all day in the high heat, and though there is bread, there is no ale, and no water to be had until they ford a river that is so churned up the water is undrinkable unless you walk a half-mile upstream. Then they are on again into the late afternoon. At last they stop by the side of the road in the town of Cheltenham, and there is more bread doled out.

'How far have we come?' someone groans.

Thirty miles is the best estimate.

But news has come back that the citizens of Gloucester have rebuffed the Queen's army, and even managed to detain some of their ordnance, and so now, perhaps, they are within a few miles of their enemy, and it is not over yet.

'So up, you lazy bastards! Come on! On your feet! There are more miles in you yet!'

And so they stagger to their feet again, and walk on. Rufus is asleep on his cart, as is Mother Pentecost. Katherine walks the next eight miles besides the cart, and at dusk King Edward finally lets his army and its followers pitch camp. They are on the common land of a village with a wooden-towered church from which friars in habits come begging – unsuccessfully – for alms for the care of lepers. She finds Thomas has been almost roasted alive in his harness, and he sits red-faced with his feet in the mud of a stream. Since Barnet he seems less enamoured of his visored helmet and it lies with the other pieces of his armour on the grass behind him, filthy and scratched, and it might be that he wouldn't mind if someone were to steal them, but the pollaxe is next to him, still oiled, and it still exudes its unsettling presence.

He passes on such information as he has gleaned.

'They are ahead,' he tells her, 'in the town of Tewkesbury. There is a crossing, but the river is too high, and crossing by ferry would take too long, and it would leave them naked if we were to come up upon them there.'

'So we have them? This will be it?'

Thomas nods.

That night they more or less sleep where they fall, and Katherine dreams that Alice lives, and needs her, and when she wakes she feels the child's loss as a constriction on her heart and lungs, an internal withering, and her tears are thick and taste of salt. Thomas is already on his knees praying and she watches him for a time with her eyes half-open in the dawn, and she ponders how far they have come, not just in the last few days, but since she first saw him, running across the snow outside the priory. What she would give for some of that snow now.

The sun is barely stirring behind the hills to the east, and the sky is almost green, shot through with rays of Yorkist sun when the rest of the camp rouses. It is a good sign, of course, of God's blessing, but also, Christ, it means the day will be long and hot.

The mood in the camp is one of solemn desperation. The last few days have whittled them to the bone, and only the very youngest of men show any spring for the day ahead. For most, whatever comes will be a labour that needs be endured. They have moved up from Cheltenham in their battles, and the men take to them now, and there are the usual sorrowful scenes of departure between those who will fight and those who stay behind, and God's blessing is called upon for the many thousands of individual acts of separation, and Katherine and Thomas take shelter in formulae and well-rehearsed conventions.

But there is something extra to this one, and as Thomas turns to find his horse, she cannot help but hurry to him one last time; she puts her arms around him and he turns and holds her tight too, and she whispers in his ear.

'Come back,' she says. 'Come back. For our sakes.'

She starts to weep and his eyes mist up too, and suddenly she wants him gone, to be away, out there, to bring an end to this, to fulfil his God-appointed role. And so she steps back, wipes her nose on a dusty sleeve and tries a smile she knows to be unconvincing, and he leads his horse off towards Hastings's tents.

Then the trumpets sound and those long banners are unfurled, beautiful pieces of work held by proud men, and the followers take their steps back, and last sights of their men are unconsciously recorded, and now there are two types of people: those staying, and those going. This latter party sink to their knees as prayers are said by a bishop with a nasal voice, and King Edward commits his cause and quarrel to Almighty God and the blessed Virgin Mary, and to His glorious martyr St George and all the other saints, and then they all murmur amen and stand and brush the dust from their knees, and finally they mount their horses, and they begin winding their way northwards, as many as five thousand of them, up the road that will take them through the flat fields to Tewkesbury.

When the last of the divisions have left the camp, the others follow on, spitting out their dust, and they alone make a solid little army, Katherine thinks, perhaps a few thousand strong, made up of women in the main, but also children, elderly men, the walking wounded, a handful of priests – none of whom talk to one another – and two surgeons with assistants and their carts of bandages and barrels of unguents and tar, which they will save for any wounded gentle.

Katherine feels underprepared, but she will do what she can with her few things and Mother Pentecost as an assistant. She has with her on the cart, alongside her own stuff, two tubs of honey and one of beeswax, a tub of vinegar, lengths of virginal linen, a small pouch of washed needles, lengths of fine hemp string that she has already coated in beeswax, what the sawyer told her was a butcher's saw, two knives even sharper than that she bought in

Lincoln, and a disc of fine grit stone with which to keep them honed. She has ewers for urine, the wherewithal to make a good hot fire, a poker to riddle it, and a device she had made by Hastings's silversmith that she will use to cauterise any of those small blood vessels. She also has five glazed pots of dwale she bought from an apothecary in Windsor who demonstrated its power on his own wife.

23

It is a distance of perhaps three miles to the horse lines, but before Thomas can dismount and prepare himself for what is to come, Hastings calls him to his side. It is still early, a beautiful day, and their shadows are long on the dew-soaked grass. Men are standing talking and laughing too loudly. Movements are jerky and unnatural.

'King Edward has asked for a plump of lances to be set up on that hill,' Hastings tells him. He points westwards to a tree-lined hillock. 'In case of ambush, such as that which nearly did for us at Towton. I have volunteered Sir John Flood, and I'd like you to be by his side.'

Thomas thanks him earnestly, and he thanks God, too, that he will not have to endure the lines again, to fight blind in that terrible helmet. By Christ, he has acquired a new respect for those who do.

'And John Wilkes will be alongside you,' Hastings adds, and there is something catching about the way in which he says this, a slight hitch in his voice and eyebrow.

Thomas thanks him again for the favour, and he wonders if Katherine is not right: Hastings does looks less exalted than usual. Can King Edward really blame him for what happened at Barnet? He was put in an impossible position. But his men did turn and run. Thomas sees there is a curious tension about them now, a self-consciousness, a quietness, as if they know they are the subject of speculation, and today they must prove themselves above all others.

Thomas leaves them with a few shaken hands and a grumble at his great good luck, and he exchanges wishes that God will go with them all, and he rides back behind the lines, past the backs of King Edward's men and the backs of the men of the Duke of Gloucester's battle on the left flank, to find Flood with what might be another ten or so men on horses, all milling around below where the ground rises in a gentle slope up to a thicket of poplars. Flood has a long spear in his hand, twice or three times his height, and he is gazing up at its point with something like wonder.

'This is more like it, eh, Thomas?' he says.

Thomas agrees that it is probably so. Beyond Flood, not yet wearing his helmet, is Wilkes. He is standing up in his stirrups and, like the rest of them, has no spurs. They do not intend to fight on horseback. He has on a dark blue brigandine, leg and arm plate, and a visored sallet similar to the one on Thomas's saddle, which he wants to delay putting on until the very last moment, and he is peering north over the heads of the men in Gloucester's battle towards the square bulk of the abbey. He does not seem very encouraged. Flood asks him why he has such a sour face, and Wilkes looks at Flood as if he is a child.

'There are more of them than us,' Wilkes tells him. 'And there's rough ground between us, tracks and so on, cutting across. And look – there's a house in the way. That is no good for horses.'

Flood is dismissive.

'We are to be up on that hill,' he says, pointing over the small stream and up at the thicket.

'That's perhaps where we'll start,' Wilkes explains. 'But we will end up either here. Or, all going well, over there.'

He points to the west, where the rivers are. Flood knows Wilkes is right, but still pulls a face to suggest he is being an old woman.

Wilkes has a horseman's hammer that looks to be of more use to a man in a saddle than the pollaxe that Thomas has strapped to the back of his saddle, along with the bow he still carries, and the sheath of arrows. Thomas loosens the blade of his sword in its sheath.

'We'd best get out of sight,' Wilkes says, and he spurs his horse up to the copse of poplars. Thomas and Flood follow. Flood is a very good horseman, or his horse is very good, and he leaps the stream from steep-sided bank to steep-sided bank while Thomas's horse steps carefully down into its muddied depths. They ride up the slope and into the shade under the canopy of fresh green leaves, where there are already a fair number of men and horses waiting. One or two have long lances, but most have horseman's picks, or flails. They study Thomas and Wilkes unsmilingly, but they greet Flood warmly, and detain him with questions about his harness and his choice of the lance. These men are excited and look as if they do this sort of thing every other day.

'Have you ever been in such a situation before?' Thomas asks Wilkes.

'It is no different from hunting stag,' Wilkes says.

So they *do* do it more or less every other day, Thomas thinks.

'You'll be fine,' Wilkes says. 'Trust in God and your own right hand. Or something.' He shoots his eyebrows. He has put his helmet on now but even with its cheek pieces pinching him from all sides, he has an extraordinarily expressive face.

From here they can see Queen Margaret's army. At its nearest point, it is about six hundred paces away, drawn up in what is, Thomas has come to see, the usual formation: in three clumped blocks gathered around numerous flags and banners to their fore, and if Katherine were here she would tell him to whom each flag and banner belonged, and therefore who they were.

'That is Somerset on the left, Prince Edward's – of Westminster – in the centre, and on the right, facing Lord Hastings's men, Devon,' Wilkes tells him.

It is somehow typical of the man that he has good eyesight.

They make their way around the back of the horsemen to the far side of the copse, on the west, where the moss is thick on the trunks and from where they can see the dark gleam of the water in the Severn, the river the Queen's troops have been trying to get across, and another river to the north, that Wilkes tells him is the Avon. Neither is as wide as the Trent at Marton, but there is no way to get across them unless by bridge or ferry or perhaps by ford. Thomas cannot help but stare at the abbey, though. There is something about it that chimes with him.

He supposes he must have seen it before, but when? Perhaps they came this way when he and Katherine and the other men whose names he has forgotten came to Wales? He thinks yes, that is it. By barge. Down the river. That one. The Avon, Wilkes has just called it. And he remembers the strangest thing: that he got lost. He was diverted around the meadow there because it was, in winter, too marshy to cross dry-shod, and so, seeking to come back to the town a different way, he'd followed a track that led him back towards the ice-rimed fishponds where he saw a boy kill a heron with a stone flung from his shepherd's crook. How strange that this is the only thing he can remember from the whole episode. No! He came back to an inn when it was already dark, and they thought he had been murdered or something.

Now when he looks over towards the abbey from this little hill instead of that scene of winter chill he can see Queen Margaret's right battle, the one led by the false Duke of Somerset. It's facing King Edward's left battle, the one led by the Duke of Gloucester, and its flank is hard against that steep-banked little stream.

'The enemy are in a good position,' is Wilkes's opinion. 'There will be no flanking them this time, as at Barnet.'

'You were there? I didn't see you.'

Wilkes shakes his head.

'I was in Dorset. Keeping watch for the Queen's fleet.' He nods at the ranks of the Queen's army. 'I brought her the news of the victory at Barnet,' he says. 'Or the loss, as she saw it. I thought I was overdoing it. I told her that it had been a massacre, and that Montagu and Warwick had been killed, and she was so scared of losing her darling boy that she was on the very brink of stepping back into the ships for France, but by the time she looked up, the French fleet had sailed off. They hated Warwick, you see? They always believed what they wanted to believe about him, and they believed he was a bad commander, because, do you remember, she'd beaten him at St Albans that time? So they thought anyone could have beaten him at Barnet. They underestimated him, just as they underestimate King Edward, and so here they are.' He shakes his head. He seems sad.

'You think it will be easily won?' Thomas asks.

'Oh no,' Wilkes says.

'But it can be won?'

'Oh yes. Much depends on how Somerset and the young Prince communicate. Or who is commanding alongside the boy. And how we – or they – deal with that rough ground. Look at those hedges. What do you think they hide?'

Wilkes is studying the difficult terrain between the two armies, the few hundred paces of country that are fissured with hedges, a copse or two, and what looks like a sunken lane cutting across the lines. It is where Thomas got lost that time, but even though it was so long ago, he can imagine what it would be like if the two armies met in such a tight space as that lane.

Their horses crop the long grasses, and are thankful for a moment's rest. Flood lingers a few paces away with the others, and has set aside his lance in favour of a flail that he is comparing to another man's hammer.

There is a moment's silence that Wilkes breaks as if he has something to say.

'So,' he says. 'Quite a year?'

Thomas looks at him. There's something confiding about the tone of his voice that is at odds with this apparently banal opening.

'Yes,' Thomas supposes. 'Yes.'

'For you, I mean?'

Wilkes is looking off into the distance, at the marshy meadow ground that lies between them and the two rivers. Thomas grunts. He doesn't know what Wilkes means.

Wilkes sucks his teeth.

'That bit,' he says, pointing. 'The meadow there.'

Thomas says nothing. It looks innocuous enough. It needs draining, but the meadow is low and probably floods every winter. Maybe it wouldn't be worth trying to drain it. Maybe rushes would be—

'I was in Lincoln,' Wilkes says, having reverted to the previous subject. 'After I saw you at Marton Hall. After Mistress Everingham's waters broke.'

Thomas can scarcely believe his ears. He is being taken back to Marton, back to the summer before Alice was born. Does he want to talk about this now? He can feel his face reddening.

'I was going on to Lincoln, after that,' Wilkes goes on. 'D'you remember?'

'I remember.'

'And you remember why? Why I was going to Lincoln? I know Lord Hastings has taken you into his confidence, and has spoken to you about the ledger. I know that finding it was part of your – your task in taking over the manor of Senning in the north.'

Thomas feels his head growing hot. The ledger! He has not thought of the ledger since – since – for months. Christ! The ledger. Here. Now. In a wood while he waits to gallop down a hill and attack men armed with bills and bows and God knows what else.

'So what?' he manages to ask. 'What of it now?'

'Well,' Wilkes goes on, 'I have likewise been looking for the same ledger for Lord Hastings. Perhaps he mentioned that?'

Thomas knows enough not to say too much.

'I know you do these sorts of things for him.'

Just then there is a ripple of pops from beyond the brow of the hill. Wilkes stretches to peer over. There is nothing to be seen.

'The Flemings are trying to goad Somerset into attack,' he supposes.

'Is there something – we should do?'

'All in good time, I think, Master Everingham.'

There is something so close about Wilkes's attention that it is almost suffocating. It is as if this whole thing – this unfolding battle – is there just so that Wilkes can get him alone for a moment.

'And I believed,' Wilkes goes on, 'when I was on my way to Lincoln, that I had found a connection – *the* connection – between Rouen, from where the ledger had been stolen, and this country. I believed I'd made a connection between a man who works for the King of France, and the man who had bought it off the man who stole it when the garrison was abandoned to the French in 1449.'

'And did you?' Thomas knows he must pretend.

'Did I?' Wilkes asks himself 'Did I? Yes. I believe I did.'

The popping continues, a ragged prickle like rain starting or finishing on hard earth. Wilkes's horse snorts and tosses his head. It is not enjoying it. But Thomas knows that the Queen's men, who have fewer guns themselves, will be enjoying it less.

'Well,' Thomas says, 'that is good, isn't it?'

'In a way it was better than that. Because, you see, we found the ledger itself.'

'The ledger itself? You found it? Praise Jesus!'

'Yes. Yes,' Wilkes agrees. 'Astonishing. A miracle. And, as you say, praise Jesus. It was hidden under a larger book, a psalter if I remember, in a widow of the parish's house.'

'Ha!' Thomas says. 'In Lincoln? All that time?'

'Yes.'

Thomas tries a laugh, but it's too dry, and he knows that is not the end of it. Now there are louder booms coming from behind the trees. Culverins, he thinks, the wheeled field guns they've brought from Windsor. Wilkes's horse continues its stamping. They can smell gun smoke, bitter as alum, drifting in the sky from the lines like fine dark dust.

'Yes,' Wilkes goes on, 'and when I was actually holding it, the ledger, in my hand, I was – you can imagine, I was pleased. I had found what I'd been looking for, for so many years, and I'd stopped the Earl of Warwick finding it, too, so I sent word to Lord Hastings and then – then I walked around holding the thing in both hands, just looking at it. And I looked at all the other books too, and how well preserved they were, but this one – well, it had a great hole punched in it, as if someone had taken a pick to it, and every edge was curled and flared, and it was so grubby, and fingered, and I thought, well, it was a ledger in a garrison, not a psalter in a church, so surely it should be like that, and surely it would be scribbled over, and have things drawn in it by a bored scribe.

'But even so, there seemed something odd about it. It was as if it was hot, while all the other books were cold. Alive, while they were dead. I know, I know it sounds strange, but that is how it felt. And I started thinking about it, and it was only after a while doing that, that – that I asked myself how came it to be that if it had been here, tucked away out of sight all these years, that I knew about it in the first place?'

Thomas is silent for a moment. His mind is still.

'How you knew about the book?' he asks after a moment. 'About the ledger?'

'Yes,' Wilkes says. 'You see, I saw then I had made a mistake. In my search for it, I had begun from one end of the trail, from where it started, if you like, but the only reason I knew it existed is because of a man named Sir Ralph Grey, who briefly had the book with him when he had been governor of Bamburgh Castle back in '64, and who tried to use it to buy his pardon for treason from the Earl of Warwick. So it occurred to me – while I was actually holding it, you understand? – it occurred to me that if he had it, and I am certain he did have it, then how did he come to have it in the first place, and why – or how – came it to be back there, *where it came from*, in Widow Daud's collection of books?'

Thomas does not know what to do. He can feel his mouth open and the spit drying. The ground seems to shrink under him. Christ. Christ. Christ. How could they have got it so wrong? Why did he not think of this?

'I don't know,' he says. 'I don't know.' His voice is creaky, dust dry. It is the smoke from the guns, of course. Wilkes smiles a little smile and exhales through his nose.

'No?' he says. 'No?'

Christ, Thomas thinks. Just how much does Wilkes know?

At that moment there is the sound of a horn from the Queen's lines. It is the signal that King Edward's Flems' handguns, his culverins and his bowmen have done their job, and they've provoked one of the Queen's commanders – Somerset probably – into attacking across that rough ground.

And Thomas knows that that is what he must do. He must attack.

'Tell me, Wilkes,' he says. 'You know that coffer? The one you found after the rout at Losecoat? The one containing those marvellous papers that proved the Earl of Warwick and the Duke of Clarence got the boy – that Great Captain of the Commons – what was his name?'

'Robert Welles.'

'Robert Welles. Him – to rebel. Did you really find any of those letters?'

'I may have done.' Wilkes smiles. Thomas sees he's enjoying this.

'You forced his hand, didn't you? He was never – I saw him – he was never going to rise up against King Edward, was he? If it wasn't for that friar, sending all those messages and raising the country—'

And then it strikes him.

'God in heaven! That was you! *You* were the friar!'

Wilkes cannot help but grin. He is proud if it. Proud of his deception.

'Christ,' Thomas says. 'You provoked the whole thing. You used Lord Welles's attack on Burgh's house as the bait to . . . Wait.'

The internal mechanism of Thomas's mind spins, locks, spins

and locks again. Wilkes stares at him with a sort of light in his eyes, waiting for him to see what is plain.

'Jesus,' Thomas says. 'You – It was you. You even got Lord Welles to attack Burgh's house, didn't you?'

Wilkes smiles and says nothing, and suddenly Thomas does not like Wilkes. Doesn't like that smile.

'You – you used Mostyn, didn't you? You – He was your man. He told you when to get Welles to attack. That day, when Burgh was away, you wanted to cause offence but nothing more.'

And then his thoughts come to rest at the end of the chain of deduction.

'And then you killed him, didn't you? It wasn't the bloody Jews. It was you. You killed Mostyn because he – what? He knew none of it was true? Or no! It was the keystone, wasn't it? He knew the thing on which this scheme was founded wasn't true.'

And now, like a sword clicking into its oiled scabbard, he remembers where he first saw Wilkes.

'You were up that bloody tree! It was you! Pruning those apple trees!'

'I've always tried to avoid bloodshed,' Wilkes says, 'that was all. I was sorry for the men caught up in this, and I was sorry for Lord Montagu in particular, whom I always admired, but if he had not come out for his brother, then there would have been no exile for King Edward, there would have been no battle at Barnet, and the Queen and her son would not be here now, and many, many lives would have been saved. When I come to stand before my Maker, Master Everingham, I will be able to say I did my best for my king and my country, and I tried to save as many lives as I could. What about you, Master Everingham? Will you be able to say that?'

At that precise moment there is a movement before them, at the bottom of the hill. A flicker of colour in among the trees of the sunken lane where Thomas remembers being lost. Few men can see it, and certainly not those on the other side of the hill, nor any among King Edward's army.

'What is that?' Thomas asks, pointing, though he knows it can only be men.

Wilkes is half-amused, as if this might be some distracting ruse. But when he sees what Thomas has seen he sits back in his saddle.

'Ha,' he says. 'Ha.' He looks at Thomas. 'They're Somerset's men, I think. Clever. They've got across the stream and – but how did they get there?'

'It is a lane,' Thomas tells him. 'It looks like a wood, but there is a lane through it.'

'How do you know?'

'I've been here before, many years ago, I think.'

Wilkes calls across to Flood, who comes over on his beautiful horse and looted saddle. Wilkes points. Flood turns, stares, stares again, then pulls his horse around. He rides quickly to the top of the hill, threading his way through the trees. He talks to a man in very fine harness with a red crown atop his helmet, wearing the white boar badge. One of the Duke of Gloucester's men. He sends a rider down to King Edward, Thomas must suppose, to warn him of Somerset's flanking movement. Somerset will catch his culverins and his handgunners, and his poorly armed archers who will have exhausted their stocks shooting over the heads of these men, and he'll appear right under King Edward's nose. He may even be aiming to finish the battle by killing King Edward.

But – is it a wise gamble? Thomas wonders. The lane, he knows, will take them across the face of the Duke of Gloucester's troops, hidden by the hedges and so on. They may emerge to surprise King Edward on his flank, but Gloucester's men with their white boar badges will be on *their* flank, and so what Wilkes says is right: this hinges on how well Somerset has communicated his plan to the young Prince Edward – who someone once said is supposed to be violent in the extreme – because if the Prince has not moved forward to back up Somerset's flanking attack, then Somerset's men will be minced between King Edward's and Gloucester's. And also, if Thomas has read this correctly, this plump of horsemen that even now is barely able to restrain itself from charging down the hill and catching Somerset's men from behind.

Thomas has almost forgotten Wilkes, when the man places a hand on his arm. It is half-confiding, half-arresting. Soft leather and steel.

'We've not long, Master Everingham,' Wilkes starts. 'So I will get to it. How did you ever come by the thing?'

'The thing?'

'I think, Master Everingham, you know by now not to fool with me.'

Thomas nods. In a way, Wilkes is showing him some respect too.

'The pardoner,' he tells him. 'We got it from the pardoner.'

'The same man who dealt in antique crossbows and pigs' bones?'

'I don't remember him,' Thomas says, 'but Katherine – my wife – she does. He – We were on a ship. He was killed. Pushed overboard by the sailors who wanted his goods, I think. They were about to do the same to us – to me and my wife, though she was not my wife then – when Sir John Fakenham came to our rescue, and he took the ship, and when we landed – in Calais – we were left with it. The ledger. But we had no idea of its . . . value. We had no idea of what it meant.'

'So you altered the text recently?'

Thomas nods.

'It only struck us to do so,' he says, 'when we saw the ink my son had made.'

Wilkes smiles.

'I saw his letters before I saw the ledger,' he says, 'but once I had seen what I was looking for, or once I'd not seen what I knew I ought, his ink and his hand came to mind. It was almost brilliant, except, of course, that it was also . . .' He blows out.

'But what would you have done?' Thomas asks.

'Well, the one thing I'd not have done is taken it north to offer it to old King Henry.'

So that is it. The mask has slipped. There is the accusation, then. The hard, cold incontrovertible truth of the matter.

'We didn't in the end,' Thomas says. He feels himself bleating, his voice pitched high and plaintive. Wilkes looks at him. He is disappointed.

'That hardly matters, does it?' he says. 'You still did it, and you still must pay.'

His words are like stones. Old, somehow. The way it always was. The way it always will be. Thomas has no reply. He knows that is true. He knows – they knew – from the moment Sir John Fakenham said the boy was a bastard that it would always end this way. He shrugs and opens the palm of his hand. They are good gloves. He is glad he bought them. Then he looks at the other men around him. Are they somehow Wilkes's men? There to help in Thomas's execution?

'I always thought it might be you, you know,' Wilkes goes on. 'I was never sure, and then, the year before last, when I came to see you, and you saw me in the woods, I thought it looked as if you had been expecting me, as if you knew I'd come – or someone like me would come – sooner or later, and I thought, well, they've got something to hide.'

'That was you? In the woods? Christ, Wilkes. You scared my wife out of her wits.'

Wilkes shrugs.

'I regret that. She is a good woman. She doesn't deserve to be caught up in this.'

Thomas could almost laugh. He could almost tell him that he has the wrong man. He should tell him that Mistress Everingham is the one that he wants, who was the creator of all this, whose plan it was.

There comes that slithering crash of surf on shingle, the din of men meeting in earnest, but from this distance the noise conveys nothing of the hair-raising terror of being there, of being half-blinded, of being half-choked, in the mad panicking rush to hit someone, anyone, before someone hits you. In a way, though, Thomas powerfully wishes he were there, or anywhere away from Wilkes.

The guns go silent, save distant pops from the right flank, from Hastings's battle. Perhaps Somerset has taken the guns and sent King Edward's bowmen scurrying? Perhaps that is all he wanted to achieve? So that the Prince and his central battle can come forward unmolested to make their numbers count? These thoughts are as distant and vague as the gun smoke itself that floats in the warming breeze.

'So what is it to be?' Thomas asks. He cannot help but look up to see any number of suitable branches from which to hang a man.

'William Hastings is fond of you,' Wilkes says. 'Fond of your wife.'

'Yes,' Thomas agrees. A tiny flame of hope rekindles.

'And I know you to be a good man,' Wilkes goes on. 'I know you tried to declaw the ledger. I know that you are on the side of King Edward, if only for your own sake.'

'Well then?' Thomas asks. Why not allow this to pass? Why does it have to end this way? He doesn't ask the question aloud, because he knows what the answer will be. Still, though, his heart picks up.

'Well then,' Wilkes says, 'what would Lord Hastings say if he discovered that I had lied to him and spared you? Not only would he have you gutted and hanged, because after all you kept the ledger from him, and tried to sell it to his enemy, he'd also have Mistress Everingham and your boy killed too, because he'd have to, you see, and he'd also have me gutted and hanged, because I would have put a lie in his mouth if King Edward ever heard of this, which he may yet.'

The flame dies. Thomas looks at Wilkes carefully. He knows his future does not hang in the balance. It is decided.

'So what are you suggesting?'

Wilkes nods at the men manoeuvring across the fields below.

'Do King Edward one last favour,' he says. 'I'll see he never forgets you. You'll get a proper burial, with a carved stone, in full harness if you like, spurs and everything. Would you like that? Ten priests to say Mass for your immortal soul. He'll knight Rufus. Sir Rufus Everingham. It has a ring about it.'

Wilkes stares at Thomas without moving. It seems everything is stilled, even his horse, and the sounds of the fighting seem to lull too, and it slowly dawns on Thomas what it is that Wilkes is offering, or asking.

'You want me to get myself killed?' he asks.

Wilkes nods minutely.

'Think of Mistress Everingham,' he says. 'Think of your boy, of Rufus.'

The odd thing about it is that Thomas almost accepts what Wilkes is saying as being the right thing. It is not merely that they all, always, knew something like this was going to happen, right from the very moment Sir John discovered the ledger's secret; it is more Wilkes's certainty. He is condemning Thomas to this death, and it is just as if he is telling him that the cock will crow at sunrise. It must happen.

Again, Thomas almost laughs, almost tells him that it was always Katherine who was caught up in this.

'You will act no further?' he asks instead.

Wilkes shakes his head.

'As God is my witness, she will go untouched, and this will end with you.'

But there is something odd here.

'So Hastings doesn't know?' Thomas asks. 'It is just you who has made this decision? Just you? You are – you are my sole judge and executioner?'

Wilkes returns a level look that brooks no appeal.

'Come, Master Everingham. It is better this way, you know it. Imagine the alternative, and thank your God you are being asked this.'

Thomas thinks. Wilkes is right, of course. Imagine the alternative. How did Sir John describe what would happen to them if King Edward knew they had proof he was a bastard? They would have their feet burned until they condemned everyone they've ever known and then they would be half-hanged, and then taken down, and gutted, and have their intestines wound around a sharpening wheel until they swallowed their own tongues. That is what he had said. Hard enough to think of it happening to yourself, but your wife? Your son?

There is a stirring among the men at the top of the field. The messenger has returned. A decision has been made. Thomas forces himself to look away from Wilkes to where Flood has raised his mace. He shouts at the men waiting just as if he were their commander, and maybe he is, that they will descend as they are formed. There is a ragged, slightly ironic cheer, and the noise of one or two lowered visors, but most men prefer to see until the very last moment, and they keep them up.

Thomas's whole body is throbbing as if he is on the edge of something – a cliff. He remembers now being a child. A boy about to jump from some gritty stones. Someone below, daring him on. Christ. Where do these memories come from?

The fighting continues away to their right. It must be Somerset's men, engaging with King Edward or with Gloucester.

Thomas gives Wilkes one last look, and Wilkes offers his hand. Thomas takes it. It is an odd, incomplete connection, two gauntlets made of leather and steel plates, no flesh. It does not feel sincere or binding.

'So we are decided?'

Thomas nods.

'Yes,' he says.

'Well then, good luck, Master Everingham, and may all the saints guide you to the New Jerusalem.'

'You too, Master Wilkes.'

Wilkes frowns and shakes his head as if he is impatient at Thomas's irony.

'One thing, though, Master Everingham. If anything should happen to me – should I, God forbid, meet my end in this field – I've left word to be delivered into the hands of Lord Hastings.'

Thomas maintains his faint smile as all hope dissipates.

Of course he has. Of course he has. Wilkes is no fool.

'Save what if Hastings is killed? What if we lose this battle? What if King Edward is killed?'

Wilkes looks at Thomas very carefully. For a moment Thomas thinks Wilkes will tell him that in the case of the Queen and Prince Edward taking the field, he has left some condemning word to be delivered into their hands, but no. Wilkes has not considered this.

'Well then,' he starts, 'in that case, you would be free of your obligation to the House of York, free, insofar as you could ever be, to live your life in King Henry's England.'

Thomas says nothing. Wilkes goes on:

'And Edward of Westminster – they call him the Prince of Wales, do you know? – he is a vengeful man. The worst of them all. How long do you think he'd let you live? How long do you think he'd let *any* of us live?' He gestures at the waiting horsemen, and then spreads his arms to indicate the whole county, the whole country, before subsiding into silence, as if his point is proven.

But there is something he does not know. Thomas wonders whether to tell him, and then cannot resist it.

'I do not think I'd need worry about that,' he says.

Wilkes hesitates before taking the bait.

'What do you mean?' he asks.

'Do you know who my wife is?' Thomas asks him.

'She is – your wife. She has nothing to do with this.' Again he gestures.

'Well,' Thomas says. 'It turns out she does.'

Wilkes looks at him.

'How?' he asks.

'Through her parents. Her father is – or was – a man named Owen Tudor.'

403

Wilkes starts. Thomas never imagined saying the words aloud either.

'Owen Tudor,' Wilkes repeats. 'The Welshman who married old King Henry's mother?'

It is gratifying to see Wilkes even slightly disconcerted. Thomas was as thrown when the Prioress told him who Katherine's family was, in the very last moments before he drowned her.

'Exactly,' he says. 'Who is her mother, too.'

Wilkes chews on this a few moments. His gaze darts about the field. He avoids looking at Thomas while he teases out the implications.

'Your wife's mother is Katherine of Valois?'

Thomas laughs.

'I know,' he says. 'It is – I don't know.'

'So she is King Henry's sister?'

'Half-sister.'

'Dear God,' Wilkes breathes and there is a long silence. Then he tries another tack. 'Ha!' he says. 'Any man might say as much. You have no proof.'

But Thomas does.

'There is an archive,' he says. 'In Canterbury. It contains all the documents. The letters she brought with her when she arrived in her priory.'

'*Her* priory?' There is a moment of blankness; then Wilkes makes the connection. 'Ah! Of course. That is where you knew her from!'

Thomas nods and then asks:

'Mostyn told you?'

'I – discovered,' Wilkes admits. 'Just before you came to kill him yourself.'

It all makes sense, Thomas supposes.

'Well,' Wilkes says, trying to dismiss it now. 'Your wife is a Tudor. So what?'

Thomas is, in truth, not sure.

'It means she is aunt to the Prince of Wales,' he points out. 'That would buy us something.'

Now that Wilkes has absorbed the knowledge, he seeks to nullify it.

'You are not going to turn on us, are you, Master Everingham?' he goads. 'You are not going to have all those men at your command suddenly turn their livery and their blades on King Edward?'

Thomas feels light-headed.

'I seek only the chance of redemption.'

Wilkes stops his sarcasm.

'You had that in mind? *Redemption*?'

Thomas shrugs. He feels desperate.

'It will make it easier,' he says.

Wilkes nods but says nothing. Perhaps he thinks Thomas is making a joke of it. Gallows humour. The sort you are meant to enjoy. But Thomas has seen a glimmer of something – some hint – within that word redemption that gives him strength of purpose. There is, Thomas thinks, a way out of this that, after all, will mean he need not die, he need not leave Katherine a widow and Rufus an orphan, and if he should fail in this, if he should die in the attempt, then at least they will be honoured in his death.

'Wilkes,' he says. 'You have done me a fine favour, and I will remember it.'

Wilkes looks concerned at this new tack, but before he can say anything, before he can verify Thomas's meaning, Flood drops his mace, and he and Thomas are buoyed up and forced on by the tide of horsemen setting off down the slope, riding ten or so abreast, fanning out as they leave the trees and start across the sloping pasture. Wilkes drops behind Thomas, in about the third rank. Thomas is aware of Wilkes watching him closely, but he doesn't care. He kicks his horse on. Ahead, hidden beyond the hedges, Somerset's men in blue and white await with their spears and bills.

24

Thomas is knee to knee with Wilkes as their horses reach the flat ground above the lane. It is damp and tussocky but the horses create a thunder and a moment later Somerset's men see them coming. Men point and heads turn. Then there's panic, confusion, and men try to run. Back up the lane! Or along the lane! But there is no give either way. The numbers are too great. The space is too tight. They turn and try to scramble away up the far bank, tussling and heaving to get away through the scrubby hedge on that side. Billmen drop their bills and amid the panicked cries no one hears the shouted orders and pleas of the commanders to stay and fight.

But now Thomas and his comrades must pull up, for the horses cannot be forced through the screen of hawthorns and down on to the fleeing men beyond. Thomas watches the horsemen throw themselves from their saddles and force their way through the thorns and spikes, immune in their plate armour, and drop down on to the poorly armed footmen beyond.

In the sunken lane, in the shadow of the trees, Thomas can see men are hacking and chopping at the billmen, who try to defend themselves, but their organisation is gone, and already the numbers in the front line are felled by sword thrust, hammer blow and spear jab.

Thomas and Wilkes stay in their saddles. There is no need to join the others in the sunken lane because already Somerset's attack has been foiled. His men are pushing and panicking and running anywhere they can: out into the front of King Edward's battle; across the field on their way back to their own lines; or pushing back up the way they've come. They sow only more panic, more confusion. Somerset's clever trick – if that is what it was – has turned against him. It is he who must rally his men now. And Thomas can see his flags and banners ahead, and he is still engaged with the fringes of King Edward's battle, and even as Thomas watches, this is astir: Trumpets sound and drums roll, and King Edward's banner and his flags are being waved about as if to impel the troops forward. Somerset will soon have precious little chance for anything other than saving his own skin.

Thomas – followed like a dog by Wilkes – moves along the line of the trees towards the mêlée where men in blue and murrey and men in blue and white are meeting now, beginning to come to blows. They are jabbing and hacking, but they are yet to move in among one another, which is when the real bloodshed will begin. The Duke of Somerset's banner is there, waving over the heads of a troop in badged jacks, who do not seem anxious to engage, and linger behind their fully harnessed commanders, who are trying to lead by example.

Wilkes hangs back, watching.

'Not going to get involved, Master Wilkes?'

'Only a fool fights, Master Everingham.'

Thomas ponders this for a moment. Wilkes is probably right, but Thomas has not much time for thought, for already to their right the Duke of Gloucester's men are pushing forward. If Thomas goes any further along this hedgerow, he will be caught between them and Somerset's men. There is no way through now to where he wants to be unless he is very, very quick, and very, very lucky. But now he sees that his plan is coming unstuck: Queen

Margaret's central battle has not pushed forward in support of Somerset, which means Somerset is absolutely at the mercy of King Edward's men, and now Gloucester's men, and Thomas will have to find another way through. Christ. He knew it would not be easy, his task, but this makes it almost impossible.

A culverin fires from across the field, a distinctly sharp crack above the shouting and the din of weaponry, and its thick smoke whorls in the already sulphurous air. It means King Edward has regained his guns, if he ever lost them, and Somerset's bid to silence them has failed. Thomas turns and watches Somerset's banner jink and dip, until it lurches decisively back towards the Queen's lines. There is a distant roar. That's it. Somerset has turned.

And now Gloucester's battle is surging forward, the white boar banner to the fore, and from here Thomas can see the little Duke is there below it, at the front in among a tight knot of his retainers, and they advance in good order, but are yet to encounter the dips, dykes, hedges and lanes that cut the field.

The rest of the horsemen from the plump on the hill have not chased the tail of Somerset's men, but are milling around the hedges of the lane, cutting at survivors and filing northwards up the lane in search of more men to kill. Now those who are lingering turn to see what is coming at them from the south, and each man can easily suppose what will happen if they do not get out of the way, and each hurries for his horse.

It seems not one of them has been killed or even wounded, and there is real joy among them. Each man is grinning. Some inspect their weapons and one man stoops to wipe his on the long grass, cleaning it of God knows what. Some stand to look back at the tumbled corpses that fill the lane, at their blue and white livery coats ripped and gore-soaked, and here and there an arm might flap and someone burble something. Men have had their helmets ripped off and they lie like acorn cups next to their dead owners, whose heads have been dished and clubbed. One of the horsemen is walking among them with a hammer, taking careful aim to silence or still those who betray their still-beating heart. Crack. You'd do it to pigs, but men?

'Back,' Thomas tells Wilkes.

Wilkes thinks he is being a coward, and you can see him thinking he will have to kill Thomas himself.

'Christ, Wilkes,' Thomas tells him. 'The fighting has scarce begun! There's still chances enough to get myself killed.'

'Come on then,' Wilkes says.

Thomas leads him and some others back up the hill to get out of the way, to gain height, to wait for more orders and get a better view of what is happening. But Thomas rides away from the others, around to the north. He wants to see Queen Margaret's army from behind. Wilkes alone follows him, until Flood appears, reunited with his spear and grinning wildly. His horse is tossing its head, rolling its eyeballs, and Flood looks like someone's idea of a god of war.

'They are routing!' he calls. 'They're routing! Somerset's men! Look!'

He points his spear beyond the hedges to the soggy meadow Wilkes had noted from above. Men in blue and white are streaming across it. They've already given up for the day and are running from the field. It has taken them an hour at the very most.

'They're trying to get to the ford!' Flood shouts. 'Quick!'

And Thomas sees this is what these men have lived their whole lives for: a rout. Every man there save him seems to know what to do, which is to gallop as fast as they can back down the slope and through the hedges towards that meadow. The hedges, the steep-banked stream and the length of track that must be traversed only serve to make the thing more thrilling, and seen from behind the mass of horses seem to pour like liquid up, over, through and along these obstacles as if they were not there.

'Christ,' Thomas breathes. His plan is unravelling before his eyes. And Wilkes too looks anxious. At this rate there will be no time or opportunity for Thomas to get himself killed.

They ride after the other horsemen, through the by now broken-down hedge, over the stream and then up and along the track. The dust makes you spit. Ahead the first of those to run are casting aside their weapons and their livery, as if they might some-how be allowed to melt into the countryside as at Losecoat Field, but here in Tewkesbury it feels very different, and everybody knows there is spite in this fight, and no quarter will be asked or given.

When they reach the fringes of the boggy meadow, Wilkes pulls on his reins and brings his horse to a stop. Thomas does like-wise. They are on the road from Gloucester, and they sit in their saddles a moment and watch as the horsemen go after the foot soldiers.

'God in heaven,' Thomas says. 'Look at it.'

'You were at Towton,' Wilkes says. 'You saw worse there, I'll bet.'

Thomas cannot recall it, but what he sees now revolts him to the pit of his stomach. There is something so barbaric about it. Merciless. The men on horses are slaughtering those trying to escape, and those trying to escape have given up all power. Most have thrown their helmets and weapons aside and all they can do is raise their naked hands to fend off blows from swords and picks and hammers. Some shriek and beg, and they throw themselves on the ground, while others try to bend away from the cutting edges, twirling in the mud, but the horsemen are too organised: they ride them down, and knock them down, raising gouts of blood that seem to linger like puffs of pink mist, and pocks and gouts of sodden flesh that leave great gouged wounds at which men stop and stare.

One or two of the horsemen have dismounted and are passing among the wounded, despatching them with single blows, as if they were chickens. But it is so much worse for there is no pity in it, only savagery, and it is unforgettably sickening to watch men be killed like this. If Thomas lives through the day, he will never forget this sight.

But still more of Somerset's men come, hoping for the safety of the river, scrabbling from the field and straight into this hunter's net to be butchered, and it is as though they think that if they can only keep running they'll escape, but they can't. The ground is marshy, and now littered with obstacles, and the huntsmen are organised and seemingly tireless, cutting across them and then circling back and catching those they missed with the first pass.

Thomas watches one man come springing from the field, peering backwards over his shoulder, as if this is where the danger lies. He's not looking where he's going; he trips over a man's leg and blunders for a few paces and then goes down. But he's up soon enough, and he looks around and sees where he's found himself, and he seems to plot a route through, and he sets off, legs pumping. But the ground's uneven. He swerves around one group of wounded where a man is on his hands and knees drooling blood, and he picks his way between three or four men who could be corpses, or soon will be, and then he sees a dismounted horseman who blocks his path to the river, but who might be got past because he's busy with his knee in someone's back and a rondel knife in their earhole. It's like he is opening a stubborn oyster shell and the man's screaming.

The man Thomas is watching now suddenly seems very aware he is not out of danger, but still he comes on, only he is tentative now, and his running is stopping and starting. He sidles at an angle, aiming to get past the man with the rondel dagger, who has just killed his target and is standing up, satisfied that his stabbing in the ear works. He wipes his knife on the coat of the man he has just killed, as if earwax is worse than blood, and then looks around for someone else to slay.

He locks his gaze with the other man, the one trying to get past. Permission is asked, but denied. The killer sets out towards his victim. His victim takes a few steps back. He casts left and right, but there's no avenue of evasion. The killer is closing. The first man has cast all weapons aside. He is wearing a jack, undyed, and russet hose. Short boots; nothing on his belt, not even a purse. His hair is slick with sweat. The killer is now focused only on him. Thomas has seen stoats kill rabbits like this.

Just then a horsemen comes thundering through the sodden field and hits the fleeing man with a pick, and he is sent slewing to the ground, bouncing once before lying still. The horseman rides on, looking over his shoulder, and the killer is on the dying man before he can move, and he has his knee in his back, and the dagger in his ear and it is over in a moment.

'Christ in Heaven,' Thomas says. Wilkes looks green too. Thomas pulls his horse around. He cannot do anything about this. It is part of war, cruel and sharp, as Sir John used to say. They turn back towards the abbey, in the direction from which men still come running. Some of them aren't Somerset's men, and instead of his square symbol of a yale, some wear what looks like a deer and others a swan, and their jackets are blue and red.

Thomas kicks his horse, forcing his way into the throng. He has drawn his sword, but no one will yet offer him a fight, for these men have only escape in mind, and they cringe as they pass him in groups of twos and threes, only anxious to be spared.

Or so he thinks.

He sees the man coming from a way away. He among them is the only one who does not seem to be running scared. He seems angry, and he is better accoutred than most of the others, who are largely billmen, in a red and white livery jacket with a feather badge, and he's carrying a pollaxe that he means to use, rather than discard. Even though he is twenty, thirty paces away, their gazes meet and lock.

There is nothing for it now, but Thomas does not want to fight anyone. Or not yet. He nudges his horse away, angling to avoid him. But the man comes after him. He is determined on a fight and Thomas's brief spell being above it all, a saddle-mounted spectator, looks to be coming to an end.

A point will beat a blade, men say, but a pollaxe will beat all else, and Thomas knows the man will first kill his horse if he does not get off and fight him. He swings his leg off and lands heavily in the gritty earth and stumbles. At that moment Wilkes seems unable to help himself, and he nudges his horse between Thomas and the man with the pollaxe, not enough to stop him, but to distract him, to make him look elsewhere for the moment it takes Thomas to right himself, toss aside the sword in the long grass and slide the pollaxe from his own saddle. Thomas notes the favour. He steps away from his horse. The thought of what a pollaxe might do in all that exposed horseflesh makes him shudder.

Now they face each other, standing amid a spinning crowd of passing men, and he's a tall man, older than Thomas, with a big, broken, sunburned nose and ginger bristles up to his crinkled eye bags. He wears a visor, which like Thomas he keeps up, and a bevor that hides his mouth. They study one another for a moment, looking for gaps in their armour. This man's got a breast- and backplate, and a plackart over his stomach, and his legs and arms are likewise encased in plate. There are few obvious weaknesses, but Thomas has even fewer.

Even so, Thomas thinks with a sudden swoop that he has not fought a man with a pollaxe since – since he cannot recall. He killed Giles Riven with this very weapon, but that was seven years ago, and Giles Riven was unarmed. Now, though, Thomas has no time to think as the man comes at him, sideways, keeping his body as small a target as possible.

But the man comes too fast. He has built up a fury from watching his erstwhile comrades deserting their lines, and he pitches himself into the fight with too much force, and from above. Thomas swings his axe up to meet this man's. He half catches the fluke, deflecting it, and then from the bind he lets the man's axe slide down the length of his own axe, and he steps back and aside, letting the man's weight carry him through after his axe.

Thomas swings the butt of his axe up and into the man's armpit, crunching through the rings of mail, and he tries to lift him as if he were a straw bale on a fork. But though the man growls and spits with pain, he's better than that, and before Thomas can drive the point home, the man has managed to wrench himself free, and he hooks the false of his axe behind Thomas's calf. Without the plates of Thomas's greaves, this would be a terrible wound, but the fluke slides up and catches and then snaps the straps holding his poleyns, his knee pieces, and Thomas must hop and spin to shake himself free and protect the back of his knee. But he is close to the man, and he can use him to keep himself upright. Then he pushes him away using his pollaxe as a staff and the man staggers a few steps.

They must start again.

But there is blood under the other man's arm, smearing the

wool of his livery jacket, and there is a change in his demeanour. He's circumspect, wary, circling now, and you can see him worried by the pain in his flank. He touches his armpit and holds his fingers up to see how bloody they are. That's when Thomas attacks. He comes from below, a series of jabs, using the axe as a spear, aiming for the throat, for the rivets in the gorget, for the joint between that and the bevor. The man staggers back, fending him off with his forearms and knuckles, trying to bring his pollaxe back down on Thomas. He strikes a glancing blow that only manages to scrape Thomas's visor down across his face, and suddenly Thomas is lost.

He hears the roar of terror in his own ears, rattling around his own cramped space. All he can see are two flat slits of light. Christ, why did he never practise any of this with the visor down? Why is he now stumbling, reeling around, unable to see where the next attack is coming from? Unable to see the man in red and white? He swings his axe wildly and sees his horse's flank. Dear God, where is he? He swipes back the visor but no! It is jammed. He backs away, turns around. Where is the man in red and white? He turns again. Christ, where is he?

Thomas flails at his visor, but it is stuck. And then suddenly everything changes. His head is wrenched on to his chest and the ground – that gritty mud – rears up at him. His feet fly and he lands with a crump on his chest. His pollaxe is torn away. He lies stunned, tasting grit and blood, seeing nothing. He cannot move. He cannot breathe. Then he feels something pressing against his backside, a foot, moving his mail skirt aside. He knows what will come next: a pollaxe fluke, straight between his legs. He rolls to the left and feels a glancing blow on his thigh. He manages to turn so that he is on his back, then his front, then his back again. But that's it. Something stops him. Another man perhaps. He waves his arms and hits something. He scrabbles for the knife in his belt. It's gone. Then there is a foot on his chest. He can feel weight through the breastplate. Thomas cannot stop himself screaming. But whoever it is bends and heaves the visor back. Thomas feels he is being strangled, or having his head ripped off. Then sunlight blinds him. He is sodden with sweat, and pinned where he is. He can see a shape loom over him, blocking the sun. It is he, the man who will kill him. Thomas sees him drawing back his arm. He knows what's in his fist: the rondel dagger Thomas lost.

'Wilkes!' Thomas screams.

But Wilkes does nothing.

Thomas thrashes. One last time. He rocks back and the man slips in his own blood that has dripped on Thomas's breastplate. Thomas rolls away, one turn, two. The man scrambles after him. Thomas can see now, but he does not need to see to feel his sword where he left it in the grass. He grabs the blade and rolls back towards his attacker, just as the man comes at him. Thomas drives the blade up under his skirt and into his groin. Both hands, everything he's got, twisting the blade. Up into the man's bladder, his guts, his belly, his heart and lungs. Thomas would drive it all the way if he could. He would see his blade point come out of the man's head if he could.

Scalding blood drenches his hands and arms and then the man falls over him, and the sword is pulled from Thomas's grip. Thomas lies there, pinned to the ground by the weight of the dying man, who arches his back and looks up and stammers something that is more like the sound of a bittern than a human, and after a moment he collapses completely. He spasms, kicks the ground, and then stills. A moment later there is a gusting sigh and a foul stench.

Thomas lies there a moment, hardly able to breathe, seeing

nothing but blue sky and the faintest twist of white cloud that drifts in the heavens. Anyone could kill him now. He is completely immobile. He sees the shapes of men – shoulders and heads – flitting past. None stop, or even glance at him. He supposes the looters will come later. He turns his head. His horse is gone. Stolen or run, he does not blame him. But there is Wilkes, too. He has dismounted and is holding his shying horse by the bridle. He is sort of smiling. It is almost as if he is pleased Thomas is still alive.

'Well, well,' he says. 'That was close.'

'For the love of God, Wilkes, get him off me.'

Wilkes comes to stand over him and looks down. Thomas looks up. They say nothing. Both know what the other is thinking. But then Wilkes bends to slide the dead man from Thomas and, once he has taken a deep breath, Thomas rolls to his feet. He is so covered with gore that he thinks he can taste it. He tries to wipe it off his breastplate and his arms, but his hands are the worst, and he just smears it about. Hastings's white livery jacket is more than half red now. Thomas looks like one of Prince Edward of Westminster's men. Wilkes steps back in disgust.

'By Christ,' he says. 'Look at you.'

Now Thomas starts trembling. His hands first, shaking violently, as with the ague. Soon his whole body is too. Then his guts rebel and he must bend double to spray scorching vomit over his sabatons.

Wilkes just laughs.

'Martial glory personified,' he says.

Thomas feels kitten-weak and needs to sit for a moment. He does so, on the body of the man he has just killed. His harness is cleaner than Thomas's. Men running past falter to look at him. He vomits again, a series of foul-tasting dry heaves.

'Like a woodlouse,' Thomas says, noting the plates of the man's sabatons. He runs his steel fingertips over the back of his sallet. Christ! There is such a dent in it.

'He caught you quite a wallop,' is Wilkes's opinion. 'He was aiming for your visor, but you turned, you see? Saved your life, I suppose.'

Men are still running past, making for the river across that low-lying meadow, and through the hedge he can see them being cut down by the horsemen with whom he'd been on the hill.

'Come on,' he says more to himself than to Wilkes. He gathers himself and his pollaxe and he sets off, on foot, against the flow of running men, along the road from Gloucester, towards the stub of the abbey tower.

'Wait!' Wilkes shouts. His horse is refusing to budge. It is terrified of the noise, the cannon fire, the charging, shouting men. Eventually, Wilkes lets him go and the horse turns and gallops back down the road towards the south. No one tries to stop it.

'Blood of Christ,' Wilkes says. 'He cost me my dowry!'

Wilkes is married? It gives Thomas a pause for thought that ends as more of Somerset's men run at them, but seeing Thomas's pollaxe, and not looking to fight any more, they swerve away at the last moment, though he can never be sure they will, so he must inch his way along the track, stopping to be ready to defend himself as each man comes on.

'What are you doing, Master Everingham?' Wilkes asks.

'What you told me to.'

'You have some – what? Some plan?'

'It is no easy matter to keep you alive and get myself killed, Wilkes.'

Wilkes allows this and they move forward, towards the stream where there seems to be a clot of men fighting over what might be a bridge. A well-accoutred horseman in blue and white comes thundering along the track towards them and, like all others, they must scatter before him. He aims a swipe at Thomas, but there is an understanding that neither wishes to fight the other and they leave one another to their fate.

There is still fighting going on beyond, and Thomas can hear that rapid snapping of a hundred weapons cracking against one another as lines meet, and the roar from a hundred throats in the distance. Banners and flags fly still, and above the sounds of the fighting drums still beat, and trumpets sound, so someone is organising attack and defence. The gunfire continues, too, and smoggy clouds billow and drift above the tree- and hedge-tops where he can see the furze of raised bills, the gleam of steel. Arrow shafts flit both ways.

But who is fighting whom?

Wilkes peers ahead to where the mêlée looks the sharpest.

'Prince Edward of Westminster,' he says. 'Pressed hard, by the look of it.'

Thomas grips the pollaxe. The blood in his gloves is tacky. His head throbs as if caught in a vice. He can hardly lift his arms. This is no way to set about it, he thinks, but he must.

'Right,' he says. 'Right. This way.'

And he steps out. Wilkes turns to him and gives him that look again. For such a clever man Wilkes is being slow. But then again, perhaps he has not heard the story of Thomas once killing the Earl of Shrewsbury? It is true Thomas cannot remember doing it, or how he did it, but it is a story that gives him hope, and Thomas needs hope more than he needs charity right now.

More men in better harness come hurrying past. Again, no blows are offered. Escape is the only thing on their minds now, that and shame, but from Thomas's right, Gloucester's men in their blue and red livery are moving up fast, and they too have only one thing on their minds: to kill those fleeing from the field; and as Thomas and Wilkes start up the road towards the abbey and the fighting, these men fall in behind them as if looking for command from someone who knows what they are doing, and before Thomas can say anything, he has perhaps twenty men in blue and red at his back, and each awaits his guidance.

Thomas leads his newfound company towards the abbey and, seeing them, the men coming from that direction – a mixture of liveries, but mostly the blue and white of Somerset, and here and there the red and white of Prince Edward – abandon the track. Some tear at the hedges to get through to the pastures and the river beyond, others turn their backs and start up the road back towards the town. Others follow. It is as if Thomas and his men have cut off the supply of deserters making for the meadows behind, and Thomas supposes he is perhaps saving their lives. Though, Christ, he thinks, looking around at Gloucester's men who've joined him, he would not count on them for mercy.

'Like herding fucking sheep!' one man laughs. He's fat and his red face is squeezed into too small a sallet, and he uses his bill to imitate a shepherd's crook.

When they see Somerset's men breaking away, they speed up, roaring and waving their bills. Somerset's men abandon the road all the faster, throwing their weapons down and throwing themselves over the hedges to break across the pastures and reach the river, as if that will save them. Some of Gloucester's men chase them, but most can see and hear that the real fight lies ahead, at the end of the road, and they stick with Thomas and Wilkes.

'Come on!' Thomas urges, waving his pollaxe as men such as Flood might, and Gloucester's men roar and surge on up the track.

And now the men in Somerset's blue and white livery are being replaced by men in the red and white of Queen Margaret's beloved son, Prince Edward of Westminster, whom Hastings once called an onanist, and Thomas begins to feel a sense of hope, for Prince Edward's men are scattering just as Somerset's have, running anywhere and everywhere other than on the road. But then, suddenly, on the bridge ahead between Thomas and the abbey, their numbers thicken, and suddenly there is order where there's been chaos.

The way is blocked. The Prince's men are not routing. They are moving back in an orderly, planned way, and they are under flags and one of those long fishtailed banners that means they can only be the Prince's household men. They will be the best he can find, there to protect him and only him, right to the very end.

Of course Thomas should have known. Of course it was never going to be that easy.

Wilkes looks at him and starts to laugh.

'You bloody fool!' he says. 'You bloody fool! Was that your plan? To be the one to kill the Prince? To claim King Edward's hundred pounds and his everlasting love? Ha!'

Thomas says nothing. That was his plan.

'Well,' Wilkes acknowledges, 'you might as well get yourself killed here as anywhere.'

He's right, of course. It was a stupid plan. Did he really think he would be able to saunter through the ranks and somehow kill Prince Edward of Westminster? Look at them! The Prince's household men are not routing, they are moving off in an orderly fashion, as part of a plan perhaps. Perhaps they even have a secondary position, another place from which to mount an attack out of defence?

He can't fight them, Thomas knows, and he hesitates, knowing his plan is come to nothing and that this is where it will end. But Gloucester's men are either blind or ignorant or utterly fearless, or maybe they are clever and they see their opportunity and seize it, for they go surging past Thomas and Wilkes, brushing their shoulders as they go, and charge at the Prince's men just as they are moving towards them across the bridge.

The thing is that the Prince's men are looking the other way, and they are not expecting this. The impact of the charge is devastating. Prince Edward's men are pinched together on the bridge, and they cannot turn to bring their skills or numbers to bear, and they can only fend off blows on a narrow front. Gloucester's men come at them in a shunting spear thrust, and they come with such force, and are fresh to the fighting, and they smash into the Prince's men with an unstoppable, harrowing fury.

Prince Edward's men manage to kill or wound the first to arrive – those who make up the point of the spear – but they take casualties too, and now their weapons are buried in the flesh of the wounded or dying men, or they are caught by those not so badly wounded, and now Prince Edward's men find themselves trapped between King Edward and the Duke of Gloucester's men, and what had been a hedgehog of bristling weapons breaks down to become a chaotic crowd of poorly sighted men weighed down by plate and carrying long poll arms struggling to keep their balance and feet as the shock of the charge passes through from front to back, left to right, and back again.

The bridge becomes impassable with those left alive fighting over the bodies of dead and dying men. Beyond it, Prince Edward's retainers are in confusion. Most of Gloucester's men are still alive, and are wading through the wounded, stabbing and hammering those left alive, and being stabbed and hammered in their turn. It is a foul-tempered tussle, a whirr of chopped blows, dagger punches and falling bodies. Thomas watches askance. He has seen something like this before. He remembers snow, and a broader river. He remembers being behind a tree with a bow in his hand. A man with a bow and two sheaths of arrows could end this fight now, he thinks, but all the arrows are shot, and the Lancastrian bowmen have run, while King Edward's bowmen are out looting.

This is it, Thomas realises. This is the moment.

He starts running. The moment he does so, with every footstep, the pain in his head blooms. He can feel blood in his collar now. His vision swims. He staggers. Christ. Christ.

'Everingham!' Wilkes shouts.

Thomas holds up a hand and it shifts in and out of focus. The pain in his head comes and goes. Each is a drawn-out hammer blow. It is enough to make him sick again.

He staggers on, one foot in front of the other. Sound changes, becomes booming, then distant. He cannot keep his balance, but on he goes and by the time he reaches the bridge he has recovered a little. His head is hot, but the pain is gone or is only present when he puts his right heel down. That is what hurts most.

The bridge is a writhing, stinking, bloody mass of fallen men. It doesn't matter what you tread on so long as you do not slip: a face might be safer than a patch of blood-slimed mud. Thomas moves forward with high knees, pollaxe head lowered to fend off any wounded man exacting revenge. He needs hit only one man who rears up in his path like a near-drowned soul breaking the surface of a lake. Thomas catches his helmet above his ear with the fluke of the pollaxe and the man goes down as if his legs are taken from under him.

On he goes. He is making for the fishtail banner beyond the bridge. That is Prince Edward's banner. That is where he will be. Blue and white, with a goat in a golden collar or something. Still waving. Still held proud. That is where the fighting will be the sharpest, that is where every action, every movement means life or death.

Thomas sees gaps open up between the Prince's men, alleyways in the line down which he might hurry, but they are quickly closed up, and soldier for soldier the Prince's men are worth two of Gloucester's, who are mostly poorly harnessed billmen. But now, from behind Thomas, wading through the carnage of the bridge, come reinforcements in the shape of the Duke of Gloucester's household men, with their superior harness and better weapons, and they are more than a match for the Prince's retinue. Thomas lets his place be taken by a keener man. He watches him trade hammer blows with another in harness with a red helmet. They are equally matched until one of Gloucester's billmen, down but not yet dead, thrusts a knife into the back of the knee of the man with the red helmet and he buckles. He is on all fours and the keen man swings his pollaxe to drive the fluke into the back of his neck and he is knocked to the ground, sprawling on the billmen below. Gloucester's man extracts his axe and continues until he slips on bloodied plate and has a spear rammed into his crotch. Another takes his place.

Thomas knows this is no time for anything but a full heart. He knows he must put everything into this or he will be killed. He roars as he storms forward, and he smashes and stabs and punches anything in his way. His visor is broken, jammed up, so men go for his face, but by Christ, at least he can see them coming!

On it goes. Swing, miss, thrust, parry, a desperate clash of helmeted heads. Butting, punching, elbowing, kneeing. The pollaxe held short for a stab into weaker, articulated plates. Pain reverberates. Up and down his arms, his head, his heart, his lungs. Everything he can see and feel is sharp, gritty, lethal. Thomas cracks the pollaxe into a visored face and does not stop to imagine the hell he has caused. He steps over the falling body.

And now he is in a tight clearing, hemmed in by the backs of men who are all turned outwards, fighting to save their lives. The noise is tremendous, the pressures are unmanageable and it is all so fast. Even those men with the banners are cutting and slashing, and beyond them a sea of King Edward's men are pressing, desperate to be the one who kills the Prince, pressing, pressing. It is almost dark with the number of raised weapons and the flailing din is hellish. They are all well harnessed, knighted men, probably lords, earls, dukes even, and here is Thomas – who at a distracted glance from below a closed visor might be wearing the red and white livery of the Prince, when it is only gore that stains him so – moving forward. And no one watches him. He knows what he must do, because, surely, only God could have guided him safe this far, and he picks out the man who must be Prince Edward, who is fighting gamely to protect the left side of his banner man.

Thomas has never knowingly killed a man from behind, but there is no time to think about this, no time to hesitate. He must kill, or be killed. If he cannot bring himself to kill the Prince, then he condemns Katherine and Rufus to death.

He hacks at the Prince's right hamstrings, driving the pick of the pollaxe through the rings of mail and into the back of his knee. The Prince rears back. He tries to slash at Thomas, but Thomas is too quick, and he drives the point of the axe through the lighter plates at the Prince's side, smashing buckle, steel, rib and flesh.

The Prince is dead, dead before he hits the ground. His banner man turns and Thomas drives the pollaxe at him too, crunching through the collar he wears instead of a bevor, and the man is dead where he stands. Thomas wrenches the banner from his hands and brings it swinging down on the man who carries the Prince's flag, so that he is plunged into confusion and is then stabbed in the armpit.

426

Within a breath the Prince is dead, and both flag and banner are gone, and the battle, if it were ever in doubt, is utterly lost.

Seeing their flag down and their prince dead, his men lose heart, and if they try to surrender, no one cares. They are killed, each one, and King Edward's men, victorious, alive, are grouped around the dead body of the Prince, over which Thomas stands, with the Prince's banner in his bloody hands, inverted, and thank God Flood is there to recognise him and to raise his hand above his head, and thank God the King's men see past Thomas's blood-soaked tabard to recognise the livery and bull's head of William Hastings. For they cheer him now, and cheer themselves, and grip one another with that savage glee that only men who have survived a fight can know.

But where is the one man Thomas needs to witness this?

Where is Wilkes?

25

They had brought him to her about an hour before noon, still alive, but with a wound to his stomach, and so not like to see out the day. She had laid him out in the shade of a wagon, and with her own hand she had given him ale spiked with the dwale. Not enough to render him senseless, but enough to soothe the pain.

'It is bitter,' he'd told her. 'I like it.'

She had laughed.

'I knew you would.'

Wilkes had tried laughing too. He was not so bad a man, she'd thought, despite what the others said about him. She'd held the mug to his lips again. He'd drunk a bit more and then had lain back and shut his eyes.

'Did you see my husband?' Katherine had asked.

He'd opened his eyes. They were curiously dark.

'I was right about him,' he'd said. 'Thomas Everingham is – He is a good man, your husband. I saw him. What he did. He is unsullied, despite – despite it all.' He'd gestured to his chest. She'd not known what he meant.

'But is he alive?' she'd pressed. 'Did you see him?'

Wilkes had drifted away for a moment, gripped by pain. When he came back he'd told her that he had not seen Thomas dead.

'So—' he'd said, as if that meant anything, and she'd supposed it did, something, anyway, and then he'd tried to shrug, but he'd started coughing. Blood-stringed ale stained his chin, his linen. She'd mopped it away with some linen of her own.

'Shall I fetch a priest?' she'd asked.

He'd shaken his head.

'Stay with me a moment, Mistress Everingham,' he'd said. 'Just a moment.'

She had paused and nodded, and settled next to him, having taken a look around the makeshift hospital, for she had other men yet to deal with, other men who needed her help. There were those with wounds in their bellies, such as Wilkes's, who were beyond her assistance; and there were those with wounds in their chests who made that strange sucking sound, and they too would all die before sundown, and for these men she had mixed a very powerful dwale and had given it to a priest, a Burton Lazar, who had come up from the village at which they stopped the night before, to administer alongside the viaticum. But there were others whom she could help – men with arrow wounds or blade wounds to other parts of their bodies, men whom she could save if she could clean, wash and stitch their wounds before the air got at them and turned them black.

She had worked at this all morning, burying herself in tasks so as not to fret over Thomas, never attempting anything that took too long, but staunching blood and cleaning wounds where she could, stitching what needed to be stitched and plugging wounds with honey-soaked, barley-filled linen wads, and all morning she had been assailed by savoury wisps of burned meat from the cautery so that at times she had felt like a pieman.

Yet kneeling in the dirt next to Wilkes, she'd begun to fear that Wilkes was trying to tell her something about Thomas in words he was weighing out for posterity. But then she had slowly come to see that she was wrong, or half-wrong: he was trying to tell her something about himself.

'Tell your husband,' he'd said. 'Tell your husband, when you see him, that I was not so bad a man as he thinks. I tried my best to avert bloodshed. I did my part to restrict the – the supply of widows and orphans.'

He had smiled at his joke and tried to lick his dried lips with a bloodstained tongue. He had been silent for a moment, gathering his strength, his eyes half-closed, his dark eyes somehow glistening. That was where the last of his power lay, she'd thought, but then he had twisted with pain and she'd wondered about more dwale to soothe these last moments.

'Tell him . . .' Wilkes had managed. 'Tell him – that I forgive him. In so far – as I am able. If he will forgive me.'

'I will fetch a priest,' she'd said.

'No!' he'd said, catching at the hem of her skirts. Then he'd grabbed her hand, and his back had arched in spasm, and he'd half growled, half roared: 'Tell him – tell him you have – tell him you have – tell him you have the – You're not to – He will understand. But tell him—'

His eyeballs were red. He was drenched in sweat. It was as if he was vomiting up his soul.

'Father!' she'd shouted to the Lazar priest. 'Father!'

The priest had come scurrying, but she'd felt the life go out of Wilkes, and by the time she looked back at him, he was dead. She'd held his hand for a bit longer, before standing up; she and the priest had stayed there, looking down at him.

'A merciful release,' the priest had said.

'He was trying to tell me something.'

'You will have to wait now, until you join him in heaven.'

Yes, she'd supposed, though there was something about Wilkes that made her think he would be made to endure many a long year in Purgatory. Then the priest had bent to close Wilkes's eyes and begin the prayers, and Katherine had crossed herself.

Now she has taken off her blood-soaked apron and left it on the wagon, and she walks towards the abbey, across the pasture towards the battlefield, leaving behind the business of the camp followers. She goes in search of solace in silence, and space, if only for a moment. She knows nothing good is likely to come of such a thing, but she is filled with memories of the past, of when she did just this, and most especially of that time after the battle of Towton, when she waited in vain for Thomas's return.

Men – and women, and children – are already out in the long grass, braving its dangers, looking for what they can find among the dead and dying, but up ahead, by the abbey, even on its steps, the fighting continues still. She can see many men in their colours still running to and fro, and the sounds of outrage are faint but somehow all the crueller, for the battle is over, and surely now it is the time for mercy.

Some of the monks from the abbey have come out and are pleading with the looters to leave their victims be. And there is so much opportunity to be had that sometimes the looters do move on in search of other prey, leaving the monks to save those whom they think they can, and pray over those whom they know they cannot.

She realises that the long grass brushing against the hem of her skirts is hazing its wool with blood and she stops and stands alone, watching, waiting, in a small clearing between the dead and the dying and the looting and the looted, and above the fresh smell of new spring growth she smells blood, and shit, and gunpowder smoke, and imagines that perhaps this is the devil's smell, and she vows that whatever else happens in her life, she will never smell this again.

Across the blood-soaked field the abbey bells have begun to ring, sharp and dissonant, and she becomes gripped by a fearful sorrow and feels the tentacles of that same terrible desolation curl up to grip her as they did when Alice died, but it is then, at that precise, darkest moment, that from the far side of the pasture she sees Thomas come walking unsteadily towards her, blood-glazed and almost demented with panic, and as he approaches she watches him wrenching off his gloves and his helmet and tossing them aside, and then his blood-soaked livery coat, and so on, piece by piece, discarded, so that by the time he reaches her in the middle of the field he wears only his hose and his arming jacket and he carries only the bloodstained pollaxe.

'We must go,' he says. 'We must get Rufus and be away.'

And she says nothing but turns to walk with him, and he puts his heavy arm across her shoulder, and he tells her about Wilkes.

'Hastings will know by this evening,' he says. 'And we are undone.'

She says nothing, but takes him first to see the man's dead body and then, while he stands there, she goes to the wagon to fetch the papers.

'He made me swear to God that I would pass them on,' she says.

'We must destroy them,' Thomas tells her. 'We must destroy them.'

'We could read them first?'

After a moment he agrees.

He opens the seal and covers the papers in a great deal of blood, but his hands are trembling too much and he complains of too great a headache, so after a moment he passes them over to her to read, and she stands a little way from Wilkes's blood-spattered corpse and looks through the papers and finds nothing about Thomas or herself until the bottom of the very last sheet of the letter that Wilkes has addressed to William, Lord Hastings. When she finishes, she too can hardly read, for her heart blocks her throat and tears her eyes.

'Say that again,' Thomas asks, for she has murmured while she read.

'He – he tells William Hastings that in the event of his death, he should rely more heavily on you,' she says, 'and on me, for doing what needs be done, but should we prove unwilling, under those circumstances it might be right Christian to let us reside in peace, unmolested and restored to our home in Lincolnshire.'

There are then tears in the eyes of both.

'He never wanted to condemn you, you see?' she tells him. 'If he lived, he would have had to tell Hastings, but if he was dead, then he wanted to spare you, in so far as he was able, in so far as it was in his power, if you might forgive him.'

'Let me see,' Thomas says, as if he does not believe her, and he tries to read through the words too, but after a moment he drops the letters and papers and falls to his knees, and it is only then she sees the wound in the back of his head.

Epilogue

Sir Thomas Everingham sits in the late-afternoon sun, playing chess with his son. He usually lets Rufus beat him, but the boy is getting too good for that, so today he does not do so. Instead Thomas watches him as his smudged little eyes take in the wreckage of his pieces on the board, and it is as if he is retracing his moves to see where he went wrong, and then when he recognises it, you can see him remembering not to make that mistake again.

John Stumps sits watching. He is the best of them all at the game.

'Got fuck all else to do, has he?' Foulmouth John always says, and the skinny boy, who is forgiven and welcomed back, and who it turns out is called John, sometimes laughs.

'But you are getting to be a very fine player, Rufus,' John Stumps says.

'Must have got it from his mother,' Jack Bradford says. He has a baby asleep on his lap and his other daughter, Kate, the girl who once breathed through her neck, sits not too far off playing with two corn dolls, cooing over them like a collared dove. Jack's wife sits nearby with her drop wheel, spinning wool into yarn. It's a comforting sound, once you get used to it.

435

After a moment Katherine comes out of the hall and sits next to Rufus. She's in her new green dress, and there is something about her that Thomas guesses instantly, though he'd never be able to say why, and he leans forward and pushes her untouched mug of ale towards her. She pushes it back at him, unable to stand its smell, and he knows, and he smiles and she smiles back at him, but it is one of those secret, careful, let-us-wait-and-see smiles, and for a moment she and Rufus look so similar he cannot help but smile a proper, happily carefree smile himself.

It is the first Sunday after the Assumption, in the year 1471, the eleventh of King Edward IV's reign, and the sun shines bright on those gathered here in the courtyard of Marton Hall in the county of Lincoln, and when it sinks, they will go into the hall, and cover the fire, and they will say their prayers and retire to bed, where they will lie watched over by the shades of men who have gone before: by John Daud, pardoner, who gave them succour; by Sir John Fakenham, knight, who knew more than ever he let on, and by his son Richard, who died blind, and of heartbreak. They will be watched over by Walter, who gave up his life for them in the Welsh mountains; by the physician Payne, who kept their secrets even to his death; and even by Lord Hastings's deep-thinking man of business John Wilkes, who knew either he or Thomas must die. They will be watched over by the shades of women, too: by those such as Nettie Bradford, who died with a crossbow shaft in her face; and by Margaret Cornford, who died in the snow, almost by their hand. And by Alice. Always Alice, their infant, whose body lies buried in the black earth of Holland, but who watches over them still.

And for as long as those sleeping under the roof of Marton Hall are able to keep the departed in mind, and offer up prayers for their souls, then such monsters as still exist in England will be kept constrained within the mind of man.

A Note from the Author

If 1469 was an odd and tumultuous year, the two that followed have to be among the most dramatic in English history: the Earl of Warwick's second rebellion in as many years failed, and he and King Edward's brother George were driven into exile where they had to make allies of not only England's oldest enemy, France, but also their own most bitter foe: Margaret of Anjou, wife of the king they'd deposed and mother of any Lancastrian hopes for the future. Six months later, and seemingly against all odds, they reversed their positions, and managed a triumphant return to England. King Edward was driven out of the country, forced to steal away across the North Sea on a ship he could only pay for with his fur-lined coat.

Old King Henry was brought out from the Tower and restored to the throne and it was as if there had never been a King Edward IV. Another six months later, though, and it was King Edward's turn to come back, sneaking in through the back door this time, at first claiming only the dukedom of York, as Henry IV had done many years earlier, but within another he had defeated in battle and killed his oldest ally, and within another he had defeated in battle and killed his oldest enemy. He was restored to the throne, and King Henry was restored to the Tower, where he was soon to join the growing number of murdered English kings.

These are the facts that provide the backbone of *Kingdom Come*, the last in the *Kingmaker* series, though readers familiar with the conventional narrative of the times – often based on *The Chronicle of the Rebellion in Lincolnshire, 1470* – will recognise I've chosen an unorthodox interpretation. This is not to suit any novelistic necessity, but because the various mysteries surrounding the attack on Sir Thomas Burgh's house in Gainsborough (still there today, and terrific to visit, incidentally), and the events that followed immediately afterwards, point to – or at least allow for – a much more interesting possibility than is usually accepted.

The basis for this hypothesis – that King Edward provoked the rebellion to force the Earl of Warwick's hand – can be found in P. Holland's excellent paper 'The Lincolnshire Rebellion of March 1470', in *The English Historical Review* (Vol. 103, No. 409). Much of it pivots on the timing of the issuing of Commissions of Array, the implausibility of those damning letters found after the battle of Losecoat, and the identity of a man named Walter who may or may not have been a churchman, but I recommend this as further reading to anyone who wishes to pursue the argument. The character of Wilkes is obviously – I hope – an invention, but it must have taken someone to initiate the plot, so why not him?

The long-running issue of the ledger is finally laid to rest, and some will be pleased to hear the back of it. Its inspiration comes from a record found in Rouen Cathedral that suggests King Edward's father, Richard, Duke of York, had been in the town of Pontoise, near Paris, during the crucial months in which his son ought to have been conceived in Rouen, where his wife Cecily passed the summer of 1441. This – along with the fact that the boy was baptised in a side chapel of the cathedral, which has been taken as a sign his mother was ashamed of him – has been seen by some as proof of the boy's bastardy, but Pontoise is in fact only ninety kilometres from Rouen, a couple of days' ride, and Edward might have been born prematurely and had a rushed baptism to ensure his entry into the kingdom of God.

Rumours of illegitimacy had surrounded Edward all his life, though, because he was not supposed to look like his father, who was short and not particularly striking while Edward was tall and strapping, and supposedly the most handsome prince in Europe. In fact, he looked similar to his siblings who were all – except notably Richard, Duke of Gloucester – also tall and fair. His sister Margaret was supposed to be 5 feet 11 inches. Such accusations were political, of course, but after his death they sufficed to prevent his sons reaching the throne until a more permanent way was found.

Given that there is a record placing Richard, Duke of York, in Pontoise in the summer of 1441, I hope it is obvious there is no record that now exists placing him in Pontours – which is the best part of seven hundred kilometres away from Rouen – and that the pardoner's double-edged bequest is pure invention on my part. Or perhaps the confusion between Pontoise and Pontours was the original clerk's?

The other long-running end that is tied up is that of Katherine's identity. Katherine of Valois was married to Henry V and mother of Henry VI, who was born in 1421, but after Henry V's death in 1422, she married (in obscure circumstances) Owen Tudor, a Welshman, who was beheaded in Hereford after the battle of Mortimer's Cross in 1461, but not before he had sired one of the most important families in English history. Katherine of Valois died, perhaps from complications after childbirth, aged thirty-five, in 1437, but there is mention of at least one unnamed daughter born in 1435 who became a nun. That would make Katherine Everingham older by five years than Thomas, and by the end of *Kingdom Come* in 1471 at the very limit of childbearing age, but there we are. It is possible. And it is why, in *Winter Pilgrims*, Owen Tudor recognised her as she stood in the crowd watching him being beheaded: because she looked like her mother, his wife.

The battle of Tewkesbury, which ends this book, also saw the end of the Lancastrian line, and the end of the middle spasm of what we now call the Wars of the Roses. It remains controversial because there is strong evidence that many – some? a few? – men were killed even though they were seeking sanctuary within the abbey. Had one of them been Prince Edward of Westminster, then you can be sure Thomas Everingham would have been there, poll-axe in hand, but despite Tudor propaganda of dastardly, heretic and murderous Yorkist activities, there is evidence that the Prince was killed in the field, during the battle itself. King Edward was rumoured to have offered a hundred pounds to the man who killed him, or brought the Prince to him alive, so there is not a doubt he would have been despatched very swiftly thereafter, but as with everything in this *Kingmaker* series, I've changed its story to match the facts, not the facts to match its story.

After the death of his son, old King Henry VI was said to have died of grief, but most likely had his brains dashed out in the Tower; and after her capture fleeing the field, Margaret of Anjou, that heroic, strong-laboured she-wolf of France, with nothing left for which to struggle, returned eventually to France to live out the rest of her life as a poor relation of King Louis XI. She died in 1482.

One of the saddest characters in this period, to my mind, is John Neville, Lord Montagu, once Earl of Northumberland, who served Edward and England loyally, remaining steadfast while his brother, the Earl of Warwick, flip-flopped all over the place, only to be demoted. If Edward had not deprived him of the earldom of Northumberland in 1470, then I imagine he would have stayed faithful and the King would not have been driven into exile in Flanders. Had Edward not spent those months in Bruges then we might not have such a magnificent royal library, or a taste for bricks, as evinced by William Hastings's unfinished castle at Kirby Muxloe, but more crucially, in the last ten years of Edward's reign, as the Earl of Northumberland, John Neville would have remained the significant power in the north, not Richard of Gloucester, and the whole catastrophe – for the House of York – of Richard III's reign might never have arisen. Well, it is a theory.

Tewkesbury was not quite the end of King Edward's troubles: he still had rebellions in the north to suppress, and in the east the bastard of Fauconberg was besieging London with some vim. Once these rebellions were put down, though, he went on to reign for another twelve years until his premature (and unexplained except perhaps as a result of gluttony) death in 1483, after which his young son Edward V became king, though he was never crowned, of course, since his uncle, Edward's brother Richard, Duke of Gloucester, took his place, and I think by now we all know how that turned out.

Toby Clements
June 2017

'An enthralling adventure story, honest
and powerful.'
Hilary Mantel

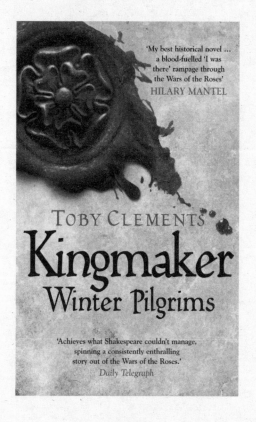

'My best historical novel …
a blood-fuelled 'I was
there' rampage through
the Wars of the Roses'
HILARY MANTEL

TOBY CLEMENTS
Kingmaker
Winter Pilgrims

'Achieves what Shakespeare couldn't manage,
spinning a consistently enthralling
story out of the Wars of the Roses.'
Daily Telegraph

Brother fronts brother.
King faces king.
The Wars Of The Roses
begins.

The first book in the *Kingmaker* series
OUT NOW

'This is history in the raw: powerful, potent stuff, always real, but always gloriously unpredictable.'
The Sunday Times

OUT NOW

The second book in the *Kingmaker* series